Red Island

A Novel

Lorne Oliver

BEWARE THE QUIET ONES

RED ISLAND: A NOVEL
Copyright © 2012 by Lorne Oliver

ISBN 978-0-9738132-3-4

To my wife and my children

Thank you for putting up with me without too much
complaining

Acknowledgements

A book cannot be written without the help of many people smarter than myself. In saying that I have to give a Big thanks to Sgt. Kevin Baillie, NCO i/c Professional Standards Unit, Cpl. S.H. Stevenson, NCO i/c Forensic Science and Identification Services, and other members of "L" Division RCMP for answering my endless questions about police procedures and the life of a cop. Any mistakes are all on me.

Brandi Oliver formatted everything and was an ear for me to bounce ideas off of no matter how much she screamed for me to stop.

And finally my deepest gratitude goes out to the test subjects who read what I had and tried their best to point out my screw ups. It is from their encouragement that Red Island is out there.

Chapter 1

Drip, drip.

I can hear something somewhere ahead. *Drip.*

I walk down an old road. The last time a truck may have come down here was last autumn. It's spring now and the snow is gone. Below my feet is last year's grass folded down from the pressure of the snow like a spongy carpet. My shoes are wet. A chill crawls up my legs inside my pants until it reaches my groin, passes to my spine and makes me shiver.

Drip, drip.

I can't hear anything else but that one noise. *Drip.*

There are no birds in the trees. Grey trees, still bare from the winter with boney fingers reaching up and out, line both sides of the road. The branches move in the wind, but I can't hear them scraping against each other. The dead leaves, still in the high branches, don't rustle. Every time my feet touch the ground there is a soft swish, more like a remembered sound, and then nothing.

All I can feel is the cold dancing on my skin and what is inside me, fear. The wind does not touch my cheek. The cold is inside me. With that is fear. The fear makes me want to look behind myself. My head won't turn.

Drip.

I see the sound before I hear it. A red drop of blood hits a small pool in the grass erupting minute drops of red in every direction. *Drip.*

I stop walking. I can't breathe anymore. My lungs feel like someone is squeezing them closed. My eyes move up. Two feet off the ground, a red drop of blood stops on the end of a blue polished toenail. It engorges itself, grows pregnant, and then drops.

Drip.

One foot is over the other like hands praying. Rivulets of red run down her legs switching direction off hairs and stubble. *How could this happen to you? Chloe. Why you Chloe?*

Drip, drip.

The wind makes her twist. My eyes slowly travel the red streams up her legs, first over her firm calf muscles and then around the boney knee and onto her thigh. *What happened to you Chloe?*

"Reid, wake up. The phone is for you."

A shiny black raven sits on a tree branch over the woman's left shoulder. Its eyes glow red.

The forest is gone. Light from the street lamps crack around the blinds covering the window. The days clothes on the desk chair are a child's boogie man. The blue light from the laptop charger glows up the wall from behind my desk. I can smell face cream, fabric softener and Hillary's shampoo. I can hear hot air being pushed up through the air vent on the floor. The cordless telephone dangles in front of my face. A foot kicks me under the sheets. The pads on the bottom are rough against my calf.

"It's work."

I push myself up with my back against the wall. "Yeah, it's Reid." I don't know what time it is or how long until the alarm goes off. I can hear the dog snoring off the end of the bed. Hillary turns the television on and right away puts the volume down. She fixes her pillows. I hear a bottle of pop open, *Pepsi* most likely. I listen to the voice on the phone. As my brain starts to register what it is saying my body wakes. My day is starting.

I respond with, "I'll be there as soon as I can," and roll onto my side to write down an address on an open notebook. I hang up the phone and turn to my wife. "Do we know a Chloe?"

The skin of Hillary's face has that red shade of someone who was just sleeping. She has a bit of sleep crud in the corner of one eye. *Proof that Sandman had come*, our daughter says. Her black hair, cut in a short angled bob, is messy from her tossing and turning but still looks good. It suits her. She runs her fingers through it and tucks it behind her ears. Her lips circle the top of her drink and she takes a good drink. It is a *Pepsi*. All she has on is a long thin shirt with panda bears wearing blue and red pajamas over it. If it wasn't for the phone call I might be inclined to slip my hand beneath the shirt and see what could happen. It has been a long time since I started a spur of the moment thing like that. There were mornings, over a year ago now, when I would get home from a midnight shift and wake her with a good tongue lashing. We now have to plan out when we have sex. We fell in love a long time ago, but only got married when she became pregnant ten years past. She stares at me for a while without saying anything.

"Chloe? I don't think so, why?"

"It was in my dream." I spin to sitting on the edge of the bed. My boxers are bunched up around my crotch and uncomfortable. I've always wanted to video tape myself sleeping to see how much I move around. I saw a program somewhere that showed people freaking out in their sleep and not remembering a thing about it.

"So now you're dreaming of other women?"

"I'm not dreaming of other women. I'm not doing anything with other women." I go to the closet and won't look at my wife.

It's April and in Canada that means it is still winter so I pull on a pair of thermal underwear first, then black slacks and a black shirt. "If it means anything she was dead in my dream." I can't look at her because I'm not entirely honest. I'm not doing anything with other women, but I've thought about it.

Instead of looking at the guide, Hillary pulses her thumb on the channel button stopping for a few seconds on each show to see what it is and if it'll pique her interest for a few minutes. You're supposed to love the little habits people have. According to the movies and books those little quirks are supposed to be what endear you to your partner. This one pisses me off. She usually pauses long enough on a show for me to start getting into it then moves on to whatever's next. She quickly passes over the shows I would watch like *Crime Scene Investigation, Law & Order*, and *Criminal Minds*. She likes the infomercials, talk shows, and reality shows. She finally stops on an episode of *Sex and the City*. She turns the volume up a little and rolls onto her side. After I leave she'll probably fall asleep with the TV on.

"You're dreaming about crimes now? I thought we moved to Prince Edward Island to get away from things like murder and death. Aren't we here so that Leigh's daddy doesn't get late night calls where he has to leave and comes home crying or drunk? Or God forbid we get one of those calls that says, Daddy isn't coming home." I can feel her brown eyes burning into my back.

"Don't start, Hillary."

"I'm going to start. You said you wouldn't get these late night calls."

"It's one call. I've had three calls in four months. You know it is part of my job. You're getting mad over nothing." I fasten a tie around my neck.

"It's not nothing, Reid. I thought you were going to ask for a desk job." Her voice has raised a little. She takes another drink of *Pepsi*. I don't want to look at her.

I say, "There are no openings right now. I'm needed in Major Crimes so that's where I'll be for now, okay." I lower my voice and say, "you'll just have to wait a little while before that happens." I won't look at her because I am lying and she'll know it. She will see my eyes move off of hers or my lip will twitch. I don't want a desk job. I like going out in the field and investigating real crimes. I would go nuts sitting at headquarters making up new reports and procedures.

Hillary says, "at least the crimes here aren't as serious as the big city." Again I don't want to look at her. I give her a quick kiss on her forehead without getting caught in her eyes. "Can you get milk?"

She does not need to know what the call was about or where I have to go and what I might see. In the RCMP strict confidentiality is first and foremost, even with your wife. To be honest, I don't stick to that as well as I should. A lot of times I need someone to talk to or I need to talk out what is in my head so that I can figure it all out. Right now what I am going to be involved with is not something she needs to know about. All it would do is re-fire our argument and give her another chance to say, *but you said you wouldn't be doing that again.* She has had enough death in her life. I have brought enough death into her life. The last thing she needs to deal with at two in the morning is death. She'll find out when she listens to the radio in the morning.

Get milk, fuck.

I go to the door across the hall, Leigh's Room is written in bold wood letters across it, and open it a crack. Leigh has her limbs all kicked around. Her legs stick out of the blankets and look like she is running. Her long hair falls across her face. I look up at the window. On the wall beside it is a large framed photograph of her riding a black and white horse across one of the beaches here on the island. Water splashes up from the horses hooves. In the dark I can't see Leigh's face in the picture, but I know she has a giant smile across it. Every time she rides her face lights up. You try and give your kids everything while really just hoping they are happy. Maybe Hillary is right and I don't give our daughter enough of my time.

I carefully close the door and head down the stairs. Time to leave the lovely family and make my way to hell.

~ * ~

"The middle of fucking nowhere," I sigh to myself and pull my car off of Blooming Point Road onto Tulloch Road. The moment I do that I am in the Tulloch Pond Provincial Wildlife Reserve. I pass two houses and the road instantly goes from pavement to gravel and then to mud. Further up large puddles span across the entire road. It has been raining for almost two weeks straight, stopping only two days ago. One puddle is deep enough to touch the undercarriage of my car. I have to fight the steering wheel. I cross a bridge, the river underneath is part of the Tulloch Pond waters. As I turn the next corner to see the growing collection of vehicles between large puddles of spring thaw waters, rain, and mud.

Sgt. Marilyn Moore stands behind her car which is parked right behind the Mobile Command Post. She looks at my car and then turns away from the bright light. Her hair dances around her head. I have to admit she looks rather sexy standing there silhouetted by my lights. I am an asshole.

My dash clock says three thirty when I turn off the car.

Outside I can hear the waves crashing against Blooming Point Beach about a half kilometer down the road. Somewhere between the beach and where we are, are the high sand dunes patch worked with grasses that are famous in scenic photographs of PEI. From November to May it is next to impossible to get to the beach because of snow and thick mud that can bog the best of trucks down. In the Spring fishermen come up here, most fish off the bridge but some will try these waters. In the Autumn hunters come down here for geese and ducks. I'm not down here for any of that.

Marilyn crosses the dirt road to the opening of a bush road that cuts off into the woods. It has probably been there for years, but few people rushing down the road in the summer trying to find the beach would notice it. Marilyn is now covered from foot to neck in a white protective suit. We call them *bunny suits*. They are to protect investigators from leaving their own traces at a scene.

"Morning," she says.

I see a light sparkle off of a new bobble on her left hand. "What's with the ring?"

"It's nothing; she quickly pulls the diamond ring from her finger and hides it inside her suit. I don't say anything about the bruise on her wrist or her red knuckles.

A small handful of RCMP officers, what we call *Regular Members*, mill around between the MCP and the patrol cars that have pulled off to the side of the road. They all wear dark blue cargo pants and dark blue jackets with slits for easy access to their gun and radio.

I walk up the back ramp of the MCP and drop my duffle bag. The long white trailer, pulled behind a black four by four, is a converted RV pull-behind trailer. At the top of the ramp, where an all-terrain vehicle would have been parked in its RV days, is a desk with radio equipment and a folding table set up for collected evidence coming in. The next room is the kitchen area, I can smell the coffee brewing, and then there is a small room that once was a bedroom and is now a mini office with a drafting table for maps and a small desk and chair. I pull my own bunny suit out of my bag and start pulling it on over my clothes.

"Hi, Reid. Sorry to wake you. We need you here." Sgt. Wayne McIntyre joins me from the kitchen area. He looks wide awake for this early in the morning. His black hair is shiny and in its proper place and his goatee is well trimmed. He has a coffee in his hand. The island's red soil, mud here in the wet spring, has splashed up his pant legs. "This is," he stumbles on his words. "I've never seen anything like this. This doesn't happen in PEI. I hate to think something like this happens anywhere." He pauses long enough to shake his head and take a breath. His hand runs down his tie and straightens it. "I want you to be the lead on this one. I haven't dealt with something like this before, you have. Moore's going to work closely with you."

I pull a black toque down over my bald head.

McIntyre continues, "A group of kids were coming down the road," he points to a red Honda Civic in front of the Mobile Unit, "and didn't like the mud so they tried this trail hoping to find another way to the beach. We have them separated in cars. The girls are pretty freaked out. I don't think they know much so I'll interview them if you want to head down to the scene."

"Find out what they saw, what they touched." I look over at the car then back. "Call *CrOps* and tell him we'll need whoever we can get. At least a half dozen here in three hours to canvas." CrOps stands for: Criminal Operations. The officer in charge of it is the one that sends other officers where they are needed.

"Time to wake everyone up, I guess."

I pull the hood of my white suit up over my toque. I just want to get down there. Something in me is saying I need to walk

11

down this road and see what is there. With a head lamp from the folding table I walk out to my partner and say, "let's go." Marilyn tucks her red wine-colored hair under her hood.

If I did not know Marilyn I would never think she was a police officer trained to fight. She has a trim body with curves in the right places standing at least six feet, a good two inches over me. She has little make-up on, as always, and she doesn't need any to look pretty. I would be lying if I didn't admit to noticing that Marilyn is a very attractive woman. I worry about her though. Her boyfriend is not the nicest of men. Worse than that, she doesn't like talking about it. In my opinion people who talk about their problems have a greater tendency to do something about it. A battered woman with a gun is never a good thing.

We put our headlight beams on the ground and walk the taped off path along the right side of the bush road. The Forensic Identification Unit, *Ident*, searched the pathway as they walked toward the scene. The old grass is spongy beneath our feet. The golden grass is folded down like a woman's flattened long hair. I can hear the water from the spring thaw and rain beneath the soft carpet. The right side of the road is lined by thick patches of thin red barked willows, with spots of aspen, birch, and spruce struggling to grow through them. An oddball collection of rubbish is scattered in the bushes from plastic bags to candy wrappers and glass bottles, everything faded. On the left side the trees are faring better, not giving the willows a chance to overcome their roots. Spotted on the ground hidden by a canopy of evergreen are tiny piles of snow not yet touched by the sun. The trees look grey. Even the evergreens in the blanket of night give off a dark grey feel. We can still feel the crisp, cold air blowing in from the shore, over the dunes, and through the willows. In another month you would not be able to walk down here without being eaten alive by mosquitoes. Some animal shuffles in the dead leaves on the tree side. There are shadows in the trees. If it wasn't for Moore beside me and the gun inside my jacket I would be sweating with fear right now. I can't stand the dark.

"What did Hillary say about this call?" I jump a little. My mind was away from where we are so much that I forgot Marilyn was walking beside me. Our feet touch the grass carpet in unison as if I am the only one here. Thousands of crickets rub themselves at the river in a giant symphony.

I sigh, "What do you think? I didn't tell her what it was about though. The last thing I fucking need is to be nagged at about PEI not being as safe a place as I told her it was."

"They have to bitch and complain about something. The other halves, I mean. I get it almost every day. Only I," I turn to her in time to see her bite her lip and look away. She pulls her face mask down over the nose and mouth.

"You need to talk?" I ask.

Marilyn interrupts me with, "We're here."

Ahead of us is a bend in the road with a lot of light breaking the black from around the bend. Large spotlights on tripods have been set up by the crime scene duo. We'll have a little light to look around the scene and see what we can find. I can't figure out why one spotlight is shooting up into the sky.

"You ever get déjà vu?" My stomach turns over. A voice inside doesn't want me to walk around the corner into the artificial light.

"No. You mean like feeling you've been somewhere before? No." Her voice is slightly muffled from behind the mask.

"Okay, let's go." I've been on this road before, but I can't say that to her. *Hey partner, I dreamed this very thing just an hour ago.* I know what is coming up, but there is no way for me to know. All I know is a dream. A chill rides up my spine. We have not been told anything about what we will find. We were told the basics – female DB found in the woods by Blooming Point Beach- no details to skew our initial thoughts.

I moved my family to Prince Edward Island for the mild weather, the quiet countrified life – until 2010 they only had Sunday shopping during tourist season and at Christmas, before 2008 they only had glass bottles – no cans or plastic -, the fresh seafood – Hillary loves lobster – and the low crime. The last thing I expected to see was a woman hanging from a tall white birch.

"Oh my God." Marilyn's words stop her in her tracks.

The moment I began walking down this road I knew what I would find. Probably even before then I knew. *Drip*

Our eyes ride the lights that are set up to the woman swinging from a tree in the breeze like a child's old abandoned tire swing. She doesn't look real. She looks like a mannequin up there as a Halloween decoration. *Trick or treat.* Her neck is stretched as long as it can without coming apart. The thick rope holds her chin upward. Black mascara has trailed down her cheeks with tears. Her eyes are closed, her lips thin, mouth open slightly. The woman, young woman, - I think she is in her early twenties – has long blond hair stained crimson so much that the blond is barely visible. Red streams of dry blood cover her naked body from cuts and slashes on her face, torso, and legs. Her skin is pale below the dark red from blood loss and lack of sun. I am guessing her natural color is still very light. I hope there is no place in the world where you would expect to see something like this. The sea wind catches her and she starts to turn. The rope creaks against the tree. It's the same sound as the tire swing in the wind. A tire swing long forgotten. We see her profile first, she is thin with a flat stomach, breasts more than a handful – one has a thin slice almost all the way around it – muscular legs, and a round buttocks and then her back covered in more lacerations. The only place not touched by the bladed weapon is a large black and grey rose with a small stem and two leaves, tattooed on the back of her left shoulder. Bright bruises of a deep purple in the middle fading to pink on the outer edges cover her body. I stare up at her, her feet at my eye level. Her toenails are painted blue. From here the skin of her face looks flawless. I cannot hear the sound of the blood dripping from her fingertips and toes into the pool of red below her because her blood no longer runs. *Drip, drip.* I hear it in my dreams. I can hear the creaking of the rope, the scraping of branches against each other, and the officers doing their work.

"Shit," is all I can say. What else is there? I do not turn away from the body but say, "she was beautiful." I probably would have taken a look at her if she walked past me on the street. When I was younger she would have been one of the girls I wanted to be with and daydreamed about when I was alone at night. She was good-looking. Now she is dead. Dead, dead, dead.

"You okay?" Marilyn asks. The smell of her perfume hits my nose and distracts me. It wakes me.

I look at her quick. "It's a bit shocking. Not what I expected to see today."

"You, and the kids in the Honda."

The only two members of the Forensic Identification Section, it's a small island, make their way around their scene all dressed in their bunny suits. They search the ground with flashlights and head lamps. Camera flashes go off every couple of seconds as they capture something. One studies the tree the rope is tied to. Greg Eckhart, the head of Ident joins us. He has a D700 Nikon around his neck and has a black covered notebook in his hands.

My mouth goes dry from being stuck wide open. I slowly, unconsciously, let my eyes trace her form. They draw lines around every vertical stream of blood that crossed down her whole body until ending at her fingers or toes where the blood fell. *Drip.* She took care of herself. She probably worked out at a gym somewhere or maybe she jogged the Confederation Trail. "She was cut while lying down. I mean she wasn't strung up first. Not for all of them."

Marilyn's green eyes stare at me over her mask asking for me to explain.

I say, "Her hair is caked in blood. That wouldn't happen if she was hanging first. The blood from the cuts to her face flowed to the back of her head and not down."

"So you don't think *COD* is strangulation?" She opens her notebook and taps a new page with her pen.

"I won't go that far. I'm not stupid." In criminal investigations you cannot assume anything. Not even if the *cause of death* looks obvious. Remember what your mom said about assuming and you and me? In investigations you cannot say anything until the proper person, in this case the medical examiner, says it is so. We cannot even say it was a homicide until the ME says so. It has to be apparent or possible. I take out my Blackberry to dictate what I see. "Victim is a Caucasian female, approximately twenty to twenty-five years of age, approximately five foot five in height and one hundred pounds in weight. She is not clothed. There is a rope tied around the victim's neck which holds the vic., approximately six feet from the ground. Rope goes over a branch high up a birch tree with the end tied to the trunk of another tree." I walk in a semicircle around the woman and the tree holding her careful about where I step. How the hell did she get up there? "Any personal effects, clothes, ID?"

"We haven't found anything yet." Eckhart pushes his glasses back up his nose with the back of his hand. "But we've only done a white light search so far. The lights are enough to see what we are doing here, but there are a lot of shadows. I'm hoping to do a forensic light search before the sun comes up otherwise we'll have to bring in a tent. Honestly, we're not finding much of anything anywhere. We took photos of wheel treads from the main road, but almost a dozen different kinds of tires so I wouldn't get your hopes up. I took a few casts of the ones I could. There isn't much mud between the grass on this road so tire tracks and footprints are obscured. Killer had to get her up there somehow so there has to be something. This isn't an easy place to get evidence from. I'm going to request police dogs come in to check the woods and maybe divers for the river."

"Time of death?"

Eckhart shook his head and raised his eyebrows. "It's been cold the past few days which would have slowed decomp. I'd say she's been up there two or three days, but we'll wait for the ME to make a closer calculation."

"Make sure you preserve the knots," I advise.

"I know how to do my job, Jacob." Eckhart watches his partner. She is crawling her way toward the body to try and go over a thick path so other work can be done. She looks at every centimeter with her flashlight.

"It's not Jacob."

"Tim, Pablo?"

Marilyn lets out a laugh. She moves her flashlight along the tree line. Eckhart plays a game with me every time we see each other where he tries to guess my first name. I promised him I would say yes if he ever guessed the right one. Marilyn doesn't look away from her light, but says, "Give it up, Greg. Even his wife calls him Reid."

"I don't like my first name. Never have, sue me." I still have trouble taking my eyes off of the hanging woman. *Drip.* "And my middle name is no better. The only thing that's good with my middle name is that it's the same as MacGyver's first name. You remember that TV show?"

"He had a first name?"

"You guys are such geeks."

Eckhart pushes his glasses up with the back of his hand again.

I look at my watch. Sunrise is in about two hours.

I stare up at the floating girl and murmur, "what happened to you?"

"Whoever did this tortured the hell out of the poor girl." Marilyn takes a grouping of photographs with her small digital camera. She looks at me and asks, "Are you sure you're okay, Reid?"

I can feel light green eyes on me. There are times when I enjoy the feeling of those eyes on me, but right now they're making my skin itch. Marilyn and I have worked in the Major Crimes Unit since I arrived in the province over a year ago and have been partners on almost every case. MCU has six officers in it and we fold in others depending on what we are working on. We deal with everything from violent assaults to break and enters involving injury to rape. For the most part we look into crimes and people's stories for other areas of specialty. Homicide falls in our scope of investigation, but killings are not a commonplace thing on PEI. Two homicides come to mind. One in 1988 which is still unsolved and that of a woman killed on the Confederation Trail in 2002. I guess Islanders can control themselves. I guess something had to let go. Just my luck.

"I feel like I've seen this before," I say quietly and more to myself. I would almost bet her name is Chloe. "Where the hell's the ME?"

"I'm coming. Don't get in a bunch." A flashlight bounces up and down in the hand of Dr. Walter Norton. He wears a big bulky jacket under his bunny suit that makes him look fifty pounds heavier than he truly is. I can hear that his shoes are soaked. Red mud is splashed up his pants. He has wavy black hair that is grey along the temples. His well-trimmed beard, hiding behind a hairnet, is white as snow with it going grey and black at the tip of his chin. He walks up in front of the hanging woman and points his flashlight up at her. The doctor is retired from general work and now teaches at the university and goes out on calls to go check out old timers who passed in their sleep. On this island there isn't much call for a doctor to check out possible homicides. He says, "I can't examine the body until we get her down. Multiple lacerations. Vaginal bruising. Ligature marks on her wrists and ankles. I need to check her over, but I would say she went through a hell of a lot of pain before she died. Any idea how long she's been here?"

"We're hoping you can tell us."

"When can I get her down?"

"We have to clear the scene, tree, rope, and even road before we can bring in the equipment to get her down. You have to give us time." Eckhart pushes his glasses again.

Dr. Norton throws his hands up. "That's going to take forever. I don't have all day to sit here in a puddle of water waiting for you guys to crawl around with your forceps looking for twenty year old garbage and fox hairs."

"Everything is possibly a clue or evidence. You're going to have to wait."

"Jesus Christ," the doctor turns and heads back down the cleared path with heavy steps. "I'm going for coffee. Come get me when you're done."

We watch Dr. Norton walk away for a while. It is a moment where we don't have to look at the woman. When we turn back she is facing us head on. The multiples of lacerations and

18

puncture wounds cover her face, limbs, and torso. I try to count, but there are too many. Too many are covered in blood. How many times can a human being be cut before passing out or passing away?

"He cut her fingernails." The woman's hands look so small dangling at her side.

"So she might have fought back," Marilyn takes pictures with the small camera she carried under her notebook.

"She might have." I go back to staring at her. I have to stare at her. I say, "It means he's smart. He knows enough to get rid of possible evidence."

"Then he's probably smart enough to not leave anything anywhere else. You don't think this is a new thing then?"

"I don't know."

"She didn't die that long ago." Eckhart starts walking back to do his work. "I'll get a dental imprint and fingerprints when we get her to the hospital, see if we can ID her. If we can't find any ID, that is." He looks at me and waits until I return his gaze. "This is going to rock the island, isn't it?"

I watch Eckhart walk back toward the tree where the rope is tied. There is not much any of us need to say. An unsolved murder occurred in Prince Edward Island over twenty years ago and people still talk about it. The papers still ask for answers on slow news days. The farmers that meet in the corner stores for a morning coffee still shake their heads and ask each other if they ever heard anything.

Prince Edward Island sits in the Gulf of the St. Lawrence where the fresh waters of the Great Lakes meet the salt waters of the Atlantic. It is 246 kilometers across and is covered in fields, patches of forest –there are so many colors of green- and small villages. Churches seem to spot the horizon over every hill. There are cattle and horse farms everywhere. People here believe in being self-sufficient with gardens, beef, poultry, and pork farms, wild mushrooms, and everything else natural anyone could want. There are potatoes in the fall and lobster in June. Then there is the debate over which is better – North shore or South shore lobsters. Beginning in May, the island turns on and the population quadruples almost overnight with tourists coming to see the home of Anne of Green Gables. There is a water park, amusement park, drive-in movie theatre, and countless beaches around the island. In October it shuts down; most of the restaurants outside of the cities and towns close down as well as anything fun to do. People have nothing left to do. The island usually has a relaxed feel, showing up fifteen minutes late is still on time, but something of this magnitude will tilt the whole island. This will change everything.

"This is pure anger," Marilyn says as if reading my mind. "This wasn't just killing, this was hate. Stabbing a few times is anger, but this went well beyond that. The killer wanted to make a statement."

"What was that?"

"That this was pure hatred."

I don't say a word. There isn't anything for me to say. She is right. Instead I think, *"And this is only the beginning."*

Chapter 2

Twenty years ago.

"Ben, change your clothes first. Ben get back here and-"

Ben couldn't hear his mother's voice. Or rather, he did not want to hear his mother. He chose a long time ago to stop listening to his parents. Nothing they said mattered out in his world. He could do anything he wanted to. Ha ha. His parents were idiots. His parents said, "Stand up to a bully and they'll back down." Bullshit. He wasn't quite sure what the word meant but it was bullshit. Most of what his parents said was bullshit. If he knew the words, he would say he was quite enlightened for an eight year old.

He was a good boy. He kept to himself in his room playing with his *Hot Wheels* and *Legos* and *G.I. Joe* soldiers having wars in the wrinkles of his comforter. He cleaned up after himself. He said please and thank you. He was a good boy. He told himself he was a good boy. No matter what he did he was a good boy.

Ben made sure to hit every puddle left over from the rain with his black Sunday shoes. His socks were soaked after the second one. He felt the chill touch his toes and shoot up his legs. He could picture his white socks, fresh on this morning, going black from the inside of the wet leather. The water and mud splashed up over the cuff of his khaki Sunday pants.

The park was only a block away from home. It was a safe neighborhood. *Ha ha.* What parents don't know won't hurt them. *What parents don't want to see will hurt you*, Ben thought.

Ben took the last puddle before the park two footed. The brown water wet his pants all the way past his knees and completely soaked his shoes through. He let out one of those pure child laughs that kids do when they reach a sudden moment of the purest joy. It was an instant of happiness – a flash in a boy's life.

The small park had a swing set with divots in the graveled ground under each swing made from years of kids dragging their feet and ruining their shoes, a couple of teeter totters, and a slide with worn out marks down the middle made up the rest. There was a lot of mowed grass around the play equipment. Houses squared the park off on three sides and the road lined the fourth. Ben liked going to the park by himself. It wasn't that he always wanted to go there alone but that nobody else wanted to go with him. He never asked, but he didn't have to, to know that they would all say no. Away from school and church he didn't talk to any of the other kids. He was strange, one had said. The park was his world. It was a place where he could run free for a little while. A place where he could experiment.

He rode the swings until he got tired of going back and forth and then climbed to the top of the slide only to sit there and wait for long minutes. He watched the cars passing by – there were four red ones – before riding down the metal slide and climbing back up again. He never went near the teeter totters. Teeter totters were for pairs. You needed real friends to do that. People in his neighborhood stayed away from him. Lucky for Ben not many came to the park after a rainy morning. Especially a Sunday morning.

He walked around the swing set kicking at the loose gravel that found its way into the grass from dozens of kids dragging their feet as they swung back and forth. Rain water had collected in the ditches under each swing. The red island dirt made the puddles red as well. Worms had found their way to the surface of the earth.

Ben crouched down beside the half empty ditch under the second swing. The wet grass soaked into the knees of his pants. His mom was going get mad. He'd end up with a smack on the bum and sent to have a warm bath, then straight to his bedroom until supper time. Then it would be the *Wonderful World of Disney* on TV, ice cream and to bed for the night. Not bad for getting in trouble.

He pushed around a worm with his finger. Their bodies had gone almost white from being in the rain water. Their bodies twisted slightly, but were too waterlogged to move much. They were like his dad after Thanksgiving dinner. They were full of water and didn't want to move. He took up a worm between his finger and thumb and rolled it back and forth. Staring at the tiny creature, something in his eyes went wild and scary. He wanted to see what was inside. He wanted to see if it still lived when it was pulled apart into two like he heard somewhere. He pushed his finger and thumb together. The worm's skin strained and then popped and his fingertips were covered in wet. He rubbed the two together as if he were trying to rub something sticky from one of them, but instead smeared the yellow and white mess of worm guts between them. Ben picked up more worms with his gooey fingers and placed them in his other palm. They squirmed and tickled. He counted ten. Ben put both palms together and pressed hand to hand like he did earlier in church. Their bodies popped between his palms. He felt their guts squeeze out of their thin bodies all over his hands.

If you looked at the boy by the swing set from across the park, all you would think was that a little kid was playing in the mud. His white teeth glowed in a big smile. You wouldn't be able to see the thoughts behind his eyes or the future he had to live. From far away he was just a kid in the mud. In that instant if you looked in his eyes you would probably have shivered.

He didn't turn around. He didn't hear anything behind him. He had no way of knowing what was going to happen so he had no reason to run.

The toe of a shoe hit Ben square in the crack of his ass. Pain shattered up through his tailbone and into his spine. He flew forward, hands first, into the ditch of mud and water. His head hit the swing and sent it flying. His hands stung. The water and mud soaked into his shirt and chilled his skin. He was suddenly aware of what the mud smelled like. The smile was gone. Now he was only pitiful.

Ben didn't move. He laid there in the red mud waiting for something to happen. He heard the chain on the swing creak. He heard feet sloshing in the grass around him. There had to be at least three sets of feet circling him. There was laughter. Lots of laughter. He hated laughter. Everyone who laughed, laughed about him. They laughed at him.

"Awww, did the little boy fall down?"

"The baby got all muddy."

"What's your mom going to say?" The boy sounded older.

Ben didn't move. He knew how this went. If he moved and looked at them he would get picked on and made fun of. He would get told not to look at them and his face would be pushed back into the muck. If he didn't move, didn't look at them, he would get picked on and made fun of, but not as long.

"Come on kid. Are you gonna cry?" A boot drove into Ben's thigh. He felt the bruise form instantly over his muscle. "Look at your Sunday best. Your mom's going to kick your fag ass." The older boy grabbed onto Ben's ankles and dragged him back along the grass. Ben felt the stains permanently grinding into his shirt. He rolled onto his back and looked up at the older kids. Two teenage boys and a girl. Their faces were blank. They had eyes, lips, and distinguishing features, but to Ben they were blank. They were faceless. They were everyone.

The girl said, "Let's leave him alone. He's pathetic enough." *Pathetic.* She laughed and then the others joined in. Their laughter echoed through his ears. *Pathetic.*

Ha, ha, ha. Look at the boy covered in mud and grass. *Ha, ha.*

Ben laid on the cold damp ground and let them do whatever they wanted to. He was too little to fight back. Fighting back brought more pain. His pants ripped and he felt the skin on his knee tear. His pants got pulled down, underwear pulled up until he began to cry. *Pathetic cry baby.* They left him alone with tears cutting the dirt that stained his face. The cuts on his knee

24

and his hands were hot and sticky. He laid there for a while before getting up and walking home.

Ben, what the hell happened to you?

How could you let this happen to you?

Let this happen? Pathetic. His mom washed the mud from his body. His Mom put band aids on his cuts. He went to bed and laid there staring at his ceiling hearing the laughter over and over. *Pathetic.*

Chapter 3

"Coffee?"

"Sure, black." I stay in the back of the MCP as McIntyre squeezes into the kitchen section and pours the drinks. Leaving the bush I counted four more of our cars, all the officers milling around and drinking coffee. Nobody else is allowed down the road toward the scene, but everyone wants to see what's going on.

Sergeant Deborah English leans against the radio desk with an oversized travel mug between both hands. She is the Media Relations liaison for L Division. It is her job to talk to the reporters and say a lot without saying a thing. Some think she got the job because nobody else wants it and she has the patience to fend off the same question over and over in English and French. Others think she got the job because she looks good on TV. Her yellow blond hair is styled in a pixie cut, short in the back and sides, longer on top in layers but nothing past her ears, and still looks wet from a quick shower. She wears the standard uniform of blue pants with a yellow stripe down each leg, khaki colored shirt with all the proper insignias, and a blue tie. She puts her coffee down for a second to zip up her thick coat. We just nod to each other.

Deb and Hillary go together to the Farmer's Market every Saturday and try to go out for drinks once or twice a month. She is a single mom; her husband left her for an old girlfriend or something. Deborah likes to deal with work at work, but Hillary keeps me up to date with gossip. It is a small island, I'm sure I'd hear it sooner or later.

"I let the kids go. They didn't see anything. They saw the body and got the hell out." McIntyre hands me a white Styrofoam cup. "So, what do you think?" Two other MCU members look back from the fold down dining table in the middle of the trailer that in a normal camper would have been used to make an extra bed.

"I think this is something that won't leave me for a while." The sadness in my voice is physically aching. It surprises me. I sip the coffee and wince at the heat burning my taste buds. At least it is something to take my mind off – *drip* – the woman.

McIntyre looks around the room and at the virgin light outside, searching for something to focus on. He says, "Any chance this is a random thing?"

"What do you think?" I know my answer. There is no such thing as a random thing. A woman does not get strung up in the middle of nowhere as a random thing.

"Do you think this is homegrown?"

"Not a clue. We need more. Do you think it is?"

He steps out onto the back ramp. I do the same and stare down the grassy side road. Dr. Norton is back down there waiting patiently with a stretcher from the ambulance. Marilyn is still down there supervising the evidence collection. McIntyre just stares down the dirt road looking at the way out.

He says, "I don't want to speculate. Not until we have an ID."

"Did you go see her?"

"No, Constable Husk was first on scene, and I instructed him not to allow anyone down there but the Ident team, the Coroner, and you two."

"Unless this girl is the bitch from hell who somebody hates with a passion, the guy who did this has severe issues. He cut her up, he stabbed her, he probably raped her; there's bruising so he beat her, and then he strung her up and left her hanging naked in the woods. He's angry and he's violent. My gut says this has nothing to do with the girl."

"What does it have to do with then?"

"Him," I say. "I think all of this has to do with him." A set of headlights are coming down the main road. "I don't know. This is giving me the same feelings I had out West."

"Who the hell is this?"

The lights bounce as the white mini-van teeters in and out of large puddles. The only reason for someone to be on this road, at this time of year, is to sit and wait for the sun to rise and the fish to bite. Only they have passed the bridge where most of the fishing happens. It could be some nosy islander out seeing what all the commotion is about. If we're lucky it'll be the killer coming to check on his hanging trophy and just hasn't noticed all of the RCMP vehicles yet. That's fantasy shit.

"I don't believe this. How did they find out so fast?" Sgt. McIntyre tosses the rest of his coffee into the brush.

"They all have scanners. You know we're lucky they didn't get here sooner." Deb walks down the ramp and straightens her shirt of wrinkles.

As if we don't have enough to deal with. The white van pulls to a stop behind all the cars and the two doors open. The passenger is a woman dressed in a nice grey suit. The moment she steps around the van, I see that her thick heeled shoes have sunk into the mud. The driver steps out and reaches back in for a shoulder propped video camera and a microphone with a coiled wire. With practice and position he gets everything set up and the camera on his shoulder as he walks. He hands the microphone to the woman; *CBC* is written on all sides. The woman bounces around the puddles. Her face is in a disgusted frown until she looks up and sees us. A smile erupts across her face. The camera man walks straight through the dirty water keeping one step behind the reporter.

I've been through this sort of thing before. I don't want to be involved with reporters and headlines and all the shit that can come with it. I take a couple of steps backward so that I am behind McIntyre.

"Good morning, gentlemen and lady," the reporter says. "Catherine Arsenault from CBC television news, may I speak with you?" She is in her forties, attractive with brown hair

29

flowing back behind her shoulders and nice eyes. She looks like a woman who had to get ready in a hurry. Her hair is a little messed and her pants, though clinging to her hips, are wrinkled. She holds up the large headed microphone in front of our faces. Her white tipped nails look new.

"About what? There's nothing going on here."

"And you are?"

"Sergeant McIntyre." He crosses his arms over his chest. He looks like a pub bouncer.

"Head of Major Crimes? And you say nothing is going on."

He nods with a half-smile. She's fishing for answers and quotes.

"Is it true you found the body of a woman hanging from a tree?"

McIntyre doesn't know what to say. Somehow reporters always get their information and get involved. This part isn't just in the movies. In PEI, they are hungry for anything big and newsworthy. They have police scanners and have been known to arrive before the police and completely screw up the scene. They have to get their stories and find out their information one way or the other.

Deb touches his elbow and steps in front of the two of us. She says, "Sergeant English, Media Relations Liaison. A statement will be made at headquarters later today, Ms. Arsenault. There's nothing for you –"

"My daughter was one of the kids who found the body, Sergeant, so I know it's there. I even have pictures of it." McIntyre and I both take a second glance at her. She looks at us with a knowing grin on her lips and one sculpted eyebrow cocked a little. "You can answer a couple of questions or I can make my own story. It is a lot easier if we work toge-"

"Don't threaten us, Ms. Arsenault. I am not at liberty to release a statement, yet. Off the record?" She waits for her to nod and the camera man to point the camera down. "Off the record a body of a young woman was found and Major Crimes is investigating. When Sergeant Reid is done with his preliminary, I will be making a statement in front of Headquarters. We will aim for around noon; until then, everything is speculation. If you show pictures then you may be damaging our investigation. We don't know if it is suicide, homicide, or accident." She told her it was "off the record," but with reporters there is no such thing. She probably has a tape recorder in her pocket or the camera is still taping voice. Deb knows this, which is why she hasn't said anything really new.

"She accidentally found herself hanging from a tree all cut up?" She raises her eyebrow again and cocks one hip. I bite my lip and try to look away from her. To be blunt, I can't fucking stand reporters. I get it, they are just doing their jobs, but when your job is to use colourful adjectives and adverbs to pump yourself up, and to stretch facts to sensationalize the story and screw up my job, then they can go to hell. It wasn't long ago that a body was found on a PEI beach and the family found out by seeing the victim's car on the news before ever getting notified. The reporters didn't care about what effect they will have on others or the investigations. It is all a big competition to have the best story and outdo the other guy. Fuck the reporters.

"All kinds of things can happen, Ms. Arsenault. Right now you are interfering with an investigation so please take your van back up the road."

"I have a responsibility to notify the public if there is a crazy maniac stringing up women on the island."

"There is no reason to believe this is more than an isolated incident."

"Can I quote you on that?"

"Why don't you screw off and let us do our damn jobs," I didn't even think the words before they are out of my mouth.

I watch the camera man's reaction. He looks from Catherine Arsenault to me with quick eyes. She probably isn't used to being told what to do. She says, "I am not going to keep quiet. I'm going to say that a body of a woman was found. I won't use my pictures, yet. Some parent out there may be wondering where their daughter is."

"All the more reason for you to fuck off so we can get some answers."

"Can I quote you on that, then? Sergeant, *Reid*, was it?"

McIntyre turns on me and stares me down. I can feel Deb's eyes burning on me. I turn and take a couple of steps into the MCP. That was stupid.

The other MCU guys are smiling at me behind Styrofoam coffee cups.

The two of them get back in the van and back out the way they came. They will probably stop by the river to give a sound bite about the RCMP making a find and being tight lipped about the whole thing. If we say too much too soon we risk hurting the girl's family and tipping off the killer so he can go into hiding. Other cases across the country have gone haywire because too much information has been given to the press before the officers had a solid case. We are only a couple of hours in. We do not have any information yet, so saying anything would be dangerous to convicting someone in the future. We'll tell them what they need to know when we feel it is right.

"Reid," Deb puts her arms out wide, "what the hell?"

"I'm sorry, I just, I don't know. I'm sorry."

"Next time just shut the hell up. It's my job to deal with these people. Did you notice the red light was on on the camera when he was pointing it down? They got everything on tape. I said, "Off the record," for their benefit. There's no such thing as off the record. Don't be surprised to find something you said on the news today." She shakes her head and walks away. McIntyre stands quietly.

Given the choice, I am not sure if I would stay on Prince Edward Island. It is a beautiful place, I have to admit that, but it does not move as fast as I'm used to. In a month the gates will open and tourists from as far away as Japan will flock to the island to play golf, eat seafood, and visit *Anne of Green Gables*. For most of the year it's a close knit community. Out in the rural area everyone knows everyone else. In the big cities, Charlottetown and Summerside, yes there are only two, and the latter barely classifies, you see new faces and a lot of ones you recognize just from being out and about. It is a good place to visit. PEI has everything you need, but not everything you want.

It is a place where strangers are usually noticed, but where the, *don't ask – don't tell* policy runs wild.

There is no need for the large lights by the time they bring the body out of the woods. The girl is in a black bag on a stretcher with an ambulance attendant on both ends. Dr. Norton walks in front of the bagged girl, Marilyn takes up the rear. She steps beside me and tells me how nothing has been found around the scene yet. They are bagging and labeling whatever they pick up but they won't know if there is anything there until they can look through it all in the lab. The doctor took a quick look at the dead body. He thinks she may have been alive when she was hanged, but that it may not be the direct cause of death. He'll perform the autopsy later and get some answers. I listen to my partner, but stare at the EMT's as they put the woman into the back of the ambulance. Everyone has come out of the MCU to watch it happen.

Drip.

I see my dream, I see her hanging from the tree, and I see her body all cut up. There's a twinge in my pants. I turn my head back to the grassy road and wonder for a second if she walked down there innocently, as if she were on a nature hike, not knowing that someone was waiting for her. I look at Marilyn and want to grab onto her and kiss her, hard. I don't want to think about dead girls any more.

"I'll ride in with her," my eyes go down to the ground. Ever wonder if the woman standing in front of you can hear your thoughts. It would be the opposite of that Mel Gibson movie. I wouldn't mind knowing her thoughts.

"Are you sure?"

"Yeah," I kick a rock into the mud. "Dispirito, you take my car back then you and Moore can look at missing persons. Focus on the tattoo. LeBlanc and Longfellow, co-ordinate with the officers CrOps is sending and canvas the neighborhood –" The two other Major Crimes officers nurse their coffees.

"As much of one as there is," LeBlanc says. One stretch of road with houses makes a neighborhood in the rural area.

"Somebody had to have noticed an out of place vehicle." I know I don't have to tell them anything. They know what their job is.

I fill Marilyn in on what happened with the CBC van and then turn to the rest of the group. "Be careful who you talk to and what you say, everyone."

"No worries. Have a good ride."

I climb into the back of the ambulance and the doors shut behind me.

I hate body bags. Body bags represent the end of things. Four smaller body bags brought me here. They put me on the island. They put me in the back of yet another ambulance with a fifth body bag.

In British Colombia I was lead investigator in a set of murders of young girls ranging from 11 to 13 years of age. The first was Nicole Tait taken from the street on her way to a friend's house. All they found that day was her bike left lying on a neighbor's lawn just off the sidewalk. She was found a week later next to the swings in a park on the same street as her family home. Raped, beaten, left to be found on the dew covered grass like some raggedy forgotten doll. She didn't deserve that.

Sara McDonald, 12, with long blond curls, last seen in pink sweat pants and a pink and white T-shirt, got into a fight with her Mom over use of a cell phone and ran away. Her Mom didn't go after her because she thought Sara would just come back when it was getting dark or when she was hungry; it was taco night – Sara loved taco night. Posters were put up on telephone poles and in corner store windows. Her Mom went on the local news pleading for people to look out for her and return her to her home. She saw Sara again almost a month later when she was found lying in the soft sand around a playgrounds slides and swings. Again she was raped and beaten. She was dressed in different clothes that were covered in dirt and mud. We had DNA, we had evidence, and we didn't have suspects.

Working a case without suspects is like staring at a crossword puzzle all day. Everything you need to finish something, to solve the puzzle or convict someone, is right there in your hands but you can't get the answers to the clues. You need more. For us, more meant other girls had to be put to slaughter.

The public thought we were moving too slow. They still hurt from the Pickton Pig farm case where over fifty women went missing from downtown Vancouver for almost twenty years and then the remains were found at Robert Pickton's pig farm. Why weren't we doing anything? We didn't care about the women since they were prostitutes and drug addicts. People don't know. They don't understand that it takes time to talk to witnesses and build evidence and plug all the holes so that a suspect can't slip through the cracks and go free. If you are building a house would you want the contractor who puts your house up in a hurry without any regard to doing it right or one who takes time and makes sure the foundation is there to hold the whole thing up? That is the whole point of me escorting the body in the ambulance. Someone has to be with it at all times so no arguments can be made about flow of evidence.

I couldn't leave the case in BC alone. I barely went home during the weeks we were searching for anything to help us. I couldn't take being at home and putting Leigh to bed while the other girl's parents had empty beds in their houses. When I did go home Hillary and I fought about why I wasn't there and how I wasn't being a good father.

After number three, we had a witness. We should have got him then. We should have had enough to make an arrest and a conviction.

I got the guy in BC. He killed one more little girl. He won't kill any more though. That's all I care to say about that.

The ride to the Queen Elizabeth Hospital, QEH, in Charlottetown takes a good thirty minutes from the crime scene so I try to get my mind to go somewhere else. I think about the bills I have to pay and the money and favors I owe. I think of Hillary. She's probably pouring herself a cup of coffee and making herself something to eat. Leigh should be off to school now. Grade four is different now than it was when I was her age. They talk about boys and she is changing before my eyes. She's too young for bras and boys. She has drama club on Tuesdays after school and horse riding Thursday nights. She's almost the same age as those girls in BC. *Drip.*

"Oh shit," I say under my breath and look toward the attendants in the cab. I look around the back of the ambulance and try naming off as much of the equipment as I can in my head. My eyes still go back to the body strapped to the gurney.

The girl inside the black bag will never get married. She had hopes and ambitions. She had dreams and nightmares. It ended on a nightmare. Who was this girl? She had a life somewhere once. She was somebody.

At the *QEH* I will follow the paramedics as they roll the body down to the basement and secure it inside a cooler. Then I will lock the cooler with an RCMP lock, seal the door with tape and wait for a constable to show up to guard the cooler and make sure nobody unofficial gets to the body. Dr. Norton will do the autopsy first thing tomorrow morning and then we'll have more to work with. Hopefully we'll have COD and weapon molds and maybe finger prints and fibers. Things don't work like they do on TV. We can't get all the answers in seconds. That is the problem with the public and their view on police investigations. Cop shows have warped them so much into thinking it only takes minutes to run fingerprints through databases and getting identification.

I turn my eyes too look out the front window of the ambulance. My eyes slowly swing back to the bag beside me. I don't want to do this again.

Chapter 4

Seventeen years ago

"Thank you for coming. I'm so sorry for the wait. Some parents just have a lot of questions to ask."

"That's no problem."

"Good, good. Have a seat. Let's talk about Ben."

~ * ~

The boy carefully looked around the corner of hay bales he piled so that he was hidden from the far window. He stared at the pyramid of doughnuts placed in the corner junction of two walls of hay, five bails high. The thought was that they could be used as a funnel to trap the creatures that got into the horse feed and garbage. The doughnuts, the plain ones left from the box of dozen, were bait. Oh if mom only knew why he cried that he wanted to pick up a dozen on the way to Grandma and Grandpa's. She'd what?

His fingers flexed around the broomstick at his side. His fingers were long and thin. His Grandmother called them piano player fingers. His feet were ready to spring his body forward like an Olympic sprinter in the blocks waiting for the starting gun. It was all about timing of course. He had missed twice before, but he learned each time. This time he knew what to do and was certain he wouldn't miss.

Ben liked puzzles. He liked figuring things out and finding the right way to get the right results. The smell of dust and straw was thick in his nostrils. It mixed and mingled with the cow dung and rotting barn boards. His ears tried to pick up every sound. Cows moved from leg to leg below him as they ate. Something was scraping in the ceiling rafters. He felt the hay scratch his face and hands. He could feel a rash tingling on parts of his body from the rough dried straw. It could be added to the rash on his groin from sleeping in the wet.

That morning he got rid of his soiled sheets and boxer shorts before Grandma noticed. She would find them at the bottom of the laundry hamper tomorrow or the next day when it was full, but he'd be gone. And what would she do? She would call Mom and Dad and they would excuse it off as he was a late bloomer. He can't help it.

~ * ~

"He's a very nice and polite boy. He is one of the few boys who uses please and thank you all the time."

~ * ~

When Ben's Dad left the Navy a long time ago he took his Navy-issue switchblade with him. It had a black fake wood handle with metal tips. The push of one button and the blade instantly arced up from the side ready to slice and stab. Three weeks ago Ben reached into the top dresser drawer in his parent's room and wrapped his long fingers around the black handle and quickly slipped it into his jeans pocket. Every day he had it in his right pocket as he got on the bus for school. He never planned on using it, but somehow it made it easier to get on the bus.

The switchblade, blade folded outward, was tied to the end of the broomstick with baling twine. He raised the makeshift spear. His ears caught a scraping noise. It was different than that in the rafters. Something was coming. His body tensed.

~ * ~

"Ben is very intelligent."

"He likes to figure out puzzles and things."

"Oh I've noticed. He is especially good at fixing his mistakes the second time he does things. He learns from being wrong and is never wrong the same way twice. Unfortunately I think the general class curriculum is a little elementary for him and he seems a little bored with some of the things we are doing. He is always reading ahead in textbooks and reads extra on the subjects we are taking so that he knows a little more before the rest of the class."

"And is that a problem?"

"It is for Ben. I think maybe he would benefit from special classes that will nurture his intelligence."

~ * ~

The bandit's face appeared in the open window. Its nose searched the air for any danger, anything at all. The raccoon scrambled over the windowsill and into the barn. It smelled the air again and quickly ran along the wall of hay toward the doughnuts. Ben's eyes widened. He suddenly forgot how to breathe. Now was not the time to be hasty.

He learned that the first time. That time he jumped out to early and the raccoon doubled back and disappeared around the edge of the hay wall and into hiding.

His fingers tightened on the pole until his knuckles were white. He had to wait for the bandit to start eating. No, not just start eating. He had to wait for the raccoon to be fully engrossed in his doughnuts so much that it wouldn't notice the sound of the boy springing to his feet and charging across at him. By the time the raccoon noticed the spear soared through the air toward its fat belly; the eleven year old boy's hand was still holding on to the other end. The sharp blade dug a centimeter or so into the animal's body. Ben pulled the spear back. The knife dropped to the wood floor with a thwack and the pole went flying out of his hands.

~ * ~

"Ben does seem to have a problem with the other kids. He seems to get picked on a fair bit, but it's all kids' stuff. I don't think there is too much to worry about. He's still well adjusted."

~ * ~

He didn't hesitate. Ben dove forward and slid across the floor on his stomach. He felt his shirt rip and his chest go raw. He grabbed the handle of the knife. The raccoon bared its teeth. A crazed growl escaped from its throat. Ben sliced through the air. He missed and sliced again. The tip of blade cut the animals black nose. It pulled back into the corner and let out a hiss. Ben hissed back.

The doughnuts went skidding across the planked flooring.

"Die," Ben screamed. He sliced again. This time he felt metal cut through skin and flesh and eyeball. He felt the blade scrape bone. *Tingles*. Blood escaped from the raccoon's eye socket. It struck forward and missed.

Ben jabbed with the knife. He felt it hit something. He jabbed and jabbed. His mouth was wide open, tongue sticking out. The sharp blade plunged into the animal. He felt it break through fur and skin and go deep into muscle. He felt the heat of blood splash over his hand. He pulled the switchblade back and jammed it forward as hard as he could. Ben was sure he felt the hard floor through the animal's body. His left hand pushed the raccoon's neck down. The other hand sliced and stabbed at it. As fast as he pulled the knife away he threw it back at the raccoon. He laughed at the sounds the animal made. He liked the feeling of blood and guts over his fingers and arms. He could tell instantly when all the life left the raccoon, but he had to keep slicing at its skin. He liked the way it felt every time the blade broke through the skin and flesh. He wanted it.

~ * ~

"Thank you for coming in. I think Ben shows a lot of promise. I think he will do some great things."

~ * ~

After fifteen minutes of sitting and trying to control his breathing, Ben pulled his shoelace out of his running shoe. He quickly tied one end around the raccoon's neck. His fingers were sticky with red. He climbed up on a couple of bails and tied the other end of the string to a nail sticking out from a post. Small bits of hay and straw stuck to the animals insides which were now out.

Drip.

He sat back down and looked up at what he had done. Soon Grandma would call him in for supper. He had to get washed up before he could go. He could do that with the hose downstairs used to water the horses and cows. He got up and left, the switchblade closed and back in his pocket.

Later on his Grandfather found the hanging corpse and gave his intelligent, well-adjusted grandson congratulations on killing one of the bandit rodents.

Ben didn't wet his bed any more.

Chapter 5

"We have an ID." Marilyn walks down the hallway toward me outside the cooler. She has changed out of her mud stained pants and into a pair of grey slacks, a blue sweater, and a grey blazer. "A missing persons report was filed first thing this morning in Calgary. They just sent it to us."

"She's from Alberta?"

One of the new constables in L Division had shown up ten minutes before. He stands behind Marilyn, trying to listen without being obvious. Every time he moves his leather shoes and belt creak.

"She's here attending University. Her parents filed a report with the Calgary detachment because they haven't heard from her in over a week." She hands me a piece of paper with all of the girl's particulars on it. I try not to notice that somehow she found the time to fix her make-up, some blush and eyeliner – like putting a spotlight on an already eye catching painting.

I slowly read it over, but still ask, "What's her name?" *Chloe?*

"Johanna Bowers. Twenty-two, five foot five, long blond hair, tattoo of a black and white rose on the back of her shoulder. We still have to wait for a DNA positive, but it looks like her. I've tried calling her cell phone, but it goes straight to voice mail."

"You have her address?"

She nods.

"Let's go then. Constable, stay by the door. If you need anything get somebody to get it for you. Call me if there are any problems."

On cue my phone rings. I take a quick look at the caller ID.

"If you don't answer it she'll keep calling you. I would." Marilyn smiles at me then picks up her speed to walk a little faster than me.

I watch her ass cheeks fight with each other inside her slacks and push the button on my phone. "Hello."

"It's been all over the radio that a body was found last night. Was that your call? I thought you said homicides didn't occur here." My wife's voice comes fast as if she's been waiting to say things and wants to get them out quickly. "You said this wouldn't be like back in –"

"Hillary, this isn't like before." I try to keep my voice low. I keep my eyes on my partner in case she turns around. I say, "There hasn't been a homicide on the island since the eighties. Most of the Members haven't worked on homicides in any of their postings. I'm the best qualified for this, and you know that. Let me do my job."

Silence. I can still hear her breathing, thinking, so I know she's still there. "Promise me this won't be like BC. Promise me you won't get that way again." She goes quiet again. Every woman's greatest strength is her silence. When she is quiet I know she is mad. When she goes quiet I start walking on eggshells, knowing damn well that anything I say or do could start her talking again. That is not necessarily a good thing.

I follow Marilyn up the stairs to the front lobby and outside the front doors. I say, "I have to go Hill. I'll call you later. And I won't forget the milk." I don't wait for a reply.

"Wife troubles?"

"I'll talk about my home life if you talk about yours."

She turns on me with glaring eyes. I try smiling, but don't know what it looks like. "At least I'm not pussy whipped."

"Just a little whipped."

Marilyn looks at me over the hood of her car. She licks her lips and says, "Maybe I like a little whipping some time."

44

I let out a laugh. *Damn.*

~ * ~

The first thing we did when we moved to PEI was take one of those horse and buggy rides through "old" Charlottetown where the driver tells you somewhat interesting historical anecdotes about the city. It was enough to encourage Hillary to learn more.

The original occupants of the island were the Mi'kmaq peoples who called it Abegweit, *"resting on the waves."* The French were the first Europeans to settle on the island calling it, Ile Saint-Jean. They settled first at Port-La-Joye, which is now Charlottetown Harbor, and began developing and farming the land. People settled along the Hillsborough River, Tracadie, Savage Harbor, and different settlements which still exist today. They were known as *Acadians.* Nearly forty years later the British came to PEI. They rounded up and deported the French from the island, whether they liked it or not. A few people stayed in settlements which are still there like Rustico, Malpaque Bay, and Souris. Many of the Acadian peoples escaped the British however and settled down in New Orleans and are now called *Cajun.* The name of the island was changed to St. John's Island and then again to Prince Edward Island in honor of Prince Edward, Duke of Kent and Strathearn. He was father of Queen Victoria and the younger brother to King George IV. The land was cut up into lots and settled by English, Scotts, and Irish. In 1864 meetings and negotiations leading to Canadian Confederation were held at Province House in Charlottetown. Industries of farming, especially potatoes, ship building, and fishing for fish, lobster, and mussels expanded. Through the years industries changed with tourism and education becoming more prominent. The island is home to the University of Prince Edward Island, Department of Agriculture and Agri-Foods, an experimental farm, Holland College which is home to The Culinary Institute of Canada, and the Atlantic Veterinary College. People still have the names of the original French settlers, but

45

now in modern times the island is a collection of races and cultures coming here for their own reasons.

Charlottetown, named for Queen Charlotte consort of King George III, has almost run out of room to expand outward. Instead they are expanding upward with lavish condos built for the elite and multi-million dollar hotels built on top of pre-existing shopping malls. Soon we'll reach the futuristic point where buildings are built on top of other building and the garbage gets tossed on those left below.

I am surprised at how much money the island has. There are plenty of farmers and college and university students struggling week to week, but there are also those who can afford six thousand dollars a month condos on the waterfront overlooking Confederation Landing and private dining in their own home made by a professional chef.

In the downtown, the old part of Char' Town, the houses are squished side by side like in London England. The further one gets away from town centers like Sherwood, Parkdale, Winsloe, East Royalty and West Royalty, the houses have yards and space.

Marilyn circles into the mid-town area of Queen Street avoiding one-way streets and the busy intersections. There is a lot of opportunity for room rentals in the city, but they are not always good.

Johanna Bowers's apartment is across the street from a Laundromat known for having drug deals out back.

Some of the downtown streets have sidewalks built after telephone and electricity poles were put in so that now the poles are actually in the edge of the road limiting parking spaces. In the winter, snow is plowed to form a center line down the streets and is trucked away during the night or the next day. It fucked me up the first winter here because I had to climb a snow bank on the streets center line to get where I was going. Marilyn tries to turn down one road and swerves back after seeing the one-way sign. The city, especially downtown, is riddled with one-way streets. She turns onto the next one, circles around, and then parks between the poles with her tires caressing the leveled sidewalk. I can see a school and a park. My first call was near here, a rape.

Johanna's building is your typical cheap ass place. It is one quarter of a house converted into four apartments. There is white vinyl siding stained near the bottom from lawnmower projectiles, Canadian flag hanging in an upstairs window, cracked eaves drooping. Nothing special. The only thing different about the place, compared to the other apartments, is that one door has been painted bright blue, I presume by the occupants. I ring the doorbell beside it.

The door opens a few seconds later. "Oh, hi," a woman stands in the doorway with a large toothy smile. "Can I help you?"

I say, "Good morning, I'm Sergeant Reid with the RCMP, this is Sergeant Moore. Does Johanna Bowers live here?"

Her smile disappears. "She does. I'm her roommate, Alex." Brown eyes dart between the two of us. She has dark hair tied back in a bun and a pair of rectangular glasses with black frames. She wears black knickers and a pink top. She quickly asks, "Have you found her? Is she okay? Her Mom's been calling and –"

"Do you have a recent picture of her?" I ask, ignoring her queries.

She stares at me a little harder making her brow furrow. "I – I do." She crosses the room and yanks a 5x7 off the refrigerator door. A second photo remains under a *Simpsons* magnet. A butterfly magnet hits the vinyl flooring and slides under a white plastic patio table. "Shit. Here. She's the blond. Obviously, I guess." Her last words trail off to nothing as her eyes drop.

The first thing I notice in the picture is the date stamped in yellow digital numbers in the bottom corner. It was taken this past October. The glossy print shows a blond and brunette posing on top of a sand dune. The blond has one arm outstretched at an angle to the sky with the other across her chest: the Archer about to let loose an arrow from her bow. She wears cutoff jeans and a white belly shirt. Over her navel is a black hand print, and there are three black claw marks on one cheek drawn with what I assume is charcoal. The brunette in a body builder pose wears a tank-top and shorts. She has a black mark drawn under each eye, football style, and three paw prints crawling up from between her breasts. They are smiling. They are happy. Good times.

Johanna Bowers – *drip* – has no blood in her windswept hair.

I feel a twinge somewhere.

Marilyn and I nod to each other. "Where was this picture taken?" I can see that it is on one of the dunes created by tides and Atlantic winds, but figuring out where on the island is impossible – at least to my mainland eyes. The tall hill of white sand has tufts of tall grass on top. The grass tries to hold onto the minute grains trying to stop the sand from blowing away. The picture is same as every dune around the island. It could be anywhere from Cavendish to Brackley.

"That's at Blooming Point Beach." Alex takes her cell phone from her pocket to take a quick look. She misses Marilyn and me looking at each other. *Coincidence?* She puts the phone back in her pocket. "It was an Indian summer so we thought we'd have an adventure and walk the entire beach and have a camp fire for lunch. That dune was by the nudie end." Blooming Point Beach is rumored to be the only unofficial nudist beach on the island. The actual "nudist" part is a twenty minute walk from where cars are parked and of all reports I've heard it is just a place where people have gone topless.

"Who took the picture?"

"Her boyfriend. Has something happened to Jo? Is she okay?"

"Alex," I hate this part, "I'm sorry to have to tell you, but we found Johanna's body last night."

"Body? You mean she's dead?" He hand instantly covers her mouth. Her eyes stare me down. I can see they are already wet with tears.

"I'm afraid so." I try to make my voice soothing. It's like telling my daughter she is going to be okay after skinning her knee. It'll all be okay Honey.

"How," she swallows hard, "how did she die? When did she – where has she been?" She stumbles back one step. I reach to catch her then pull my hand back as she catches herself. Tears start running over her cheeks.

48

"We were hoping you could help us with some of those questions. Can we come in?"

Without a word Alex backs herself into one of the chairs that match the patio table. She bangs her elbows down and holds her head in her hands. She begins to sob loudly. Her body jerks. Marilyn sits in the chair closest to her. I sit on the other side of my partner.

I look again at the photograph. Johanna had a flat stomach and strength to her arms. She was in shape. She looked confident and strong. How did this happen to her?

When Alex calms down a little Marilyn asks, "How long have you known Johanna?"

She puts her glasses down and wipes tears from her face with the heal of her palm. "Jo, she likes – liked Jo. She didn't like Johanna. We met first year. We were both at the Veterinary College. We got an apartment together after winter break so we've been living together a year and four months, except for a month last summer when we both went home."

"And when was the last time you saw her?"

"Over a week ago." She pulls her cell phone out again and quickly looks at the screen. She quickly types something into it, presses send, and places it face down on the table next to a lavender scented candle in a glass bowl. "It was last Tuesday. We had a small argument so she went for a walk to cool off. She didn't come back. I thought maybe she stayed at a friend's or her boyfriend's. Then she didn't show up for classes. Her Mom called on Friday and I –" She stops and puts all concentration on a silver watch around her wrist. She turns it round and round.

"You what, Alex?" Marilyn's voice is very soothing. I'll let her do the questioning until the time comes to be an ass.

Alex looks up. She stares at my partner and says, "I told Jo's Mom that she went out and didn't say that she was gone since Tuesday. I didn't tell her that until this week when she called again. If I had told her then maybe she would –" She puts her hands over her face and sobs into her palms.

After five minutes I tap the photo on the table top. "You said Jo had a boyfriend?"

49

She sucks back some snot and runs her hand across her nose. "Not really. Not anymore."

"What does, *not really*, mean?"

"I don't know."

"And what does that mean?" I'm getting really annoyed with this and I can hear it in my tone.

"Anything you can tell us, Alex, will help us figure out who might have hurt Jo."

She looks at Marilyn again. She says, "His name is Mike Valance, but he wouldn't hurt her." She checks her cell phone. Her voice drops. "They were fighting and broke up, I guess, because Mike and I," she looks down and shrugs her shoulders.

"And Jo found out. On Tuesday?" Marilyn asks.

Alex nods her head.

"How did she find out?"

"She read texts on my phone." She flips the phone on the table.

"Okay, you're going to have to tell me in detail about that last day you saw Johanna." Marilyn readies a pen over her notebook. "I need to know everything."

I push away from the table. "Where do I find her bedroom?" Alex directs me to a room just around the corner from the kitchen. My eyes flash at the second photo on the refrigerator. The two girls and two guys all standing on top of the dune in different stages of catalogue poses.

As I flip the light switch my phone starts to ring and I jump, a little. It is LeBlanc and Longfellow reporting they are not finding much with the neighborhood chats. They talked to someone in every house up to five kilometers away in every direction or left calling cards on any doors where no one was home. I tell Longfellow to continue with the extra officers and for LeBlanc to go to the Atlantic Veterinary College and see what people think of Johanna Bowers. I'll call CrOps and get some officers to meet him there to help question everyone. Then we'll all meet back at HQ to debrief McIntyre and then English before she updates the press on the front steps.

Jo's bedroom looks typical on the surface. The bed was made. Three large body pillows are near the headboard. There is a four drawer dresser with make-up scattered across the top in front of a large mirror, photographs tucked into the frame. Jo and Alex at a bar, Jo and a guy standing in the ocean, Jo on a horse, a young girl that looks a lot like Johanna playing soccer. A desk in the corner has different text books on it – papers, a laptop computer folded shut, binders, and notebooks. There are clothes scattered about on the floor and over the back of a chair in front of the desk. On her walls are drawings and pictures of different animals. She was your typical Canadian girl next door.

I take a quick look through the clothes filled closet then move to the desk drawers. Nothing special there. Junk stuff people don't throw out, bills and paystubs from a downtown clothing boutique. Then I go to the dresser for a quick look through the drawers pushing aside different clothes items. In the top there is a small pile of condoms and, underneath thongs and panties, a black vibrator, but nothing out of the ordinary. *Nothing*.

"So what time exactly did Jo leave here Tuesday night?" Marilyn gives me a nod as I walk back in the room."

"Seven thirty, quarter to eight."

I stand behind my partner. "Did she ever say anything to you about any bad feelings she may have had or anyone watching her?"

Alex says, "Not to me. There are creeps when we go to the bar that we might see a few times, but she never said anything. Should I be worried?"

"I wouldn't be," Marilyn says.

I ask, "Do you know anyone who wanted to hurt Jo? Did anyone not like her?"

"No, everyone loved her. She was popular. Nobody would want to hurt her. Do you think someone we know did this?"

Nobody wanted to hurt her but you fucked around with her boyfriend, eh? I think it to myself but say, "Just a standard question." I turn to my partner, "Do you have everything?" Marilyn nods. "Good. We are going to go. We'll give you our cards. Call us if you think of anything, no matter how small."

The moment we are outside I ask, "Did you get this Mike Valance's info?"

"He works at this restaurant a couple blocks away. It's a breakfast and lunch place. You want to go talk to him there?"

"We've got till eleven to get as much as we can then we have to go for a debriefing. Let's go."

~ * ~

I do a quick count as we walk into the restaurant. There are twenty tables and only one is empty.

I worked in a restaurant washing dishes when I was a teenager. The kitchens are always hot from the ovens, deep fryers, grill, and stove top. There is a noisy exhaust fan above everything, but all that does is pull out the smoke and some of the heat. The rest lingers in the air and soaks through chef coats into the workers skin. Their sweat runs down their bodies underneath collecting in puddles between their legs and in their shoes. I hated that job. The only relief was when I was sent to the walk-in cooler or freezer to get something. I always had trouble finding it.

We walk through the long restaurant and through the kitchen doors without anyone asking one word. Immediately I recognize the young man from the photograph in Johanna Bowers's bedroom. He stands behind the grill. He wears a white chef's jacket splashed and stained yellow, red, and different shades of brown to grey. A backward baseball cap covers his head.

The man beside him is wide in the belly and thick in the neck. His chef's coat looks like it has not been cleaned in over a week. He barks out orders for two orders of French toast, one with no cinnamon, and eggs Benedict. In their menu it is called a Southwestern Bennie.

"Excuse me," a waitress pushes past us, grabs plates with food on them, and heads into the dining room.

"Are you Mike Valance?"

He looks up from the grill. "Yeah, that's me."

"If you don't work here can you get out of the kitchen," the Chef says as more of a statement than a question.

"Sergeant Reid, RCMP," I show my credentials. "I need to speak to Mike Valance." I try to add confidence and power to my voice. I look quick at the knife beside the grill. The blade has to be at least ten inches long with a yellow handle.

The Chef says, "It's going to have to wait until after service."

"I need to talk to him now. It's very imp-"

"It'll have to wait." His voice rises.

Mike looks from his chef to me. He doesn't know what to do. I can feel the sweat forming under my suit.

"Look, we can step outside and talk now or I can cuff him and drag him through the dining room." I stare across at the Chef. I'm in no mood to deal with any Gordon Ramsay wannabe. One of us has to give, and I know damn well that after twenty four hours my chances of getting a killer drop immensely. He makes a head move and Mike turns and walks to the back. We follow him out a door with a glass window into the cool morning air. I stand closest to him and a little in front of Marilyn. It is my turn to ask the questions. "You're Mike Valance?"

"Yeah," he instantly pulls a pack of cigarettes from a pocket in his apron and lights one. Black hair sticks out of his hat. He has a square jaw, a piercing in one eyebrow, and his bottom lip seems to stick out a little. His body is solid in the shoulders and torso, built like a football player. He then produces a flat iPhone and thumbs a button for the screen to wake-up.

I shake my head. I don't really want to deal with this, not today. I ask, "When was the last time you saw Johanna Bowers?"

He doesn't look away from the phone. "I saw her not this past Tuesday, but the Tuesday before that. Tuesday night." He looks up. "Is this about her missing?" And back down.

"What can you tell us about that meeting?"

"Meeting? It wasn't no meeting. She came by my house –" All of his concentration is on his touch phone. I can see his eyes moving as he reads something. His eyes slowly turn to me. His mouth is open, lip sticking out. His facial color instantly fades. "She's dead? Alex texted me that she's dead."

Marilyn says, "Yes, she is. We're very sorry."

"You think I did it?"

"Did you?" I ask.

"No." He spits.

"Know anyone who would?"

He shakes his head. His lips grip the cigarette and he sucks hard. He stuffs the phone back in his pocket. His eyes are glossy. His hand is shaking as he pulls the cigarette away.

"So do you want to tell me about the last time you saw Johanna?"

He drops the white tube to the ground, stares at it for a minute, and then crushes it with his black kitchen shoes. He says, "It was Tuesday. She walked to my place."

"Where do you live?"

"Three blocks from her." He tells us the address, Marilyn writes it down. He speaks in a quiet voice so I can barely hear him over the exhaust fan. "She was mad. She didn't even come in. She just yelled at me in my doorway. Then she slapped me and left going back toward her place. Until Alex told me she never showed I thought Jo went home."

"So what time was that?"

"I don't know, like, eight-thirty. I was watching the hockey game."

I ask him what the fight was about.

Mike watches his foot draw circles on the ground. The smell of smoke and fryer oil is thick in the air. I suddenly realize I haven't eaten yet today. "Jo went home for Christmas and Alex stayed here. And we were drinking. And it happened, you know."

"Was that the only time?"

He sucks his bottom lip in and bites it. His cheeks turn a light pink. He looks up at Marilyn. His eyes drop. What kind of shit is going on in this guy's head? When I was in my early twenties I would never have even thought about cheating. Of course now that I'm in my late thirties – *asshole*. He looks up at me with a side glance. I see a lot of myself in him, only who I am now, not when I was his age.

"What do you want me to say?"

I want you to say that you at least feel guilty about it, little shit.

"I regret it, but it happened." He shrugs his shoulders.

"Regret only happens once." Of course this is from the guy who hours ago was staring up at a hanging dead girl thinking about how gorgeous she was and getting the beginnings of a woody.

He stares at me a long time building his thoughts. I can't tell if this guy wants to hit me or just wants us to go away. I stare back. I am not like him. I am not.

"Did you and Jo go to Blooming Point Beach much?" Marilyn asks.

It takes him a few seconds before twitching. He says, "We liked to go out there a few times during the season. We last went there in like October or November. Alex went with us. It was pretty much whenever I could get my Dad's car."

"You don't have a car?"

"No."

I can feel Marilyn looking at my back.

"When was the last time you used your Dad's car?"

"I don't know, like a month ago. I hit a parked car and took out a taillight so Dad hasn't let me use it since. Can I go back to work now?"

"You don't seem that heartbroken."

Mike stares at me again. His eyes are still wet. His bottom lip quivers. "What do you want me to say? I have to work, don't I? I work two jobs because I'm saving money to go to school. I work here Monday to Friday and then at *Civilizations* on the weekend and some weeknights if they are busy. I'll cry later. Okay?"

I step a little closer to him. "I want your Dad's phone number and address. I want your boss's name at Civilizations." I open my notebook, shove it into his hands, and give him a pen. I stare him down the whole time. I want to hit him. I want to make him care. When he is done I say, "I'm going to keep in touch with you."

55

He pushes past me knocking my arm. I take a deep breath and count to five. "Let's walk around."

"You were starting to scare me a little bit." Marilyn walks quickly at my side.

"Why?"

"I didn't know where you were going there for a while. Usually I know what you're going to ask next. I didn't."

I jam my notebook up under my arm pit, put one hand in my pants pocket and the other on my gun. At the car I stop and look back. My head spins. Images of Johanna hanging in the woods, Johanna and Alex standing on a dune, Marilyn's ass cheeks rolling over themselves, every woman I have ever seen naked all run through my head in rapid snap shots. And then I see Hillary.

I turn to look down the road at Charlottetown Harbor. The Delta Hotel is in my way. "Things aren't that great at home. He just made me think of things."

Marilyn is quiet, but I can tell she is rewinding the conversation over in her head. Do I want her to figure it out? Maybe that was why I said something. She touches my arm, my fingers tense on my pistol. "Did you cheat on Hillary?"

"No." My voice has no tone.

"Did she cheat on you?"

"No." I turn and look her right in the eye. Her red hair dances a little in the breeze. It frames her face. I look away quick. "Have you ever cheated on Chris?"

"No. If I did he'd-" She catches herself.

"We should get going."

Without another word we slide into the car. Marilyn pulls us onto Queen Street heading up the hill. After a while we cross over the University Avenue and keep heading uptown. I fight the urge to flip the finger at the CBC building. University is the "main strip" of Charlottetown PEI. It has the city's only Burger King, only full-fledged MacDonald's, there is another one in a corner store and one in Wal-Mart. Every big mall in the city can be reached off of University. Depending on the time of day it can be the busiest and slowest street in the city. Ten-forty on a Thursday is not one of those times.

I call Civilizations Restaurant to ask about Mike and get a message that nobody will be in until noon. I leave my name and number.

As we crest the hill and pass the KFC the traffic begins to slow almost to a crawl. There could have been an accident up at the intersection of University and Belvedere. I can actually see people in the cars ahead of us rubbernecking to see what is going on across from the *Indigo* store. HQ is across from Indigo. As we get closer we see the minivans with different logos on their sides pulled into every space available around the oval in front of RCMP Headquarters.

"Shit."

Marilyn signals and slowly turns in. I count the different painted logos. CBC television, CBC radio – English and French, CTV news, The Guardian – PEI's official newspaper, *covering Prince Edward Island like the dew*, The Global, Canadian Press, plus more that are from other news agencies. The reporters and camera people are all milling around their vehicles getting ready for Sgt. English to step out and tell them what is going on. They all turn and watch us circle around the building toward the parking lot in the back. I try not to look back. I want to sulk down in the passenger seat and hide on the floor mat. I see Catherine Arsenault glaring at us as we get behind the corner of the building and disappear.

The HQ building is an L shape of red brick with lines of windows on the first and second floor. Off to the side is a long white building we affectionately call *The Condemned Garage*. There are other RCMP detachment buildings across the island, but this is the main building. It has three levels. The basement houses Computer Analysis, the janitor's office, a large industrial shredder which destroys documents in every direction, a small gym, and Special I. Special I is a secured and secretive section – don't ask, don't tell. The main floor houses the Crown Court Liaison, Major Case Management, Drug Enforcement – probably the largest unit, Major Crimes, Sgt. English' office, Emergency Preparedness, and Community Policing. The second floor has a training room, Informatics Manager, Internal Services, Human

Resources and Recruiting, Telecoms, the CO's office and the CO's boardroom.

There are pictures along the corridor walls of PEI the way it was, an aerial shot of Charlottetown, a couple of the musical ride officers all dressed in their red serge uniforms and on horseback in front of Province House downtown, and the HQ. On the second floor, above the photocopier is a large stuffed head of a buffalo. My daughter saw it during our Christmas kids party, screamed and ran away. It matches the RCMP's emblem found above the front door.

The emblem above the main entrance is a buffalo head surrounded by a circle and then a wreath of maple leaves. Below it on a scroll are the words *Royal Canadian Mounted Police*. Above the whole thing is a crown representing Canada's connection to England and their Queen. Written in the circle around the buffalo is, "Maintien le Droit" – Maintain the Law. That says about it, doesn't it?

I walk in the CO's conference room on the second floor with my notebook in one hand and a cup of slow roasted coffee from the one cup machine in the lunch room. Marilyn comes in with a herbal tea and sets her laptop up in front of her. Dispirito sits beside her. I sit across from them. LeBlanc and Longfellow sit to my right. McIntyre and the CO – Command Officer – are already in there. Superintendent Barry Tulloch – CrOps officer, sits on their other side with a notebook and a Blackberry in front of him. He is the officer in charge of police operations so if you need twenty officers to blanket the area and spook out your suspect, he's your guy. As soon as we are done getting all of our information out there English will come in and we will tell her what she needs to know. Then she will meet with Kam Wallace, our Media Relations Consultant, speech writer, before going to talk to the reporters. Eckhart comes in and falls into the closest chair. He wears a pair of dark blue sweats. RCMP is silkscreened across his chest in bright gold.

"Let's get this going then." McIntyre says. "Who wants to tell us the basics?"

"I will," Marilyn says. She relays the main facts that we know. Body was found, call came in...my mind drifts away. I try making a list of what I have to do next and where to go from where we are, but I come up blank. I have no fucking clue what to do next.

"Reid?"

I look at McIntyre then scope out everyone else. "The last report we have of Johanna Bowers being seen was a week ago Tuesday. Unless you guys found anything at the school."

"No, we did not." LeBlanc's French accent is thick. "Nobody has seen her in two weeks. The teacher said the last time she was in class was that Tuesday."

I continue by telling them about the fight with her roommate and boyfriend. "What did you two find out?"

"No one reported any suspicious vehicles or anything out in Blooming Point." Longfellow runs a hand through his hair. "No more than usual. Locals say that once the weather changes cars start heading to the beach by the dozens whether they can make it all the way or not. Stereo's blasting at night, people yelling out windows. Nobody saw anything suspicious though. There are still a couple of places we have to go back to because nobody was home."

"At the Vet school everyone we talked to said Miss Bowers was a nice person. Good student. Nobody knew her that well," LeBlanc says.

"Eckhart, your turn." McIntyre's arms cross over his chest.

He pushes his glasses up with the back of his hand. "We found a lot of trace evidence at the scene, but I'll be surprised if any of it is relevant. A lot of it was garbage from years past. There were no obvious fibers or hairs on the body on first inspection." He takes a manila folder from a leather case and passes it to me. I take the pictures out and spread them on the table. Everyone takes turn passing them around. Eckhart continues without pausing, "We'll be able to look closer at the body during the autopsy first thing in the morning. The PD's are searching the woods now for anything." I had a call that the Police Dogs had started their search. "We have a lot of shit to go through. Some of the trace I am sending to the lab in Halifax. We were able to get a positive ID from Calgary with the fingerprints I took from the body and the fingerprints from one of those child find kits the parents still had. She is Johanna Bowers." He pushes his glasses up.

I sit quietly and listen to all of the talk back and forth. This is the first murder on Prince Edward Island in a long time. Like my case in BC, I have nothing. I really don't know where to go from here. I have no idea how to solve this.

"Reid," Staff Sergeant Oliver taps the table. "What do you want from me?"

I look up. For one moment I feel like just shrugging my shoulders. Instead I say, "We need to check with anyone patrolling out there over the past few days, anyone giving out traffic violations. We need to get security tapes from the four stores on St. Peter's Road heading into Charlottetown and out to Mount Stewart. Offer something up on Crime stoppers as soon as possible. I want guys going back to the houses where nobody was home. Get everyone talking to their sources. Somebody saw something. Someone is talking out there."

"I'll do what I can from my end."

"Good," I say. "Longfellow, can you be the *Files Manager*?"

"No problem." The Files Manager spends his days scanning all of the info and reports brought in by the field officers onto the computer. It is then all put onto discs and can be given to the crown prosecutors instead of giving them boxes and boxes of paperwork.

"Ah, Reid," Dispirito stares at one of the photographs. He has it close to his face. He puts it down and looks at me. "These cuts, they look familiar to me. I've seen a similar pattern."

Chapter 6

Fifteen Years Ago

"Look at the one coming from this way."

Ben's dad looked up from the lawn mower, first at his son and then the way he was looking. The June sun made his sweat drip from his eyebrows. A young girl walked on the sidewalk toward their house. She was probably in her late teens, but he pretended she was in her twenties. She wore a purple and blue summer dress with blue jeans underneath and black boots with two inch heels. The dress was cut low at the chest, but she wasn't well developed. Her long black hair bounced behind her shoulders. She was good-looking.

"Nice one, pass me the five-eighths."

Ben did as he was asked. He looked down for a second at what his dad was doing with the lawnmower blade. He slowly let his eyes roll up so he could see the girl from under the bill of his *Toronto Blue Jays* baseball cap. He didn't move his head. There was no way she could have known he was looking at her.

He liked the curve of her boot from toe to heel and then the way it hugged her ankle and firm calf muscles. He liked how the hem of the dress fluttered above her knees. His eyes followed as it went in at her waist. He liked how the fabric was tight around her small breasts. It probably pulled against her nipples and made them hard, exciting her. He liked the black crescent moon hanging from a long chain around her neck. It bounced from tit to tit before finding refuge just below her dress in the crevasse between her tiny mounds. He liked the white creamy skin of her almost bare shoulders. Only spaghetti straps marked her perfect flesh. He liked how her face and features were almost Asian. She had large maroon lensed sunglasses covering her eyes. He guessed they were brown, deep mahogany, and her eyebrows were probably plucked and sculpted into perfect arches. He liked the constellation of freckles across her cheekbones. Ben liked the way her bangs fell delicately on her forehead and the way her black hair danced behind her like a gymnasts ribbons. He liked the way she moved and the way she walked on heels like she had worn them since birth. So many of the women dad pointed out as having a nice ass or great tits walked in heels like they needed training wheels. This girl had confidence. He liked that.

He let his eyes follow her without moving his head. Her heels clicked on the sidewalk. He liked that. Ben pulled the bill of his hat down a little.

She looked in his direction and smiled.

She smiled at Ben. See, he wasn't pathetic. She liked him. She thought he was cute. This older girl smiled at him.

He looked up and watched her walk away. Her hips swayed with confidence. Her shoulders were bare except for the thin dress straps over them. On the back of her shoulder was a picture of fairy with colorful wings casting a spell with a wand tattooed into her skin.

"All done," His dad's voice knocked Ben out of his trance. "Finish the lawn and don't hit any more fucking rocks." He picked up his tools, wiped his face with his shirt, and marched into the house.

Ben flipped the mower back onto its wheels. He put the lever onto the picture of the rabbit, pushed in the primer bubble three times, and pulled the chord. The small engine burped and coughed, but it still fired to life with a loud roar.

When he looked up the girl was at the end of the street. She quickly crossed, in his mind Ben still heard her heels clicking, and disappeared behind the house on the corner. Ben pushed the mower. Cut grass spewed out the side funnel. He kept the push bar low.

The girl lived in her parent's house two streets down, three houses over. Her house was red brick with fake white shutters on either side of the windows. There was a flower garden along the front of the house that needed to be weeded. It had wild pink roses, dragon lilies, and yellow and red tulips in the spring. A batch of chives flourished on the corner. Ben mowed their lawn once a week. The parents and younger brother had a bedroom upstairs. The girl was on the main floor in the back corner. Her window was above a flattened out patch of rhubarb.

When she was in her room she often locked the door and pulled her top off. Sometimes she took her bra off and threw it on the bed.

Ben had the mowers push bar pressed against him below his waist. He let the vibrations course through his body. As he got hard inside his jeans he adjusted the metal bar so it vibrated against his manhood.

The girl moved a lot when she slept. Ben took walks without his parent's knowledge. And he saw her kick her feet in her sleep. He stood on tiptoe, his feet on rhubarb leaves, and looked through her window. The cold evening air pressed against him. By the time he would return home the evening dew would be soaked into his clothes. She moved and turned in her sleep. The blankets slipped down. Her small breasts appeared. All he could see for sure was the dark circles around the nipples. It excited him to the point of his knees feeling like water was in them. Her hand brushed across them. A white heat flared in his abdomen. A something moist erupted in his pants making him wet and sticky, but he couldn't stop watching her.

Ben felt the burning heat in his groin. His knees want to buckle. He bit down on his bottom lip. He pulled his shirt out of his jeans. His eyes looked around to see if anyone was watching. There was a sudden explosion of warmth and wetness beneath the waist band of his jeans. It squirted up above them and under his shirt. That sudden jolt excited him. It thrilled him. Ben wanted more. There had to be something more than just that.

He tried mowing a little longer until he felt wet running down his thigh. He turned off the machine and went inside.

"I have to pee," Ben called out after his Dad asked what was wrong.

He went to the bathroom and quickly stripped from the waist down. He rubbed at the white goo squished against his lower belly. He dug some out of his navel. He rolled his briefs into a ball and stuffed them in the small bathroom garbage can under tissues balled in snot and his mother's *Maxi pads*. He stuffed his jeans in the clothes hamper under two of his dad's shirts and his mother's housecoat. Ben looked in the hallway then crossed to his room. He put on a new pair of briefs and a pair of sweatpants.

At night Ben sat on his bed flaking off dried semen from his belly. He liked that girl. It wasn't enough though. There had to be more. There had to be a greater feeling than looking through a window or the vibrations of a lawn mower. It wasn't enough.

Three more years and he would find something more.

Twelve years after that and he would find what he was made for.

Chapter 7

"What pattern?" I take the photographs. Johanna Bowers's torso is there with cuts and stab wounds covering her.

Corporal Dispirito leans over the table. He pushes the 8x10 picture to the table. "You see the cut around the breast, the slices on her stomach, and these, like, hesitation marks on her neck?"

I nod.

"I was called about a violent rape almost six months ago and the vic had the same sort of cuts, especially the one around the breast. She was really upset about that and thought nobody was going to want her again." Dispirito sits back down. "Marilyn and I took the call. You were out of town for two weeks.

"If I remember correctly we didn't find any fibres on her either. There was spermicide, but no sperm or foreign fluids." Eckhart pushes his glasses.

"Did it go anywhere?"

Dispirito shakes his head. He says, "No suspects, no DNA, no witnesses, and pretty soon there was no victim. She didn't want to be involved with it any more. She just wants it to go away."

"I want to see your file on her." I push away from the table.

"Reid," McIntyre runs his hand over his goatee, "Marilyn and I will talk to Deborah and Kam. Let me know what you want to do next."

It is sad, but rape is a big, yet hidden crime on Prince Edward Island. The young adults on the island like their drink and drugs and with that comes stupid actions. Date rape happens often without anyone reporting it. Over the past couple of years there was a serial rapist who attacked women on the Confederation

Trail; the trail crosses the island. It used to be train tracks and is now a gravel covered trail used for exercising, biking, hiking, and on some nights, just before dusk, attacking women trying to stay in shape. The rapist was caught. The worst part of it is that a rape victim doesn't want to have to remember and recall what happened to them. They just want it to go away.

Al Dispirito stands six-four with sandy hair that falls back into place every time he moves. He has a scar on his right temple from an accident when he was on RCMP peace keeping duty in Haiti. He is your typical poster boy. He is a good-looking guy in and out of uniform. I follow him down the stairs to MCU. LeBlanc and Longfellow stick close behind.

"Her name is Sierra West, nineteen, from Summerside." When Dispirito talks deep dimples appear on either cheek. "She was in Charlottetown with two girlfriends to celebrate her birthday. They checked into a hotel, went for dinner, and then went bar hopping. *Olde Dublin*, *Globe*, and then *The Velvet*." He pauses long enough to pull the file out. He hands it to me and I dig out the photographs taken at the hospital. "At the Velvet she got into a fight with one of her friends over a guy. She left the club saying she was going to get a cab back to the hotel. A guy offered her a ride. She was raped and cut up then dropped off in the parking lot of her hotel. The sicko actually dropped her off at her hotel."

In the pictures the girl's brown hair fell over her face. Mascara streaked down from her eyes. There were bruises on her temple, mouth, and over her torso. There were three small shallow cuts on her throat where someone may have held a knife to control her. There was a slice around her left breast, almost enough to take it off, and cuts to her stomach. They were only slices to her flesh, no stab wounds and nothing too deep to cause anything serious. There were no ligature marks on her wrists or ankles.

"What makes you think this has anything to do with Johanna?"

"Besides the cut around her breast? Sierra couldn't remember much because of how much she had to drink, but she remembered

66

some of what he said." He leans down and flips through pages. "Right here, he said, she wasn't the one. He told her she was practice and that she was lucky. I don't know how lucky she was."

"I want to talk to her." I say.

~ * ~

Summerside is Prince Edward Island's second-largest city. It is 53 kilometres away from Charlottetown down Highway 2. As long as there is no construction the trip does not take long, but it seems like they try "fixing" up the road every year. Just a couple of years ago they cleaned up the Hunter River junction and rid the main freeway of tire-killing potholes. The drive is a scenic one with the rolling hills, patches of forest, spotted with churches and farms with grazing horses, cattle, and llamas. After making the turn at Kensington you pass the Haunted Mansion – an old house made up inside with flashing lights, loud sounds, and scary dummies to frighten people for nine bucks. We took Hillary's nephews there last summer. Then you pass the Cavendish French fry factory before getting to the small city. The entire section of highway smells of fry oil and chips. Summerside has a little bit of everything. We pass the entrance to the hospital. The city has a lot of shopping, a lot of restaurants, and a beautiful waterfront and boardwalk.

We take my car. I drive with Marilyn beside me and Dispirito in the back. I asked LeBlanc and Longfellow to look through old rape reports to see if anything looked similar to what we had before us.

Every fifteen minutes or so something comes on the radio about the body being found in the Blooming Point area. Foul play is suspected. The name of the young woman cannot be released pending notification of next of kin. The police are following leads. It is then followed by CBC news reporter Catherine Arsenault saying that she spoke to an eye witness who claimed they saw the woman hanging from a tree. *Fucking reporters.*

"I called her on her cell phone to let her know we were coming. Turn right up here. She's at work and can only give us a little time, but she is willing to talk to us. She is a strong woman, I'm telling you."

"Did you tell her why we were coming?" Marilyn asks.

"I didn't want to scare her. She has to live with what happened to her, she doesn't need to live with what might have happened."

Marilyn and I wait outside of the grocery store Sierra West works at while Dispirito goes inside. It is very warm for mid-April with a cool westerly wind. Marilyn takes her white framed sunglasses from her eyes and uses them to push her hair back to the top of her head. Her red wine-coloured hair poofs up a little, but she still looks good. The wind tosses it in the back. She asks, "What are you thinking?"

"If this pans out this guy has been doing this for a long time, he may not have been killing, but he's been getting ready for it."

She checks her watch and slides the other hand in her blazer. "Do we need to talk about what you said earlier?"

I nod at someone walking past. "What was that?" I wonder if she is playing with that engagement ring in her pocket.

"You're life at home. We're more than partners, Reid. You can talk to me."

"Here he is." Saved by the bell. I know that if I talk about what it is I am feeling things will probably get better, at least in my own mind, but it's getting myself started that is the hard part.

Dispirito walks out beside a young woman who looks almost ten years older than her nineteen years. Her brown hair, masked by gentle curls, looks dull and tired. Right away I look to her throat. There above the collar of her uniform shirt are little lines, still pink with white edges, where a knife was held against her and pressed hard enough to draw blood. She leads us around the corner of the building. Her arms are tight around her body. When she stops she tries to look us in the face. Her eyes are tearing up. There are grey bags under them. The wind blows her hair into her face. She doesn't try to move it.

"Sierra, these are Sergeants Moore and Reid. They have a few-"

"This is about that body, isn't it?" She looks at each of our eyes in turn. Hers have lines of red in the whites. Then she looks around us and behind herself.

"It is. Can you tell us about what happened to you? Do you remember anything about your attacker?" I try my best to make my voice as soothing as possible. It is a completely different approach from what I used with Mike Valance. This girl is still hurting.

She took a deep breath. Her eyes glassed over and her expression sank. "His breath was minty." Her voice was so soft I had to strain to hear her. "It smelled like he just brushed his teeth. And he smelled like soap, like he just came from the shower. He asked me if I needed a ride somewhere. I was drunk. I was upset. I didn't get any bad feelings about him. He wasn't a creep or anything. He looked like a nice guy."

"What was he driving?" We know most of the answers from the original police file, but asking again doesn't hurt. Something else could be sparked now that she has had a long time away from the actual event.

"A SUV. I don't remember the colour or anything. I had a lot of tequila and a Jager-bomb. We were all doing shots all night. I think I fell asleep in his car. The rest felt like hours and hours, but it wasn't that long. I think I fought him because he hit me again and again. Then I stopped fighting. He put himself in me. He held a knife to my throat while he did it. Then he cut me up." She stares out at the parking lot. Her head turns to look behind her then she stares out again. Her voice never changes tone. She is absent from what she is saying. "He cut my stomach and then he put his hand over my mouth and he cut my," her arms go tighter around her body, "he cut my breast. I started to beg him not to hurt me and he hit me again."

"What did he say to you?"

She looks around. "I'm not going to kill you. You're not the one for that. Practice makes perfect. Then after he threw me out of the SUV he said I should feel lucky. I have to get back to work. I have to get back."

"Did he have an accent? Did he sound like he was from the island or from away?" Anyone not born in the Maritimes is *from away*. Nobody likes to admit that Islanders are prejudiced, but people from away are treated differently. People *from away* rarely get into leadership roles in community groups or have trouble getting a helping hand. I've had people look at me with a strange expression and say, "Oh, you're from away?" The easiest way to tell is by the way people talk.

"I, I don't know. I have to go to work." Her feet scuffle, but she doesn't walk away.

"What did he look like?"

"A nice guy. To me now he's every guy who talks to me."

"Is there anything you can remember that you didn't tell the police before? Are there any details at all? Hair color? Eye color?"

She looks in my face. Large tears are getting pregnant in her eyes. She says, "I relive it every night when I try to go to sleep. No, there is nothing else. Did he kill this girl?" One tear releases and streaks down her face.

"I don't know," I reply.

"Will you stop him?"

"I don't know." My voice drifts off to nothing. Sierra stares into my eyes for what feels like minutes then turns and walks toward the store entrance. The last ten feet she runs. I can't tell her what I really think, but somehow she probably knows. There may not be an end.

It takes five minutes before I speak again. "Let's head back."

~ * ~

"We have gone through the files for the last five years, yeah. There are six more cases involving a knife." LeBlanc fans the file folders out on his desk in the MCU office. "They, ah, go from a knife on the throat to lacerations."

"You think it's the same guy?"

70

I say nothing. I sit in his chair and open each file and read what is there. Hand written and typed reports, photograph after photograph. Two of them involve an SUV, four of the women tested positive for the date rape drug *Rohypnol*. All of them had elements of violence and a knife. The attacker liked to hit in the face and stomach. He either held a knife against their throat or had it where they could see it. The two women raped the year before Sierra West were the only ones cut. Before that it was just threats of cutting and death.

The Major Crimes office is basically one large room. McIntyre has his own private office and the rest of us have desks in the main room. The floor is a generic grey and black carpet, and the walls a dull beige. On our walls are large bulletin and white dry erase boards. They are the best things for figuring out crimes so that everyone can see everything at once and hopefully find a connection. Right now, most of the boards are empty. One by the door has a list of court dates and which investigator is supposed to attend.

McIntyre walks out from his office and stands behind me. He leans over my shoulder to take a look.

Longfellow puts his coffee down on the table. He shoves his hands in his pockets. "None of the victims can give a good description of the attacker. The ones that had the drugs can't remember much of anything and the others had their eyes taped or were knocked out and came to with something covering their eyes. I don't know, man, it doesn't sound like the same guy to me."

I look up at him. Something inside of me churns. There is a burning in my chest that is ready to explode. "Right now we have nothing. Everybody loved Johanna Bowers. She was an outstanding young woman, top student. We could bring in her boyfriend and roommate, but all we're going to get from them is that they fucked up. They screwed each other and got caught. Whoever this killer is, he didn't just start with Johanna Bowers. These guys evolve."

"What do you mean?" Marilyn asks.

"I mean these guys – rapists – they evolve into killing."

"We have one body, Reid." McIntyre puts his hand on my shoulder.

I put my eyes down at the table. "I've studied these guys, Wayne. They evolve. This guy has been raping people. He told Sierra West that he was practicing. He was building himself up. There is a pattern."

"Where? I see a girl snatched on the Confed Trail five years ago, grabbed from behind and hit over the head, raped and let free. This one was slipped Rohypnol at a house party, raped with knife marks on her throat. This one picked up hitchhiking on Highway 2, knocked out, and duct taped. I don't get the pattern, Reid." McIntyre puts his arms out.

"It's right –"

"I see six unsolved rapes."

Dispirito interrupts, "Seven. Don't forget Sierra."

McIntyre stares at him for a moment. I am about to say something when he starts again.

"Seven unsolved rapes. A couple may be similar, but for the most they are completely different. I don't want you to go down a wrong path and forget about this girl."

I rub a hand over the stubble on my head. Sweat is breaking from my pores. I can feel all eyes on me. I bite down on my tongue. There is no way I can *forget* about this girl. If anything she is going to haunt me.

In my head I start to count. *One, two, three.* Mom used to count when she was mad at something I did or said. *Four, five.* She said by the time she got to ten she usually calmed herself enough. *Six, seven, eight.* I nod my head. Fucking guy wakes me up in the middle of the night because I know what I'm doing then won't let me damn well do my job. *Nine, ten.*

"I want us to look into a pattern." I stand to look down at the table. I try not to look at my boss whom I want to lash out and strike. "My gut says this guy has been evolving into something. Let Dispirito look into it." Now I look at him. He looks back and begins a battle of eyes. The first one to look down loses the power.

McIntyre looks at the table.

"He's got the rest of the day to look into some pattern of evolution. After that, it's done. The rest of you get me something on this murder. I want it solved." McIntyre spins on his heel and returns to his office. The rest of us stand for a few minutes, each looking down at the files.

I spin around and fall into my chair behind my desk. All I have is a desk with a laptop computer, a black desk lamp, a phone, an in and out stack box, and a photo of Hillary and Leigh in a gold frame. One extra chair sits in front of the desk. The screen saver for my computer is a picture of me in the early years of my career dressed in red surge on the back of a black horse, Titan, captured in a fast turn. Dirt flies up from his powerful hooves. For three years I was part of the *Musical Ride*. I had the opportunity to travel all over the world. I have been an RCMP officer for sixteen years, since I was twenty-two, with postings in Saskatchewan, Ottawa, British Colombia, and now here on the island. I still haven't found the place I am most at home. The red light on my telephone is blinking fast.

"What do you want to do?" Marilyn wheels her chair over and sits in the space across from me. She slides a shoe off, lifts her foot onto the opposite knee and starts massaging the sole.

My finger floats over the messages button on the phone. I'm willing to bet there is going to be one or two from Hillary and then probably reporters trying to get a scoop. I can push the button and listen to what everyone wants. Answering calls could take me through the rest of the day and help me to forget everything for a while. It still won't change anything. It won't help.

I stand up quick. My head twists and spins for a second. I say, "Get LeBlanc and Longfellow. We'll canvas every house between Johanna Bowers' place and Mike Valance's. Somebody might have seen her. Looks like you're feet are going to hurt some more."

We are not even close to the exit and I see Sgt. English walking down the hallway toward us with a purpose in her step. "Reid, I need to talk to you." I look at the others and tell them I will meet them outside. "Any idea if this is homegrown?"

"We're working the case, Deb. When we know something, you'll know."

She is a shorter woman. "Do you have anything? Catherine Arsenault is pressing for info." The worst thing about my wife having a friend that is good-looking who I work with is that my wife has a friend that is good-looking and that I work with her. It's one of those situations where a man just has to keep his eyes on the ground.

"Screw her." I look up at her eyes quick.

"She says she has crime scene photos and will release them if we can't give her anything. I'm trying to keep her back, Reid, but we might have to give her something."

"What do you want me to give her?" My arms fly out to the side. "I don't know anything. I have to go."

I am half-way out the door when I hear, "Your wife wants you to call her," from behind me.

~ * ~

"What are you doing here?"

"I live here."

"But what are you doing here?"

"What do you mean?"

"I didn't expect you home."

"Better push the boyfriend out the window."

Hillary's lips quiver for one second.

I put the carton of milk on the small table by the door with my keys and slip my shoes off. I haphazardly toss my blazer on a chair. It slowly slides then plops onto the hardwood floor.

"Come on, move your nose." Our brown and white Welsh springer spaniel lifts her head to look at me with drooped eyes. Once I fall to the couch cushion beside her she places her head on my lap and goes back to sleep snoring like an old grandma who really needs to blow her nose. The end of her nose is white with small brown spots then she's brown with white up her front legs and over her shoulders and along her whole belly with brown over her back. Her ears sit flat. She's one of those dogs you see on pictures of hunters walking through fields looking for pheasant or going duck hunting. Most of the white on her is stained red from the island sand. I drop my socks, damp with sweat from walking up and down the three blocks between Johanna's and Mike's, to the floor. My muddy clothes from this morning are in a plastic bag on the passenger floor of the car. Sure as shit, Hillary is staring at my two socks sitting in a snake curl beside my feet. My eyes lock on the television. She has been watching one of those *reality* TV shows.

"Shush, I thought you wouldn't be home until much later or tomorrow."

"Sorry." She's right, I shouldn't be home. I should be chasing some lead somewhere, but I don't know where to go. I don't have any leads to chase. Mike Valance's whereabouts the night of the murder at Civilizations Restaurant has been confirmed. The neighbourhood canvas has given us nothing. Lab guys are pulling a blank. We have twenty-four to forty-eight hours to get our best evidence in any case and we can't get anything. We have no suspects. Where the hell was this girl for a week and a half?

Our dog, Frix, rubs her head on my leg until I scratch behind her ears. She moans and rolls to give me full exposure to her belly.

Hillary sits in my lounge chair, one bare leg curled under her, the other sticking out bouncing unconsciously. All she has on is one of my sweat shirts, RCMP in gold over black. Turn my head to the right angle and I can see that that *is* all she has on. This should be turning me on. My wife is an attractive woman, sexy, firm, waxed – I should be ready to explode. I can put it down as it has been a long day or I've seen death today and listened to a story of rape. Maybe it has nothing to do with any of it. Maybe I am not turned on by my wife any more. That happens right? You put this same situation fifteen years ago when we were first starting out or eleven years ago when we first said, "I do," and I would be pushing the stool and laundry away and diving face first between her thighs, hands clamping her bare ass and pushing me in further. Instead I'm scratching my dogs head thinking about whether I should bother picking up the electric bill off the coffee table or just let Hill deal with it.

She doesn't say anything until the next commercial. "Are you alright?"

"I'm tired." I scratch Frix's head. The old pup snuggles herself deeper into my thigh.

"I mean mentally."

"I'm fine."

"Did you want to give Dr. Ferron a call? It's four hours earlier in BC." Hillary turns the volume down on the television. Her signal for, *I want to talk*.

My head feels too heavy for my neck. "I don't need a fucking shrink." Too harsh.

"You damn well did the last time." Hillary throws the blue jeans she just folded onto a pile on the large foot stool. It teeters to the side, but does not fall. She grabs a shirt from the basket beside her.

"That was different, Hill. It was kids. And I killed a guy."

"But you had to."

The show comes back from commercial and we both automatically go quiet. I stare down at the Wii system beneath the television. Leigh's Christmas present. She barely uses it now.

Did I have to kill him? He tortured and murdered four little girls. I can still remember his eyes glaring at me across the room. Now at night when I just fall into the opening stages of dream I see his white eyes. It usually startles me awake. I wanted to kill him. *Did* I have to?

"Leigh sleeping?" Above the television is a framed photo of me in my red serge standing with my horse. Next to it is another framed photo of Leigh smiling from the back of a grey pony. If you want to be part of the musical ride you have to do it early on in your career before getting promoted to sergeant, so Leigh was still four years from being born when I was part of it. I have taken her to see the ride and visit the horses though.

Hillary nods her head. She folds a tiny bit of cloth and puts it on the same pile as the jeans. It is not cloth, its underwear. Tiny black boy-cut briefs with white lace around the edges. Why is it the older my daughter gets, the smaller her underwear gets? Hillary says, "She had a rough day. Her friends don't like her any more. *Not hardly*, was what she said."

"That will change tomorrow."

"And then she got upset because you didn't make her riding lesson." Here comes the guilt, enjoy the trip.

"For Christ sake, Hill, a girl was murdered."

"I know that. I'm just telling you about her day, like you asked."

Bullshit.

"She has another lesson tomorrow if you have the time."

I push the dog off my lap and get to my feet. She stands there looking at me with her sad eyes and droopy jowls as if to say, *what the fuck asshole.* She takes her spot at Hillary's feet. "I'm going to bed." I pick up my socks and head for the stairs. My feet pad across the hardwood. On the third step I spin around and go back down. My hand slaps down on the milk carton. "I got the milk."

Hillary says, "I already picked up a jug after the riding lesson."

Of course. I put my one litre carton of milk next to her two litres in the refrigerator. On the rack below is a plate of fried chicken, boiled potatoes, and frozen vegetable medley covered in cling film. I made a sandwich in the kitchen at work so I'm not hungry. Something else to make me feel guilty. I close the door and head upstairs for a shower and bed. Tomorrow is the autopsy.

Chapter 8

14 years ago

Her heeled boots clicked on the cement sidewalk. The wind blew against her face sending her black hair dancing out behind her. She pulled her small black coat in tight. *Click, click.*

Ben watched her cheeks make a figure eight in blue denim as she walked. How many times has he followed her? Watched her? He remembered that day last summer when she looked at him and smiled. *Click.*

He missed her most during the winter. It was too cold to look through her window, and someone might have seen his tracks in the snow. He had to find other ways to release what was inside him. He found the videos and books in his parent's closet behind the box of old board games. It was spring again. Girls were wearing less. They walked around teasing him. She teased him in her tight jeans, her hair falling free.

She looked at her watch. This wasn't right. She could feel his eyes on her. It made the hairs on her arms tingle. She fought the urge to run. She didn't want him back there anymore.

Ben could smell her. The wind carried her perfume and the scent of her shampoo all the way back to him. He smelled coconut. It made his insides burn. There was a twitch in his pants. *Click, click.* As she passed a telephone pole he started counting seconds. A block ago he was twenty-two seconds behind her. Fifteen seconds. He was getting closer.

Click, click.

The girl turned the corner and disappeared behind a garage. Her eyes looked back the second before she was gone.

Ben hurried his pace. He had to catch her. His feet hit the ground hard. What was he going to do when he caught her? He wanted to take her coat off and feel her top in his hands as he ripped it in two. He wanted to see her small breasts, squeeze them in his hands. He wanted to see her naked body up close. He wanted to touch her, feel her milky skin against his, and taste her. She was to be his. What if she fought back? He felt the switchblade folded and quiet in his pocket push against his thigh in response to his thoughts. She'd listen if he showed that. She'd listen or she'd get cut. She loved him though. She smiled at him. He wanted that. He wanted her. He had to have her.

The sidewalk flew up and hit Ben hard in the back. The back of his head erupted in pain. The front of his face vibrated. Blood rushed from his nose. Hot red ran quickly across his cheeks and into his ears. He tasted the salty sickness in his mouth and deep in his throat. He coughed and choked and tried spitting it out. The world was wrong. Everything was standing up above him. A curtain dropped. His world went black.

"Grab his –"

Voices.

"–heavy for –" Far away. "–perve."

Something wet on his back.

Don't you pull my leg, Benny.

"What – do?" Sweet voice.

"Hurry."

The curtain fluttered. There were clouds and blue.

Internal heat exited through a crack in the back of his skull. He felt scrapes and wet over his entire back.

"Is this enough? What are we going to do?"

Ben opened his eyes wide. Figures stood above him. He couldn't make out who they were. His vision was still blurred with blood and pain. His shirt was up in his armpits, his back bare against wet grass. Rocks dug into his skin. There was no concrete sidewalk behind him anymore. He had been dragged away. Where was he? Who was there? What were they going to do? He had to move. He had to get up and get out of there. He tasted his own blood in his throat, that wasn't good. He sat up quick.

"Stay down." A boot hit him and knocked him on his side. He felt the sole touch rib. "Where were you off to, b'ye?" That was a man's voice. He sounded older than Ben's fourteen years at least. He could tell from the way he said, *by* instead of boy, that he was probably from Newfoundland.

"His name is Ben." He knew this voice. It was a girl's. He had talked to her enough to say hi. She smiled at him. "He mows our lawn."

"He likes to look t'ru your window too. Don't you, b'ye? You little shite." Ben smelt his hot breath. He felt the guys spit hit his ear.

There were more there; four people in all surround him. He felt them more than saw them. His vision was still blurred.

"Hey, b'ye," too loud, right in his ear. His head rang. Ben felt the man's lips, and something else, touch his ear. Whiskers, he had whiskers. A Newfie accent and whiskers.

A hand gripped Ben's throat. A knee pushed down on him. Fingers pushed on his larynx. His eyes opened wide. He couldn't breathe. He wanted to fight. The pressure on him was too much. He had to get is arms out. He had to get a hand free. Get the hand away from his throat. There were voices. The others were saying something, but they sounded far off.

"You pervert."

Spit splashed his face and his eye. The hand let go. Ben gasped for air. His lungs tried to pull in as much as they could. So much it hurt.

He was hard. Ben didn't know why, but he was excited and hard. And his insides burned. It was more than his lungs wanting air. He wanted death. He wanted to feel blood on his hands. If he could only get the knife out. He could cut them, slice them, he could make them pay. There were three of them. And *her*. Would he be able to get the three before they stopped him? Ben would cut them and then he would have her. He would have her like in the videos. He would have her like how he saw the Newfie had her.

"The kid's had enough, man. Let's go before someone sees."

A foot hits Ben's thigh. Nobody walked away. "Dis kid is a fucking peeping Tom. Who knows how long he's been watching 'er. I saw da pervert watching us, fuck. Maybe you get off on that b'ye, but not me."

Ben rolled onto his back. He stared up at the man beside him. He was a mountain above him. His face was covered in whiskers and sweat. His blue eyes were red with anger. Ben had seen him. Ben had seen him from the rhubarb patch pushing himself into her. Ben saw them both caked with sweat. Her nails scratched the muscles of his back. Ben imagined it was him. He imagined her moans and her calling his name. He heard it. He imagined what it would be like to bite her shoulder on climax, the one with the fairy tattoo, and taste her blood. Ben saw his eyes. His blue eyes had turned to the window and stared at Ben's. He didn't stop, he didn't yell out, he smiled. He got off, exploded, inside her as he stared at Ben. He liked it.

"You saw me." Ben said. It was a statement, not a question.

A foot hit his stomach. He fought back the urge to vomit as sour bile and blood collected in his throat.

"Stop it. Let's go."

She doesn't want them to hurt me, Ben thought. She wants to save me.

"Are you going to do something? He watches you in your sleep. His spunk's probably all over the wall outside her window. Do something."

Ben looked into her eyes. She loved him. She would smile and walk away. She knew he watched her. She liked it.

"Step on him. Grind those heels into this shit b'ye."

She lifted her foot and pushed her spiked heel into the left side of his bare chest. Ben started to scream. The heel, scratched from use, pushed down into his skin and muscle. He heard his skin begin to tear. His hands tried to push the leather boot off. He could smell it. She pushed harder.

"You leave me alone, you pathetic pervert freak," she screamed down at him. She didn't love him. "You're pathetic." She twisted her heel into his chest and stepped off.

She hated him.

It was all her. It was her idea, her plan. She tricked Ben by smiling at him. She got him to follow her and had the Newfie waiting. She wanted to hurt Ben. She hated him. She thought he was pathetic. *Pathetic*, she said that word.

The four of them walked away. Laughing.

Ben began to cry. He rolled onto his side and curled into the fetal position as sobs raked his body. His hand awkwardly tried to pull his shirt down. The mark on his chest, the size of a spiked heel, beside his nipple leaked blood into his shirt. The scrapes on his back stung with sweat. His nose had stopped bleeding, but was packed with snot and blood. The crack in the back of his head was a sticky mess. He didn't know what to do.

She looked back over her shoulder at the boy curled on the grass. She didn't mean for this to happen. She didn't know if he had looked through her window before her boyfriend saw him. She didn't know what would happen and then she felt like she had to do what her boyfriend wanted. She didn't know what she was setting forth. She didn't know what she was letting loose.

Nobody knew.

"Chloe. Come on."

Chloe.

83

Chapter 9

"What time is it?"

"Early. I have coffee on."

"I know. I can smell it." Hillary moans and pushes herself up.

As Hillary enters the kitchen she wraps her housecoat tight around her body and sits at the table. The chair scratches the floor as it shifts under her weight. She lifts one foot up on her knee and fixes the housecoat to cover as much as she can. "Where are you going so early?"

I tighten my tie and take a quick look at my reflection in the window. I say, "Briefing with McIntyre. Then I have an autopsy to watch. Do you want a cup?"

"Sounds like fun. Please. Do you think you'll be free for lunch?" Frix comes in the room. Her nails click on the floor until she lies next to Hillary and rests her head on her bare foot.

"Probably not, if I am I'll smell like the inside of a body. It's like a pigs burp. It'll make you want to puke." I hand Hillary her mug that reads, *World's Greatest Mom*. She takes it from me, wrapping her hands around it and inhaling the aromas.

"You don't have to be so graphic, Reid." She crinkles her nose and sips her coffee.

"Well it's a fact. The smell is amazing. And it sticks to everything. You've never smelled anything until you've smelled the inside of a body."

She shakes her head. She takes a big drink of coffee. "If you're around the Urban Eatery in the Confed. Mall at twelve thirty, and don't smell, look for me. I should be there somewhere."

I was pretending to be asleep by the time she came to bed last night because I just didn't want to talk. I asked her if she was alright and then rolled over. "Hill, I'm working a murder case. I doubt I'll be free. I'll try." I sip my coffee from an oversized mug. I lean against the counter.

"Did you have any more dreams last night?"

"What? No." I didn't dream because I barely slept. Every time I closed my eyes I saw Johanna Bowers swinging in the breeze. *Drip*.

"You were tossing a lot."

"I have a lot on my mind." A lot of those things have nothing to do with work. How do you tell your wife that you have some sort of feeling inside yourself that feels like you are unsatisfied with life? "Did I keep you awake?"

"A little."

"Sorry, I should get going. I'll call you if I can make it or not." I kiss her cheek and leave without another word. At the front door I look back. Hill is engrossed in pleasing the dog by scratching the back of her ears.

The morning is cloudy and cool. Perfect day for what I have to do.

~ * ~

Inside the Major Crimes Unit office a white board on one of the walls is already dedicated to Johanna Bowers. Her name is written in bold black dry erase at the top. The picture of her and her roommate on top of the dunes at Blooming Point Beach is taped beside her name. On the left side is a brief write up on the details of how and where she was found. Her roommate's and boyfriend's names are listed on the right. There is not much else to write down. We have no real suspects. We have no murder weapon. We do not even have a definite scene. Corporal Gordon Longfellow is at his desk with an espresso. McIntyre's door is open. I just stand and stare at the white board for a while. There have to be answers there somewhere.

"Reid," McIntyre calls out from inside his office. "What time is the autopsy?"

"First thing." Dispirito left rape files on my desk. A yellow post-it on top says he flagged anything that was common among them. I try looking through them.

"In my office."

Time for the Triangle.

The Command Triangle is a term used in major case management for the top three people running a serious case. At the top of the triangle is Sgt. McIntyre, the Major Crimes commander. One point is the lead investigator and the third is the File Manager. Together we will meet every morning and discuss what has to be done throughout the day to end this thing. From there we can delegate who needs to do what and figure out if we need extra resources.

"Where are we?" McIntyre motions for us to take the chairs in front of his desk.

I shrug my shoulders. "I'm hoping the autopsy gives us something. I don't have any suspects right now. Dispirito found some commonality between the stranger rapes, I want the guys to go back and canvas the houses leading out to Blooming Point and write down every vehicle everyone has seen. Let's see if we can get the video tapes from the Confederation Bridge and get pictures of every car on and off the island for the past week. I want to run this through *ViCLAS*."

"You think this is from off island then?" There is hope in McIntyre's eyes. I'll bet he got in to work to a half dozen phone messages, and just as many emails, from reporters about whether this is a homegrown thing or not.

ViCLAS stands for Violent Crime Linkage Analysis System. It is a police computer database for tracking violent crimes and criminals across the country. If you have a rapist who says, "You like that bitch?" repeatedly to his victims, you can put it into the database and hopefully you'll find out that another crime somewhere else had the same commonality. Nova Scotia RCMP had a rapist who wore a black hooded sweater, slapped the victim in the face, and wanted them to scream. They put the particulars into ViCLAS and it turned out that there was a similar case in Alberta. The investigators pooled their information and were able to make an arrest. In our case we can put in the brutal stabbings, the cut around the breast, and the naked hanging and perhaps we will come up with something. If there is a similar case somewhere else then at least we will know it is not homegrown. That, after all, is the main priority for Islanders.

I tell them I am not sure where the killer is from. "We need to get the autopsy done and see if there is anything there. Then we'll have to start going over everything again. Somebody knows something. Somebody has said something to someone."

"Alright, Gordon can send out electronic messages to everyone telling them what to do. You head to the QEH. We're releasing her name this morning and we are going to ask for tips on the Crimestoppers line."

~ * ~

"Morning, Sean."

"Not even close," I say as I greet Eckhart.

"Ian? Ziggy?"

"Now you're just being silly."

"Alice?" Eckhart pushed his glasses up with the back of his hand. He is already dressed in his white bunny suit.

"You should give up while you're ahead."

"Moonbeam?"

"Oh jeez."

As soon as Dr. Norton arrives we can get under way.

An autopsy is not a fun thing to be at. And it doesn't take two minutes like on the television. There are a lot of tedious things which have to get done. We all get dressed in the white bunny suits and collect in the morgue with the body that has been locked up since yesterday. Photographs are taken of the body. Each cut and stab wound has to be photographed three times – overall, mid-range, and then close up.

88

Eckhart goes over the body slowly to see if there were any fibers or particulates missed in the field. He cuts the rope that's still attached to her neck, away from the knot and places it on a side table with plastic underneath. She is weighed and measured and placed on a stainless steel table with raised edges. Then Dr. Norton washes the body to clean off the blood. Eckhart stares at the knot and waits.

"I count thirteen stab wounds and over twenty-seven other lacerations on the front ranging from six centimeters to twelve centimeters long. Lividity has set in. There are multiple bruises on the torso and legs that were not completely there at the scene."

"Look at this." Dr. Norton has her rolled onto her side so that he can see her back. "There's bruising on her back where blood collected internally. She died lying down, probably just moments before she was strung up."

"Lucky her," I mumble. "Can you approximate a time of death?"

"I'd go with two to three days. Probably closer to the three mark. Some of the lacerations, however, have dried blood and are at different rates of healing or infection so I would say she was cut up for a few days prior to death. I will do a vaginal examination and then we can see what's inside."

I stand off to the side taking notes in my book, trying not to look up as the doctor conducts the intimate exam.

Finally he says, "Vaginal bruising, lubricant and spermicide, no evidence of body fluids."

"I'd say ligature marks were made by something like a leather strap. It's too thick to be rope. There's no residue from tape." Eckhart and the doctor are not really working together, but they are not working against each other either. Together they do their jobs and help each other out with opinions and ideas.

The last autopsy I was at was the little girls in British Columbia. I stood there in a daze watching the poor children be cut up. They were desecrated by their killer and then taken apart by a doctor looking for why. *Why* is the big question in these things? Why did they have to die? Why did this girl have to die?

"Here we go then," Dr. Norton says. He makes his incisions and I try my best to zone out.

Eckhart hands me the jar of Vicks VapoRub. I put a small smear above my upper lip. The goal is to give me something else to smell. Eckhart puts some on but the doctor doesn't. Doctor Norton makes incisions and then goes at the body with the circular bone saw. It's like listening to a dentistry nightmare. The saw cutting into the sternum and through ribs makes a similar sound to a giant drill digging into the very back molars of your mouth. It echoes off the walls and makes you close your eyes, and imagine being in that chair just so you forget for one moment what is really happening. Then the smell wafts through the room. The Vicks doesn't even come close to keeping it away. It gets in your nose and sticks to the tiny hairs. There is nothing like the smell of someone's insides. It is this vile disgusting stench that you know the moment it touches your nose that you are smelling death. Years later I may forget the vision of Johanna Bowers swinging from the tree all cut up and bloody, and I may forget what her insides look like all weighed, measured and sitting on a table, but I know that one night I will wake up in the middle of the night from a bad dream and this smell will be all that I remember.

An autopsy is painstakingly slow. Everything has to be documented. Dr. Norton talks into a recorder as he moves along. He is looking for cause of death. Eckhart searches for anything that could help us find the killer.

Two hours is a long time to be in a room with a body. Your mind plays tricks. Sounds come out of the body and you swear she is alive, or you see things move. Pretty soon you start to panic inside the bunny suit, and all you want to do is get out.

"He cut the lung." I step up beside Dr. Norton. He holds the woman's lung in his hands. "One of the stab wounds punctured her lung. She basically drowned in her own blood."

"That's COD then?"

The only things I can see of Dr. Norton's face are his eyes and nose. His beard is covered in a facial hair net. "That is my opinion," he says. "The stupid thing is that if the killer only

90

waited a few hours, one day tops, she would have bled out. She had lost so much blood that she was as good as dead."

"Let's talk this out." I close my book, with my thumb keeping my place, and cross my arm over my chest. The other arm rests on it and clicks a pen absently. Eckhart pushes his glasses up. He stands beside a table with his camera and Ident. Kit. Dr. Norton stands with his gloved hands in the air. I say, "The killer strapped her down and cut the rat shit out of her. He raped her,"

"Probably before he cut her up." Eckhart pushes his glasses.

"She was raped numerous times," Dr. Norton adds.

I continue, "So she's raped, cut, stabbed, and beaten. Then he stabs her lung and instead of praying for her life, she starts choking on her own blood. She dies. He has to do something with the body so he hangs her up in a tree for the fun of it. It doesn't make sense. He would have to be covered in blood and yet he leaves no sign of anything."

"You're missing one thing." I look at the doctor questioningly. He adds, "The why. Why did he kill her? Why did he hang her up in a tree?"

Why?

~ * ~

"I have a list of cars for you." Marilyn is sitting outside the morgue waiting. "Ugh, you stink. The boys went back to Blooming Point and knocked on some doors again. This old guy, who wasn't home the last time, was there. He writes down every new car he sees go by."

"Really? Why?"

"Twenty years ago someone's house got broken into or something. The officer at his door got the full length story." Her hair is tied up in a bun. Her bare neck disappears inside a shirt with two top buttons open.

"So we have a list of cars that went to the beach?"

"Don't get too excited. We have a list of some of the cars which passed his house. He lives over four kilometers away from the scene so all we know is that these cars went past his house.

No proof they went to the beach at all. And they were all in the daytime and there isn't that much detail" She opens her notebook. "Red Sunfire, old blue pickup with red back quarter panel, grey sedan, red Ford pulling a boat trailer, grey SUV, grey Volkswagen, green car, turquoise minivan, small blue SUV, green Chevy twin cab – it's a long list."

I unzip the bunny suit and push the hood off. The stubble on my head is covered in sweat. I can't smell anything the foul stench of death. "It's a start. We have COD." I fill her in on what we discovered through the autopsy.

"A couple of answers and a lot more questions."

Investigations are all about answering questions. You have a puzzle in front of you and by chipping away at evidence and finding clues you try to answer the two big questions: who is the killer, and why did he or she or whomever kill? You have to answer a lot of smaller questions to get yourself there. We answered who the victim was, Johanna Bowers. We know when she was last seen, a week and two days before she was found. Now the whole mess is trying to figure out what happened to her between the time she disappeared and the time she was found in Tulloch Pond Provincial Wildlife Reserve. I have to figure out what questions we should be answering next to get us there. It is like putting together an elaborate riddle with no known solution. You repeat it over and over again inside your head until your brain feels exhausted. And here we are, with only half the riddle.

As soon as I have the bunny suit off we walk out into the fresh air. Marilyn tells me I still stink. I say, "I see you're wearing your ring again."

She looks at it and puts her hand in her pocket. "People wear rings, Reid."

"True, *engaged* people."

"Your point?"

"No point. If you're engaged you should be proud of it, shouldn't you? You should be showing the ring off not hiding it in your pocket."

"I am proud." She does not look at me. Instead she walks quickly staring ahead. She practically jogs up the stairs. "I just don't want to talk about my personal life."

"Why not?" What I really want to ask is if she forgot to wear it home and if Chris threatened her. Or did he perhaps hit her? She's a cop. She knows how to hide bruises. Plus I'm sure Marilyn is not the first woman he's brutalized. I bet he knows where to hit that won't leave visible marks.

"I don't want to, Reid. Do you want to talk about you and Hillary?"

"Only if you talk about your life. Question for question?" We go through the front doors into the warm spring air. I look at my partner for an answer. She shrugs her shoulders. "Do you really want to marry him?"

She takes her sunglasses from her pocket and slides them on. The lenses are light enough that I can see the outline of her eyes, but I can't see where she is looking or the emotion inside them. "I'm not sure. My question, do you-"

"Wait a minute," I say cutting her off.

"What?"

"That wasn't a real answer. I'm not sure? Come on." My car is on the opposite side of the parking lot from where we are headed. I don't really care.

"I'm not sure. That's it. Part of me wants to say no and part of me still thinks I can turn him around and change him."

"Come on Marilyn, you can't –"

"It's my turn." I close my mouth and nod. "Do you really plan on cheating on your wife?" I feel her eyes on me behind the white rimmed glasses.

I should have guessed that this game would make me uncomfortable. I was never good at *Truth or Dare* as a kid. I usually picked truth because the dares my friends came up with were disgusting or embarrassing as hell, but a lot of times there is a little truth that you do not want to deal with. When I was younger, my friends and I were the types who liked to exploit the hidden secrets. This right here is a truth I'm not sure I am ready to deal with. I rub my hand over my head. "I don't know what I want to do. I'm going through one of those midlife crisis things."

"You're not old enough yet for one of those midlife things."

I stop walking. Marilyn stops and looks at me. I slowly turn and look around the parking lot. All of the different cars outside the QEH and any one of them could be the killers. I look at my watch. "My turn. How often does he hit you?"

"He doesn't hit me." She watches a car pass.

"Bullshit."

"Reid don't get all high and mighty with me. Cheating on your wife isn't any different than a little hit now and then."

"How do you figure?"

"Cheating is like an emotional hit. The pain isn't physical but the pain doesn't heal either. Maybe I like it rough. Maybe I like getting hit. You don't know much about me."

I take a look at my phone. I say, "Fine. Forget it then. Your question."

She shakes her head. "No, I'm not playing any more. I'm going back to HQ. What do you need me to do?"

"I don't know." I really don't know. Officers are out there doing everything that has to be done and we are not getting any farther. "I'll meet you at headquarters," I say. I turn and walk across the parking lot towards my own car. There is still time before I am supposed to meet Hillary. I don't know if I want to. Marilyn has me thinking. I haven't even cheated yet and I feel bad about it. I feel guilty for thinking about it. *Screw her*.

I head back to the office.

~ * ~

"Sergeant Reid, can I talk to you?"

"You know how this works Miss Arsenault, you talk to Sergeant English."

Catherine Arsenault had been waiting in her car in the parking lot behind the headquarters building. The moment I pulled in she got out of her car and ran between the other vehicles to catch up to me. She was by herself and didn't have a camera, but she did have a tape recorder in her hand.

"I'm just asking for one minute of your time," she says. Her voice sounds a little desperate.

I get my access card ready. "No comment."

"I'm going to release pictures of the scene."

I stop at the base of the stairs but don't turn around. "Doing so will compromise our investigation. Talk to Sergeant English beforehand."

"I'm going to tell people about your case in BC. Islanders will want to know who is trying to figure out who killed one of their own. They don't trust people from away."

I slowly turn to look at her. My first thought is that she looks pretty. Her hair is parted and drapes over her shoulders. A brown leather jacket falls to her upper thigh and is tied around her waist. "Those girls don't need to have their lives thrown into the spotlight again. Their families don't need it. They don't deserve that. You leave them the fuck alone." Too loud.

Marilyn gets out of her car and crosses rapidly toward us. "What's going on?"

"I meant that you shot the killer." I saw her thumb twitch on a button of her recorder. Marilyn scratches to a stop between us. "Islander's might care to know that a killer is looking for a killer."

"I'm not a killer. It was a good shoot. Self-defense."

"Was it?" She gives me a mischievous smile. I try staring at her eyes, but in my head I want to look away. She couldn't possibly know anything about what happened on the other side of the country. The suspect and I were the only ones there at the time. He is dead. I don't talk about it. Of course, reporters are slippery.

Marilyn's hand grabs my arm. She pulls me toward the stairs. "Let it go, Reid."

"Talk to Sergeant English." I shake my arm loose, run up the stairs and flash my access card in front of the card reader.

~ * ~

"I found a couple of similarities," Dispirito says the moment I walk into Major Crimes.

I'm dressed in my workout sweats. I showered downstairs at the gym, threw my suit into a plastic bag and left it out in my car's trunk. Catherine Arsenault is gone. "What kind of similarities?"

As I said, rape on PEI is higher than most would think, but rape by a stranger is very rare. In most cases it is someone the victim knows, a boyfriend who can't take no for an answer, a relative, a friend. On an island as small as PEI, rape by a stranger is hard to get away with because everyone is known by someone. There are even rapes against men but few are reported. In this world things seem to only be getting worse.

Dispirito leads me to one of the white boards on the walls. I have to look up to look him in the eye. "I wrote it down. Three women said their attacker smelled good. He smelled fresh, he had minty breath. A couple said their attacker was in a dark SUV or van. Almost all said their attacker used a knife. Some were cut. Sierra West is the only one who had the cut around her breast."

"So we're looking for a nice smelling guy in an SUV or van with a knife fetish."

"Who went from being what rape victims called a nice guy to being extremely angry?"

"That's what makes me think we are dealing with different attackers here." McIntyre stands behind us. "These ones say he smelled like soap and mint. This one didn't say that but he used a knife. Nobody was seriously cut until Sierra West. If your rapist is the killer then what made him so violent?"

"I'll be sure to ask him when I find him." This is probably too snotty to say to my boss. I go sit at my desk. The light on my phone flashes. Marilyn looks at me from her desk. "Anything come in from ViCLAS?"

"Not yet. Nothing is coming in from the phones either. It's like this guy doesn't exist."

I look around the room. I stare across at the boards on the walls and all of the notes listed on their white surfaces. When I worked on the case in BC, I studied serial killers. I read information on Ted Bundy, the Green River Killer, and anyone else known as a sadistic killer. I wanted to find out how their minds worked. I wanted to find out how they went about picking out their victims, taking their victims, and what they did to them. People don't even know the true brutality these killers put their victims through. I read about what makes a serial killer do what they do and how they go from being an innocent child to a heartless murderer. I have that feeling about this case. It's either going to go unsolved or something else is going to happen. Something else has to happen.

There was a serial killer born on Prince Edward Island, but all of his five killings were done in Toronto. He killed his lover. While doing life in prison other evidence was found that made the police able to charge him with four hooker killings in 2010. They even checked his DNA with the unsolved PEI killing from eighty-eight but it was a no go. It remains unsolved. The fact that he killed the five in Toronto was the big thing here. That sort of thing would never happen on the island. *Never*.

"He exists," I say without looking at anyone. "He is out there on this island and he is going to do this again."

"Don't even go there, Reid."

"What? Somebody who tortures a girl like this and hangs her up is going to do it again. He had fun with her. He would have gone on torturing her if he hadn't stabbed her lung."

"You have no proof of that. You have no reason to talk about it or speculate. Deal with facts Reid." McIntyre cradles a mug of coffee in his hands. "I want facts. Get me facts on this guy."

"From where? We don't have anywhere else to look. We have to wait for lab results now and that might take over a week, and even then we won't have anything." I look at my cellular phone. It is almost half past twelve. I never called Hillary. I pick up the desk phone and start dialing. Time to face the music I guess. I look up at McIntyre and say, "We're going to need something big to just suddenly jump out at us before we can end this." I look down at my desk and hope McIntyre walks away. "Hillary, it's me. I got held up, I'm sorry." My eyes move up to look over at Marilyn.

~ * ~

The Circle K Ranch is a good forty minute drive from Charlottetown toward Summerside, off the main highway and into the back roads that cross the island at strange angles. Four months after moving to Prince Edward Island, Hillary and Leigh announced to me that we were buying a horse. It was a brown and white American Paint Horse, the white taking a saddle shape on its back. The white also fades into the brown in what is called lacing. The horse's name is Dakota, but we named it *Trouble on Horseback* for the English shows during the summer season. I argued about purchasing it, but not for long.

I can see the horses in the fenced in fields long before getting to the ranch. I pull onto the long driveway. Kenneth Oliver's horses are out in front of the large square house. He's ridden horses for recreation and competition for years, now he's retired and rents out spots in his barn for people to board their horses and gives them a place to ride in his indoor and outdoor arenas. I park beside my wife's car. The only other vehicle here is the owner's black Chevy pick-up and his grey mini-van. Past the house is a three door garage to one side and two barns starting at the end of the driveway, all of which are white with green trim. The older one, used for storage, is on the right. An old truck sits between the two barns. It has a chain conveyor reaching into the back of it from a window in the new barn. Horse manure fills the back of the truck and spills onto the roof and down the windshield onto the hood. Grass grows out of the pile on the roof like crew cut stubble, and there are two tufts of grass and wildflowers that have started to grow at the base of the windshield like the truck's green eyes.

"Spring's coming, I think." Kenneth walks slowly from the house toward the field. He wears western boots, blue jeans with a brown leather belt, a large belt buckle that reads *OLIVER*, and a denim shirt with the sleeves rolled up to below the elbows. He has a little roundness to his stomach, but his arms look strong. He does all the work in the barn himself. He cleans all the stalls and turns out the horses in the morning, then he puts out their grain and brings them all in at night. When we first met him he told us he didn't know the age of his dog because it wasn't nice of a man to ask a woman her age.

"Let's hope so. You're running late today?" I know Oliver usually sticks to a strict timeline.

"A little, yep," he says the last word as he breathes in. It's one of those things Islanders do. "So are you I think." He walks past the manure truck.

This is not the closest boarding place to Charlottetown, not the cheapest, but it is the nicest barn I have ever been to in my life. It is a large square barn with thirty stalls along an S shaped hallway and a small arena. The first concrete hallway leads straight from the driveway to the arena. You can tell the walls were painted white once, but dust and time has made the walls grey. Kenneth's stallion lives in a stall on the right with a pregnant mare across the open space. The first thing I notice is that it doesn't smell like a barn. The country music station, *95.1 FM CFCY*, plays out of a small dust covered clock radio. The sliding door is open showing the dirt filled indoor arena. I turn left and follow the hallway. Stalls line the left side. Each stall is twelve feet by twelve feet with a small dust covered window in each behind metal bars. The barn side of the stall is solid on the bottom with metal bars reaching up from chest level to the ceiling. A couple of them have name tags hanging from the metal bars telling the name of the horse and the name and number of the owner. Faye owned by Cheryl Goettlicher, Darlgonic Autumn Breeze owned by Sarah Stokes. Wood holders keep riders equipment opposite the stalls. Saddles, bridles, reins, and helmets. I can hear Leigh and Hillary arguing up ahead. I walk past a second radio playing the same country station. Thirty-two meters down I turn right into the last hallway. Outside the far opening is the giant outdoor arena that Leigh likes to canter Dakota around. A third radio plays across from their stall. The radios here play constantly night and day.

Hillary stands outside one of the far stalls. She gives directions to our daughter inside the stall with the horse.

"I know, I know," comes out from inside.

Hillary looks at me. "Your father's here."

"Hi Dad," a lone voice floats out of the stall.

"You missed her riding. And we're almost ready to go."

I shrug my shoulders, "you know how cases like this can be."

"I know exactly how a case like this can be." Hillary crosses her arms over her chest after pushing her short black hair behind her ears. "Are you any closer?"

"No." Abrupt. "How was your ride, Leigh?" I join her in the stall and run my hand along Dakota's strong muscles. Is she brown or white? She has white socks on all four legs. On her right fore leg the white runs up in a thin strip then splits in two. One line fades into the brown of her back while the other strip circles over her neck where it splits again; one line goes under her belly and up half-way on each side, the other goes up the left side of her neck. There is a thin faint line of white down her nose.

"Is this going to be a long case?" Hillary asks.

"Great. I cantered and did some jumps. Can you come next week?"

I look at Hillary and give her a nod and then turn to answer Leigh. "I hope so, babe."

Chapter 10

Ben remembered the day in flashes, little snippets of time made up his memories. They were vibrant and full, but the parts that sewed them together were fuzzy or not even there. Those bits did not matter in the long run. The flashes were what made the story. They proved it wasn't his fault. None of it was his fault.

~ * ~

Twelve years ago

Julie Gallant always smelled of coconut. He remembered that smell.

That was one of the things Ben knew. Ben knew he didn't like field trips. He enrolled in the business class because his mother said he would need the knowledge in the future. She wanted him to be a business man, not a blue collar worker like his father. He knew he didn't want to go see how real businesses worked. He knew he didn't want to ride an orange bus across town and sit through boring presentations all day only to get back on the bus for the ride back to school for last bell. The green vinyl bus seat was cool where no one sat beside him. It creaked like a fart when he moved, Ben knew that. And he knew Julie Gallant smelled like coconut.

What he did not know was why the smell of coconut was getting thick in the air and why his ear was getting wet.

He didn't want to turn around. He waited to get on the bus last and took the only seat available. He saw them all there behind his seat as he slid over next to the window. Julie Gallant and Sonja Rufo sat directly behind him. Their boyfriends were in the next seat back. The cool kids. The popular kids. They felt better about themselves by picking on others. He knew that too well.

There was laughter.

"Something wrong, Benny?" One of the boyfriends.

Pathetic.

"You wanna say something? Eh? I didn't think so." The other boy.

"Something stinks." Julie Gallant. More coconut wafted from behind Ben. He felt the back of his hair go wet.

Laughter.

He tensed up. He looked for a road sign so he could figure out how much longer he was going to be in the bus. There had to be at least fifteen minutes. On the inside he was panicking. He heard breath coming in small quick breaths. Something more was going to happen. He had to get out of there. He couldn't see the teacher's head at the front of the bus. In the mirror at the very front he saw the driver's eyes were on the road ahead. There was no place to go.

"What smells?"

Please don't do this. You're going to embarrass me. Ben felt the panic swell inside him.

Ben's body tensed again. He stared straight ahead. He felt eyes on him from every direction, every direction except from the teacher in the very front seat.

"Let me." Sonja Rufo. The scent of something floral mixed with the coconut.

Pathetic.

More laughter. This time it came from other places on the bus.

"Do it." Whispered from the guys.

"I can't."

"He won't do anything. Do it."

Ben heard a noise and then felt something on the top of his head. It was cold and moist. He felt a hand push down and smear it in. He couldn't move. He was too afraid to move. Some of it fell to his ear and slid down until it dropped to his shoulder. He felt his eyes swell up. He couldn't cry. He couldn't face any more humiliation.

There was laughter all around him. It echoed in his ears. Something in him wanted to strike out.

"What's wrong, Benny? You want to hit her? You won't fucking touch her."

"What are you gonna do, Benny?"

Pathetic.

"No woman would let him touch her."

Laughter.

Ben leaned forward. His hand pushed the blob off his hair to his forehead and let it fall. The white mixture went splat on the floor and splashed out. Some got on his running shoes. He tried to think of what it was. His hair was matted to his head. His breath came out through his nose loud and hard. He bit down on his lip. He didn't want to cry. He couldn't let them win.

Pathetic.

~ * ~

The moment the bus dropped them off at the school Ben headed for home. *They shouldn't have done that*, he thought.

Ben swung his backpack. It hit a telephone pole and bounced back. He had his hood pulled up over his head. His shoulders were hunched down.

Fucking assholes.

He smelled of coconut, flowers, and sweat. All he could taste was coconut and blood from biting his lip.

Pathetic.

His feet shuffled on the ground. Ben picked up a rock as big as his hand without a thought. He left the sidewalk and followed the trail, made by countless kids walking and biking, down the slope beside the highway. It was faster than taking the long way down to the lights and then cross. When he got down to the bottom the street towered above him on the left, houses were behind three rows of trees on the right. It was like walking through a deep canyon. The path cut a thin grey strip through the grass.

What are you gonna do, Benny?

A girl walked toward him. Her short hair bounced. He didn't know her. She looked older. She had full breasts and soft hips. She had headphones over her ears.

Nothin', that's what.

Ben felt the sick burning in his stomach. He didn't want to go home. He didn't want to see his mother's face. Kids will be kids. *Bullshit.* He stayed in the bus until everyone left so that he would be behind them and they would hopefully never look back. He could have gone in to tell the teacher, but she would have laughed at him. They were all laughing at him. He heard them in his head. They were gone, but he still heard them. He didn't want to hear them.

Laughing.

You stink Benny.

How could someone do that?

Ben put his head down. He put his hand behind his back. His face burned. They couldn't do that to him. It had to stop.

Benny the Stink.

He felt the girl look at him. Was she laughing? His head was down so all he could see were her shoes. They were those slipper type shoes. She didn't have on socks. It had to stop. He looked up. The path was empty.

Pathetic.

Ben spun on the ball of his foot. His arm stretched out. It swung with his momentum. His fingers flexed on the rock. His eyes went wide. He held his breath. His penis moved with excitement.

What are you gonna do?

The rock connected. The girl's head flew sideways. For a second it looked as if it would leave her body and then she followed. Her body lifted off the ground. It flopped in the air like a doll. She hit the grass, rolled twice then stopped.

Ben looked up and down the path. He jumped over her body. Blood escaped from behind her ear. He knelt down and grabbed her jacket at the shoulders. His feet slid on the ground. His butt hit the ground hard. He got up again and tried to get footholds. He had to get to the trees. He felt her hot blood on his hand. He heard the cars up above. A dog barked.

He felt himself hard in his pants. He looked down at her. A moan escaped her. He crouched beside her body. One knee touched the ground. His hand pushed her jacket aside and cupped her breast over her blouse. It was smooth and firm. Ben felt a rush inside him. He wanted this. He wanted her. This was his world. He was in charge. Ben ripped at her shirt. Buttons flew loose. He pulled until her bra was left. The excitement rose. The thrill. The tingle.

His ears picked up sounds. Voices.

~ * ~

Ben didn't open his eyes. He was wide awake, but stayed motionless on the living room couch. Last night he stayed up watching Kung-fu movies on the late night movie channel. His mother told him to go to bed, but threw her arms up and went to bed herself when he ignored her. He fell asleep with the television on. It was now off.

His parents were in the kitchen. It had to be close to six because his Dad was still there. Ben's father always waited for the six o'clock news on CBC radio to hear the weather before he left for work at the factory.

The radio was loud because Ben's father didn't hear so well. Ben listened eagerly.

Last night was the best sleep of his life. He felt spent and fully relaxed. He never made it past the hero being banished in his movie. When he closed his eyes he was out. If he dreamed he didn't remember and it was not enough to wake him in the night.

"Our top story this morning, a Charlottetown woman was attacked yesterday afternoon while walking home."

Ben felt that tingle again.

The radio said the police were looking for a Caucasian male in his late teens to early twenties wearing a dark hooded sweatshirt. Anyone in the area who may have witnessed anything is to call in.

Ben listened with eyes closed. He heard his mother tsk and his father growl.

"Who could do such a thing?"

Ben had to be smarter. The sweatshirt, it had a sports teams name across the chest, was in a garbage dumpster behind the *Esso*. He was too smart for this. He had to learn. Clothes had to be disposable, no insignia. He had to be stronger. He could barely drag her a few meters into the trees. He had to get his nerves out of it. The voices were nothing but he ran. If he was going to do this again he had to get better at it. He had to fix mistakes. Only then could he take it farther.

He wanted that high.

Pathetic.

They'd all learn. He was no fool.

He wanted the thrill and wanted to live.

What are you gonna do Benny?

Whatever he wanted to.

Chapter 11

I look up from my desk. It isn't even lunch time and I'm tired. I have been tired for a long time. It's been two weeks since finding Johanna Bowers and I am nowhere. The crucial first forty-eight hours went by in a blur of frustration. Now my desk is littered with lab reports from Halifax about the meaningless samples taken from the scene, lists of a decade worth of garbage found in the woods, lists of obscure vehicles people may or may not have seen go toward the beach the week prior, statements from all the people between her place and her boyfriend's – a couple may have seen a woman of Johanna's description walking and crying, but nothing is connecting. Dispirito and Marilyn have gone out and re-interviewed rape victims that may be connected – McIntyre doesn't have much faith in that direction. We even brought in the boyfriend for a polygraph, which he passed with flying colors. I am so tired.

"Do you know what today is?" Marilyn says to no one. Her red hair is up, a little of the ends flare out the side and a couple of strands fall down beside her face.

LeBlanc says, "May 1st?"

"Besides that."

"The first official day my daughter is allowed to start planning her birthday." Leigh woke before I left the house and made a point of telling me. She wants a party at the *Cari* pool at the University of Prince Edward Island and then for three friends to sleep over. The movie consists of popcorn as a snack, veggie burgers with spicy curly fries, ketchup, and then cake and ice cream for dessert. Chocolate soya milk, that her mother got her hooked on, to drink. Chips with onion dip as a late snack.

"The ferry started running?" Dispirito

"Yes, but no. It's the first day of lobster season." Marilyn gives them all a large smile.

"Oh yeah."

"My father and brother are both going out today. So you are all invited to my parents place this weekend for the first lobster feed." Marilyn says.

Lobster season on the North shore of PEI runs from May to July. The life of a lobsterman goes up and down with rising and falling prices. The lobsters on the North shore have thick hard shells compared to the soft shelled ones fished off the South shore in mid-summer. The debate continues every year about which tastes better. I've had them from both sides and no matter where they are from you put them with some melted butter and it's all good. Of course I am "from away" so what do I know?

"Everybody up," McIntyre flies through the door of his office. He has a piece of paper in his hand. My stomach jumps. He looks right at me and says, "We have a body."

I am on my feet. "Where are we going?"

"Port-la-Joye."

"The historical park?"

I unlock the bottom drawer of my desk and take out my Smith and Wesson 9mm pistol. I attach it to my belt and take up my notebook. "Marilyn I'm riding with you," I say.

"Dispirito with LeBlanc. Longfellow you're with me. The body is right in the main park where the old fort used to be. Ident is on the way. The press is already there but we have them held back. The MCP will be there by the time we are." McIntyre follows us out the door. "I want everyone on this. I'm going to get you all the help you need.

"As long as nobody gets in my way." I have never felt this intense before. I actually stop to face him. My eyes burn. "I want this guy."

"It's only been two weeks. Would he kill this soon?"

"Bundy waited a month between kills. He started in late winter and then by June he did three women, two in one day. This guy could be crashing. We have to stop him now." I turn back and head for the exit. I want to get out and in the car. I can feel my blood racing through my arms and legs.

Behind me McIntyre says, "I guess you're right, we have a serial killer."

"He's not a serial killer until he kills three," I say over my shoulder. I'm going to stop him before he gets that far. One serial killer is enough for one career.

Port-la-Joye was the first French settlement on the island. Michel Hache-Gallant, a surname still found all over PEI, lead the settlement in 1720. In 1758 when the British took over control and the French abandoned the settlement. Fort Amherst was built in its place. It was the islands defense against anyone coming into the harbor. Within ten years the capital city site was selected across the harbor. Currently, reverting back to its original name, Port-la-Joye is a National Historic Site used for school fieldtrips and picnics. Over the past few years classes from UPEI have gone there to dig up parts of the park trying to find artifacts from when the French occupied it, including the site of the Hache-Gallant homestead.

From the boardwalk in Charlottetown you can see the grassy hill where the settlement and fort are located where the West and Hillsborough Rivers open up to the Hillsborough Bay and the Atlantic. To get there you have to take the long way around. As we cross the bridge over North River I take a look at the *Cow's Ice Cream Factory* and remember that Leigh wants to go there this summer. We drive through the town of Cornwall, turn left at the *Subway*, and make our way through the backwoods.

"How are things at home?" Marilyn asks.

"What?" I blink fast and come back to where I am. I watch the kids looking over the bridge crossing West River. During the summer, they jump off into the water. "Things are fine. What? Why?"

"Trying to get your mind off things. What do you think we'll find?"

"A dead girl who went through a lot of pain."

At Fairview the highway changes to a piece of highway patched together one pothole at a time for years. The island is cut into small areas or townships. Your area becomes part of your address. The areas range in sizes from just signs on the roads to larger ones with community halls. From Charlottetown to the park we pass through Cornwall, Meadow Bank, New Dominion, Fairview, and then Rocky Point.

As we pull onto Blockhouse Road I can see the news vehicles collecting up at the next intersection where two RCMP cruisers block the entry to the park on Hache Gallant Lane. Reporters and their crews stand on the side and in our way. They slowly move so we can pass. Cameras fire up. Questions are thrown out.

I look out the passenger window at Catherine Arsenault as we slowly cut through all the people. Our eyes meet and hold each other. She has trashed me in the news. She has questioned my ability to handle this case with clear objectivity because of what I did in BC. She has been saying that I did not have to kill the serial killer in British Colombia. She hinted at it being a police cover up to not charge me with the killing.

"You okay?" Marilyn touches my elbow.

I flinch.

"I'll live," I mumble. I turn and look out the front window. "You know all she said about me in the news? My own daughter Googled me to see if it was true. She asked me if I had to kill the man."

"What did you tell her?"

My eyes watch the pavement in front of us. The grass is cut five feet on each side and then long grass left over from last summer takes over. Right now the tall grass is green at the bottom with the silvery blades from last year sticking up like a dye job with darker roots. Up ahead I can see the Visitor's Center with its brown cedar siding. It is small and flat to resemble some of the coastline cliffs of red clay. The building blends in with the thicker woods behind it. "I told her what I told everyone else, it was him or me."

"Was it?"

"Was it what?"

The Mobile Command Post is sitting in the parking lot pointing out toward the park. An ambulance sits next to the curb out front of the Visitor Center, Island EMS written in green and yellow on its side.

"Was it a good shoot?"

I turn and look at her. I say, "Does your boyfriend abuse you?"

She looks at me and forgets about the road ahead. Marilyn looks back out the windshield and quickly says, "Yes. Was it a good shoot?"

Port-la-Joye-Fort Amherst National Historic Site has three small lighthouses on the property along with a Visitor's Center and a small house which was one of the first homesteads on the island. The main park area is a large circle of green grass. Behind the visitor center is a patch of forest with hiking trails leading down to a small beach. You park your car out front of the center and then follow a concrete path past information signs telling you about the history of the site going back to the Mi'kmaq Indians. Past a tiny pond, believed to be larger in the days of the French fort so that it acted as the fort's fresh water source, is a higher mound rising up from the grass. There is an outer and inner circle of raised ground covered in vibrant green broken only by the pathway in. The center has rises and dips of ground where buildings had once stood. Last year we came here with Leigh's school. Hillary said she wanted to come back some day.

Eckhart and his partner are already in full white Bunny suits slowly making their way toward the center fort area on the walking path. Four other people in white suits walk in line with them on the grass creating one line of evidence search. They put flags every few feet on the outer edges. As soon as they are done, the MCP can drive on the grass and get close to the actual body site.

All of us are out of the cars before they stop. McIntyre starts barking orders at some of the officers standing around to go help push the reporters further back. He wants someone to block the barely-there access road that we saw coming in leading down the side of the park.

Marilyn and I go to the trunk to get out our equipment. A strong wind shoots through the thin trees and up from the bay. Marilyn's hair is tied back, but still blows around into her face. I stare at her green eyes. For a moment I hate her for asking if it was a good shooting. For a longer moment I hate myself. I don't want to talk to her about it. I don't want to talk to anyone about it. I talked enough when I was sent to the fucking shrink out west. Without a word I turn and join McIntyre. I won't look at my partner though. I know it is still in her pretty head.

"Reid, did you ever meet Constable Justin Earnshaw? He was first on site."

Earnshaw introduces us to the workers at the park who found the body. "I got here shortly after nine and went right in the Visitor Center." Daniel MacDonald wipes his forehead with a square of paper towel. His orange hair puffs out beneath a khaki baseball cap with a Canadian flag it.

"Who was the last worker here?"

"I was. I clocked out at five last night." He looks quick at his boss then down to the ground. He's lying, but we can deal with that later. I'm sure he just doesn't want to get in trouble for leaving early.

"Nine to five. There's nobody here at night?" I have my hands in my pockets. Marilyn has her notebook out.

"No, there's never been any need to. There is nothing here to steal and not much to vandalize. The Visitor Center has an alarm." Hanni Van Uden is the curator of the historical site. She knows everything there is to know about the fort. Most of her summers are spent educating any visitors who stop and ask. "We only opened up the park officially last week so we were lucky anyone was here." They both wear green pants and shirts with Parks Canada written over their hearts.

I ask Daniel to continue. "When I first got here I noticed the crows flying around, but I didn't think anything of it. I went inside and made coffee and checked the phones. And I went on the computer for a bit. When Hanni arrived she asked me to go see what the crows were going after."

"Crows are carrion birds. They go after any dead flesh. I thought maybe the coyotes got to a raccoon or something."

"I walked straight down the path, and then I saw the body right in the old fort. She's naked and there's blood. When I saw it I ran back." He wipes his head with paper towel. It is soaked right through. His body shakes.

I head down the path walking slow behind the Command Post as it moves down the searched path. Eckhart and the others are inside the high ridge going all the way around former fort.

"What are you thinking, Reid?" McIntyre steps beside me. We watch the officer in charge of the MCP set it up. He lowers the back ramp. "Do you think this is the same killer? The body's not hanging from a tree, it's not a secluded place."

"There hasn't been a homicide in Prince Edward Island in over twenty-five, twenty-seven years and now there's two within a couple of weeks. You really think this is coincidence?"

"We don't even know if it's homicide yet."

I look from McIntyre to Marilyn. "What do you mean? I can see the body from here. She didn't get naked out here in the middle of nowhere and just drop dead." I step beside the trailer and look forward at the site of the fort. Eckhart and the others are slowly making their way around the inside of the fort toward the inner circle. "This is homicide. This is the same guy. He's gone from a body in the woods to one out in the open because he wants to make a show. This is homicide, Wayne."

"Suit up then."

Marilyn and I pull on our bunny suits over our clothes. Booty slippers cover our shoes. I pull the hood up over my head, it was shaved yesterday. Marilyn tucks her hair inside her suit. Now we wait for Eckhart to give us the okay to move forward into the fort.

The body is almost in the direct center of the old fort. As I walk through what was the threshold to the fort I stare at the body laying amongst the dips. Things that look like sinkholes go around the inner "walls," each representing where a building had once been. The woman is laying face down, her head turned to

113

the side. Her tan colored skin has cuts all over the backs of her naked legs and torso. Her buttocks are round; her calves are those of someone who runs. Her long dark hair is a mixture of blacks and browns. It is cast to the side and covers most of her face. Both arms are up over her head. She has bruising under the blood. The only part untouched is a tattoo of words on the back of her shoulder. "Herois do mar," there is an olive branch underneath and then more words, "Saudai o sol que desponta, Sobre um rider te porvil."

"She's got a tattoo," I state.

Marilyn leans past me. I can smell her perfume. She says, "Heroes of the sea. Salute the sun that rises over a smiling future." She turns and looks at me. Our faces are awfully close to each other. I turn and look at Eckhart who has stopped to look at us. Marilyn looks at him. "What? My grandmother is Portuguese. That's an old Portuguese proverb."

She takes a quick picture of it with her phone.

Eckhart pushes his glasses up with the back of his gloved hand. "We haven't found anything yet. We can't even definitely decide what direction the killer came in. There was no blood along the path. I'm guessing she was a dripper. Give me some time and we'll flip the body."

"What's with the extra help?" I nod towards the extra Ident crew.

"McIntyre had them sent over from Halifax to help with going through all the garbage and crap from the first scene. We're lucky they are still here." Eckhart goes back to the body. He slowly moves over her with his flashlight checking things out.

The wind swirls over the tops of the outer structure and threatens to push us over. I can smell the salt in the air. The only places we can see out of the fort are down the path toward the MCP and the Visitor Center and out the other side to see a view of Charlottetown. From here you can make out the high steeples of St. Dominics Basilica church and the generic red brick walls of the Delta Prince Edward Inn. New condominium buildings have popped up in three places along the waterfront. There are no cruise ships in, but soon you will be able to sit here and watch them go straight by as they come into the harbor from the Atlantic. About forty-five or more cruise ships come in through the summer with probably over three thousand people on each. From here you can really see how small Charlottetown is. It's no Vancouver.

"How long is this going to take Eck?" I ask.

"I don't know Dick." He looks up at me to see if there is any reaction.

I shake my head.

"I have to bring in a dark tent so I can use the UV lights," Eckhart continues.

I stare down and watch him do his job. He searches every inch of the woman without touching her like some high school party game to see how close he can get. I look over the body. My eyes trace her legs and roll over her ass cheeks. They slide up the small of her back to her neck. I can picture the killer's nose and lips barely touching her skin as he moved over her tied down body. I look over her arms to her hands closed together, fingers curled. He cut her fingernails again. The remaining nails are painted red and chipped. I try counting wounds but give up. There are too many.

"She's different," I say out loud, but to myself so that I can hear my thoughts. I kneel down close to the body on the balls of my feet with enough room to allow Eckhart to do his job.

Marilyn adds, "Yeah, she's a brunette this time."

I don't look away from the body. "There's that. Johanna Bowers was trim. This woman is in shape, but she's round in places. Her butt is bigger and her hips wider. He changed his victim. Most serial killers go after the same type."

"This isn't a serial killing." Marilyn stares down at me.

I look up for a second, then back to the young woman. *I have a feeling* is all I want to say. It is strange for me to even think it. Somehow, I know there are going to be others. If we don't hurry, this is going to be a lot worse than my case in BC.

The wind cuts through the bunny suits and then our clothes. It comes in from the last stretch to Hillsborough Bay and hits the top of the hill with full power. The French picked this site

115

because it gave a good view of the two rivers and the water leading out of the harbor. I can imagine soldiers up high watching what is going on in the water, and the Mi'kmaq natives camping down near the woods, farmers bringing in products.

When we were here with Leigh's class last year the wind was strong enough to send a couple of hats rolling over the grass. Any evidence like loose hairs has probably blown away. This guy is too intelligent. Killers like this are not usually smart, but are very intelligent.

Marilyn folds her notebook in half and tries to balance it on her forearm with her fingers trying to hold down the paper; the tips go white. The page corners twist up in the wind. She carefully draws the scene out in black ink.

"This damn wind," she re-adjusts the book. "It's fucking cold."

I rise up, my knees ache. "What do you think?"

She stops drawing. She looks down at the body and lets her eyes stay there. "It could be a copycat. Maybe someone saw the opportunity to kill off a girlfriend or something."

"It takes a lot of anger to brutalize someone like this."

"It's a different victim type, different scene, different placing of the body,"

"His signature is the brutality." I fold my arms across my chest to hold in some heat. My eyes ride over her body again, from the back there are signs of rape. "I bet the breast is cut around."

"I didn't know you were a betting man, Reid." Dr. Norton walks over the grass toward us. His bunny suit flaps violently in the wind. He wears a hair net around his beard. "You get on the island and the whole place goes to hell, eh." He looks at me and I guess he sees something because he quickly says, "I'm kidding. Are we ready?"

Eckhart says, "Bring in a backboard and we'll turn her over."

With a wave, one of the ambulance attendants brings the board to the outer edge of the fort. Eckhart and I take the backboard from him. Eckhart positions himself at the victim's head, Dr. Norton at her feet, and I hold the board as they roll her toward it. Blood covers her entire torso. The left breast has a long thin slice completely along the base. When it was attached her breasts were a good size, more than a handful. Her body was so similar to the other victim. I look at her face. She was pretty before the killer took a knife to every centimeter of her. Her dark eyebrows are trained to mid arches. Her skin is smooth and was at some time clean. Her hair is caked onto her face in thick clumps. The bruising over her body and on her legs suggests she took an intensive beating. The violence between her legs was deadly. She went through a lot. *Drip.* The Doctor leans in and does his work with Eckhart watching every move; Marilyn and I stand back.

"From liver temp, I'd say she died between eight and ten hours ago. From the amount of blood loss she was laying here when she died."

I look at my watch, "She was put here between two and four in the morning."

Dr. Norton moans as he stands up. "I'm amazed she lived. Some of the cuts and bruises look older."

"What's that?" I look at Marilyn. Her arm is stretched out pointing down at the victim. "You can hardly see it."

The blood from her breast has washed over her stomach like a giant wave. There is something underneath. *Drip.*

"Some writing, I can't make it out." Eckhart leans over the body. He moves in and out like an optometrist studying a retina.

"Let's clean it off so we can read it."

Greg Eckhart looks up at me. His glasses are stretched down to the tip of his nose. He says, "It'll have to wait for the autopsy."

"We can't wait."

"We can't clean the blood off on site." Eckhart gets to his feet and stands between me and the body. He pushes his glasses up.

"We don't have anything, Greg. This could give us –"

"I have to follow proper procedures."

"Fuck procedures." I feel my eyes get wide. "I need to know what that says."

"Reid, we have a chain of custody. We have protocol. We can't just screw everything up so you can read this."

"I want to know what this says."

"What happens when we get to court and shit gets thrown out because we jumped steps?" His hand jumps and pushes his glasses up.

I step closer to him. I can feel my own breath reflecting off his face. "Take your pictures, get your samples, and make it so I can read what's on her."

"Back off Reid."

I stand there a few moments. I don't know what to do. Marilyn touches my arm. Dr. Norton stands back and looks between the two of us. I look into Eckhart's eyes. I know he is right. We can't risk doing anything that will jeopardize a future trial. I turn and walk off toward the entryway to the fort. Instead of heading to the MCP, I turn left.

At the corner of the fort is a monument erected in honor of the *Great Acadian Upheaval* when the English came from New England and kicked the French off the island. Some of the French, now called Acadians, stayed on the island in small pockets, most of which are still there today with strong hold on their Acadian heritage. During the upheaval they went back to Europe, to other parts of Canada, and to the southern United States like the city of New Orleans where they became known a Cajuns. The monument has a cross with a map showing where the Acadian's were sent all above a five pointed star.

I stare at the monument but wonder who this woman was. I wonder how she moved, what she looked like when she walked. How did her ass move? What did she like to do? Johanna Bowers – Jo – liked adventure. She liked climbing on the beach dunes, putting charcoal drawings on herself and taking silly poses for the camera. What was this girl like? Because she is a *was*. She is past tense. She will never be again.

I push the hood back off my head. The wind cools the sweat on my skull. I'm suddenly ice cold completely throughout my body.

The girl no longer has a name. She had one at some time. *Chloe.*

"You alright, Reid?"

"What?"

"You good?"

I nod.

Dispirito leads the way into the MCP. "No ID yet. We called Charlottetown Police, but nobody has any missing person's reports matching her description, yet."

"What's going on?" McIntyre joins us and makes himself a cup of coffee.

I take my bunny suit off to the waist. "There's something written on her stomach under the blood. Eckhart won't clean it up so we can read it. He's right." I fucking hate that he is right. We could clean up the blood to find out that the words on her stomach have to do with some stupid sex game and have nothing to do with who killed her. It could just be another tattoo.

"Reid, here it is." Marilyn takes long steps up the back ramp and pushes her Blackberry in my face. "Eckhart took his samples and cleaned the body up a little so you can read what it says. This is serious."

On the small square screen are words written in black marker on a tanned stomach with blood all around and between the words and letters. It is block capital letters about a centimeter or so tall in black marker. I hold it close to my eyes.

YOU MISSED ONE. Underneath it read, *3231 BPR.*

Chapter 12

10 years ago

"Hi," smiling.

"Hi," straight faced.

"Hi,"

"Hey,"

"Hello,"

"Hel-lo," wink. "That's stupid."

"Hi, I'm Ben," *suave*.

"I'm Ben." Smile.

"I am Ben." *Too forced.*

"Ben's the name."

"Ben," head nod.

"It's Benjamin, but they call me Ben," *corny*.

"Hi, I'm Ben," little smile, bite of the bottom lip. *Very innocent*.

He ran his hands through his brown hair, still wet from the shower. It was cut short. As he ran his hand through it, the strands spiked up in all directions. His ears stuck out a little. Water dripped down onto his shoulder. He had bags under his eyes. He adjusted his glasses. He had to move his head to see through the steam fog. His cheekbones were high. His chin was pointed like his mothers. He had thin lips like his father. His top lip was almost completely hidden. There were no scars, no birthmarks, his skin was smooth. His mother was a firm believer in scrubbing his pores clean with *Oxy Clean* scrubs every night and every morning. It gave him baby skin. He knew he wasn't good-looking, but he wasn't ugly. He was average looking. All that was needed to make him good-looking was confidence.

"I'm Ben, how are you?"

"How you doing?" *Too Joey from Friends.*

"I'm fine."

"Good and you?"

"Hi, I'm Rick." *Not realistic.*

"I'm Webster."

"I'm Tom." *Possible.*

"My name's Tom."

"Tom."

"I love that dress."

"Nice eyes," *too serial killer.*

"What's your sign, baby?" *Cheesy.*

"Hi, my name's Ben."

He stood before the full length mirror on the back of the bathroom door fully naked. His shoulders were small and hunched forward a little from years of trying to be invisible. There was a round mark, the size of a spiked heel, over his left nipple. A few hairs pushed through down the center of his chest. His arms had been growing. He was up to one hundred push-ups a day. His stomach was flat. If you looked hard enough you could see the six pack forming from his regimen of daily abdominal crunches. There was a hairy patch between his legs with a limb that measured seven inches when excited. He had to shave all of that to not leave hairs. His legs were hairy, except for circles on each knee cap. They were strong and firm. He ran everywhere. He didn't like his feet or the hair on his toes. He was thin and light. He was average. Average build, average height, average weight. *Average. Pathetic.* He stared at his naked body. It was blossoming into something more than average.

"Hi," his voice was louder and it shook. "My name is Ben." *Stronger.* "And I'm going to FUCK you whether you like it or not." Spit flew from his thin lips. He grinded his teeth and stared into his own eyes. He couldn't see in them what he would become. He couldn't see what others were going to fear. He knew how to hide it. He studied what to do and how to not leave signs. He was going to be known.

The island was *his*.

Chapter 13

"*You missed one.* What does that mean? What did we miss?" Marilyn.

"Another body?" Dispirito

Instantly I look through the windows for more crows collecting over dead flesh. The only crows around seem annoyed with our presence.

Marilyn puts a hand through her hair. "Do we even know if this is part of all this?"

"It is," I quickly throw out.

"It could be some stupid game she was playing with a boyfriend." McIntyre puts his coffee down on the counter.

"This is him." I slam my hand down on the counter. His coffee does a little jump and splashes over the rim.

He and I stare at each other for long moments.

"This is a game. This is his game," I say.

"What are you talking about?" Dispirito absently rubs the scar on his temple.

"He knows we're not even close. He thinks he can do anything and still be safe. He thinks that writing a note, maybe giving us another body is safe because we have nothing. He thinks he's too smart for us to get anywhere near him. Other psychos have done it."

In the late sixties a killer calling himself *The Zodiac* terrorized Northern California by killing a confirmed seven people over a short period. He claimed to have killed over thirty. The real psychological game was sending letters to the press with psychotic puzzles that nobody has yet deciphered.

McIntyre says, "I'm still not convinced this victim is from the same killer as Johanna Bowers. It's completely different."

"This is him." This time my fist hits the counter. A crack echoes through the tiny room.

"Reid,"

I look at Marilyn quickly to quiet her.

I take a breath and push it out through my nose. My hands flatted down my shirt. My knuckles are now screaming out in pain, but I can't show that. "This is him. He's now killed two, maybe three. All I'm asking for is the benefit of the doubt, Wayne. If we find something in this girl's life that might say something different we'll look at it as hard as anything else. This is him."

He nods. "Okay, where do we go from here?"

Dispirito takes Marilyn's Blackberry. "What does 3231 BPR mean? BPR? Could that be his initials?"

"Would he really leave us his initials?" LeBlanc asks.

"If he thinks he has us by the balls he would." Marilyn.

"The BTK killer left notes with his victims. He signed them BTK. But that stood for Bind Torture Kill, not his name." Dispirito flicks his head moving his blond hair.

"You and Reid need a new hobby." Marilyn has taken off her bunny suit. She leans against the entryway to the back of the MCP where the radio station is and the evidence table.

"It's an address." We all look at LeBlanc sitting at the table. "Don't you remember, Al? 3231 Blooming Point Road. It's a house we didn't go to. The driveway is grown in. Neighbours say it is abandoned three or four years now."

"You didn't go to it." I glare down at him.

The Frenchman stares back up at me. "It is an abandoned house. We were questioning people, not looking for anything."

"Fuck sakes," I grab onto the top of my head and walk into the front room. I know he is right. Put in the same place I would have done the same thing. There was no reason to go up to the place and look around. I still need to get it out somewhere. "Fuck."

I walk back in the room and give a head nod to LeBlanc. He nods back. All is good.

"Let's calm down," McIntyre takes his stance as the leader. He has to get us all together and set us on the right path. Set us on a path at least. He crosses his arms over his chest and looks at me. "What do you want to do?"

"We're going. Marilyn and I in one car and Dispirito and LeBlanc in another. No radios. I don't want the reporters to beat us there and screw everything up," I say.

"I'll get the ERT team out there." McIntyre takes out his phone.

"No, I don't want them." The *Emergency Response Team* is the RCMP equivalent of SWAT. For going into violent situations they are more equipped with better weapons and stronger armour than regular members have. Right now I don't have the time or patience for them. I want this guy. "This isn't going to be dangerous."

"What are you talking about? It could be a trap. You could walk into a place strapped with explosives or something. No."

"He's not a cop killer, Wayne. He kills innocent girls. He ties them up and tortures the hell out of them. He's not going to go face to face with us." I look at McIntyre and wait. I know he has a job to do and he has to follow procedures.

He straightens his tie. "I'm putting them on standby."

"Let's go." I lead the way out of the Mobile Command Post and down the paved trail toward the Visitors Center. "I'm going to get the guys on the road blocks to stop the press from following us," I call back over my shoulder.

Marilyn and I walk a few meters ahead of everyone else. She says, "Are you okay?"

"I want this guy. He's only just beginning."

~ * ~

Almost a week after finding Johanna Bowers' body there was a memorial service at the Belvedere Funeral Home in Charlottetown. Her parents were on the island waiting for Dr.

Norton to release the body so they could take her home to Calgary for a proper funeral. Marilyn and I decided to go to show respects and look for any possible suspects. Some killers liked to visit the funerals of their victims in order to continue their fantasy. Seeing the grief was a sick exciting game for them.

"This is police work, Hillary, you shouldn't be there. What if we see a suspect?" I tightened my tie and checked the mirror to make sure everything looked straight.

"I remember what you were like after the funerals in BC."

"Hill, that was different."

"You got piss drunk, came home, left your gun where Leigh could have got it, and passed out. I'm going with you. If you see someone and have to do something, then I'll back off." Hillary sat on the edge of the couch. Her short black dress rode up her legs past her knees as she reached down to put on black heels.

I put my jacket on. In my pockets were my *ID*, handcuffs, phone, and gun. "It was out of her reach."

"It was out in the open." She stood and flattened out her dress. "Is Marilyn going?" She led the way down the stairs. The babysitter sat at the kitchen table setting up a board game for her and Leigh to play.

"Of course she'll be there. She's my partner. She has to be there." I tried to look at her face but couldn't see any signs of anything. "Why do you ask?"

As soon as we were outside Hillary said, "No reason. You spend a lot of time with her."

"We're working an important case."

She moaned agreement.

Marilyn stood outside the funeral home when we pulled in. She was dressed all in black – pants, shirt and jacket. She said how much she liked Hillary's dress. Hill smiled at her and said a simple thank you.

We stood outside and watched the people who came. Most of the veterinarian students came and walked in small groups. Some of them didn't look too sad, but that was probably because there were a lot of them that didn't know the victim. Other people came with sombre expressions. They filed into the funeral home.

Johanna's father met everyone at the door and thanked them for coming. Her mother and sister were inside. They had a flight back home in a few days with their lifeless daughter and sister. I tried to spot anyone out of the ordinary, anyone who looked happy instead of sad. Most everyone kept their gaze at the ground. Mike Valance, her former boyfriend, arrived with Alex, the roommate. They didn't hold hands, but walked close together with their fingers barely touching. Neither said anything to us. They barely said a word to Mr. Bowers.

Marilyn tapped my elbow and pointed in the direction of the entry into the parking lot. Hillary watched our interaction and followed our gaze. The CBC News van pulled in and found a spot. Catherine Arsenault stepped out dressed in an elegant black dress with her hair done nice for the camera. Her driver/camera man started filming the people as they arrived. I hoped she was going to stay outside for the service.

We were the last ones to enter and sat in the very back. I watched everyone. Everyone there seemed to belong. They were there because they cared for Johanna. Of course that didn't mean that her killer wasn't there.

Hillary rested her hand on my thigh. I caught Marilyn looking down at her hand.

A pastor spoke about death and that life was precious and how this act was senseless. Her teachers and some of her classmates said words about how she got along with everyone and how great her future looked. Her family went up and her father thanked everyone for coming out, her mother was silent. Her sister, who looked a lot like Johanna, talked about how life was when they were growing up.

Afterward there was food and chit chat about the Stanley Cup playoffs and what the weather was like. Barely anyone spoke of Johanna.

~ * ~

"You okay?"

"What? Yeah, I'm fine." We are on St. Peters Road heading out to Blooming Point. "Pull over to the store up ahead. We can get our vests on and plan it out." I get on the phone and call the boys behind us to follow us into the parking lot. We park off to the side and all put on our blue Kevlar vests on over our shirts then get our jackets on overtop. Marilyn's jacket is too tight to put on over it. I find it surprising how much of her figure disappears once the vest is on. She's just one of the boys. "Do you guys know anything about this place?" I say once we are ready.

"No, we had no reason to check it out." LeBlanc states.

I nod. "We go in standard formation. From there we decide how to go. Probably Marilyn and I will hit the house with you two covering. I bet the worst we find is a note pinned to the door saying, made you look, but you never know."

I heard a comedian on *Just For Laughs* once that said police officers are problem solvers. We go in and solve people's problems, then move on to the next one. The part where our jobs get dangerous is when people don't like the solutions we come up with. We put our lives on the line, hopefully for the better. It is our job to be out there and say, "No, you can't do that." It is our job to stand between the boogie man and the rest of the people. We are the soldiers against the dark.

Dispirito and LeBlanc pull off to the side of the road ahead of us. This stretch has no other houses on it. There is a house as soon as you turn on either end of this stretch, but none look down in this area. It has thick forest on either side. The blue and white sign at the end of the driveway with 3231 on it is bent almost in half from snow plows taking it out.

We pull onto the side of the road and I am out on the grass with my 9mm pistol ready. I instantly take a one knee stance with my right hand holding the gun, left hand cupped around it. The side of the road beyond a ditch is all forest of aspens and evergreens. The small driveway cuts into it with tree branches reaching over like a long archway. Single branched willows and thorny plants spot the driveway that has not been used in years. Off to the left I can see a corner of a house through the trees with

130

virgin leaves. I feel a tap on my shoulder; I move forward crouched over with my gun ready. The others move forward, a few steps behind and off to the side. The driveway goes fifteen feet and then turns left. A tall white pine tree blocks our view of the house. The branches, with three inch long green needles, hang down in sheets. I slide a little over so I can see everything.

The open yard is in the shape of a D with us on a lower curve. On the upper curve, diagonally off on our right, is a small white shed being sucked in by the forest. Trees grow on three sides. There is a white barn like building by the upper end of the flat part of the D. Between us and that are four fruit trees. Their branches reach out far from the main trunk. On the lower part of the D is the house. The walls are made of fake brown logs stacked on top of one another. A deck is attached to the front. The roof goes in different angles. Facing us is an octagonal window on the second floor, it is open slightly. On the ground, at the bottom corner, is a hole in the wall opening to the crawl space underneath the house. Thin trees are encroaching on the far sides. Besides the buildings, there is nothing left to let anyone know that people had once lived here.

I look at Dispirito, point to my eyes and then motion my hand toward the small shed and barn. I motion LeBlanc to check out the hole into the crawl space, was it made by an animal or someone who wanted to steal the copper pipes that made up the houses plumbing. I also point up and to the back silently telling him to keep his eyes on the octagon window above and the back corner of the house.

I move forward with Marilyn behind me and off to one side. The others sidestep away to keep their eyes on their assignments. The side of the house with the deck has one door on the side that looks like it may have been the front entrance. A willow has grown up and leans in front of the door, blocking it. The deck, once stained green, is flaked and dry. The first step calls out the moment my weight is added. On the deck is a glass door with a large window on the far side. There are small windows up above us on the second floor. With my pistol in both hands, I move forward. I step over a hole in the deck. The boards crack. I put my back to the wall. Marilyn does the same. My head snaps around. The inside is a hardwood floor living room, no furniture, with a black cast-iron fireplace and an island blocking off the living room from the kitchen. The refrigerator door is wide open. There is a back room through a doorway. There is no dead body.

My mouth is dry. I can feel the sweat collecting beneath my vest. From here I can see Dispirito under a fruit tree. I can't see LeBlanc. My body goes tense. I can feel my knees shake. I'm afraid.

I reach my hand across to try the doorknob. It turns, the door opens inward. There is a rush of stale air followed by a stench that makes me want to vomit the moment it touches my nostrils. It sticks to the hairs in my nose. I move in with my knees bent. There are stairs behind the door going up. I point the gun up the stairs, can't see more than a few steps up, and move forward toward the back room. I can hear Marilyn behind me. I look behind the kitchen island. It is a nice little kitchen. There is an open door on the side under the stairs. Inside is an empty bathroom. My pistol leads the way into the back room. It is a laundry room. The machines sit there silent and waiting. There is a back door leading out.

"Clear," I say and head back into the main room. Marilyn falls in. I can picture myself halfway up the stairs and suddenly seeing a gun and feeling the blast of a bullet in my chest. I can picture myself flying back down the stairs, my arms flailing all around, knocking my partner down. I want to tell her to go outside and wait. I don't want her to follow me and get hurt. I need to go. *Drip.*

The smell of death and decay is strong at the base of the stairs. It could be a dead animal. A wounded raccoon could have found a hole into the house and died upstairs. I'm not that lucky. My Smith and Wesson leads the way. Where it looks, my eyes look. Both of us look up the length of the stairs. My ears strain to hear anything. The only sounds are our shoes on the wood steps. Marilyn's breathing comes hard. Sweat appears on my arms and is instantly chilled. A step creaks. From the top of the steps I can see three doors. Two are closed, the far one open. Marilyn tries the closest door. It opens into an empty bedroom.

"Clear." *Drip.*

I move down the hallway keeping close to the wall. The smell can practically be seen wafting down the hallway from the room with the open door. It reminds me of bile stench that exploded out the moment the Doctor cut open Johanna Bowers. *Drip.* We have to check the last closed door before going any further. Each of us takes a position low on either side of the closed door. I keep my eyes on the open door and reach up for the door knob. I turn and push. Marilyn follows her pistol into the room. She checks the open area and then the closet.

She taps my shoulder and says, "Clear."

Drip.

"Both of them are small rooms. That must be the master."

I move forward. I can feel the smell on my skin. It is worse than the stench of rotting garbage.

I see the dark marks on the floor and walls. Light comes in through the slightly open octagonal window. Something creaks.

I cover my mouth. My stomach lurches. There's fire and acid in my throat. My gun goes down to my side. *Drip.* She is there in the air above the floor. Her body sways in the breeze from the window. A rope is tied around her neck and to a ceiling fan. Her neck looks abnormally long. Her body is caked in dried blood. Her body is cut up far more than the other girls. Her stomach had been cut open letting the insides hang out. There is a long slice across her neck. Her arms hang down at her sides with palms open forward. There are cuts crossways all down her legs.

"My God," Marilyn puts her hand over her mouth. "Reid,"

There is blood all over the room. The hardwood paneled floor is permanently stained in a deep red brown. The blood splatter is all over the white walls. The killer must have been swinging the knife wildly.

"Reid."

Her face points down at the floor. Sandy hair hangs down around her face. Her blood has long stopped to drip from her wounds. *Drip.* Her toenails and fingernails are painted black, ends trimmed. Her breasts are larger than the woman we found this morning. She was probably healthy, in shape, sexy. I imagine she had been anyway. Now her skin is in dark shades in places and is dry and tight. Where her intestines are showing the area is green and rotten. I take a step. I want to see if she has a tattoo on her back shoulder.

"Reid."

"What?"

"There's something moving."

"Where?" I bring my pistol up and ready. I sweep the room and see nothing.

Marilyn's face has gone white. Even the colour has left her lips. She says, "On the body. Something is moving on the body."

Little white maggots crawl and wiggle over the woman's body. They come in and out of every open wound. As I watch a few maggots drop off her body where they can't hold on. They join a collection of them on the floor beneath her. Other insects crawl on the wounds and fly around the room. A group of something eat away at soft tissue in one eye. A small group of flies collect on a splash of blood in the corner. Only now do I hear the constant buzz of thousands of insects echoing through the room. I feel the threat of sick enter my throat again.

"How long do you think she's been here?"

"Before Johanna Bowers," my voice sounds like it is from somewhere else. I want to run down the stairs and out into the yard. I can't. I have to look at her. I have to find out her story and tell the world. I have to try and find some explanation for this. "Go tell the others we found her. Get them to check out the other buildings. And call McIntyre." I don't know if Marilyn argues. I don't hear anything except the bugs eating their dinner and the rope creaking.

Chapter 14

Three Months Ago

Ben sat on a hardwood floor with his legs crossed meditation style. He had the point of the hunting knife dug into the floor in front of him. He turned the weapon around in a circle and let it spin with his finger on the end of the handle. His grandfather showed him how to sharpen the blade with a whetstone a long time ago. It was back in his days of killing raccoons before they could go after the chickens or the garbage cans. Covering his hand was a black leather glove. He wore a black sweatshirt and black sweat pants, pretty generic. Over top he wore a yellow plastic slicker. It was held tight at his wrists and ankles by rubber bands. His shoes were cheap hiking boots bought at a department store, one and a half sizes too big. On his head was a backward baseball cap. Before going out he brushed his hair with a thick bristled brush to get out any loose hairs. Ten years ago he found his destiny. Since that moment he put himself into school to learn how not to get caught. He was a walking encyclopaedia of criminal forensics.

The girl made a noise. Her bare leg moved. Ben saw the patch between her thighs. It was a little darker than her sandy hair. She was bleeding from there. She was bleeding from her behind. She was bleeding from the small cuts he had made on her legs and body. Just the thought excited him.

The first time he had sex was ten years ago. She was blond too. He crouched down in a cluster of evergreens along the Confederation Trail. She jogged toward him. Her arms pumped at her sides. The muscles in her thighs jiggled. She wore plaid shorts and a baggy sweatshirt. Headphone wires dangled down from her ears. She didn't know he was there. He had been hiding there for over an hour watching people go by. There was a couple walking with a baby carriage, a man that jogged by himself, two women ran by together. This one was alone. There was nobody in either direction. Ben lowered the mask over his face so that all that was left were a pair of eyes and his mouth. His fingers flexed around a two by four. Ben nodded in time with her feet hitting the gravelled path. He held his breath. He stood. His arms swung the board. She never saw it coming and didn't have the time to react. The board hit her flat in the face. She heard her own nose crack at the same time her feet went out from under her. Her body flew through the air, her hands flailed. She hit the ground and slid off the far side into the grass. She didn't move. The only sound that was made was when her body hit the ground. Ben was on her. He slid his hands under her shoulders and dragged her into the woods. His hands wouldn't work properly. His thumbs and fingers felt like they were swollen as they tried to work the buttons on the front of her shorts. He curled his fingers over the top and yanked them down. They fought with her wide hips for a moment then went down. One hand grabbed onto her panties, white and thin with tiny blue and red flowers, and pulled them down. She was trimmed with a thin strip down there. A moan escaped her throat. Blood ran from her nose and mouth where teeth were missing. Ben pulled his pants down to his knees. He fumbled around with the condom package. He had practiced this in his room. He knew how to get it on. Then he was in her. He pushed three times and came. It was done. He put the condom and wrapper in a plastic shopping bag from his pocket and walked into the woods. His Dad's car was parked two kilometres away, far from the trail. The girl was found twenty minutes later by joggers. She never saw the man who raped her. Ben never even knew her name.

"Help me. Please." The girl rolled to her side. Her arms were duct taped together behind her back. Her toes, nails painted blue, tried to push at the floor. They slipped and fell flat. "Let me go," she said softly. "Let me go," she yelled. Spit and blood flew out from her blood caked lips.

"Where would you go?"

"Just fucking let me go, you fucking freak." Her feet kicked at the floor as she tried to turn herself over. Ben sat just out of her reach. He smiled a little as she tried to kick at him. She was weak. She was losing the strength to fight. Soon it wouldn't be any more fun.

His clothes were disposable. This woman's clothes were going to disappear. He never took trophies like some idiots. He didn't let anything become personal. It was an addiction he had to fill. He wasn't going to let something like getting caught stand in his way.

"Why are you doing this? I don't know you. Just let me go." Her voice was back to begging. It was getting close to daylight. He had to decide what to do with her. He'd only held a woman a few hours before. He had this one here for almost twelve hours. It was cold in the room, but Ben didn't feel it. He was sweating inside his clothes. She shivered, her lips were blue, her skin pale from blood loss.

Eight years ago he tried to change. He knew what he had done was wrong. He had done it two or three times by then, but he knew it was wrong. Something in him wanted, no needed, to do it. He needed that fix. The sex didn't last that long. It was the excitement of waiting to get hold of the girls and the possibility of getting caught that was the thing he craved. He knew that by number two or three, whatever. For one of them he even had to hold his hand over her mouth as someone went by. He saw that they were wearing *Nike* shoes. It was that close. Thoughts like that made his hand busy in his bed for many nights.

Eight years ago Ben met Shannon in school. He was at the university for computers, she for business. He saw her in the computer lab struggling over a project she had due. She was a little round with large breasts and a roll to her belly. She had shoulder length blond hair that looked like it was cut with hedge clippers; it had uneven cuts all over. Ben was certain when her hair was first cut it looked great, now it was grown out and not maintained. She had nice blue eyes. She wasn't like his other girls. She was nothing like Chloe. She was nothing like the others at all. He knew before he sat down beside her and offered to help that he wasn't going to hurt her. She was going to show him the way and help Ben stop hurting girls.

"Hi, I'm Ben."

The police were looking for him. Ben wasn't stupid. He knew what he had done was wrong. The trick was not caring. It was his world. The first one was great. The next he saw fear in her eyes and it was better. At night he pictured those eyes or the thin white panties with blue and red flowers as he relived it. Shannon was supposed to help him. Shannon was supposed to set him on the right path and show him real love.

The first time he went in to kiss her Ben saw curly white hairs under her chin. The first time he put his hand down her pants he found out her *silk* wasn't groomed. He talked her into shaving that. He tried talking her into getting a tattoo on the back of her shoulder, but she hated needles. He did it gentle and slow with her. Any time he started to thrust hard or bit down on the big circle around her nipples she complained about it hurting. Ben let her push him away. Though he wanted to fight her, wanted to slap her in the face and have her submit – his teeth ground and he got a look in his eyes that he was certain frightened her – he didn't.

The girl kicked out at him. Without a thought Ben leaned forward and flicked his wrist. The tip of the knife caught the bottom pad of her foot. An inch long cut pulled open and blood ran out.

She screamed, "Stop it. You prick. Let me go."

Ben smiled wide with perfect teeth. He said, "My mom always told me things could get worse."

On their year anniversary Ben took Shannon out for dinner. He took her home and gently took her clothes off. He kissed her neck and shoulders and back. He laid her down and made love to her. She came. He didn't. In the past year the only time he came was lying next to Shannon thinking about the fear in that girl's eyes. As soon as she was asleep he got up, pulled on a pair of blue jeans, and a sweatshirt with no logo on the front. He put on his hiking boots and walked out the front door, grabbing the keys to her father's pick-up they had borrowed for the evening.

He pulled up outside a bar and waited. He didn't know what he was waiting for. He watched the boys and girls going in and coming out. Most were no older than his twenty years. The girls were dressed tight. Their jeans and pants and skirts and shirts barely held on around their bodies. One stumbled away from the herd. She looked back and yelled something. Her fingers went up in the air. She wore heels at the end of long legs that came out of a black skirt. She pulled a small jacket around her. She walked away from the bar. Ben pulled away from the curb.

"Hi," he said out the window. He raised his voice, "My name's Ben. Hi, you look like you need a ride." He showed a little smile, nothing too confident.

"I don't know." She smiled. Her drooping eyes looked behind her. She was almost at the end of the block from the bar and none of her friends were following.

"Look," Ben leaned a little out the driver's window, "my girlfriends going to kill me if she finds out I drove a hot girl home, so if you don't want the ride that's cool. I just wanted you to be safe." He faced forward. His hand put the truck in drive.

"Wait."

Ben was smiling inside. *Hook, line,*

"I could use the ride." She climbed into the passenger seat. *Sinker.* "And it's woman."

"What?"

"You said your girlfriend will kill you if she knew you drove a hot girl home. I prefer woman."

"Right." He put his foot on the gas.

Her name was Rachel Howe. She could barely stay awake. Ben dragged her to the back of the truck by her hair. He pushed her skirt up. There was nothing underneath – *fucking slut*. She struggled, only a little. Then Ben pulled the knife from his back pocket. He pushed it against her throat. He saw panic in those eyes. He saw terror. He came that time. He back handed her across the face, changed condoms, and did it again. This time he

139

pushed the knife so hard he saw blood. He left her outside her place. She never reported it.

Ben watched a tear run down the blond girl's cheek and fall to the hardwood flooring. It quickly disappeared in a puddle of blood. A constant moan left her. She was in pain, but not afraid.

"Things could always get worse," Ben repeated.

She turned to look at him. Her eyes stared as if trying to understand. She had to breathe with her mouth open because her nose was broken from where Ben punched her yesterday and blood outlined each tooth. He could count the cuts on her body on one hand. He knew what was coming. He knew with Sierra West what was coming. He probably knew a long time ago.

"How the fuck can this get any worse?" She watched him get onto his knees.

He started tapping the floor with the knife. His eyes were down on the spot where the blade tip hit the floor.

"Are you going to kill me?" She asked. "Then fucking do it you pathetic –"

Ben looked up. The girl's expression instantly changed. Her next words got caught in her throat. She saw something in him. It just got worse.

He lunged forward. The tip of the knife pushed the skin of her calf. It popped and the blade sunk in. She screamed. He pulled the knife out and plunged it into her thigh. She tried to kick with the other leg. He sliced her knee. He didn't feel the blade cut her. A three inch line just appeared out of nowhere and blood began to pour. She screamed. He sliced her arms. He sliced her hips. Ben jumped over her like one of those flying monkeys in *Oz*. His face went into a *Joker's* smile. Wide eyes took in all the blood. Perked ears heard her screams and the sound of knife on skin. Sierra West didn't call him pathetic. None of them did. Chloe did. He held onto her left breast with his free hand, his thumb and finger pulled at the nipple. He opened his mouth and let out a yell of satisfaction as the hunting blade cut under her breast. They both screamed together.

Ben stumbled backward and fell to the floor. Breath went in and out fast. He didn't know how much time had passed, but he was sweating. She was covered in so much blood you couldn't see every cut. She was still alive though. She moaned and wiggled on her slippery red. Ben looked up at the dormant ceiling fan. He had a rope. He wanted to tie her up there where he could finish the job. Let her live with the embarrassment. He didn't care if she was dead yet. He just wanted to slice her more.

A noise tried to roll its way out her throat. "Stop." So much blood. "I have a daughter. I have a child."

Ben crawled towards her. The plastic slicker was now red. He felt wetness inside his briefs that had surged out when he almost cut her fucking tit off.

"What's that?" He knew he was smiling. He couldn't help it.

"I," gurgle, "have," a large bubble of thick red rolled out of her mouth and down onto her throat, "a daughter."

Ben flexed his fingers around the handle of the knife. With his finger he drew three circles around her navel. Her stomach muscles twitched.

"No, you don't." His eyes moved from her flat stomach to her eyes. His grew instantly wide and focused. He never saw such fear or terror. This was a new world. Evil was there watching. He wanted to see her eyes. He wanted to see her reaction when he raised the knife over her stomach and said, "I've been watching."

Chapter 15

I sit in my car parked in the lot behind the headquarters building in Charlottetown. My eyes are closed, head back. It's been a long twenty hours since the woman was found in the park. Her identification came through very early this morning as Nicolle Teresa Pereira. She was arrested once so her prints were in the computers. I was able to get a couple hours of restless sleep in the very early hours and then a quick shower before coming back here. We had to wait at 3231 Blooming Point Road for Ident to finish out at Port-la-Joye-Fort Amherst Historical Site before they could make their way to where we were. By the time they showed the smaller command post was set up. The reporters made it there first. Marilyn made me sit in the car and wait. I wanted to look around.

A knock on the window makes me jump.

I turn to the side window to see a pair of tight black pants. As the woman leans down I see it is Catherine Arsenault. Her hair falls down to frame her face, it glistens with moisture. I get a good view of her cleavage down a baggy sweater. It is too early for this.

She holds up a microphone in front of my view and waggles it. "Sgt. Reid, I have some questions for you."

I push her back with my door. Outside the cool drizzle in the air wakes me. Catherine's camera man stands a few feet back. More reporters are coming around the building.

"Sergeant, is it true that all three murders are connected to each other?"

"You know I can't say anything. There'll be a briefing later."

"Sgt. Reid," a man with a large microphone attached to a case by a cord comes to a halting stop in front of me. He has a *Mario* mustache. "Is there a serial killer loose on the island?"

A car honks at the new intrusion in our parking lot.

"Do you have any suspects?"

I move to my left and suddenly someone is in front of me. Rain falls down my neck. I fight the urge to just push everyone down and run for the back door.

"Have you identified the new victim yet?"

"Did the three victims know each other?"

I step sideways between two of them. There are now at least a dozen people all pushing microphones in my face. Camera operators all try to manoeuvre themselves for the best angle. I recognize some insignias from national and bigger centre presses. "We are following leads. Someone will speak to you later," I tell them.

"Is the killer local?"

"Are these random killings? Should Islanders be worried?"

"Should tourists stay off the island?"

"Do you think this will hurt tourism on the island?"

How the fuck should I know? I can't say it. I have to stay calm.

A hand grabs my wrist. I look down at white tipped nails. I look up into lovely eyes. "What are you going to do when you find the killer," Catherine Arsenault asks.

"Excuse me? Who do you think you –"

Sgt. Longfellow steps between the reporter and me. His hand touches my back and pushes me toward the stairs. He says, "Sgt. English will make a statement to the press later. Let us do our jobs. Let us through, come on." Close to my ear he adds, "Don't let her egg you on. She wants a sound bite."

I look back at her and shake my head before disappearing inside.

"Morning Reid, let's get this started right away. I know you have to get to the hospital." McIntyre is waiting in Major Crimes with a cup of coffee in his hand.

"The fucking reporters were waiting for me Wayne. That Arsenault lady grabbed me. Can I charge her or something?"

"They attacked me to. Forget about it. She'll just use it against you anyway and we don't need any more bad press. The frigging Premier called. He wants progress reports on this thing."

I hang my jacket on the back of my chair, then I slowly find myself in front of the white board with all of our information. Overnight, the notes and photos tripled. "Marilyn's supervising the autopsy. They should have started by now. The doc's doing them back to back. I'm not in any rush to smell like Jane Doe."

"Still no ID?"

"Not that I know of," I look at Longfellow who shakes his head. He's pouring his own cup of coffee.

He says, "Dr. Norton said he could estimate the time of death to be between two and three months ago, approximately. There's been no missing persons report with us over the past six months matching her description. We checked with all the other police departments across the island and all say the same thing. Other provinces and cities are checking their files to see if they can find anything."

"What are the chances she's from away and the killer brought her here? Maybe he's from away?" McIntyre strokes his chin. He is way too excited.

"I don't know." This killer is a local. I would bet anything on it. I'll need some sort of proof before saying anything concrete.

"Let's start with the other victim then."

I pour myself a tea and take a long drink before starting. I take out my phone and read what the computer guys sent me. "Nicolle Teresa Pereira, age twenty. She had a record two years ago for possession with intent, that's how we could ID her. No record before or since."

"What do we have on the third victim?"

Longfellow starts, "The house she was in is owned by an American business man in Boston. He bought the house four years ago and has only been up here three times since then. He is waiting for the market to recover before trying to sell it."

"Good luck with that now."

"Unless we missed someone else, she has to be the first." I run my finger over the pictures of Jane Doe. She did have a tattoo on the back of her shoulder, three hearts stuck together by a dagger. Fitting. "This killing was brutal. I mean, he ripped her guts out. He did Jane, liked it so much that he took his time with Johanna, and then he liked the attention she got that he killed Nicolle and left the message so that he could get a name for himself. He's grandstanding."

"And we have no suspects?"

"Charlottetown Police gave us a list of people who are violent, but there has never been anything like this on the island." Longfellow can't bring himself to look at the pictures of the Jane Doe crime scene.

I pull the cap off of a dry erase marker and step up to an empty white board. "Victimology is this,"

"We're not going to work on the suspect anymore?" McIntyre says.

"We don't know anything. In BC we didn't have anything so we worked on the victims and were able to get the suspect through that." He nods and waves a hand. I continue, "He likes them in their early twenties, good-looking, athletic," I write each word in red. One on top of the other. "They all have a tattoo on the back of their shoulder. Hair colour is different, but they are all Caucasians. He likes to tie them up somehow, rape them, stab and slice them, then hang them and kill them."

"Except Nicolle Pereira."

"They are all found naked, no clothes, jewellery, or belongings found. We know from Johanna Bowers that he used different edged weapons. One probably a hunting knife, one smaller."

"But we know nothing about him?"

"We know he gets off on this. He rapes them and wears a condom. He may have raped," I hold my hand up to stop McIntyre from arguing, "before. And we know from people who live on Blooming Point Road that they remember an SUV parked on that stretch of road by the house for at least two days. Colours range from dark red to black, but they all agree on an SUV. You know why they don't find serial killers? Because they're every guy. They're the average Joe. They had Ted Bundy's first name, description, and description of his car but still nobody could place him. He was a nice guy. He'd never hurt a fly."

"This isn't Ted Bundy."

"This is a sadistic killer, who's getting out of control."

"What do you mean?" McIntyre stares at the boards along with me.

I go and sit at my desk. I say, "I think he killed Nicolle Pereira just to leave the note on her stomach so we would find his first victim. It's a game for him now."

"Reid don't start going places where we don't have any facts to go. Go to the autopsy then talk to the next of kin. We're going to have to make a statement sometime today. Get as much as you can, as fast as you can."

Before leaving I check my messages. Two from Johanna Bowers' mother asking if these girls have something to do with her daughter. She wants me to call right away. She wants some sort of closure. She wants something I can't give her.

~ * ~

"My God, it stinks in here."

"Decomp, my friend. Dead bodies smell. All those fluids and gases trying to get out all at once make a wild soup. The vaporub is on the table." Dr. Norton doesn't move his eyes from his work.

Eckhart stands on the opposite side of Jane Doe from the doctor. Marilyn stands a little behind him. The back of her gloved hand is pressed against her mouth. She looks at me with wide panicking eyes. Though most of her is in a white bunny suit I can tell her skin is green. I put a dab of vaporub under my nose. A bucket of the stuff can't mask this smell. I feel it seeping through the suit, through my clothes, and onto my skin.

"You've been missing all the fun, Gerard."

"Wrong again, Eck."

"We checked over victim number one,"

"Nicolle Teresa Pereira, got the ID this morning."

147

"Okay," The head of Ident pushes his glasses up with the corner of his camera. "We went over her already. The big difference between her, Johanna Bowers, and Jane Doe here is the ligature marks around the neck. She didn't have any. Something similar between her and Jane, but not Johanna, is a shoulder was recently popped out of joint. It looks as if they had their arms behind their backs and something violent popped them out." He shows with his own arms how the women may have been tied up.

"Did you find anything else about her, or the crime?"

"She smoked. So young to have such damage to her lungs." Dr. Norton keeps his head down. "And her neck was stretched from hanging for so long. I'm sending samples of the insects to a Forensic Entomologist at the University of New Brunswick to narrow down a better timeline."

"There is something that is significant to the Nicolle girl that none of the others have." Eckhart walks to the walk-in cooler. The gurney in there has a black body bag on top. He unzips one end. Nicolle Teresa Pereira sleeps inside the bag. "See here?" He points at the side of her head. He says, "She has a rather large contusion here to her head. Dr. Norton is pretty sure this happened first. None of the others had this. This is probably how he took her."

"That's good, this is really good." I write the notes down in my notebook. I hope to hell this takes us somewhere.

"I haven't dealt with this kind of a case before, Tony. No? We go through training and shit, but this is all new to me. I don't want to miss anything." He pushes his glasses up.

"We'll get this guy. Something on one of these bodies is going to get us there. Just do your job and we'll have him. This cooler's fucking cold, man."

Marilyn moves her hand away from her mouth long enough to ask, "What do you think?"

The thoughts are all clicking in my head. Wheels are turning. Something has to work. Something has to happen. "I don't know," I say. "I think the only reason this Nicolle girl was killed was to tell us about Jane. He wants to be known. He's going to fuck up."

"How many more is he going to kill before that happens?" This time Dr. Norton looks up from the insides of Jane Doe and stares right at me.

~ * ~

"Did you get much sleep?" Marilyn's voice echos from the bathroom in the nurse's locker room. She just finished her shower then opened the door to talk. I remember dating this girl named Sonja when I was in my late teens. We went hiking through mountain trails all day then I took her home. Her parents were out. She told me I could stay for a while and then said she was going to take a shower. I sat on the couch and patiently waited for a five minute conversation after, but I wondered then and I still wonder if her saying, "I'm going to take a shower," was an invitation instead of a statement.

"What? No, not really. Tossed and turned. You?"

"I woke up Chris and he was in the mood to fight, argue, so I didn't get any sleep. What did Hillary say?"

I lean against the wall outside the bathroom door with a bottle of *Pepsi* in my hand. I say, "Nothing. She didn't know I was home. I called her earlier and said I probably wouldn't be home."

"How could –"

"I slept on the couch. She's been a little, I don't know, suspicious or jealous lately so I didn't want to wake her and start a fight. She knows it's the job, but she still questions things."

"Should she be suspicious or jealous?" Marilyn's voice seems to bounce around the entire room.

I nod at a pair of nurses getting their cigarettes from their lockers. I turn to the door and say, "I haven't done anything." *Yet.*

"But you've thought about it."

"Just thought about it."

"And talked about it to me."

The two women leave and we are alone again. "They're only thoughts. It's not like I have a woman picked out and everything."

"Don't you?" She walks out of the bathroom to the table in the corner. Her hair is a darker red from the damp. She has changed into charcoal pants and a white sweater top. She pulls her hair up in the back and ties it off. She stuffs the sweats she wore under the bunny suit in a plastic bag.

I see the line of her thong as she bends over to pick things up. "No, nobody's picked out."

She turns to look at me. Black lace shows over the low neckline of her sweater from an undershirt. She says, "Maybe you should flash your gun and badge around here. I'm sure you'll pick up a horny nurse."

"I don't think that's what I want."

"Do you know what you want?" She puts on her brown leather jacket and ties it off at the waist. It falls enough to cover her ass, not enough to cover her legs. "How do I smell?"

"Like a woman should. Me?"

"Like a man."

"Is that a good thing?"

"It'll do." Marilyn straightens my tie. I feel a tingle.

"I don't smell like dead, do I?" She was in the autopsy room for a few hours and I was in there thirty minutes, so I didn't shower. The last thing I want to do is smell like shit and rotting guts while talking to Nicolle Pereira's parents.

"You smell fine."

We take the Bypass to Brackley Point Road and head out of town. The airport is quiet. The restaurant and gift shop only open when a *West-Jet* or *Air Canada* flight is due. There is no reason for anyone to be there in between. Not long after leaving the city, the scenery along the road becomes fields with little patches of trees and a lot of houses. Next there are cows and horses. Then comes the bed and breakfast signs and other signs offering cabins for rent or RV parking spots. Further down the road are small hotels, bigger hotels, and the Brackley Drive-In Theatre offering two pictures a night from May to September. The very end the road becomes a provincial park where people can pay to go swimming at one of the nicest beaches on the island. Everything costs a little money.

Nicolle's father owns a small house with a large garage beside it. A sign that reads *Pereira's Garage* stands beside the driveway. As we pull in a large man with a bald head looks around the side of a GMC pick-up. He is dressed in blue coveralls stained with oil and some other substances. He has scruff on his tanned face. A younger man with tattoos down one arm comes around behind him.

"Did you see the address?"

I nod at Marilyn. "Mr. Pereira? I'm Sgt. Reid with the RCMP; this is my partner Sgt. Moore. We're from Major Crimes. Can we talk to you for a minute?"

He never leaves from the cover of the garage. He waves a hand for us to come over then pulls a rag out of his pocket and turns back. The air is still damp and cold. We walk into the garage. I can smell oil and gas. Shelving units line the walls with a lot of different parts, and tools hang below them. Two large red *Snap-on* tool boxes sit along the back wall. There is a hydraulic lift off to the side. *K-Rock* plays on the radio. Mr. Pereira disappears around the front of the truck behind the propped open hood.

"Mr. Pereira, we need to talk to you about Nicolle Teresa Pereira. Is her mother here?"

"We're divorced. She lives in New Brunswick now. What did Nicolle do now?" He keeps his head in the engine. In the creases of his fingers you can see old oil sitting there. "It was her old boyfriend that screwed her up the last time. This is Wade Reader, her new boyfriend. He works here fixing cars."

"I'm sorry to tell you both this, Nicolle's body was found yesterday."

He looks up into my eyes. Sweat covers his face. Instantly his skin goes from tan to white. "Found? You mean that she's dead? That body in the park? The girl that was killed? That was Nicolle? No, no," he stumbles back until he is up against one of the shelving units. Something falls over and slams into something else. "You're wrong. She's like her mother. She's a gypsy. She just took off for a few days." He stares at us for a long while. Neither of us says anything. There is nothing for us to say. He starts to raise the can of Coke to his lips then lets it fall to his side. "Are you sure?"

The boyfriend lowers his head and begins to pace the length of the garage. His baggy camouflage shorts hang low at the waist and are down to his knees. I recognise a coy fish on his arm with blue and white waves taking up most of the sleeve. There is another tattoo on the back of his right calf and one circling all around. There are nickel sized holes in his ear lobes with black rings holding them open. His eyes are instantly moist from overloaded tear ducts.

"We ran her fingerprints and found an old charge," Marilyn says.

"Her boyfriend had her hold onto his stuff and she got caught with it. It wasn't her fault. What happened to her?"

"That's what we have to figure out. What can you tell us about Nicolle's life?

"She worked at a grocery store, she took off on these trips without telling anyone, and she liked to run. She had wanderlust; always has. When she was a kid she went for long walks in the woods without telling anyone. Her Mom left three years ago and Nicolle moved out two years ago to her own place in, ah, Charlottetown. We talked, but we didn't really see each other that often. Wade can tell you more."

We all look at the man in his early twenties and wait. He looks at us but doesn't say anything. "Well?" I ask.

"I don't know. We liked to work out together and watch movies and stuff. Are you sure it's her? She's been depressed lately. When she's depressed she hops the bus and goes away for a couple days. Maybe she just –"

"We're sure. When was the last time either of you talked to her? Mr. Pereira?"

His big hand digs in his pocket for a pack of cigarettes. He walks out into the drizzling rain without looking to see if we are following. "She came out for dinner last weekend." He lights his smoke and sucks in hard. "She came with Wade. She complained about her job, talked about the last *NASCAR* race, and she said something about wanting to do liquor tasting at the liquor stores."

I turn to Wade. "And you?"

Wade adjusts a worn baseball cap on his head. The Portuguese flag sits across the front. "Something like five days ago. We talked on the phone and she said she was going for a run. We don't really talk every day and we've been busy here. I've been calling her, but she was supposed to be working late every day so I wasn't –" He stops and wipes a hand over his face. Oil streaks over his cheek. "If I had gone to check on her maybe I could have stopped this."

"I don't think there is much you could have done." The strong looking tattooed guy holds his hands over his face and walks to the back of the garage.

When we get back in the car, Marilyn drives. We back out past the fire number, 1323, and onto Brackley Point Road heading back into town.

My phone rings as Marilyn asks, "3231 Blooming Point Road and 1323 Brackley Point Road, what are the odds?"

"Slim, very slim." I push the answer button on my phone, "Reid."

"It's Dispirito. You should come down to Victoria Park area. Charlottetown PD got a call about some blood that a little kid found on one of the bush trails. Nicolle Pereira lives five blocks east."

"We're on our way there. Call Ident. If city PD get in the way, call McIntyre down and sick him on them." I push a button. "Go to Victoria Park. We may have where Nicolle was abducted."

"He screwed up? You think we'll be able to pinpoint where the others were taken?"

My phone rings. "I don't know." I look at the number then push the button to ignore. "I want to try something later before theorizing."

"No wonder she's suspicious if you never answer. That was Hillary calling, right?"

"She's going to ask when I'll be home."

153

"So tell her you don't know. You're on a high profile case, she'll understand. Maybe she just wants to hear your voice."

I turn out the side window and watch the trees and houses go by. Farmers are preparing their fields. Within a month or so, roadside stands will pop up offering potatoes and other vegetables and fruits for sale. You are expected to be honest and leave the correct amount in a little money box. Fucking trustworthy Islanders.

I push the button on my phone for Hillary's cell. She answers on the second ring.

"You called?"

"I wanted to see how you are. You didn't say a word this morning." Hillary sounds like she is concerned.

"I didn't want to wake you."

"Did you eat something? You know how you forget when you're on a case."

My empty stomach growls in agreement.

"You lost almost ten pounds in BC," Hillary reminds me.

"In BC," is how we refer to the serial murder case on the West coast. We both know what we mean. I lie and say I ate.

"Is Marilyn with you?" she asks. Her voice is probably dull with no inflections, but what I hear is, "is *Marilyn* with you?"

"She's my partner, of course she's with me," more for the woman in the car. I might have put too much attitude there. We both go quiet.

The car goes past the *Coke* bottling plant and then the airport again. There is noise on the background of Hillary's end, but I can't make it out. Someone talking.

"Leigh go to school?"

"She wanted to know where you were. I know you are busy, but you should try coming home to see her."

"I will, I will. I have to go."

"Call me and let me know if you'll be home for supper."

~ * ~

154

Victoria Park, back in the 1800's, was known as Government House Farm on Fanning Point. Over the years it transformed into being Charlottetown's favourite place to go for a walk or have summer fun in the grass, in the pool, or on the playground. Prince Edward Island's Lieutenant Governor's residence is still on the property. Along the coastline is a boardwalk where dozens of people go walking or running every day. During the summer it is impossible to find parking here. There are, behind the kids' playground equipment, a collection of woods with trails worn down over time to the tennis courts and skateboarding park. It is not the place to be after dark however. I have heard stories of men being raped in cars. But that's the underbelly, the never discussed part of Charlottetown.

Marilyn parks the car on the main street between the boardwalk and the park. Across the strait we can see the green of Port-la-Joye Fort Amherst Historical Park. Another coincidence. We follow a city police officer across the park and into the woods.

Dispirito nods to us. We all stand outside of the yellow police tape. Eckhart is inside the tape along with someone I assume is from the Charlottetown Police. We are on the edge of a trail that opens up to a rough road where utility trucks come down as a shortcut through the back end of the park.

"There's blood," Dispirito starts, "and skid marks like someone fell. Over on this side there are some drag marks that stop on the road. Something happened here. You think maybe this was our guy?"

"Eck, I need to know if this is her blood."

"You'll know when I know, Horatio."

One of the city cops leans in to Marilyn, "Is his name really Horatio like in CSI Miami?"

"We're going to her apartment."

~ * ~

Five blocks east and we are at Nicolle Teresa Pereira's apartment. It is the basement of a three story house. Her father

155

gave us the spare key she gave him for safe keeping. Anything to help us find the killer of his little girl.

The apartment is a one bedroom place with cheap carpeting, forever pushed down at the door, with a musty smell and feel. With Charlottetown being a university and college town; a lot of houses have been changed into apartments. A hallway runs from the front door to the back wall. A living room is first off the hallway on the right, then the hallway opens to a kitchenette area with linoleum floor. A bathroom and bedroom are through two doors on the right from the kitchen. A small bookshelf in the living room has a collection of books on witchcraft, vampires, and Wiccans. Candles sit on every surface, some half gone with decorated collections of formerly melted wax around their bases. The Portuguese flag covers one wall. The top shelf of the bookshelf is an assortment of empty alcohol bottles. The kitchen is a mess. There are dirty dishes piled in both sinks. A bowl of fruit on a tiny table has three fruit flies circling above. I notice two things of interest held to the refrigerator door with colourful magnets. One is a calendar. April is still showing with hand written numbers on each date up until three days before she was found. Underneath it is a street map of Charlottetown with a line made in blue marker making a path through the city streets, including a detour through Victoria Park.

"She was healthy. She exercised. Look, she was up to ten kilometres a day. If this is her path it took her straight through the park right where the blood is."

"Her mobile phone is here on the table." Marilyn inspects the red cell phone. The front slides up to show the keys to type messages.

"What woman these days leaves their cell phone at home?"

"One who doesn't want to be bothered while she runs?" Marilyn replies.

"And thinks she'll be home shortly."

"Did you notice her windows? None of them have curtains. Anyone could have been watching her."

I can feel the excitement growing inside of me. In my head I can see this guy. I can't make any details out, but I can see this fuzzy image of the killer. He's getting closer. We're getting closer to him. I say, "He does that. He watches them. He has to know their every move. I don't think he wanted to kill Nicolle this soon. She was a message."

"To who?"

I look right in her eyes. "To us. Let's look around some more, then I have something I want us to do."

~ * ~

One hour later we stand on the street between the apartments of Johanna Bowers and Mike Valance. We walk for a while, both watching the houses on either side. You can see the blue screens of televisions in living rooms.

I stop and turn to my partner. "Scream."

"What? Are you kidding?"

"Scream and watch."

Marilyn stares at me for a long while. She gives me a little smile, sucks in some air, and lets out a loud yell. We both watch people come to their windows and look out, some on the ground floor, some from the second floors. The point is: they looked out.

"You see, I was right."

"So she didn't scream. I don't get it."

I smile and flash my eyebrows. "She didn't scream because she had no reason to scream. Johanna Bowers knew her attacker. I've been thinking about this since we found out Nicolle had a head contusion. I'll bet you Johanna went willingly."

"That's a pretty big statement, Reid."

"Somebody remembers seeing her walking and crying. Nobody saw her disappear. Why?" I wait but Marilyn doesn't respond. "Because nobody would really notice a girl getting into someone's vehicle willingly."

"And Nicolle?"

"I don't know. But he obviously was watching these girls. I bet he followed Johanna and knew that she would be an easy target. She was crying and distraught and obviously in need of someone. Then Nicolle, he picked her because of her father's address, I think."

"And Jane?"

Without a thought I say, "Same as Johanna, she knew him."

"We don't have any proof, Reid." She puts her hand on my arm and rubs up and down.

I look back at the houses. Some of the people are still looking out at us.

"Somebody knows something. Somebody saw something." I take a breath and let it out slow. "You can't fucking throw a rock in the ocean off the East Point without someone in West Point hearing about it at the corner store. I can't believe somebody doesn't know something. You can't do this without talking."

"Calm down."

I look into Marilyn's light green eyes and try to will myself to calm down. If we don't stop this guy he is going to kill again and again. It has become a game for him. The police are so pathetic that he had to tell them where the first body was. He has us by the balls. He can do anything he wants right now because we don't have a clue. I have theories but no facts. I really don't know where to go from here.

Chapter 16

3 Weeks Ago

Ben reached over the dashboard and turned down the radio. The news said nothing about him. They said nothing about the woman. They knew nothing about him or her. Something there was wrong. He wanted them to know what he had done. The world hurt him and he wanted them to know what he was capable of. Maybe he had to tell them. They had to know first, and then he had to frighten them. They had to be scared every day.

He looked down the street and saw what he was waiting for. A smile formed on his face. Maybe he needed something else to get everyone's attention.

~ * ~

It was an Indian summer. Ben felt the ocean air against his skin and with every breath he could smell and taste it deep in his throat. The beach sand spewed up from his feet. It stuck to the sweat on his chest and back. His arms pumped at his sides. He liked running because it cleared his head and gave him a chance to think about how he was winning. It was his world. He made the rules. If he wanted to run in October then it shall be warm because he says so. It was almost time to turn around and head back to where the dirt road ended on the other side of the dunes and the Tulloch Pond Provincial Wildlife Reserve began.

The sound of a girl's laughter made him look over at the dunes. Two girls stood on top of the dunes, two guys were at the bottom. The girls jumped and screamed like they had just won a king of the castle contest. The tall blond spun around. Ben's eye caught something on the back of her shoulder. She took a pose with one hand stretched out toward the sky, the other across her chest. The other girl took a body building pose and one of the boys took a picture. He wanted to see what was on her back. He had to see it.

He ran for a little while longer then circled back closer to the dunes.

"Hey, come here," One of the guys waved Ben over. Perfect. "Can you take a picture of all of us?"

"Sure. Just push the button?" The boy explained how the digital camera worked. Ben looked around at everyone. The blond girl had a black charcoal hand print over her navel and claw marks down her cheek.

"We're going to climb up to the top of the dunes, okay?"

Ben nodded and smiled. He kept his eyes moving. No need to let them catch him staring at the blond. All four of them started climbing up the dunes. He watched the blond climb. Her backside filled out a pair of cut off denim jeans. Her back muscles flexed under a white belly shirt that did little to disguise her figure. Blond hair circled around her in the wind. It was there on the back of her shoulder, a tattoo. It was a black and grey rose with a stem and two leaves. It was lovely.

He took the picture. At the same time he burned the girl's face into his memory. Later after Shannon fell asleep he would be able to recall every bit of her face and body. He'd see the tattoo and imagine his lips moving over it.

"Hey, thanks man. I'm Mike, this is Johanna,"

Johanna.

"Alex, and Ted."

Johanna. Chloe.

"I'm Ben." *Johanna.* "Great weather, eh?"

"Amazing." Johanna gives a huge smile

The whole conversation was mottled into quick words and phrases. Trained ears pulled out what he needed.

"You come here in summer?"

"Ever camp here?"

Johanna was the name.

"You live near here?"

"Charlottetown."

"I'll see you around."

He listened, he watched, he learned. Johanna and Mike were an item. Alex and Ted, not so much. Johanna and Alex were really close. Both were students at UPEI. They all lived in Charlottetown.

Ben ran back toward the only road in. There he could look through the windows of any cars parked there. People often left things out in the open. Mike Valance left a bill from Maritime Electric sitting on the dashboard. All Ben had to do was look through the window to get his name and address. As soon as he got home Ben searched the name Mike Valance on *Facebook*. His profile wasn't blocked. Anyone could look at his status – gone to the beach with my girl and friends – his job, his relationship status, look through his pictures, and go through his friends list. Johanna Bowers was number six. Her profile was limited. He could see her profile picture, her holding a guitar and looking into the camera all sleepy eyed, and had the option of requesting her be on his friends list.

He wasn't stupid. Where would that get him? Blocked out completely, labeled as a creep to be avoided at all costs. They would all give him suspicious looks and if anything happened his name would be on their lips.

Timing was everything. The moment he saw her he knew she was going to be one of his prizes.

~ * ~

Johanna jogged from her apartment and down Queen Street. As soon as she was a half block away she stopped running and pulled her jacket in around her. Ben knew where she was going.

~ * ~

161

Ben saw her as soon as he walked into the small breakfast and lunch place. He had never been in there before. He heard only bad things about the food. Johanna sat alone at the counter in front of the service area, kitchen behind that, with her back to the door. Ben sat at a table close to the entrance. He ordered toast and a coffee from the waitress and unfolded the morning newspaper.

He knew from Mike's profile on *Facebook* that he worked here. He figured he would have to follow Mike after his shift, see where he lived then go there from time to time until Johanna showed up. He didn't know she'd be right there, on his first try.

He had to remain calm. He couldn't let on that he was watching her. She had to think this was just some chance encounter. Ben walked in here for some toast and coffee. Nothing special. She didn't need to know that he was thinking about what she looked like naked or how she'd tense up as he held a knife to her throat. He wanted to feel the blade cutting her skin. She was the one. She had to be the one. The other girl would be second. He wanted this one. Johanna.

Mike appeared from the back and leaned over the counter so that his lips were close to Johanna's ears. She smiled and laughed. With a kiss the boy returned to the kitchen and the girl stood. She walked towards the door. Ben held the paper a little lower. He looked up through the top of his glasses. Her blue jeans hugged her hips. They rolled with each step.

"Hey, from the beach right?" Her hands went to her hips.

Ben smiled and let the newspaper rest on the table. "Yeah, what was your name again?" *Smooth.*

"Johanna," her head tipped to the side, "Jo." She liked him. She wanted to be casual with him. "Small island, eh?"

"Yeah, I just came in for breakfast."

"Mike works here. He's a chef." He's barely a cook.

"I didn't know. I just happened to be downtown and wanted a place to sit. What are you up to?"

She twists a little. "I have to go home and then off to school. I'll see you around, okay?" Her hand taps the table and she heads out the door. Ben turns slowly and looks after her. She turned left to go up Queen Street.

Ben slowly folded his newspaper. He left a five dollar bill on the table, pushed away from his table, and walked out the door. He could barely see Johanna's – Jo's – white jacket up the street. He got in his SUV and began the job of frog hopping after her. He drove slow and then pulled into a parking spot before passing her so that she wouldn't see him. He saw her turn up her street and stopped at the corner to see what house she went into. Ben circled the block and came down the one-way street from the other side, but parked as far away from the building she went into. He climbed into the back seat with tinted windows and waited. He had time. People rarely noticed a strange vehicle until they had the reason to notice.

~ * ~

Ben knew where she was going. She looked like she was crying. Her arms were still wrapped around her body. A hand went up and rubbed her cheek every few seconds. Ben felt a tingling inside his groin. This was going to be the night. He missed it last time and had to settle for who was supposed to be number two, but tonight he would have her. *Johanna. Chloe.*

~ * ~

"How do you feel about me, Ben? Really?" Shannon sat across the table and stared him down.

Ben shrugged his shoulders. He stared at his fingers playing with the salt shaker.

"Are you going to answer me?"

"What do you want me to say?" He was thinking of tattoos. Black and grey roses and three hearts stuck together by a dagger.

"What are we doing, Ben? We've been together for eight years. What are we doing? Are we going anywhere? I want to get married. I don't want to be common law the rest of my life." Spit shot from her mouth. He felt the venom from her eyes.

"I've been applying for jobs off island." Shannon didn't wait for him to say anything. It was pointless. Ben just played with the salt shaker and kept his eyes down. "The first one that offers me something is the one I'm going to take."

Ben turned his head away from her. "I thought you loved it on the island."

"I can't stay here like this. I need more. If I have to go somewhere else to get it, I will."

Ben twisted the salt shaker in his hand as close as he could get it before any salt fell out of the holes. *The fucking bitch.* What made her think she could just decide what she wanted to do with her own life? *Pathetic.* Those other girls didn't get to run their own lives.

Shannon pushed away from the table and stood. Her hand hit the table top. She said, "Do you love me? We barely make love any more. You don't show me any passion. You barely kiss me." *Pathetic. You're pathetic. Pathetic.*

Ben got to his feet. His chair teetered on its hind legs. His hands locked around Shannon's upper arms. She made a noise. He pushed her back against the refrigerator. His mouth went over hers. He tasted coffee. He felt something rise. He wanted to hurt her. Ben moved his mouth to her neck. He bit flesh. His hands pushed and squeezed her breasts. *Pathetic.* He pushed her legs apart with his knee. He was going to fuck her. He was going to make her scream.

"Stop. Ben, stop." Shannon pushed him back until he hit the table.

Ben stared at her. He didn't know who she was. He wanted one of the others. She was Shannon. He stayed at her place often, and slipped out in the night. Her parents lived out by Blooming Point Beach. People knew them together.

Shannon stared at him with her eyes and mouth wide. "What are you doing?"

Ben stumbled back away from her and out the door. His eyes couldn't focus. He didn't know if he was breathing. He got in his SUV and started the engine. He had to find something. In front of his eyes he pictured Shannon covered in blood. He saw cuts and slices over her body. Then she was Chloe walking down the street, a strap crossed over the tattoo on her back. He pictured her in the back of the SUV, hands and feet taped to the corners. He felt himself fucking her. He felt his hunting knife slice through the skin around her breast.

Ben blinked fast as Sierra West screamed.

~ * ~

"You bastard. No, leave me alone. Leave me alone." Johanna ran away from Mike's place. The cook stood there and watched for nearly a minute. As he turned back to the inside of his place he brought his cell phone up.

~ * ~

"I don't get you Ben, I really don't. You've barely spoken to me for three months. I can't deal with this anymore."

It didn't matter what Ben was staring at, in his mind all he saw was making girls pay. He missed that look Sierra West gave him as he sliced her chest. Pure terror. She thought she was going to die. She wasn't the one though. He needed more than that. Johanna was going to be the one.

"Are you even listening to me?"

Ben looked at Shannon. He wanted to say no and see her eyes change. He wanted to kill her.

Shannon said, "I'm not doing this anymore. This is pathetic."

Ben reached down and flipped the oval coffee table into the air. Magazines and old mail danced for a moment in the air then rained down to the carpet floor. "You don't call me that." Ben pointed at her and screamed. There was fear in those eyes.

"We, we're done Ben. I'm leaving the island."

~ * ~

165

Ben sat in his SUV down the street from Johanna's. He couldn't have Shannon. He didn't have Chloe. He wanted to see terror. He wanted to be satisfied.

Johanna, Alex, Mike, and three others walked out of the apartment and headed down the street. They were all dressed up. Johanna wore a short black skirt. Mike held her hand.

Ben wanted this. He had to do something – he had to feed this hunger. He wanted to taste her, feel her breath quicken. He wanted to feel her body tense and hear her moan and scream and try to get away. Only he couldn't. He had to. There was always the other one. She would have to do. He had the place picked out. Johanna could be number two. And he already had number three picked out. His hunger would be fed.

~ * ~

"Jo? It's Jo, right?" Ben called out through the open passenger window. Johanna looked over at him. Nothing in her face showed recognition. "I'm Ben, we met at Blooming Point."

She nodded and tried a smile. Her eyes and cheeks were red from crying. She had her arms around her, hands hid in her sleeves. She waved one hand and started back walking.

"Are you okay? Have you been crying?"

She stopped and turned. She said, "I wouldn't be the best company."

"Let me buy you a coffee, and you can tell me your problems. I may not know the answers, but I'm a good listener." He smiled. "Come on, pretty girls shouldn't walk around crying."

She looked up the street one way and then back. She didn't have any direction to go. She smiled a little and climbed into the SUV.

Chapter 17

My foot scrapes sand across the sidewalk that someone named Jennifer carved her name into when it was freshly poured. Everything on the island seems to be covered in this fine beach sand silt.

"So, what do we want to do?" Marilyn tightens the belt around her. She rides her hand back over her hair and shakes it out.

I don't know what to do. This thing is eating at me like grains of the beach sand stuck in the toe of your shoes. It grinds at your toes until you are so frustrated you'll stop anywhere to bang the dirt out. I have to bang the dirt out.

"What we need is Jane Doe's real name," I say.

"Well we don't have it, so what do you want to do?" She checks her phone.

I stare down the street in the direction of Johanna Bowers' home. The place where she felt safe. She should have been safe. She walked down here to go to her boyfriends, to go home, to go where? What did she do? If the killer knew her, how did he know her?

"We have to get into these girl's lives. We need to know their schedules. Where were they morning 'til night? Where did they go? What did they do? What restaurants did they go to? What stores did they frequent? Did they go to gyms, parks, bingos, *what*? All three of them have *something* in common."

"Tattoos. They all have tattoos on their backs. Maybe they all got them at the same place."

"Call Dispirito. Have him and LeBlanc visit every tattoo place in the city, on the island if need be. Tell them to show the ladies pictures and the pictures of their tattoos." I am getting excited. Things are clicking in my brain. We're hound dogs on the hunt. "You and I are going to Johanna's place again. After we're done with her life we'll dive into Nicolle's. I want to know these women better than I know myself."

After just a couple of weeks, the outside to Johanna Bowers's apartment looks dark and flat. Or it could be the way I am feeling. The world is grey and flat. This guy is getting to me.

Mike Valance answers our knock on the door. He lets out a blast of air. He takes a quick look over his shoulder and says, "What is it now?" We pulled Mike into the headquarters for questioning last night to see if he knew anything about Nicolle Teresa Pereira or Jane Doe. He almost threw up at the pictures of the mystery woman.

"We came here to talk to Alex," Marilyn says. "Is she in?"

He looks back over his shoulder again. "She's not in the mood for visitors."

"She better get in the mood," I state plainly.

"Look, she's scared. She thinks this guy might come after her now and no offence, but you guys don't know shit." He looks quickly at Marilyn and then stares at me.

"We need to talk to both of you to understand who Jo was. We think she may have known the man who is doing this or she met him somewhere. If we can go over her daily schedule then we can narrow down where she may have met him," Marilyn says

"Will he come after me?" Alex stands at the entryway to the rest of the apartment. She looks pale. Her hands are hidden inside the sleeves of a sweater. Her hair lays flat.

"Can we talk to you about who Johanna was?" I speak up. I can't tell her if this guy is going to come after her. The truth is I have no idea. She nods and we enter the apartment again. Dirty dishes are piled in both sinks and spill out onto the counter. There is a pile of envelopes on the table addressed to Johanna Bowers. Alex sits in the same chair she sat in the day we came to give her the news. Mike stands behind her, arms crossed in front of him. "Do either of you know where she got the tattoo on her shoulder?"

"Calgary, I think."

"I thought she said West Edmonton Mall. It was somewhere out there before she came to the island." There goes that connection.

Marilyn sits at the table. She makes a little space amongst the mess to put her notebook down. I pace the kitchen. Out the window is the small back yard with a fence blocking off the neighbors. The killer could probably have stood behind the fence and looked through, but his back was open to the people on the other side. A dozen windows looked in the apartment's direction. Any one of them could have someone looking our way.

"What was her day like?"

Alex rubs her arm with the heel of her hand. "She'd get up early and get ready. Then she would wake me up and walk to the restaurant to see Mike and have breakfast. I like to sleep in a little. She walked back here after breakfast and we went to classes. After classes we would come back here."

"Maybe she would come to my place if I wasn't at the other restaurant. Jo's life was school and me. Mostly school."

"When did she have time for this?" I tap my finger tip on the photograph attached to the fridge door, the one of Johanna, Mike, Alex, and her date.

"When the work was done she made sure to go out and have an adventure," Alex says.

I stand with my back to everyone and stare at the photograph. "So she didn't go any place? She didn't frequent any stores or do anything?"

"I don't know." She pulls at her shirt. Mike keeps his eyes on her. "She liked the Farmers Market on Saturday. She went to the Dollar Store a lot. We get our groceries at the Co-op. What do you want?"

"Did she belong to a gym or go swimming?" Marilyn asks.

"The university gym, but she barely ever went. She swam in the Cari pool a few times, the ocean in the summer."

"Did she wear tank tops a lot? Or shoulder straps?"

"Why? What does that have to do with anything?"

"We're trying to narrow down why he's going after these girls. We have to look at every angle."

"You think she dressed sleazy? You think she asked for this?" Mike states defensively and puffs his chest up.

"No, of course not, Mr. Valance." Marilyn changes the tone of her voice to stop him before he goes somewhere. "Just like us bringing you in, we have to check things out."

"This picture," I put my nose up close to the photograph on the fridge door.

Johanna had the charcoal marks on her like the one we borrowed the first time we were here. I stare at it for ten minutes every morning trying to imagine what she went through the week she was missing. Alex had her marks. Mike had black hand prints all over his bare chest and abdomen. The extra man had streak marks over his face and chest. A large arrow pointed down into his shorts. I imagine he probably drew it on his own stomach.

Mike says, "It was at Blooming Point last," and Alex stops him and tells him we have the photograph of the two girls.

I move the rock magnet, the word FRIENDS carved into it, and take the picture in my hand. "Who ah," I start.

The house phone rings. Everyone, even Marilyn, jumps. Alex picks it up. She muffles a hello. I gather it is her parents worried about her, but the only end of the conversation I hear are barely coherent mumbles and sounds. This girl is losing herself the way Hillary is afraid I will lose my own self.

"Everything alright?"

She nods her head. Her bangs fall down in front of her face. She doesn't waste time placing them back. "Mom thinks I should come home. She's worried."

Marilyn catches my eyes with hers. She nods her head to the door, international sign that we are wasting time here. "We should get going. I think we have enough."

I return the photograph to the refrigerator door and place the rock *friends* magnet on its corner. At the door I turn back to Mike

170

and Alex. "That picture, who –" I point at the photograph and everyone fallows my finger, "who's the second guy?"

Alex moves a little closer to Mike. I wonder if they are officially boyfriend and girlfriend now. "Ted Mosby. He was a friend of Mike's."

"He moved to Fort McMurray a month later to work as a cook."

"Thanks."

There is always a fear after you are done asking someone questions. Did we ask the right ones? Did we miss something that would have opened it all up? I tell the others to let it go. They have to forget about what may have been asked or seen and work with what they know, what they have. Not me. I'm *Sgt. Cool*. I deal with what is on my notebook pages and solve the case. Bullshit. Inside I work over everything until I have seen everything I can and until I have a list as long as my arm of questions I should have asked. I'm doing that now.

I call McIntyre and get him to kick whosever ass he has to kick to get us Nicolle's phone and bank records. I'm afraid we've missed something somewhere. There has to be some connection among the three women.

If half a dozen officers showed up at the RCMP HQ gym there wouldn't be enough equipment. We have a stationary bike, treadmill, weight machine, and then some free weights and mats to stretch on. It has enough to keep us in shape. The Fitness Centre at UPEI has this times ten. We walk in the large, well lit room and stand at the front desk waiting. There are bicycles, treadmills, cross-trainers, stair climbers, and rowing machines. On one side is a collection of free weights and different equipment like medicine balls, stability balls, and different things that I wouldn't know how to use.

Marilyn flashes her credentials at the guy behind the desk and asks for the manager. He stutters for a few seconds before marching across the room in search of the manager.

I walk slowly through the equipment. I look, listen, and smell.

The room stinks of sweat, plastic, and metal. Metal clinks against metal. Skin tears off of plastic seats, bound by sweat, and people let out cries of pain and moans of some sort of exercise high. Television screens flash silently as captions scroll across the picture. Most people are dressed in tees and shorts, some in more, some in less.

A guy walks in front of me and gives me a nod. A yin yang symbol with a bonsai tree growing from the top is permanently drawn into the skin of one muscled arm. Around the room are more tattoos on calf muscles, ankles, and arms.

A blond woman marching on a stair climbing machine is dressed in tight shorts and an orange tank top. She has something on the back of one shoulder. As I get closer I see it is *Winnie the Pooh* hugging a honey pot. A second woman, on a treadmill this time, has something all the way across her shoulders. All over the room are people, women with tattoos. All he had to do was walk in the room and he could scope out what he wanted.

"According to their records Johanna hasn't been here since September. No record of Nicolle Pereira. Reid, you hear me?"

"Look over here." I pull Marilyn in close, my body over laps hers. I feel her buttock flex against my thigh. My chin barely touches her shoulder. I point across the room to the *Winnie the Pooh* woman. "There," over to the one with – I think they are wings across her shoulders, "there." Another woman turns around. "And there." Something is tattooed on the back of her shoulder. "He had an open menu right here in front of him. All he had to do was pick which tattooed one he wanted."

"You think this is how he found Johanna?"

It is pretty wild. What are the chances? I say, "I don't know. It's possible." I'm second guessing myself. "Let's check out the gyms near Nicolle's place and see if we can get lucky." We head out to the car.

I can picture this guy, this killer, sitting on a stationary bike looking for his prey. Everybody gawks at women in health clubs, so he wouldn't be out of the ordinary. He could pedal away at the back of the room waiting to find a tattoo. The guy in BC who killed those kids – who I killed – liked walking his dog in the park. He hid behind aviator glasses. Behind dark lenses he searched out the little girl who's mom let her go just a little too far, away from her watchful gaze. There was always a mom who didn't pay attention. She was usually too involved in her conversation. Parks were safe. *Sure Honey, go see the doggy.* So anyway, like I was saying – ripe for the taking. The PEI Killer, as one paper is calling him, has his own shooting gallery. He finds them, he finds some way to approach them, he sets them at ease, and then he puts them through the worst experience of their lives until they are dead, dead, dead.

I want to kill him.

"Reid,"

"What?" I snap.

"Your phone." Only now do I hear it ringing.

Before I can say anything, McIntyre is screaming back at me through the lines, "It's about time. I got the I.T. guys to email you Pereira's records."

"Anything on Fitness Centers?" I ask.

"Oh Jesus," there is a short pause as he scans the lists in front of him, I assume. "Atlantic on Kent."

I whisper the name of the club to Marilyn as we climb into the car. "We're going there now. Gyms give him the opportunity to see tattoos."

"The other guys haven't come up with anything. They found one tattoo place that recognized Pereira, but nothing on the other two."

"Okay. Get them to go over her calls and charges for like, five days prior. Maybe something will jump," I say.

"This doesn't look good, Reid. The CO got a call from the Premier's office. They want an update as soon as we have something. What do we have?"

Nothing.

"What do I tell them?"

Tell the Commanding Officer to tell them to fuck off and let us do our job.

I put my hand on my forehead. I can feel my brain pulsing through my skull. "Tell them we're working on it. We're building a case. I don't know, Wayne, baffle them with bullshit."

"You let me know when you know something." As McIntyre hangs up the phone I catch him calling me a son-of-a-bitch.

The phone rings again and I answer.

"It's Eckhart. I put a rush on some blood samples. I think we found Johanna Bowers blood at the the Blooming Point site. In the first outer building."

"So she was there?"

"I won't have the DNA check back for a week, but it is her blood type. I'm guessing that was where some of her torture took place. There are still a lot more samples to check out, but I thought you'd want to know."

I hang up the phone and look at Marilyn. "Supposedly Ted Bundy had sex with his victims days and weeks after he killed them. He would go back to where he left their rotting corpses and do his thing or even just lay with them."

"Okay and you're telling me this why?" She slams her door and leads the way across the street. I have no real interest right now to watch her wiggle.

"Eckhart thinks this guy had Johanna Bowers at the Jane Doe site. I'll bet he got off on her reaction. I don't know why he changed with Nicolle, but she was lucky to not go through what Johanna did."

We enter Atlantic Fitness and Marilyn asks for the manager while I look around. In the first seconds I see a woman with a tattoo on the back of her shoulder. Her ponytail brushes over it like a horse tail as she jogs on a treadmill at an incline. I weave myself through the maze of equipment and bodies. The work day is over with so everyone is coming for a stress relieving workout before going home and dealing with more stress.

"Nicolle was a member here. Manager's records say she was here four days a week. The last time was two days before."

"She was here. He was here." I bring Nicolle's picture up on my phone and start asking everyone if they saw her. The pony girl shakes her head.

A guy with glasses says, "No, I've never seen her."

"She looks familiar."

"Did she make a complaint about guys staring? There are always guys staring. I'm married."

"I haven't noticed anyone watching me," the other girl with the tattoo on the back of her shoulder.

"He was here, Marilyn. He watched Nicolle here," I say.

"Johanna's not a member and none of the workers recognize Jane Doe. What's the connection?" Marilyn replies

"I don't know." I turn back to the room from the entry way.

The blond with the ponytail continues to jog, the guy at the free weights stares at his biceps as he curls, the guy in glasses pedals on a stationary bike while watching the news, two women practice yoga on the mats, people are running, walking, exercising and minding their own business. They are safe. "He was here," I say

~ * ~

I drop my keys by the door. Frix comes up demanding a scratch behind her ears. As soon as she gets it she turns and trots away shaking her little nubby of a tail.

Marilyn took me back to headquarters to get my car. We think sleep will be a good thing. First thing tomorrow we will comb through the Atlantic Fitness membership lists, assuming we can get them. Either way sleep will do us good.

"Daddy." Leigh runs down the stairs and wraps her arms around me. This is one of those grand moments in a father's life when you think: *this is why we had children*. It's like those nights when you wake as your little angel is crawling into bed because she had a bad dream and the only thing that can keep her safe is Daddy or when they say they love you for no reason. She leads the way to the living room and curls up on the couch. Her long brown hair is in a mess of waves; she hates brushing it. Her fingernails show the final remnants of a nail polishing experiment at her friend Sarah's – one different color for each nail. She smiles with two big front teeth.

175

"How was your day?" I ask. I sit beside her and stretch my legs out in front. Frix digs her way underneath.

"Good. How was yours?"

I don't know how to answer this so I shrug my shoulders.

"Did you catch the bad guy?"

Hillary walks into the room, hands damp with dishwater. She wears short white shorts and a thin white shirt that I can see through. Her subtle tan and short black hair makes the white stick out. The moment she gets home she likes to change into something she will be comfortable in. Suddenly, I feel like all eyes are on me. Is *daddy* going to be home for a while? "Not yet Honey."

Hillary goes back into the kitchen, her bare feet pad on the floor.

"What are we watching?" I ask.

"The Big Bang Theory," Leigh replies.

"What's this?" I push Leigh's sleeve up to her elbow. A crude picture of a snake is drawn on her forearm in red and black marker. It is coiled by the elbow with its split tongue sticking out near the wrist. "What is this?"

"What? I was bored."

"You were bored? You were bored so you drew a tattoo on your arm?"

"Yeah, so," Leigh pushes away from me and sits in the corner of the couch. She pulls her sleeves down, puts her chin in her hand, and stares at the television.

"That's a stupid thing to do," I tell her.

"Why?" She doesn't look at me.

"Because you, you," I don't have a fucking clue. How about because a fucked up killer is torturing and killing girls with tattoos on their back? *Which has nothing to do with a forearm.* I try and think up things my mother would have yelled at me. "You could poison yourself and people will think we don't know how to teach you to wash. Go wash it off."

"No," defiant. Her lips pout and her eyes stare straight ahead.

"Go wash it off."

176

She crosses her arms in front of her and mumbles, "I don't want to wash it off."

My teeth clench tight. "Go wash it off." I sit square facing her. I can feel anger burning inside of me. There are things you can't yell at a nine year old, no matter how much they are acting like a defiant stubborn teenager. The noises in the kitchen stop.

"No."

"I'm not asking you Leigh, I'm telling you. Go wash it off." I'm almost at a full yell.

"It's my body and I can do what I want with it," Leigh says.

"Excuse me?" I get to my feet. My ears are burning. I'm beyond thinking about what I should or shouldn't be saying. "Your body may be yours, but your mother and I own the rest of you. I told you to go wash it off. Now go." Spit flies from my lips.

"You don't have to spit." Leigh glares at me.

My arm flies out with a solid finger pointing the way. "Go." My teeth grind together. My breath goes hard through my nostrils. Leigh pauses for just a moment and then runs from the room. Her elephant feet stomp the floor. A door slams. I'm pretty sure it is her bedroom and not the bathroom. This infuriates me. The one and only time I ever slammed my bedroom door when I was a kid resulted in my Dad smacking my ass so hard I had to sleep on my side. Then he popped the hinges and I didn't have a door for a few months. No kid of mine is going to slam a door in my house. No fucking way.

"Reid," Hillary stands by the kitchen door. "Calm down."

Unbelievable. "She's got a piss poor attitude. She slammed her door."

"And she's not one of your criminals you can bully around. It was just a drawing on her arm."

"Hillary," my hands are in tight fists at my sides, "it's more than just a drawing. The killer's targeting girls with tattoos. I told her to do something and she flat out defied me. When I was her age I was scared of my parents. I did what they told me."

"When you were her age kids didn't know about rights and protecting themselves." She crosses over to me and puts her hands lightly on my forearms. "Now parents are afraid of their kids. The Wendle's across the road, they had child services come by because their son told the school his dad was hitting him. He later admitted he didn't want to mow the lawn like his dad told him to. It's a different time, Reid."

"Is it better or worse?" I can feel my whole body calming down. I don't want to argue any more. My teeth hurt from grinding together. Once again Hillary has shown me that she knows me better than I know myself.

"Depends on what side you're sitting on. Why don't you sit and I'll get you something to eat. We can watch some TV and relax." She looks at me with her brown eyes and waits for me to nod before going on.

The best times my wife and I have ever had have been just sitting and watching television. Hillary has a glass of wine. I have a small glass of the moonshine made on the island. We watch a couple of comedies. She does have a great laugh which gets more full bodied the more wine she sips. There are snorts involved and her head flies back. Her short hair bounces around and finds its way back.

Leigh kisses us each goodnight. Her pajamas have long sleeves pulled down over the heels of her palms. I fight the urge to get her to pull them up. She quickly returns upstairs to go to bed.

Hillary picks a medical drama for us to watch. We sit close, she in the corner of the couch, me on the middle cushion. She puts legs over my lap and rolls her feet around. My hand sits on her inner thigh and rubs the smooth skin. She doesn't make a sound, but moves so that my hand slides a little more inside. Eventually she pulls it in deeper. It feels nice, it feels comfortable. By mid show my fingers slip inside her shorts. A moan escapes her throat. Hillary closes her eyes and leans her head into the crook of my shoulder and neck. I can smell cookies and vanilla in her hair. It makes me hungry, but not for food. My index finger caresses her smooth waxed area until it becomes moist. Two things that won me over when we were just dating were that she, back then, shaved down there and she never wore underwear. Her tongue licks my neck below my ear.

"Mmmmm." Hillary tightens her lips on the skin of my neck. She says, "Maybe we should take this to the bedroom."

"Why?"

"What if Leigh comes down?"

"She won't come down."

She tries pushing my hand down and away. I put on more pressure to keep it there and lean over to kiss her chest. My teeth grab a nipple through her shirt and give a little tug. It goes instantly hard. She sucks in a quick breath. Her whole body wiggles. She cups my face with both hands and pulls my mouth to hers. Our tongues caress each other. She locks her lips around my bottom one and pulls. "Someone might see us through the window," Hillary whispers between kisses.

"This from the girl who used to get a thrill from the idea of getting caught."

"Now I'm responsible." My finger slides inside her and my mouth attacks her breast. "Oh, God." Her body gives in to me. She doesn't try to stop me from pushing her shirt up over her chest. My mouth takes in her breast. I want to have all of her. Her hand goes under my shirt, fingernails scratch my stomach, and every bit of abdominal muscle tightens to the point of hurting. She is a beautiful, sexy woman. She moves it down and strokes the monster inside my pants. I know it wants to burst out, but it's been a while and I have to make sure she is happy. I push her hand away from my stomach and trail my lips down over her taught abs. She has a small mound left over from childbirth, but I like it. I barely touch her skin like a silk teddy. I don't know how there is any way I could not want her. She lifts her hips so I can pull her shorts down and off. My hands start at her ankles and rub the muscles of her strong legs. Her back arches as my tongue touches her moist womanhood. Her thighs push on both sides of my face. She lets out a scream. Her hand grabs at my hair and pushes me in deeper.

My cell phone rings and starts to vibrate across the coffee table.

I sit up and wipe the wet from my chin. Hillary lets out another moan. Her whole body twitches. She's lost her breath. I take up the phone. "Reid."

"Get your ass to HQ. The killer called the tip line. He gave us Jane Doe's name." McIntyre hangs up his end.

I push Hillary's leg off of me. "I have to get to work. We might have a break," I say.

"Are you serious?" Hillary lies on the couch with her shirt still up under her chin and nothing else on. I am suddenly not in any mood for sex. I'm still hard, I just don't want to. I can't.

"He called the tip line."

"And it can't wait?"

I put my phone in my pocket. "Hill, there are lives –"

"Just fucking go." Hillary picks up her shorts, stands and lets her shirt fall down over her breasts. I watch the curve and bounce of her ass as she walks away. From the stairs she says, "Say hi to Marilyn," over her shoulder.

Chapter 18

5 days ago.

"It has been nearly two weeks since the tortured and brutally murdered body of Johanna Bowers was found hanging from a tree in the Blooming Point area and police are no closer to finding who is responsible. Sgt. English, Media Relations Liaison for the Charlottetown RCMP, states that investigators are following several leads. Lead investigator, Sgt. Reid of the Major Crimes Unit, refused any comment.

"Sgt. Reid transferred to Prince Edward Island RCMP from British Colombia two years ago where he was involved with a series of murders where the victims were four little girls between the ages of eleven and twelve. Reid came into notoriety with the shooting and subsequent killing of their one and only suspect in the case. The murders did stop, but there is still a question as to whether this Mounty got his man. This is Catherine Arsenault, Charlottetown."

When he finds the killer of Johanna Bowers will he shoot first? Of course, in order for that question to be answered Sgt. Reid will first have to find suspects

Ben stared at the television set. There was little around his apartment. It was decorated to look normal. Couch and lounge chair, a tall lamp, coffee table with a scattering of popular magazines, small entertainment center with television and three disc changer stereo, a stand-up CD and DVD holder – most of which he had not listened to or watched. On the walls of his living room were photographs of wildlife and scenic views he had taken and framed. Three large ones crossed one wall in a line showing parts of the sun setting into the ocean. There are no pictures of family or friends, except six of Shannon strategically placed around the apartment so that he sees one everywhere he goes. By the front door his shoes are neatly placed together along the wall lined up perfectly. There is a glass bowl on a tiny stand holding his SUV keys. His world is tidy and organized. There is very little which is left out of place.

Reid.

In the corner is a bookshelf with an array of novels and books ranging on a wide selection of topics. Most he had not read. In his world everything was in order.

Reid.

The police were nowhere near finding him. His world was safe. He could continue doing what he was doing for a long time. He was smarter than them. They hadn't even found the other body yet.

The news was onto talking about a house fire in Crapaud.

Ben liked games. It was too soon, but he could make life interesting. Maybe Sergeant Reid wanted to play. He could leave him a note. If Reid wanted to join Ben's world he had to learn who was in charge and who controlled the game.

He checked his watch. Nicolle would be going for a jog soon. He only introduced himself at the gym. Ben bumped into her once, said he was sorry and went back to his workout. He watched her from a distance and two more times found a way to graze against her or bump his behind into hers.

"I guess if we keep bumping into each other I should at least introduce myself. I'm Ben."

"Nicolle, I'm sorry."

"No, it was my fault." He smiled and they both went back to their machines.

Ben wasn't sure if she was going to be one of his special girls, but this Reid pushed up his schedule. *Reid.* He had to take her. He had everything he needed in his SUV. He knew where she jogged. He had to be quick. Strike fast, strike hard, and get her out of there. Ben pretended to be tying his shoe with a baseball cap pulled down. He looked over his shoulder and watched her black and brown hair toss around and her breasts heave and bounce with each step.

He rose and swung.

She dropped and slid across the ground with a thud scattering dead leaves. He knew where he'd leave his message. Reid would get it. He'd figure it out. Catherine Arsenault was going to tell everyone what he did.

The first step was to leave a note. The second was to change the game.

~ * ~

May 2nd

Ben got out of his SUV and followed the others toward the back of the building. He held his Pentax camera up in front of his face. Some of the others had video cameras, some carried microphones attached to packs on their belts. Catherine Arsenault leaned down to the driver's window of a black Pontiac. A few paces behind her stood a man with a video camera. As the others got to the car everyone started throwing out questions.

Reid. He was there. His shaved head, his blue eyes, his strong shoulders. All of him was there in front of Ben. He snapped a picture.

Ben shouted out, "Do you have any suspects?" He kept the camera on one eye to hide his face. "Have you identified the new victim yet?"

He bit his lip. He didn't want to smile. He couldn't smile. He couldn't show him who he was. Reid pushed between Ben and a real reporter. Ben noticed he smelled of *Old Spice*. He was going to go home and print out the pictures and study them. Reid was one of his special girls now. He came into Ben's world and he had to play the game.

"Ms. Arsenault, can I ask you a question?" Ben walked one step behind the reporter. She turned to look at him. Her brown hair danced against her shoulders. He got lost in her lovely eyes. Does she have a tattoo? "I'm from Halifax and this is the biggest story I've been on. I just want to know if you know where Sgt. Reid lives so I can get some background."

She stopped walking and looked Ben over. She said, "I probably shouldn't tell you but his wife's name is Hillary. That's all I'll say."

Ben nodded and watched her walk away. That was all he needed to know.

~ * ~

Later on May 2nd

Ben looked down from the television in the corner of the gym. His legs slowed a little on the stationary bike. *Reid.* He was there. What was he doing there? He slowly made his way through the machines and people. He showed everyone a photograph. Another officer stood by the front counter talking to the workers. She was interesting.

He was too close. Ben studied how to not get caught. He didn't make a move without making sure he didn't leave any evidence. How the hell were the police here? How did they find him?

"Have you ever seen this girl in here?" *Reid.*

Ben pushed his glasses back up his nose. Nicolle stared back at him from the square photograph. Ben instinctively said, "No, I've never seen her," and continued with his pedaling.

Reid walked around some more. At the front counter he turned back to the room and swept everywhere with his eyes. Ben was sure he saw him. He didn't say anything because he wanted to play the game. He was going to play all right. This was Ben's world. Ben controlled what happened. He tortured Johanna Bowers and licked his lips every time she begged him to stop. *Reid.* Ben was going to make his life change. Reid was too close. He had to think about other things in his life instead of who Ben was. He was going to be tortured.

Chapter 19

I walk the halls of headquarters and enter the Major Crimes offices. At this time of night there is nobody in the building except up in Telecoms where the 911 calls come in for half the island. HQ is eerie at night. Some offices have motion sensor lights so that when someone walks past the door the light turns on. But still there are no people moving from office to office and there are no noises except creeks and clicks and computer cooling fans turning on with nobody around.

I enter major crimes and am met by the bitter smell of coffee. Dispirito puts a brown take-out cup in my hand, and LeBlanc lingers over a box of doughnuts.

"I figured we're going to be up all night," Dispirito says.

"I'll put some money in the coffee jar. Marilyn's not here?" I check my watch. It's nearly midnight.

"Not yet. Gordon's in the can," Dispirito explains

"Everybody here?" At the same moment McIntyre enters the main room from his office and Longfellow comes in from the hallway.

"Marilyn's not." I keep my eyes on the door.

"She didn't answer her phone," McIntyre grumbles. "You'll have to fill her in. This fucker's getting bold. He's challenging us to catch him. He gave us Jane Doe's name as Casey Marsh and then laughed at us."

"Are we sure it's the real deal?"

"Here, listen." McIntyre clicks something on the nearest computer. In a few seconds a voice starts coming out. The first thing I notice is how calm and monotone it is. He's just some guy talking.

"I think you are looking for me."

"Sir, you do understand that this is a tip line for the recent murders? Do you have something that will help the police?" The tip line operator on the recording says.

"You don't understand I'm the one. I'm the one who killed the woman on Blooming Point Road and Johanna Bowers and Nicolle Pereira. Do you understand?"

The operator stutters with his next sentence. "Ah, yes, sir. Could I get your name?"

There is a little laughter across the line. He says, "Are you serious? Look, I left Johanna Bowers hanging from a birch tree." His tone never changes as he talks about what he has done. Listening to him I can tell he is smiling as he talks. "Her tattoo was a lovely rose. Nicolle Teresa Pereira, I love how the news gives her full name, was a message to the police. It was pathetic that they didn't find the first one. But believe me she would have been there sooner or later. Nicolle's tattoo was educational, I liked it. I noticed there was nothing in the news about the tattoos so I suppose that is your," he pauses as if looking for the right words, "hold back info? If you want to walk in my world, you better pick it up. Are you recording this?"

"Excuse me?" The operator questioned.

The killer raises his voice, "Are you recording this? I'm going to tell you something important for you to tell Sergeant Reid. Are you recording this?"

"Ah, yes," one of the operator's goals is to not let the caller know that every phone call is recorded, "yes sir you are being recorded."

The man on the other end of the line, I would guess his age to be mid-twenties by his voice, says, "The first woman's name was Casey Marsh. The tattoo on her back is three hearts on a dagger. It represents her parents and sister who died in a car accident. Reid would never figure it out so I have to tell you. *Pathetic.* You tell him to come and get me." He stops talking but we can hear his breath coming over the recording. He is excited. He's enjoying this. "I'll be in touch." The recording stops. Neither of us says anything. What are we supposed to say? I've never dealt with anything like this. In BC we were able to use evidence left at the scenes and body dumps and video from where the guy took the girls. We have nothing. The killer is feeding us our evidence.

"Holy Fuck." Dispirito.

I stare at McIntyre. He has to be thinking the same thing I am. He used my name twice. This could get personal, and that is not a good thing.

"Your name has been in the news. You're the one people know when they hear about this case. It means nothing," LeBlanc says.

"It's past midnight now," McIntyre starts. He strokes the end of his goatee. "Dispirito, LeBlanc find out everything you can on Casey Marsh. She's the first so she's going to have something connecting to him. She's our best chance of finding this ass. Special-I is already trying to get where the call came from. Reid, listen to this ass until you have the whole thing memorized. He has to be telling us something about himself. We'll have a triangle meeting at six. I want this guy caught today."

The other two start work on their computers going through every database we have trying to find out who this Casey Marsh was. I sit at my desk and listen to the killer three more times. By the third, it is me he is talking to. He sounds average and normal. There aren't any rough throat noises like the killers in the movies. He sounds more like the kid behind the counter at Burger King. He calls it his world, superiority complex. He laughs and sounds excited, so he enjoys this whole thing. Knowledge of the victim's tattoos could be from prior to him taking them or could be information he got out of the women while he had them. He uses the word pathetic twice and the way he says it, emphasizing all of the sounds, he likes the word. "Come and get me," indicates he thinks this a game or sport. "Hold back info," knowledge of police procedures. "She would have been there sooner or later," means he was watching her. It was not a random killing just a *sooner than he wanted to* killing. "I'll be in touch," could mean that he is going to call again or that he is going to kill again.

187

I push the sweat from my forehead back into my hair. The only real thought in my head is that this guy used my name twice. To me that says he feels a connection towards me. Or like LeBlanc said, he just knows my name from the news and is using it because that is all he has. I sit back in my chair and look around the room. Marilyn should be here dealing with this crap and telling me I'm letting him using my name get to my head.

I get up, "Guys, I have to go home and make sure things are smoothed over. I'll be back as soon as I can." Dispirito and LeBlanc nod their heads at me. Longfellow has already gone home. He'll be back first thing in the morning making sure he has all of the reports from all of us.

"Bring back more coffee."

In my car I lean back in my seat and close my eyes. I don't know where this investigation is going. In most cases we want to be the ones dictating how it goes and the path it takes. We are five steps behind this guy and he is the one dictating what information we have. It sounded like he knows who I am. He could be watching me. He could be here in the dark.

My eyes open. I spin around in the driver's seat to see 360 around the car. The hairs on my neck stand up. I check the back seat. I stretch to see the back floor. Nothing. I push the power lock to secure the doors. My blood pulses through my neck. My heart is racing. I hate the fucking dark. Things hide in the dark. I look out across the fields of the experimental farm at the Farmer's Market building on Belvedere Avenue. My imagination has the killer standing in the field, grass growing around his feet. He is dressed all in black. He stares across at me, he can see me from that far away in the dark. In one hand he has a long bladed knife. It drips blood into the grass. The teeth in his smile glow in the moonlight. His eyes are dark holes that lock onto my own eyes.

I start the car. The image disappears in a bath of headlights. The dark has scared me since I was a child. Carrying a gun doesn't help.

Marilyn lives in the Sherwood area. To get there I have to drive around the experimental fields and past the Farmer's

Market. I didn't have any intention of going home. Marilyn always answers her phone. If she didn't answer her phone during an important case something was wrong. Going to her place after one in the morning is wrong. I'm not an idiot. Her boyfriend runs her life and treats her like crap. I am pretty sure he hits her. Hillary would understand why I'm going there so late. I'm sure she would.

Her lights are on. I sit outside for a while and watch the windows. Only one shadow crosses the light.

Marilyn answers her phone this time, probably because my name popped up.

"It's me. Are you okay?" I say after a moment of silence.

"Where are you?" Her voice sounds strained like she has been crying.

"I'm outside actually. I wanted to check on –"

"You can come in. Chris isn't here." We both hang up our phones.

The cool night air wakes me up the moment I step from my car. There's a Dodge Charger parked up the street, a Kia SUV drives past. A house across the street still has lights on, another up the street has the blue glow of a television in the upstairs window. I shouldn't be here. Something is tossing around inside of me. I can feel a tingling rising up from my thighs. I look around to again to see if anyone is there. What the fuck am I doing? Marilyn opens the door when I am three feet away.

"You alright?" I walk in past her. I can smell wine thick around her.

She shuts the door and says, "No." She chokes back tears and snot. "Chris is gone."

"You said that."

"No, he's really gone. I told him to get out. He packed a couple of bags and left." She rubs the palm of her hands across her eyes. Her makeup is smeared. Her left cheek is puffy and red. There is a little spot of dried blood sitting at the bottom of one nostril. I also see her knuckles look scraped and red. "He," she chokes, "hit me. Slapped me across the face."

189

"Hard enough to make your nose bleed, eh?" I shove my hands in my pockets.

Marilyn moves from the front area to her sunken living room. I try not to watch the curve of her hips and ass in the green hospital scrub pants. I try not to, but I also notice she's not wearing underwear. Her place is artsy. There are paintings in the wall and different artistic touches all around. I don't see much of Chris here.

"I hit him."

"Really?"

She drops onto the love seat. She leaves enough room for me to sit right next to her. I don't know if I should. "Sit down." Marilyn tries to smile up at me.

I slowly sit beside her. Our thighs are touching.

"He slapped me hard enough to make me fall back and then he yelled at me not to talk back at him. I jumped up and punched him in the jaw like three or four times. I told him he had fifteen minutes to pack and get out."

There is a glass of white wine on the coffee table. Her engagement ring sits in an ash tray next to it.

I don't know where to put my hands or eyes. With my right thigh touching hers my right hand has nowhere to go. I place it across my lap. I can smell her. I can feel her. My mouth is dry.

"That's good," I say. "You don't need him screwing up your life."

"I know."

We both look at each other. I look into her light green eyes. The red wine waves of hair frame both sides of her face. Her tongue comes out and licks her lips. The pink tongue and slightly darker lips. There is a twitch in my pants. I'm not sure what is happening here. This has to be in my head. I don't know if I would want this.

"McIntyre called us in. The, ah, killer called the tip line. He gave us Jane Doe's name and challenged us to find him. He used my name."

"I'm in no shape for work right now. I can't let the guys see me."

190

"We have a triangle at six."

She puts her hand on my thigh. My skin jumps and dick twitches. "Let me get some sleep and clean myself up and I'll be there. A girl has to put on some makeup to hide the bruises." The tears well up in her eyes again. One lets loose and runs down her cheek over the bruising mark. Without a thought my hand flies up and my thumb wipes it away.

"Do you think you could hold me for a little while?"

I don't say anything.

"I just want to be held."

Marilyn's head falls to my shoulder. I awkwardly move around to get my arms to circle her. Things start to grow. Her arms wrap around me. One of her hands grasps the back of my neck.

I try to think of other things. I shouldn't be here. But at the same time I was asking and hoping for this. I'm an ass. Marilyn is vulnerable and drunk. Right here I could probably push something. I'm pretty sure she wants something to happen. She wants me to kiss her. Fuck Hillary. I feel fingers squeeze the back of my neck. Fuck the past ten years.

I get to my feet. "I should go."

"You can stay." Marilyn's green eyes are getting pregnant with tears again. I'm suddenly aware of the fact that my hungry penis is at the same level as her face.

~ * ~

"Let's get this going. I have a meeting with the CO, the mayor, and someone from the Premier's office at nine so I need to know everything. Reid, you tell me where we're at." McIntyre stands in the middle of the group office area with his arms crossed over his chest.

I look at my watch. Ten after six and still no Marilyn. "We don't have much on this ass. I think we know how he found Nicolle Pereira at a gym. If I profile him, he's in his late twenties or early thirties. He drives something that won't get noticed but can hide another person well. If he is the same guy who's been

191

raping women for years, then he's a nice guy not great looking but not a stereotypical movie type bad guy either, he's average. From his phone call I think he is confident. He thinks he's too smart to get caught. He knows about police procedures and how to leave a scene without leaving any sign of himself. He stalks these women. He knows them. He watches them for a while and knows their routines. I think the tattoos are important to him. When we find out where this Casey Marsh lived I bet we'll have his hunting area. Lastly, he has something to do with the Blooming Point area. He killed Casey Marsh out there. He tortured and killed Johanna Bowers out there. And it's no coincidence that Nicolle Pereira's fathers address is the same numbers mixed up and the same initials as where Casey Marsh was found."

"If that is the case then are you sure her tattoo is that important?"

"If I'm right he was hunting for women at Atlantic Fitness when he found her. I'll bet he gets names and Googles them and has some way of finding out whatever he needs. Nicolle Pereira is dead because she had a tattoo and where her father lives. I don't know if she would have lived if she only had one."

"So he got lucky?" Dispirito bounces his eyebrows.

I nod. It does sound farfetched when you have it all together. But then a serial killer right here on the "Gentle Island" is farfetched.

"So that's it? No fingerprints, no hairs, no fibers, no notes of guilt? The only proof there really is of a guy out there doing this and not some Mikma ghost getting its revenge is his bullshit phone call. Am I right?" McIntyre rocks on his heels, but otherwise doesn't move. Little droplets of sweat form on his forehead. I'm pretty sure the man got his position because he looks tough. "I have to go tell these people that tourist season is coming and we have no fucking idea who this serial killer is. A shitty tourist season could kill the whole island. I know you're not from here, Reid, but Islanders depend on tourist dollars."

"What do you want me to say Wayne? Do you want me to lie to you and say, I don't know, that I have a list of suspects and I'm looking into alibis before I make my next move? I can bullshit it if you want."

"I'm sorry." He moves his hands to his hips. He still looks tough and scary. "The pressure of these suits calling and emailing is getting to me. Keep chipping away at it. What did you guys find?"

The door to the offices opens and Marilyn shuffles in. She keeps her head down with her hair hanging on both sides of her face. She makes apologies and quickly sits at her desk and turns on her computer. I try catching her eye. She doesn't look at me.

"Casey Marsh was twenty-five when she died," Dispirito states. "That makes her the oldest victim. It was hard to find anything on her. What we got the most from was actually from Facebook. We have her address so we'll go there as soon as we're done. She was originally from North Bay, Ontario. We have a list of people she knew on the island, so we're going to start waking people up. Otherwise, she was a ghost. The only phone in her name was a cellular pay-as-you-go that is out of order. She worked at the *Holiday Inn* as a housekeeper. I have to wait for the managers to get in."

"We were able to find that her parents and sister did die in a car accident last winter. It was blamed on black ice," LeBlanc adds to the conversation. "We woke up as many people as we could, but we still have to wait for others to rise. We called the Ontario Provincial Police, and they're working on getting more info."

"Okay, Reid and Marilyn, go to Casey Marsh's apartment. Bring Eckhart in to look around. Dispirito, LeBlanc, work the computers. As you get something, feed it to the others and we'll change things as we go. I want something big on this case. If you can get something before nine you'll make me a happy man." McIntyre spins on his heel and heads for his office. Before going through the door he says, "Marilyn, come in my office first."

She quickly gets to her feet, still not looking at me, and walks into the boss's office. This time she pushes her shoulders back and picks up her chin. At some point I guess we are supposed to talk about what happened during the night. We don't have a choice. If she doesn't want to look at me then how are we supposed to talk?

My computer pings signaling a new email. I open the window and bring up my email. "Hey, Special-I found out where the phone was this shit called from. Oh fuck."

"Where was it?"

"The," my mouth can't form the words. My mind is having enough trouble grasping what is written there on my computer. He could have been there. Maybe I wasn't imagining anything.

"Reid?"

Dispirito, Longfellow, and LeBlanc are all staring at me. "Sorry, he used the payphone across from the experimental farm fields outside the Farmer's Market. He probably sat there and watched us all show up." He could have even walked across the field dressed in a black coat with a knife in his hand staring into my soul. My whole body shivers. I pick up the phone and dial Eckhart's number. He answers, groggy and already pissed off about an earlier call about Casey Marsh's apartment. I tell him to meet us at the pay phone in thirty minutes.

~ * ~

"You ever going to talk to me or no?" I stare out the passenger window of the car across the field to the back parking lot of headquarters. Outside the driver's side is the Charlottetown Farmer's Market building. The walls are wood paneling painted green, and there is red tin on the roof. There are two yellow pillars outside the main entrance at the back. The entrance to the parking lot is one of Charlottetown's many round-a-bouts. The guy had a perfect seat to watch us all show up in the middle of the night like his personal little puppets. *Dance cop man, dance.*

And then he moved in for a closer look and watched me leave for Marilyn's from the field.

Marilyn opens her door and slides from the car. Eckhart pulls the Ident van beside us.

"Somebody owes me a butt load of overtime. How about you two?" Eckhart says through the window.

"We work for the thrill of the chase?"

"You want me to buy that, Phil?" He pushes his glasses up. His partner gets out of the other side. They start pulling on their bunny suits and getting their equipment ready. "Do you know how many hours we've been putting in? Not to mention having to organize all the extra help I've been sent. So this guy called you, eh? That's new."

I slide my hands in my pockets. Marilyn stands quiet with her hands in her jacket pulling it tight around her body.

"He's got us working our asses off today. Maybe that's what he wants. He wants us all working on so much information that we can't concentrate on anything that will help us. By the way, Ashley found something at the Jane Doe scene," I say.

"Casey Marsh, the killer says her name is Casey Marsh."

"Right, well Ashley," he nods toward his partner, "found a void in the blood. Something small. Like the size of a nickel. We took a closer look and saw there were two other marks in the dust on the floor. In the outer building where we found Johanna Bowers blood we found dry flakes of Jane, Casey Marsh's blood. I think whatever was in the first woman's blood was brought to the other scene."

"Any ideas?" I'm running out of my own.

"I'm guessing tri-pod. Maybe he filmed the torture or took photographs. Hopefully, you'll find something later you can shove in his face. You ready?" Eckhart's partner nods her head. "I'll call you if we find anything."

I give him a nod. "We'll meet you at Casey Marsh's apartment."

~ * ~

The landlord is already there standing outside the apartment door. It is one side of a house with white vinyl siding tarnished with green algae from the salty sea air. There's a ten speed street bike with the front wheel and seat missing chained to a support pole. The support pole holds up a small roof above the tiny platform outside the door around the back of the house. The tiny

195

back yard is completely fenced in leaving the driveway as the only access. Marilyn parks the car beside a red Volkswagen. As we get out, the landlord lets out a gigantic yawn and checks his watch.

"Mr. Nowe?" Marilyn asks.

"Are you now going to tell me what this is about?" The others had her address. From there they found out who owned the home and woke him up. He's a round man. His beard is shaved so that the chin is hairless.

"I'm sorry, Mr. Nowe, but it is a sensitive police matter. Is this the apartment of Casey Marsh?" I try and smile. Marilyn and I have been driving around in silence for the past hour or so waiting for people to wake up. I tried talking to her but she wasn't having it. She only gave me nods or shoulder shrugs. Over one hour of awkward silence feels like days.

"She owes me a month's rent. She wrote me all those postdated checks and the one for last month bounced. If the one for this month bounces I'm getting rid of her stuff and renting to someone else."

"When was the last time you saw Casey?"

"I don't know," he shrugs his shoulders and folds his arms across his chest. "Four or five months ago. My tenants give me postdated cheques and I don't come see them unless something goes wrong in the apartment. Casey broke her key in the lock and needed a new one so I came by. Was she one of the dead girls? Oh my Lord." His face goes instantly white as the realization flows through him. "She was so nice and so hot. She was quiet. I don't think she made many friends here. I have to drive by here on my way to work and on my way home and there was never anyone here. Real shame. She was all alone here. Her boyfriend brought her to the island and then left her for some blond girl in a pink spandex outfit. I think that's what she said."

He doesn't have the name for the boyfriend. Mr. Nowe unlocks the front door and then goes back to his VW to sit and have a cigarette. He tells us he doesn't want to enter.

The apartment smells stale, that's the first thing I notice. There are three pairs of women's shoes inside the front door, all

196

the same size, piled on top of each other. It is like we are walking into some place stopped in time. Nothing has happened here for months. We will walk through carefully and then Eckhart will come and do his thing.

The first room is the kitchen. There are dishes piled up over the top of one sink. Food has dried on to their surfaces. Small fruit flies dance in circles above them. The countertop is mostly clean except for a toaster with crumbs scattered around it. Dark pellets of mouse poop are also scattered around. Marilyn looks at the photographs taped to the green refrigerator. I look through the mail on the tiny table. There is nothing newer than three months ago.

"I think we have a timeline," I say. "The last dated mail is February 11th."

"These pictures look like they span her whole life. These must be her parents and this one her sister. There's a couple that look more recent but nothing I can see of the boyfriend," Marilyn says.

"So you're talking now?"

She shakes her head. "Reid, I'm not dealing with this now."

"I was just making a comment." I walk into the living room. There is little here to see. An old style television sits on boxes from *MacDonald's*. If it is anything like my first apartment, the boxes are filled with books and VHS tapes. There is a brown and tan couch with ornate wooden arm rests but no legs. Beside it is a small square table made of old looking wood. On ledges, window sills, and beside the television are clowns made of ceramic, fabric, and plastic.

"I hate clowns," Marilyn says. She slips into the bathroom and comes back out. "There's more clown things in there. Only one type of shampoo, one toothbrush, no men's shaving equipment. There is a cat litter box though and a dish with a little food left in it."

"Where's the cat?"

There are more clowns up the stairs to the second floor. Some are smiling, some crying, some holding balloons, and even one on a unicycle. I am guessing these are something she has been collecting most of her life. Perhaps they reminded her to smile even when a simple and stupid accident can take away your entire life in a second. The top of the stairs open to a large open concept bedroom. There is a small bed here with no frame, just a mattress on floor. It is made neatly by a woman who cleaned rooms for a living. Maroon striped sheets were tucked in with hospital corners and a white comforter with a coffee looking stain near one corner, covers the top. A table matching the one downstairs, except with two levels, sits beside the head of the bed with a lamp, digital alarm clock, and a copy of the novel, *Just By Accident* sitting on top of a PEI tourist guide. Different articles of clothing are spread over the floor and a small dresser beside the door. A tan cleaner's uniform sits on a dining room chair, the only other piece of furniture here. A laptop computer sitting on the stained hardwood floor is plugged into the wall socket beside a tall window.

Being here is giving me the creeps. I can't get the feeling out of me that he is somewhere watching us. Watching me. I've heard of stalkers putting tiny video cameras in their victim's houses so they can watch them every second of the day. What if he has cameras in here now? He's getting under my skin. This is what he wants. He wants me to be on edge. I don't want to be here.

"We have a woman's wallet here on the dresser." Marilyn unsnaps the folded black wallet with two fingers. She opens it slowly. "Casey Marsh's Ontario driver's license." I feel my phone vibrate before it starts ringing. "I guess we wait for Eckhart now."

"Hold on." Unknown number. "Hello?"

"Are you busy, Sergeant Reid?" The man on the other end sounds young.

I watch Marilyn move around the room. Her fingertips float above objects.

I say, "Yes I am. Who am I talking to?"

"You don't recognize my voice?" says the voice on the other end of the phone line.

"Who is this?" I demand.

"You know who it is." I can hear him smiling. I snap my finger and get Marilyn's attention. I mouth to her that it's the killer.

"Why don't you tell me your name so we can talk proper."

"Why don't you tell me your first name? Don't be pathetic, Sgt. Reid, it doesn't suit you. Are you at Casey's apartment? I was never there so you're wasting your time."

"Why should I believe you?" He won't let me try and talk nice to him so why not be an ass.

He breaths hard into the phone. "You can't help it, same as them." He sounds calm. He knows he is in full control of this game. He has me over a barrel and he's fucking me hard in the ass. "I'm a nice guy. Nice guys never hurt anyone. I just wanted to check up on you."

"Why these girls?" I ask.

"I'll make you a deal, Reid. I'll answer your question if you answer one of mine."

I went through the hostage negotiation course a long time ago, but everything I learned is not coming to my brain. I can't think of how to talk him down. If he was a jumper I would probably tell him to just get it over with. I'm forgetting to listen to other noises behind his voice. I'm not concentrating enough on his words and not looking for patterns or hidden symbols in his speech.

I stare at Marilyn on the phone with Special I. Her green eyes stare back at mine for the first time today. I can see some worry in those eyes. *Why the hell is this guy calling you, Reid?*

The small cellular phone feels heavy in my hand. This guy with the pleasant voice and hard breathing, as he is getting more excited, is about to lead me on whatever path he chooses. I'm no longer in charge of anything. It's a terrifying feeling.

"What's your question?" I keep staring at my partner's eyes.

He smiles brighter on the other end. It's a feeling that I have. He's enjoying this. He wants this. "All I want to know Sgt. Reid, is what is the name of the horse your daughter is riding in the framed picture on the wall? The black and white one?" He lets out a little laugh.

"Excuse me?" My brain flips through pictures. What the hell is he talking about? How would he know anything about my daughter?

"What's the name of the horse, Reid?" His voice yells into my brain. *Dakota.*

I push the hang up button on the phone. "He's in my house." I know my legs are doing something but they are working on their own. I don't care what else is happening. I hear Marilyn run down the stairs behind me. Half of me hopes she doesn't get in the car. If I see this man in my house I have to kill him.

She climbs in the passenger side. She says something to the big man sitting on the hood of his VW. Our flashing lights and siren come on. I can hear the wailing somewhere in the background. My brain doesn't work around what corners to turn or what streets to take. I just end up going in the right direction.

The picture of Leigh on a black and white horse named Dakota hangs on her bedroom wall right beside the window. It faces her bedroom door. The only way to see it is from inside the house. *Inside* the house. Inside *her* bedroom.

I picture myself slamming the car in park without touching the brake. I push through the car door and instantly my gun is in my hand. I hear Marilyn running behind me calling for me to slow down. My hand opens the door. We move from room to room and then up the stairs, pistol always entering first. I picture myself turning into Leigh's bedroom. The photograph is there on the wall beside the window. Leigh sits on the back of her black and white paint as she trots down the beach. Sand flies up from the horses hooves.

I'm there. I wasn't picturing it, I was doing it. I am standing in the doorway to Leigh's room, my hand falls at my side heavy with the Smith and Wesson. Marilyn is talking behind me. Frix is barking from outside the house inside the fence. He was here. He was in my house.

"Reid,"

I blink.

Marilyn is right in front of me. "Where are Leigh and Hillary?"

"Leigh's in school. Hillary's at work."

In fifteen minutes Leigh is in the back of our car. She keeps asking what is going on. I tell her it's nothing for her to worry about, but every time she asks again I can hear the strain in her voice. She's ready to cry. Five more minutes and we are at the bank Hillary works in. As I walk through the glass doors she looks at me from behind the counter. I look around the room. My pistol is inside my pocket with my hand caressing the handle. Four people are in line to see a teller. None of them are the right age. None of the people up at the counter are right.

"What is this?" Hillary holds up a brown envelope before I can say a word.

"We have to go." I tell her.

"What is this?" she demands.

"Hillary, this is serious. We have to go. I don't know what it is, okay? I don't care what it is. Leigh is out in the car. We have to go."

She pulls out three photographs. Each one is stamped in yellow with the time and date on the lower corner. They show me going into Marilyn's apartment last night.

"What the hell is this?" My voice goes up high.

Hillary pushes her hair back from her face. It just falls back with a couple of black strands reaching in front of her eyes. They glisten with moisture. "They were dropped off five minutes ago. You want to tell me about them?" She looks to the side to see if anyone is watching. "You leave me and go to her?"

"Did you see who dropped this off?"

"What? No."

"We have to go."

"What are you talking about, Reid? I'm working. And this crap shows up. Do you know how this makes me feel?"

"Hillary,"

"Just go Reid."

"Hillary," I yell it out. All eyes turn to look at us. I lean over the top of the counter. "You can come with me now, or I'll climb over there and arrest you. Leigh is in the car. Come now."

Chapter 20

May 3rd, 8am

Ben picked the photo from the printer. He had the latest software for printing out digital photographs. He was good at what he did. He wasn't sure which was his hobby: photography or killing. In high school he was in the graphic arts club and learned all about developing real film. He made the walk-in closet in his bedroom at his parents' house into a dark room and developed his own pictures there. *Chloe.* Some of them were in his new apartment.

The photo in his hand was good. It was from a distance but it was still great quality. He got a good angle on the woman. Thanks to his inheritance from Grandpa passing away twelve years ago and the selling of his old farm, Ben had cameras, lenses and a printer with the best software. He sold his pictures to magazines and books and did work at different events. This one was magazine quality.

Hillary Reid arched her back up with her elbows pushing off the arm rest, her mouth was open, her hand reached down between her legs and pushed Reid's head down. He got in close enough to capture her hard nipples. Her hair was scattered over her face. She had good skin and dark eyes. Usually Ben didn't like girls with short hair. She liked it nasty though. He didn't know if she had any tattoos. He might have if they weren't interrupted. Too bad for her; her husband was dedicated to his job. Maybe Ben should have given her a visit. *Chloe.* She wasn't his type. He placed the photo on top of one of Leigh Reid getting on the school bus.

Ben lifted the large framed middle photo of the sun setting into the ocean off the coast of Prince Edward Island, a dark angled fence post is in the foreground, and turned it around. He set it on the couch with the back looking out. Ben moved along the wall and took down the two side photos of the extended horizon and did the same. Ben had a secret. He knew he shouldn't have all of it there. If the police ever caught on to him, basically if he let them, or any person he let into his life were to look at the back of the photos, it would be his downfall. He told himself he would get rid of it before the police got close enough. Ben framed the photos himself. On the back of each he had a cork board. On the cork boards he had pictures of women. They went back for years.

The middle one had all of his women. Chloe asleep in her bedroom, developed in his closet darkroom. There were pictures of the women he had raped. Some were taken before, but most were taken days or weeks after. Rachel Howe was there. Sierra West looked tired and drawn out with no make-up to help her pale skin. Three pictures showed Johanna Bowers. She walked down the street. She laughed at a table in the university library. The last one showed her swinging in the late night wind with her toes pointing down to the dew covered ground. Casey Marsh was there. She was there in different stages too. There were pictures of her from before he took her, one of her in the housecleaning uniform, to when he had her tied down and naked, to when she was first bleeding, and then one of her after she was gone. Between the two women was one of Johanna and Casey together – one dead, one dying. Nicolle Teresa Pereira's picture was there.

With metal thumbtacks Ben secured his new photographs onto one board. Reid caught in the middle with the press pushing in on him, Hillary Reid, Leigh Reid waiting at the curb for the bus – her hair blown to the side with the wind, and Sgt. Moore in her loose top and green hospital scrub pants taken from outside her window. He had pictures of the two RCMP officers as they kissed. He knew what happened.

The left over pictures on both the left and right cork board were pictures of what he called potentials. They were of women he had seen and got interested in. *Pathetic.* One was a mother of two – thin with a little mound at her belly, sexy, fair-haired. She had a tattoo of a cross and rosary beads on the back of her shoulder. In the picture she was wearing a spaghetti strap blouse in the mall. For her he told her he took pictures of children for advertisements and wanted her number. Ben knew where she lived, what she drove, that her husband was a trucker who was away days at a time, where her kids went to school, and the dirty secrets she kept when her husband was away. There was a brunette that had stars on her shoulder. A redhead, more blonds, more brunettes. Ben knew something about all of them. He knew how to get to them. *Pathetic.*

~ * ~

May 3ʳᵈ, 5pm

"So are you going to talk to me before you go, Hill?"

"I don't know, Reid." Her arms are pulled tight around her body. She stares off at where Leigh is playing cards with Dispirito on the row of blue chairs, but I'm willing to bet she can't see her.

We stand close to each other but away from everyone else next to the display dedicated to the history of Maritime Airways. The Charlottetown airport is never really a busy place compared to airports in other cities. One plane is landing, so people are showing up across the building to wait for loved ones, and then on this side others are waiting to get on the same plane once it has been cleaned and refueled. The plane is going straight from Charlottetown to Toronto. Hillary and Leigh are going to meet Hill's father there and then spend the night at a hotel close to the airport. In the morning he will drive them the three hours to her parent's house. They will be safe there.

"Nothing happened, Hillary." I have my hands shoved in my pockets, shoulders slumped forward. I don't like having people looking at us and wondering what our business is about. Of course I can't actually see anyone watching us. Dispirito looks up from his card game once in a while. Two plain clothed officers we borrowed from the drug unit are here keeping their eyes open for anyone suspicious. One sits on a high chair in *Budley's Restaurant & Lounge*, the other keeps checking his watch where he stands leaning on the barrier between departures and arrivals. Marilyn and LeBlanc are outside the airport sitting in their car watching everyone. "I went to her house to see if she was okay. She and Chris were fighting a lot lately. He hit her last night," I say.

"She's a cop, Reid, I'm sure she can handle herself."

"She may be a cop but she's also a woman."

"You noticed." She looks at me.

"A woman who loves a man is still a woman. Maybe she was a cop second. You could smack me around all you want and I would never pull a gun." I watch Hillary watch our child. "You know I love you, right? I didn't fool around." It would take something special for me to admit that I have thought about cheating. I know it's the unfaithful man who says, thinking about cheating and actually going through with it are two different things. I'm not going to tell my wife that Marilyn and I kissed. I'm not stupid.

Hillary turns to me. She pulls her arms tighter around her. "I know you love me. But I also know that you've been different ever since BC. Last night was the first time in a long time you started anything with me. And then you just got up and left like you flipped a switch. Do you know how much that hurt? Then I get pictures of you going into Marilyn's. Do you know how much that hurt?" I give her a nod. Tears fall from her brown eyes and streak down her face then get pregnant again on the edge of her jaw. "Maybe we need this time away."

I bite my lip and turn to look at what is going on across the terminal. This son of a bitch is ruining me.

Hillary said the guy who delivered the envelope with the photographs wore a baseball cap and aviator sunglasses. There was nothing special about him though and she didn't think she could identify him. We are waiting for the bank's security camera footage. We won't get a look at his face. This guy is playing with us.

"We have to go through security. Leigh, honey, come on."

She runs over and wraps her arms around me. "Are you sure you can't come, Daddy?"

I get down on one knee and tell her I have to stay to catch the bad guy. "You take care of Mom and I'll see you soon."

"Will you go check on Dakota?"

"I will. You be good for mom. Come on, you have to go."

"I drew this for you at your work." Leigh hands me a piece of paper with the RCMP logo on the top. There is a rainbow made with different colored highlighter pens and some words roughly written underneath. *Hearts heal from lots of rainbows. Rainbows are good luck for everyone. Everyone loves everybody around them.* She wraps her arms around me, tells me she loves me, and brushes her lips on mine.

I put my arms around Hillary and we place our lips against each other. It's not as warm as I had hoped. I wave to them the moment they turn back at the doorway leading into security. Two plain clothed officers already went through ahead of them, with no guns, just to watch everyone. They will get on the plane to Toronto and then get on another plane to come right back to the island. Charlottetown does not have tunnels to the planes like real cities. When they have to board they will walk out onto the tarmac to the plane and up the portable stairs to the *WestJet* plane.

The moment the plane starts rolling toward the runway I turn to Dispirito, "let's get to work."

"You okay?" Marilyn leans against the front fender of the car.

I shrug my shoulders. "A psycho killer is fucking with my life. What could be wrong? Let's go to Maypoint."

~ * ~

May 3rd, 11:30am

Ben looked out the sliding glass doors to a back deck and a fenced in yard beyond. A black and white dog sniffed the ground and walked in a circle. It didn't care about the stranger in its house. Ben turned away from the glass patio doors. The Reid house was clean and well kept. He walked around the dining room and kitchen letting his gloved fingers caress the different surfaces. There were family pictures in frames all over the surfaces and up on the walls. A wood block held knives. Plastic horses lay on their sides on the dining table. It was so different from his childhood house. This house was loving and warm. It had the scent of ocean freshness.

He walked through the kitchen. Someone had toast with jam this morning, but didn't put the knife and plate in the sink. There was only one coffee cup, it still had the dregs inside. Someone had cereal. *She* probably had *Banana Nut Cheerios*. In that cupboard is also an open box of *Lucky Charms* and one of *Frosted Mini-Wheats*. It was a mother and daughter alone in the morning because the man of the house was off fooling around with his partner. *Pathetic*.

Ben liked watching Reid and his wife last night. *Chloe*. It was like the old days when he stood outside a girl's window and watched her boyfriend fuck her. Ben took his pictures then sat in his SUV as the cop drove away and imagined himself climbing on top of his wife. He bet she was tasty. *Pathetic*. What an idiot this Reid was.

He walked through the living room and stood for a moment looking at Reid's awards and certificates framed on the wall. There was one there for stopping the killer in BC. The *Playground Killer*, was what the newspapers called him. Ben needed a name. *The Prince Edward Island Terror*. It had to be something connecting him to the island, but still being menacing enough to terrorize the people. Reid had a $123.34 bill with Maritime Electric. Leigh won ribbons for riding. She was a cute baby.

Upstairs he walked through the master bedroom. He sat on Reid's side of the bed. He looked through the dresser drawers. Reid wore boxer briefs. Hillary Reid had some thongs, colorful panties, and a lacey black pair, but there weren't any in the hamper. In the very back of her drawer was a toy, a little finger vibrating toy in a black leather case. Hubby was away far too much. He needed to take care of what was his. Ben touched all their clothes. He knelt down and looked under the bed. Dirty socks, a pen, pair of slippers on her side, a fly swatter, and dust bunnies. Hillary had a *Karen Brichoux* novel on her side of the bed on a nightstand. He opened the closet and ran his hand along their hanging clothes like a kid running his fingers along a fence. He smelled Reid's aftershave and Hillary's perfume. The latter was something with a touch of vanilla. Hillary Reid had a lot of shoes on the floor and in boxes. She had a pair of black boots with five inch heels. He imagined her with those and only the black lace panties on. She had a lot of dresses, Reid a lot of blazers, and ties on one hanger.

All Ben needed to see in the daughter's room was the picture next to the window. If he was a dad the worst thing to know right now was that someone was in her room. His daughter was getting close to the age of the girls killed in BC by the *Playground Killer*. *Green Gables Slasher*.

"Time to make a phone call."

~ * ~

May 3rd – 6:10pm

"Eckhart." The Maypoint detachment is out of Charlottetown on highway one heading toward Cornwall. It's next door to a Chinese restaurant. Ident's office is at the back of the building. Marilyn and I make our way through the cubicles and through the open office door. There are two desks in the main room. A corner room right by the door has a map of the island and a large flat table. One side room has white boards like our office and a light wall like the ones hospitals use to look at x-rays. At the far end of the room is a thin, long, corridor used for fingerprints and photographs. Besides Eckhart and Ashley, I count eight other people in the room. Eight more than what they usually have. I don't know them and I don't care to. "What do you have for me?" I ask.

He looks at me from the computer. "What d'you mean?" The back of his hand pushes his glasses up his nose. "I told you this morning we didn't have anything." He shakes his head and looks around at everyone else. .

"What have you been doing then? I need something on this guy." My voice echoes in my ears.

"What do you want me to say?" Eckhart puts his hands out.

The surface of his desk is covered with a lot of things that have nothing to do with police work. His name is on a piece of wood. There are a couple small photographs and three toy cars.

"I want you to do your job and get me some hard facts on this son of a bitch. I need it now," I snap.

"Don't raise your voice at me, Reid. In the past three days you've given me two murder scenes, two victim's houses, your house, and a payphone. There's only two of us that actually work here. Even with help from Halifax, we're still buried. This doesn't happen on the island. We're not equipped. We have to wait for everything to come back from the Halifax lab."

"You don't know what you're doing."

"I know exactly what I'm doing, but this doesn't happen here. It never has," Eckhart protests.

I grab one of the chairs in front of his desk and shove it out of my way. It rolls until it hits something. Marilyn makes a noise behind me. All movement stops. "I don't care about this backwoods place. I need fingerprints. I need DNA, hair, cum stains, anything. This guy fucked these girls until they were bruised and you don't have anything on him?"

Eckhart pushes his glasses up. He stares at me from his seat. "He wiped the phone down at the *Farmer's Market*. I printed the weather guard around it and found twenty-five different sets of prints. They're going through the computer now. There's so much shit from every scene that we're spinning. Samples were sent to Halifax, but they won't be finished for a week or two. You know how this works Reid. It's not like *CSI* or *Law & Order*. We don't get lab reports before the second commercial break you know. We're doing what we can."

Marilyn's hand tightens around my arm. My whole body shakes. I want to twist out of her grip, grab onto Eckhart and shake him until results come out. What the hell is that going to do?

"It's like this guy is weighing us down with so much crap that we can't focus on anything."

I stare at him. He stares back then pushes his glasses up his nose. I feel a tug on my arm. Marilyn pulls me out of the office and I follow her like a puppy scolded for running two yards away. My eyes stay on Marilyn's heels, but I know everyone is watching me. "Somebody's watching me. I've got no privacy." My feet scrape the floor. The moment we get outside the cool air opens my eyes. I still can't think things out. My family is gone, our dog is at Sgt. English's place and I can't go home. I feel like the killer's eyes are on me. He knows my every move.

"You have to pull it together Reid."

I look at Marilyn.

"LeBlanc texted me that the fitness place has that list of members for us. They're sorting through it now."

I nod. I look back over my shoulder. As we get in the car I take a quick look at the back seat.

~ * ~

May 3rd, 2:12pm

Ben walked through the mall with his hands in his pockets. They still hadn't turned off the heat for air conditioning, so it was a little too warm inside. He stopped to look at the display of discounted books, placed on a small table, by the bookstore entrance. He lifted one up to eye level and pretended to read the back while watching the people walk by.

By now Sgt. Reid's world was out of control. Life wasn't going to stop for him.

She came in from the Queen Street entrance, walked past the bookstore and the table of discounted books towards the stairs to the second level. She wore blue stretch pants that hugged every centimeter of muscle in her legs. Under a red jacket she wore a grey sports bra. Ben knew it left enough room to show off the Pegasus tattoo on her left shoulder. Her light brown hair was tied back. She had an *iPod* with headphones in her pocket. Ben left the books and followed her up the stairs. She was going for her work out like she did every second day. Her name was Kathy Welsley. Her birthday was September 12th. She was twenty-four. She had gone to Bluefield High School. In the past three years, she had vacationed in Cuba, Edmonton, and New York. *Facebook* was an excellent source of information. All Ben had to do was look at her profile page. He talked to her once or twice so she accepted him as a friend without question. She knew him. And yet she didn't even notice him outside the bookstore. *Pathetic*. Ben followed her across the causeway and licked his lips.

~ * ~

May 3rd – 8:23pm
"This is going to take all night," I say.

Marilyn leads the way down a stone path to the three story apartment building. The bottom is beige siding with the upper two floors done in red brick. The roof goes off in wild right angles in all directions. The base makes a horseshoe around a communal courtyard and loop driveway. I count six balconies along the front of the building. It sits in the back of two mini-malls and off to the side of the *Atlantic Superstore*, one of the biggest grocery stores around. The two mini-malls are some of Hillary's favorite places to shop. Around *ISE'S sports bar* is a large two part mall. *Smitty's Restaurant* and the *Bargain Shop*. The right angled side goes *East Side Mario's*, ISE'S front entrance, *Dollarama*, then *Jumbo Video*, a hair salon, a kids clothing store, and *Pizza Delight*. The other mini-mall on the side of the Superstore's parking lot has *Better Living*, a furniture rental place, *Bulk Barn, The Brick, Reitman's*, and *Indigo books*. Across University Avenue is the RCMP headquarters. We turn and watch a car speed into the parking lot from Queen Street. The large lot is speckled with pot holes and broken asphalt.

"Do you want to cut this short and finish talking to these guys tomorrow morning?" She waves the list of male members from Atlantic Fitness. We have talked to three men already. Two thought they recognized both Nicolle and Casey, but only one

212

tried talking to either. LeBlanc is doing an in depth background check on him. "We're by HQ anyways."

"Better to get it over with. He has to be here somewhere. Oh wait," I jump forward and catch the security door as a woman and her two daughters come out. The two little girls stare up at Marilyn and give her a smile. The mother smiles at me.

"Nothing like catching someone by surprise." Marilyn slips past me.

"Do you want to bet his first question will be, *how did you get in the building?* If we can't find him on this list, then I don't know where else to look."

"You think he would actually give a real name and address?"

"He's untouchable right."

She leads the way into an elevator. "Ben Cooper lives on the top floor. 3F."

~ * ~

May 3rd – 8:27pm
There's a knock.

Ben stares at the front door. His spoon stops. Milk drips off of it onto the table beside his bowl of Frosted Mini Wheat's. He waits patiently. Nobody rang the security buzzer for him to check who it was and allow them access to the building, so maybe they got the wrong apartment. They'll figure it out in a minute.

A second knock.

Ben rises to his feet. People don't interrupt his world. *Drip.*

Nothing in the apartment is out of place. The large photographs are back up on the wall with everything out of view. *Knock, knock.* Perhaps it is Shannon. *Pathetic.* Maybe she's come back and she's ready to fall in line.

He looks through the peep hole. *Drip.* Sgt. Reid. Sgt. Moore faces straight on to the door behind him. *Drip. Drip. DRIP.* The world spins. His head feels like it is suddenly full of water. He steps back from the door. What the hell is going on? Panic threatens his body. He feels it come up from inside and circle

213

around inside his skull. What are they doing here? What do they know? His body sweats. Should he climb out the window?

Stop. Control yourself Ben. They know nothing. He takes a breath and feels the calm sweep down through his body. This is *his* game.

He puts his hand on the door knob and turns.

"Can I help you?" Ben smiles.

"Ben Cooper? I'm Sgt. Moore, this is –"

Ben says, "Sgt. Reid. I took your picture."

~ * ~

May 3rd – 8:30pm

I stare into the brown eyes of Ben Cooper. The florescent hallway light reflects off his oval glasses. His short brown hair is spiked and held in place with gel. He has high cheekbones, bushy eyebrows, smooth skin with a few old acne scars and a pointed chin. His thin lips form into a smile and his upper lip almost disappears. There is a thin film of sweat below his nose and on his forehead. He looks like an average guy. When would this man have taken my picture?

"I'm a freelance photographer," he says as if he is reading my thoughts. "I was outside the RCMP headquarters yesterday morning taking pictures and asking questions for the National Press." He rocks back on his heels and smiles at me. I stare at him a little longer, his smile slightly fades. Is there anything in that?

"Is that so?" I don't remember him.

"This is the biggest news story to hit the island since the fathers of confederation met to form Canada, right? I just really wanted to be part of it and see if I can make some cash from the news. Sounds sleazy, I know." He smiles again and looks over my shoulder to Marilyn.

"We don't judge, Mr. Cooper," I say.

"Call me Ben." He smiles with teeth and lets his eyes look over Marilyn from top to bottom.

"We need to ask you a few questions, Mr. Cooper. Are you a member of the Atlantic Fitness club on Kent Street?"

His eyes widen. "Atlantic Fitness, yes. I go there three or four times a week. I like to ride the bikes, watch Sports Centre, check out the scenery, you know."

"No we don't. Can you tell us?" Marilyn stares him down.

"Sure, come on in." The room is very clean. It is a very normal looking room. Matching couch and lounge chair, coffee table with scattered magazines on it, a single plate and glass empty are on a small dining table. Marilyn stays close to Cooper as I slowly circle the room looking at the photos on the walls. There are a lot of wildlife and scenery pictures in frames. Three large ones of the sun setting around the island sit on the walls above the couch. In one corner are two photo lights and a tripod set up with no camera on top.

"I like to watch the ladies exercising," he says. "I know that sounds sleazy too, but I'm a guy."

"You live far away from Kent Street don't you? Aren't there closer gyms?"

"There are. I like the atmosphere of that one."

"I have some pictures here, Mr. Cooper, can you tell us if you've ever seen these women. Maybe at the fitness club." Marilyn pulls photographs of all three women out of a manila folder and shows them one at a time.

"I saw this one here. Long time ago I think," he says, pointing to one of the photos.

Marilyn tips is so that I see he pointed to Casey Marsh. She asks him if he is sure.

"I just remember noticing that she wasn't around. I figured maybe she just switched the times she worked out or something," Ben replied casually

"Was that because you were bugging her? Or was somebody else? Would she have a reason to change her workout times?" I stare at him without letting my gaze waver.

He looks at me. The ends of his mouth go up and his head shakes. "I don't know." He looks back to Marilyn, "I've seen this blond one," he flicks the picture of Johanna Bowers, "she's the woman found in the woods a couple of weeks ago. I never saw her before if that's what you mean, and this other one I told Sgt. Reid that I didn't remember seeing her." All eyes look at me and I look back. "At Atlantic Fitness yesterday, you showed me her picture. Coincidences, eh?"

I nod. I don't remember seeing him there either. How could I not remember seeing him twice? This time he stares at me a little longer. Long enough so that I feel uneasy and look away. The hairs at the back of my neck stand on end. I look out the window that faces the mini-mall. I don't know what to think of this guy. He's nice. He smells nice. Who said that before? The only photos around that are not of scenery or far off people are of the same girl.

"This your girlfriend?" I ask.

"Yes, she is. She was. We broke up recently. It still hurts so I haven't taken the photos down."

"Thank you for your time, Mr. Cooper. If you can remember anything please give us a call. Here is my card." Marilyn passes the small paper to him.

He takes a look at it, runs his thumb over her name, and flips it around in his fingers. "Sure no, no problem."

"Thank you." I put out my hand and he takes it. His palm is hot and clammy. His fingers grip hard and squeeze. His eyes meet mine. He looks into me. He knows me. There's a tingling down in my groin, but I don't know what it means. If I was a woman I might feel a little creeped out the way he has been looking at Marilyn and the way he probably looks at other women. Is it enough of an uneasy feeling to mean he is a serial killer? Probably not. Our hands drop and I follow Marilyn into the hallway.

Before we get into the car Marilyn calls LeBlanc to tell him to do a background check on Ben Cooper.

~ * ~

May 3rd – 9:04pm

Ben closes his door behind the two police detectives. What the hell were they doing there? He knew he should have used a fake address. Would that have helped? How much did they know? Were they just fishing or were they trying to get his reaction to something? They couldn't possibly know that much since they left. They didn't ask about his whereabouts during any times. They didn't know anything.

Drip.

Reid knew. Reid looked at him and saw through into his soul. Reid was taking over the control of Ben's world. How dare he? Ben's teeth push down into his bottom lip. He tastes his own blood.

He crosses the room and stares out over the mini-malls roof top. Across University Avenue he stares at the RCMP Headquarters. *Drip.* It is *his* game. He has to take control.

~ * ~

May 3rd – 10:45pm

"We've barely made a dent in this list."

"Do you want to call it quits for tonight? I don't really want to be waking people up all night."

"That's fine," I check my cell phone. "We have a couple leads so far."

"Where are you sleeping tonight?" Marilyn turns onto Grafton by the *Confederation Center for the Arts. Anne of Green Gables, the Musical,* would be starting there soon and running for the entire summer. That play has been performed there since dirt was invented. I know deep down she is just being curious, but a little part of me is hoping she wants to offer me a spot at her place.

"I don't know. I might just go home," I say.

"With this guy out there going into your home? Don't think so. You can come to my place and sleep on my couch if you have to."

"Yeah, Hill would love that."

217

"Don't tell her." My phone rings. "Let me guess, she's psychic and that's her now."

I smile over at her. "Reid."

"Sgt. Reid, its Catherine Arsenault from CBC news."

"Call Sgt. English," I tell her.

"No," her tone of voice is very strong and demands attention. I shut up. "I'm calling out of courtesy, Sergeant, I didn't have to. I could just let you hear about it in ten minutes on the news like everyone else."

Hillary does this too and I hate it. She'll say something full well wanting me to ask what it is she hasn't said so that she is dominant and I'm dependent on what she has to tell me. "What are you talking about Ms. Arsenault?"

She lets out a little sound of triumph. "Your killer sent me an email twenty minutes ago. He says he is only just beginning and is going to paint the island red with blood before he's done. I'm naming him the *Red Island Killer*. Kind of poetic considering if you don't catch him soon he will kill the entire island since the tourist season will be dead."

"You can't run with this. How do you know it's even him?"

"Oh, I know and I am running with it. In fact I'm live in one minute. I thought you should know."

~ * ~

May 3rd – 11:10pm

Ben sits back in his lounge chair with a smile to his lips. *The Red Island Killer*. He likes it. It's his world. It is his game. Life is but a stage, and each of us has a part.

218

Chapter 21

I test the water coming out of the main faucet before turning on the shower. The old hotel pipes whistle. The hot water hits my body and instantly my muscles want to give in. It wasn't until getting to the hotel last night that I realized how tired I was. I locked the door and checked my phone to see if Hillary called and for some reason I missed it. Then I dropped to the bed, and instantly fell asleep with all the lights on.

My hands rub *White Rain* shampoo into the stubble on my scalp until it foams. I scratch the foam in behind my ears like Mom always told me to do. The spray pelts against my chest. My hands move from my armpits to chest to groin spreading the soap around. My fingertips caress the small scar in my abdomen left over from my run-in with the Playground Killer in BC. My only other substantial scar is on my right thigh where I got kicked when I was with the musical ride. I squeeze my muscles to try and alleviate the pains. It has been a while since I put some serious time in the gym. I still have good muscle tone, but I should probably see if the guys want to go a few rounds in a boxing ring somewhere just to get some work in.

The hotel room door is locked, dead-bolted, and chained. I thought about moving the dresser across the room to block the door but I'm a cop. I shouldn't be terrified. I shouldn't be looking over my shoulder. I shouldn't have to check the back seat of my car before getting in. I shouldn't see a shadowy figure with a knife when my eyes close. The bathroom door is locked. My Smith & Wesson 9mm sits on the back of the toilet under a folded towel just outside the shower curtain. In the night I woke suddenly and my hand went instantly to my hip. I fell back asleep, as restless as it was, with my pistol under the pillow.

I want this guy. He knows how to play us. He knows how to play me. When I was a teen and my parents went out of town leaving me alone, someone called and hung up when I answered. It scared me. How dare they? How dare that reporter put it out there for everyone to hear and read. I don't want to think about what today is going to bring us all. The island is going to panic.

Soap seeps into my right eye. Both close on instinct. I swear I hear the door open. I can feel him enter the bathroom.

He's here.

I push my face into the waterfall and rub my eyes. In my mind I can see his silhouette through the white shower curtain.

Oh god, he's here.

My throat constricts. I can't breathe. He has a knife. *Drip.* I pull open the curtain with eyes wide, fist up high ready to fight. Both retinas burn from the soap. There's nobody in the bathroom with me. The door is shut and locked. I take a breath. My knees tremble like there is Jell-O inside. Water splashes out onto the white tile. My ears perk and strain to try and hear if there are any noises out in the room. It's stupid, I know. I can't help it.

To finish showering my head, I lean back so that the water falls over the back of my head while my eyes can stay open. Now this guy has me feeling like a total idiot.

~ * ~

The Red Island Killer is emblazoned across all of the morning newspapers in the hotel lobby. The Guardian says the Red Island Killer has the island 'paralyzed with fear.' The Globe and Mail asks if Prince Edward Island RCMP can handle the case.

As I pull my car into headquarters the press vans are parked on the grass going around the building. They have multiplied since the last time I saw them. My foot pushes the gas down. I circle the building fast and don't brake until I'm ready to park. Catherine Arsenault stands by the back stairs. The moment she sees it's me she bends down and places her take-out coffee on the

220

ground. Her camera man does the same and adjusts the camera on his shoulder. Catherine stretches out her microphone cord.

"That's littering." I point to the coffee cups as I rapidly walk toward them. "You better pick those up or I'll get an officer out here."

"Sgt. Reid, what is happening with the Red Island Killer case?"

"The what?" I walk around them and take the stairs two at a time.

"Can I get a comment about his threat for the people of PEI? Can you do this job?"

I stop at the top of the stairs. I know I shouldn't say a word. I should just flash my security pass over the scanner and walk in, go make myself some slow roast coffee, check my email to see if Hill sent me anything, and start my day. I should. I can already hear McIntyre calling me into his office. I slowly turn and take a step down. Catherine's lips slightly turn up at the edges.

"You were completely irresponsible for putting that out there. How's that for a fucking comment. If there's a god damn panic all over the island then you're the one to blame for it. You wanted my fucking comment, there you go." Spit flies from my lips.

There's a flash of yellow hair in front of my face. I feel hands with fingernails grab my arms and push me back. "Come on Catherine leave Sgt. Reid alone," English says to the reporter then turns to me, "Go inside Reid," back to the reporter, "He's been putting in a lot of hours. He's tired from working hard on this case but he's here pursuing this killer relentlessly. The RCMP are putting everything they have to this case and utilizing every resource at their disposal. I will make an official statement at nine o'clock."

I walk through the back door to the headquarters building and all voices fade away.

"Thanks for the save," I say when Deborah comes back in through the door. I catch a quick glimpse of Catherine Arsenault bending down to pick up her coffee.

"Don't thank me Reid. She's going to run your comments you know."

"She's irresponsible. She should have come to us first."

"You know how they work. They have to be the first ones to get the story and it doesn't really matter who gets hit in the crossfire. Just smile, say no comment, and do your job."

She runs a hand back through her hair. Her hands quickly straighten out her uniform. She has to make a press conference so she needs to be in her crispest blue pants with a yellow stripe down each leg and a tan shirt. Our blue and yellow day to day uniform is nice, but our red serge can make someone quiver. Early on in our relationship, I remember Hillary coming to bed wearing my Mountie Stetson, black utility belt from my serge uniform and nothing else. Deborah English is hot to begin with, more so in a uniform. Of course if I were to come on to her she would be in touch with Hillary before I could feel bad.

"Have you heard from Hillary?" English asks.

"Not yet." I tell her.

Her eyes look down quick to the floor.

"What?"

She looks back to me and lets out a breath. "She sent me an email. She's good. Leigh's good. She asked me to keep an eye out for you and make sure you remember to eat."

And make sure I'm not fucking my partner in the hallway.

"I'm supposed to remind you to go see Dakota. She won't tell me what has her so mad." She looks at me with a little hope that I'll spill what asshole thing I did, but I didn't do anything. "I don't know what she's mad about, but don't let the job get in the way, Reid. Russ left me because he felt he couldn't compete with the job. He loves his daughter and says he still loves me. We just got to a point where I would rather work than spend time with him and he couldn't handle it."

"Deb, you know what I'm trying to do. Sometimes other lives have to come before those around me. I have to go."

There is nobody else is in the main area of Major Crimes as I walk in. McIntyre's light is on. I sit my jacket over the back of my chair and take my place in front of the white board. There are pictures of all three women from when they were alive and vibrant to when they were found with the life taken out of them. We have a copy of the photo from Johanna Bowers' refrigerator of her and her friends at Blooming Point Beach. Above them is a timeline of estimated times and actually known times. Below the photos is everything we know for sure about each victim leading up to when they were last seen until they were found. There is more under Johanna and Nicolle's pictures than Casey's. On the right side of the board Longfellow has started writing a list of suspects. It is a short list. All are from the Atlantic Fitness list. We have cleared Johanna Bowers' boyfriend and the boyfriend of Nicolle Pereira. In the middle in red marker is the list of what we know about the killer. There is a lot of empty white space on the board.

My head fills with questions with no answers. Who is this guy? Why did he pick these girls? Where did he find them? Did he see Casey and Nicolle at the gym? Johanna never went there so where did he meet her? We know where he grabbed Nicolle, but where did he grab the other two? What was the significance to the tattoo on the back of the shoulder? Was there significance? Why does he almost cut off their left breast? We know where Casey was killed and where Johanna may have been tortured, what about Nicolle? Where did he kill her? Why is he fixating on me? What is his sick game? So many questions.

"What are you thinking?" McIntyre.

I keep staring at the board and say, "You don't want to know."

"We're making progress." He steps beside me and takes a bite of his morning bagel.

"Not enough. Not fast enough. Not for the island expecting him to go around the whole place killing everyone."

I keep my eyes on the board half hoping something will flash or glow or fall off and tell me what to do next. It's kind of like in school back in the day when I would stare at my papers hoping that an essay would just appear out of nowhere. This isn't like the movie *Seven* where the killer just walks in and says, I did it. He's going to stay out there and play me as long as he can string it along.

"We should put Atlantic Fitness under surveillance. We could put some plain clothes guys in there watching whoever is watching everyone else."

McIntyre shakes his head. He moves over to the coffee pot, puts a brand new white filter into the machine, scoops in the coffee grounds out of a *Folgers* tub, sprinkles in a little salt from a shaker, and fills the water reservoir. "We have no proof that this guy even finds these women there. We don't know why."

"It's the tattoos, Wayne. He has to see them somewhere. Where else in the winter is he going to see tattoos?"

"If this guy knows their routines who's to say he hasn't been watching them since the summer? Johanna Bowers didn't go to that gym. Where did he find her? Maybe he saw the tattoos in the summer and he has been stalking them ever since. It could have been any time. He could have been on the beach the day that picture was taken."

"But –" I start.

"I can have units go by there. Maybe get city police to go by, but we're not putting people in there," McIntyre says, cutting me off.

McIntyre tells me as soon as Longfellow arrives to come in his office and get the triangle started and over with so we can get the day going. The Premier of Prince Edward Island has people calling the Commanding Officer every day, Members of Parliament have called, the Mayor of Charlottetown, the tourist board calls. Everyone wants this done with. People are watching the summer tourist season slowly preparing itself to die as long as this killer is out there. I check my phone messages. Reporters wanting a sound bite, a constable in Manitoba looking for background on a suspect for a case he is working on. There is nothing from him. I stop on the last message. It came in last night shortly after the evening news. Mr. Pereira's voice cracks with emotion. He saw the news and wants me to find this guy. He says, "Put me in a room with him and let me do what you did to that guy in BC." I have to listen to the message again. Does everyone think I shot the Playground Killer because I wanted to see him die? That's not what happened. I didn't see it like that.

It was me or him. It was something that had to be done. This time I will bring this guy in. I'm going to end this.

Longfellow comes through the door. He doesn't have the time to put his stuff down before we are summoned into the Major Crimes leader's office.

~ * ~

The others roll in. We are already back at our desks starting with our own days. LeBlanc got a haircut. He gives me a grunt and goes to check his computer. Dispirito comes in singing the latest annoying jingle from a local radio commercial. Something about a local real estate guy who will sell your house today. Right away he starts asking about the news reports and the possibilities of what our killer may do.

"Red Island Killer, that's pretty catchy really, when you think about it. The island is red from the red sand and clay, he makes his vic's bleed so he's making the island red."

"And the tourist industry is about to go to shit and will kill the island. I know." I sit behind my desk and rest my head in my hands.

"Your puppy run away?" Marilyn puts a mug down in front of me. The smell of slow roasted coffee fills my nose. I'm instantly awake. I take a quick inventory of her face looking for any new bruising. There is none.

"What?" Marilyn looks at me.

"How was your night?" I ask and watch her eyes. I really am asking if Chris came home and if she was stupid enough to let him back in.

"I just went home, showered, and went to bed. How was the hotel?"

"Quiet." I could tell her about my freak out, but I would have to fight off her insistence that I should see someone.

I saw Dr. Ferron in British Colombia after the Playground Killer case when I shot the main suspect. I had nightmares afterward of the little girls calling for help. *Chloe.* I don't want to see a head shrinker again, especially if it isn't the victims haunting me this time. I'm not going to see a psychologist because the killer is haunting me. "I have to go see Dakota sometime today."

Marilyn stares at me for a moment. Normally I like staring into those light green eyes, but with everyone here I'm uncomfortable.

"Can I come with you? It's been a while since I've gone horseback riding," Marilyn says.

I give her a nod. Some past fantasy about cowgirls flashes through my head. "Let's go finish these interviews."

"Reid, Marilyn, wait up." LeBlanc jumps from his desk and sprints to the printer. "Backgrounds on your interviews from yesterday. Ben Cooper is clean, no priors. Brady Golding has an old charge for assault on a woman, but it was dropped before ever going to court."

"Good show. We'll call you with new names as we get them."

In the car I call the Charlottetown police and talk to the detective who was involved with Brady Golding when he was arrested three years ago and get the whole story. He was the one who said yesterday that he tried talking to Casey and Nicolle. There was a disturbance at the apartment shared by him and his girlfriend. The two of them were drunk and he got angry about some guy she talked to at work. Words were said. Actions were done. The neighbors called the police and Golding was arrested. His girlfriend refused to take the charges any further so everything was dropped. He hasn't done anything since. In fact, we knew from talking to him yesterday, the woman he assaulted was now his wife. She wasn't home and he wanted us to not let her know that he was talking to other women. He swore he was just talking and wasn't looking to hook up with anyone. I don't know whether to believe him or not.

Marilyn and I spend the next couple of hours hunting down the men on the list from Atlantic Fitness and asking them if they knew any of the women. The important part for me is to watch their faces as we show them the photographs. I watch their eyes, lips, nostrils, cheeks for any sign of change. Just a little twitch of recognition could mean something. We go through five interviews before finding someone who shows any sign of knowing them. The other men may have noticed them but it looks like they never spoke to them. They went there to work out and went home. If they checked out one of the victims asses while doing so, doesn't mean they had anything to do with their deaths.

"Do you recognize this next name? Ted Mosby, where have we heard that?"

Marilyn looks away from the road to the paper. "Check my notes. Check the last interview with Johanna Bowers's roommate and boyfriend. I think that's where it was."

I flip through her notebook. She is a lot better at taking notes than I am. Everything is dated and written in that lovely flowing handwriting that women have. "Ted Mosby, the former boyfriend of Alex who was in that picture at Blooming Point beach. He left for Fort McMurry Alberta to work as a cook a month later. Why does a guy in Alberta pay monthly memberships to a gym in PEI?"

"Did I ever tell you that I used to work in a restaurant?" Marilyn leads the way into *Giorg*, a fine Italian restaurant on Victoria Row. In a couple of weeks they will place tables halfway into the street with a black gate around them. In the summer part of the street gets blocked off to traffic so that a fountain can spray up out of a sewer grate, live music can be played in a small gazebo across the street, and the four restaurants can spill out. Marilyn did tell me that she had worked in a restaurant as a waitress. When she punched a guy for touching her ass she decided to get out and take the RCMP aptitude test.

"Is there a Ted Mosby working here?" Marilyn asks the hostess

"He's in the kitchen," She smiles with white teeth. This is one of those places visited by business types for lunch so of course she is good-looking.

"Can you ask him to come out here please?"

She takes a quick look around the room. Lunch is slowing down so there are only a handful of tables remaining and nobody waiting to be seated. She nods and heads to the back.

Most places along this street are longer than they are wide. The only windows are on the street side so they are dependent on artificial light. This one is dark with single square lights in the center of the table and wall lights spread along the sides. It is very intimate. Soft guitar music plays out of hidden speakers. There is a long oak bar along the side with a high wall of wine bottles behind it. During the afternoon, this is the restaurant you go to if you have clients to impress or pamper. In the evening, this is the place for proposing marriage or celebrating anniversaries or just spending a bundle on really good food. Hillary and I talked about coming here, but that was as far as it went.

The hostess comes back followed by a tall thin man. He was over six feet tall. He wears checked pants and a white chef's jacket with a couple of smears across the front and a black beanie cap. He takes a side towel from his shoulder and twists it around one hand.

"Can I help you?" He asks.

"You're Ted Mosby?" I ask.

He nods. "Sergeants Reid and Moore from the RCMP. Have you ever seen these women?" I hand him photographs of all three women.

"Ah, what is this about?" He has a thin nose and thin, almost hidden lips. Long fingers take hold of the photos. There are red scab marks on the back of his left hand and a band aid on the middle finger of his right.

"Can you just look at those please." Marilyn and I already talked about this before getting out of the car. We didn't want to tell him that we knew he had an association with Johanna in case he didn't say anything about it. Her picture was in between the other two.

He slowly flips through the pictures. I watch his face for any twitch or tell that he recognizes them. He spends a long time on Casey Marsh, his breathing changes a little. He passes through

228

Johanna Bowers quickly; I notice a twitch of eyebrow. At Nicolle Pereira's picture his eyes widen and nostrils flare. He says, "I know all of them."

There's a connection.

"What is this about? Johanna was killed right?" He looks at the hostess who pretends not to listen. Mosby puts his mouth close to my ear. "Do you think I have something to do with this?"

"Maybe we should talk about this outside, Mr. Mosby."

"I haven't seen Johanna since like October, November. Did Alex send you here?" The hostess looks from him to us. Customers are now paying attention.

I give a nod toward the door. "Let's go outside and talk."

"We're just asking questions Mr. Mosby. Nobody sent us here." Marilyn says as she follows us into the street. We quickly cross over and stand beside the back entrance to the Confederation Center. "Why would Alex send us?"

His eyes are as wide as they can be. He looks from Marilyn, to me, to up the street, and down at the ground. In the cool spring air, today's temperature is around thirteen degrees Celsius, sweat breaks out over his face. "I didn't do what she said." His voice is still a sharp whisper though there is nobody near us. He runs a hand back over his head pulling off the black cap and letting loose a bushy mop of blond hair.

"Why don't you tell us your side of the story then?" Hillary is much better at this than I am. She has tricks to make anyone think they are telling her something she already knows when she has no idea.

He looks around to make sure nobody is listening. I can see the hostess looking from inside the restaurant.

"I got rough one night so she called rape. She never called the cops but Johanna wanted her to. When I called Johanna a bitch, Mike and I got into it, so I thought it best to take the job in Fort McMurray and get out of here. I couldn't make it out there so I came back in January. I haven't talked to any of them. I didn't even know they knew I was back on the island."

"Come on Ted. Mike works in a kitchen just half a block up Queen and you're saying you haven't seen any of them?"

"Okay, I've talked to Mike. I didn't talk to the girls." He wipes sweat from his forehead with the side towel. He smells of garlic and onion.

"What about the other photographs? You said you knew them too."

"Oh Jesus," He pushes both hands into his hair and pulls on it. "I met them at the gym. This one, her name was umm, umm, Casey I think, she was quiet. She was hot though so I tried talking to her. She seemed cold so I didn't want to push it at all and I left her alone. I assumed she switched gyms or something cause she just stopped coming. This one I know for sure. This is Nicolle. She was a big flirt, but as soon as I asked her out she told me she had a boyfriend. Are these the other two girls? Jesus, I didn't do anything. You have to believe me." His face contorts and he looks like he is ready to cry.

"Can you tell us your whereabouts the night of April thirtieth?"

"April, that was, okay. We lost a cook two weeks ago so I've been working the late shift and then coming in in the morning to do the lunch shift. I probably clocked out at ten, ten thirty, went home to crash and then was back here for ten in the morning."

Fuck.

"You work twelve hours a day?"

"I get like two or three hours off in the afternoon between rushes."

"Thank you for your time Mr. Mosby. We may have to ask you some more questions later. It's a bit cliché, but please don't leave the island without giving me a call." I give him a nod.

We watch Ted Mosby wipe his forehead and cross the street to the restaurant. We will have to talk to his boss and make sure of the times he works but it doesn't look good. It is hard to disappear long enough from a kitchen to kidnap a woman, let alone rape, torture and kill them while still having the energy to work another twelve hour day. At least that's my theory.

Before getting in the car I slam my hand down on the roof. "He felt right Marilyn. Damn it." We both climb in.

She says, "You thinking he's pissed off about Johanna wanting Alex to call the cops that he now hates women?"

"Maybe he wanted to kill her but needed to practice a little. Then he kills Johanna, from the torture and the fact that he had her for a week he obviously enjoyed it. Now to get us away from that, he quickly did away with Nicolle and is making these threats. It would all fit –"

"If his job hours fit," she finishes my sentence. "What if he has a partner?"

"What if? I'll call McIntyre and see if we can get surveillance on this guy." I watch the front of the restaurant as I wait for the boss to answer the phone. I'm not sure how to characterize the feeling inside me. Part of me wants to believe this cook has something to do with the killings. He's the only one so far with a connection to all three women. He had some sort of motive for at least one of them. He just didn't have the time.

Marilyn and I spend the rest of the day finishing our list of men who frequented the gym. Some recognize one girl or the other, but none show any reaction to all of them. I'm tired and frustrated. We completely avoid headquarters. I don't even want to drive past it in order to stay away from the press vehicles. All those reporters asking me questions that I too want answers to makes me sweat. Do we have any suspects? Not really. We have people of interest but are they really suspects? Are we any closer to finding out who did this? No. Can we prevent the killer from taking more lives? Not at all. Right now it is his island and he is free to do whatever he wants. Do I think he will live up to his threat of killing more and painting the island red with blood? Yes I do. And there is nothing I can do about it.

"Oh no," Marilyn pulls the car up outside her house. A black truck sits in the driveway. She wanted to change before going out to the ranch. "It's Chris."

"Do you want me to come in with you?"

"No, I can handle it." She gets out of the car keeping her eyes on the front door of her house. When she is halfway up the walk

I get out and lean back against the car keeping my eyes on the same. When Marilyn is almost at the door Chris pushes out the door with a full duffle bag over his shoulder. I can only hear muffled sounds and nothing I can make out. Chris looks over his shoulder at me. Marilyn pushes him away and goes inside the house. He gets in his truck and pulls out of the driveway. Our eyes lock on each other as he pulls out. Ten minutes pass until Marilyn comes out wearing faded blue jeans, a grey knit sweater, and western boots.

"Everything okay?"

"He was picking up some of his things. Can you drive?" She places the car keys softly in my hand. Her hip nudges me away from the passenger door. She opens it quick and is inside leaving me alone and a bit confused.

We ride in silence. Marilyn sits with her head resting on the head rest, turned to the side. I drive and try to keep my mind on the road ahead. Instead I keep seeing images that I would much rather forget. Johanna Bowers' body floating above the ground, her toes pointing down. *Drip*. I remember getting a tingling from looking at her naked body and imagining it without cuts and blood and death. Nicolle Teresa Pereira lying in the grass, the wind taking her hair. *Chloe*. I can almost smell the thick stink of decaying flesh with Casey Marsh hanging amongst the smell, cuts and slashes all over her once lovely body. I imagine Him walking silently through my house, Frix in the back yard barking at the house but not knowing why. I can picture him flipping through our mail tray, and looking through the photo albums in the living room. He walked in my daughter's room, ran his hands over her things. I turn the music up and rub my eyes.

As I drive under the wrought iron K in a large circle, I think of Keanu Reeves' line in *Bill and Ted's Excellent Adventure*, `Strange things are afoot at the Circle K.'

We park along the fence and I go to collect Dakota from the far pasture. All of the other horses try to follow us out of the fence, but Marilyn closes it quickly and refastens the chain. In the stall, I start brushing her down with the curry comb in circles to get rid of most of the dirt and dust. I pass it off to Marilyn on the other side while I continue with the hard brush.

"I'm a fool, aren't I?" Marilyn combs Dakota's mane while I dig through the wood box we have across from our stall with some of our equipment in it.

"What's that?"

"Why am I so upset that he was getting some of his things? He said he was sorry but he didn't ask to come back," Her eyes droop with sadness. "Shouldn't I be happy?"

I fix the saddle pad and saddle on Dakota's back. "I don't know. Shouldn't I be missing my wife? Instead I'm thinking about a killer and hanging out with you," I fasten the girth under the horse's belly.

I finish tacking Dakota and then lead her to the outdoor arena. Marilyn puts her foot in the stirrup and lifts her other leg up and over the saddle. The leather creaks and clicks. The denim is tight over her leg muscles and curves perfectly around firm ass cheeks. She makes a kiss noise to induce the horse into a walk. After one lap she gives a little kick in the horse's flanks to push it into a trot. She holds the reigns with delicate fingertips as her body bounces with the beast's rhythm. One more squeeze and Dakota opens into a gallop, her hooves thunder on the sandy ground, her nostrils flare as the air goes in and out in loud snorts. Marilyn's red wine-colored hair flows out behind her as her body bounces on the saddle. She deftly commands the horse to make turns and do sudden stops then start again. As she goes by, dirt flying up from the horses hooves, I see Marilyn smiling with large white teeth. Everything else slips away. I hang off the white fence around the arena and watch her for a while. There's no death here.

Chapter 22

Ben turns his KIA Sorrento off of Queen Street and onto Kent. He pushes the brake to stop for an elderly lady crossing the street without looking down the one-way where cars come from. Parked in front of the Community Policing office is a city squad car and an RCMP cruiser. In the basement of the building is his fitness club. Traffic starts again and Ben moves on. He looks over at the police officers standing on the sidewalk talking. Their eyes move around to look at everyone walking by and the group of smokers outside the *Tim Horton's*. They don't know who they are looking for. They know where Casey Marsh and Nicolle Theresa Pereira came from.

They know. *Reid.*

Ben checks his side mirror. He changes lanes. He goes through the intersection of Kent and University, passes *Lot 30*, and signals to turn left at Prince Street. His eyes flip to the rear view mirror. *Maritime Electric* is on his right. *Hunter's Ale House* is across the street on the left side of Kent. On the right side is the nightclub *Velvet Underground*. Outside there was where he found Rachel Howe, Sierra West, and two others. All of the parking spots around the area are taken as the early evening crowd looking for steaks mixes at Hunter's with the evening crowd wanting drinks starting to roll in. As soon as the light goes green his foot pushes down on the gas pedal. The dark grey SUV moves on without anyone around knowing what is amongst them.

Pathetic.

Reid.

He licks his lips. His hand rubs his neck muscles on the right side until they hurt. Nobody on the sidewalks turn his way. They will pay attention to his actions more than to him.

The day after Reid and Moore came to see him and he sent the email to that Catherine Arsenault lady at CBC he sat himself in a coffee shop. He sat at a small table with a cup of coffee, breakfast burrito, and a *John Grisham* novel that he had no intention of reading. He listened. The topic of the day yesterday was the Red Island Killer and how he was going to rain blood on the island. People were scared. People were mesmerized. This morning the topic was when will the Red Island Killer take his next victim? He heard doors and windows being locked all across the island. If only they knew who sat amongst them. He was invisible to them, but they were all waiting to see what he was going to do next. He had them. It was his world. His next move would be all the talk around the corner store coffee urns.

They didn't know anything. Reid was the bad one. He was the one making Ben go after more. Nicolle wouldn't have been dead if the police did their jobs right. Reid. He wouldn't have had to put an island wide threat out there if Reid hadn't knocked on his door. His hunger had subsided. He was happy with what he had done. He could have gone months without needing to feel the heat again. Reid has him on fire. He's waited just over a week and he's hungry again.

He tried working the past week. He went to Halifax and took pictures at the *East Coast Hair Show*. He drove around the island trying to calm himself taking spring pictures of animals coming out of hiding and plant life starting to bloom. All he could do was picture what things would be like dead. At least three of the hair models had tattoos on their shoulders. Oh he was hungry. He had to make a statement. He had to show them it was his world.

Reid.

Two blocks up ahead he can see her standing on the corner. She has on black pants and a baggy dark jacket with a hood pulled up. She leans back on one leg with the other foot pointing up in the air, the foot balancing on a three inch heel. He can see the red ember of her cigarette. *Pathetic.* She holds a bag over her shoulder. Ben pulls the car next to the curb. He keeps his eyes on her as she jogs across the street. She gets in the passenger side, pushes her bag down at her feet, and pulls her hood down. Fingers with white tipped acrylic nails comb through her fair-hair letting waves flow out over her shoulders.

She turns to Ben and says, "Hi." She smiles with big teeth. Her nose seems to have a ball at the end and her chin comes to a point. Her lips are painted bright red. Blue eyes are lined in black with her eyelids dark and smokey. Underneath the jacket, which she zips down before fastening her seatbelt, is a white tank-top. A multi-green rock hangs from a leather strap around her neck. She smells of citrus and strawberry.

The SUV pulls away from the curb.

Heather Blais, maiden name Colicchio, twenty-five year old mother of twin girls, age four. She works a couple evenings and most weekends at *Giorg Restaurant.* Her husband drives eighteen wheelers all across the Maritimes and Quebec. He is gone for a few nights a week. Heather is young. She got pregnant, they got married, and she still has things she wants to do. When her husband is away she likes to play. After having the twins she got herself on the treadmill and got herself back into shape. She likes to smile and flirt and push things as far as she can go. The one thing she makes sure of is to tell her lovers that it is only physical. That way she can keep it away from her husband. She's safe that way.

"So where are we going?" She folded her hands in her lap.

Her husband left last night. Ben sat in his Sorrento down the block watching him leave.

Her husband grabbed her by the back of her head and kissed her full on the mouth. There were tongues and words of love. Ben waited forty minutes before calling her.

"Hey, it's Teddy," that's how she knew him, "I was wondering if you thought about me taking pictures of your daughters? I'd like to see you tomorrow, if you're free."

They met in the morning and Ben took pictures of them playing. He made sure to take pictures of Heather and flirt with her telling her she was beautiful and sexy. *Drip.* She agreed to meet up later. She told her Mom that she was going out with the girls and would be back late, then walked up the street so nobody would see who was picking her up. Nobody knew who Teddy was. She didn't even know who he was.

"Out by Blooming Point. My family has a cabin there. I thought I could make dinner." He keeps his eyes on the road ahead, but gives a smile.

She's like Reid. She doesn't have a clue. *Drip*.

She starts talking about her day. Ben doesn't listen. His mind is off on a run through of everything he has to think out. This one is going to make a mark. This one will put Reid in his place.

They pass a large house on the left with a two car garage and giant yard of grass circling the house. In the fading light of day they can see a wooden swing-set in the back and with a clothes line from it to the house. The fields with patchwork forest changes to high walls of trees on either side. Down further on the right is 3231 Blooming Point Road. Ben turns left off of the main highway onto a gravel road that suddenly cuts into the forest wall of pines and naked poplars and birch. The Sorrento teeters in and out of old potholes. Heather makes a little sound of surprise. Trees line both sides of the road like a giant fence. The sun has gone down. It is even darker in the tunnel. The headlights cut through the dark. They turn right. Here a bunch of small roads go off in different directions leading to cottages along the bay. No cars are around the buildings, no lights are on. They can see the vast open space of dark that is the bay. Lights from across the bay dance off the calm water. He pulls up to a white mobile home. It has a wooden deck along the length of it, flower boxes outside the windows, a big carved sign above the door saying, WELCOME. Heather comments on how sweet it looks.

"This is great," she says outside of the SUV. "I guess nobody will see us here."

"Just like you asked. Nobody will be in these cottages for a couple weeks." Ben walks up beside her and a little to the side. He can smell her. He can taste her in the back of his throat. "I have a surprise for you."

"Oh," Heather starts to turn. Then there is blackness.

~ * ~

"Beer Reid?"

Marilyn's brother pulls a bottle of Keith's from a cooler now mostly water instead of ice. I shouldn't, considering I have to drive back to Charlottetown from Rustico, about twenty-six kilometers away, but I take it and twist the top off. I've had too many beers already. The golden nectar cools my throat. Little spirals spin inside each temple. My head feels heavy on my neck.

Her parent's house is a two-story farm house built over one hundred years ago. The open concept dining room and kitchen, like a lot of old island homes, is the largest area in the house. In the Maritimes the kitchen table is where the family and friends meet. The east coast is known for having kitchen parties with fiddle players and a lot of food. The fireplace, at the center of the room, has a small fire inside. The large wood table where the family ate most of their meals together is scattered with plates and bowls almost empty of a variety of potato salad, coleslaw, broccoli salad, rolls, melted butter and cold lobster cooked earlier. The walls are eggshell with natural wood baseboards and trim. Marilyn's brother brought daisies for the table. Her mother has potted plants and ivy all around the kitchen and house. It's a pleasant house. It's a place that has family and friends around and it's a place you know a serial killer would never come from.

I lean against the door frame leading to a small sun room. All of MCU is here. McIntyre, along with his wife, had his fill of lobster and salads then left. He needs sleep in order to deal with his daily meeting with the CO. LeBlanc is the only one left. He sits at the table dipping more lobster into the melted butter. I barely ate. I'm from the west. I don't get the lobster thing. To me it is an indulgence for special occasions, not an everyday thing.

Trying to be subtle, not sure if it's working, I keep my eyes on Marilyn. Maybe it's the alcohol, but I enjoy looking at the curves of her legs and buttocks.

After seeing Dakota last week, Marilyn and I drove back to Charlottetown. We went to her place and talked over coffee, French fries, gravy, and a ten piece from KFC. Nothing went on. We talked about our childhoods and I told her all about my relationships from Debbie Weeks chasing me around the trailer park when I was five up to Hillary and how we met. Marilyn told me about her life and what lead her to an abusive guy like Chris. The night ended with long minutes of us looking at each other and not saying a word. Since then we have barely talked about anything besides work. Hillary called the next day.

She and Leigh tell me every day that they want to come home. "We could stay in a hotel or maybe you could get a guard on the house."

"Hill, it's not safe."

"He hasn't called you again."

"No, but it still isn't safe. He was in our house, Hill. It's just better for you to stay there for now. We're working as hard as we can."

Hillary sighed and got quiet for a while. She quickly said she had to go to sleep and ended the call.

Perhaps that's something I should do.

"I should get going," I say to no one in particular. A couple of eyes turn my way. LeBlanc, and Marilyn's brother are busy debating about hockey teams. Marilyn and her mom look at me. "Sandra, thank you so much. The food was great."

"I'm sorry your family couldn't come," Sandra Moore gives me a hug and kisses my cheek. I take a whiff of her short red-wine colored hair, the same as her daughters. "Are you sure you want to drive home, honey?"

"Yeah I'm fine." I put the beer down. I smile at the ladies and give them a nod. I walk outside and stand looking at the ocean over the roof of my car. Here on the island you're always ten minutes from the coast. The water is grey, almost black. There is no moon to glow off of it; the stars don't even reflect back. A small sailing boat sits out there, almost motionless, barely visible in the dark. I wonder if this killer ever takes the time to stare out at the water.

"Reid." Marilyn walks down the rock path to the driveway. She wears heeled boots and tight blue jeans over her long legs. "Are you sure you can drive?"

I stare at her for a moment and can't say a word. She has make-up on around her eyes and lips. Her hair is loose and flows in waves and curls around her face and onto her shoulders. A low cut blouse draws my eyes down to her cleavage. I blink and look up. Her light green eyes look deep into mine. She has a slight playful smile to her lips.

"I'm fine," I say.

"My parents have a couple spare rooms. I'm spending the night."

I have an instant image of me trying to sneak around the house in my underwear unsure if I should or not. "I can't, really. I don't think it would be a great idea."

"I'm not going to molest you Reid."

It's not you I'm worried about, I think but don't say. I can smell her perfume. My groin tingles. I can picture myself kissing her neck. My hands unbuttoning her blouse. Her breasts falling out. "Really, I should go. I'll see you in the morning." I get in my car, turn the engine over, and back out.

I'm a married man. I have a lovely wife who loves me and is gorgeous and sexual. We have a daughter. I get onto highway six and cross through *Oyster Bed Bridge*. Hillary was the woman I wanted to marry. Why the hell can't I be happy with what I have? Something in me wants something else. Something in me isn't happy I guess. It should be. I made the vows.

There's a woman running. She's running through the woods. Trees slice at her naked body.

There's a light. It's chasing her. It's going to get her.

She has to run. She can't.

Chloe.

A horn blares.

My eyes flash open. I pull the steering wheel to the right. The horn goes off again. A truck goes past me as I pull out of its lane. I swear I can see the driver's face. He has a beard and glasses and a foul mouth. I blink fast. My arms feel like rubber.

I straighten the car out and for a moment drop my foot from the gas pedal.

The sleep is gone. I rub my eyes and try to laugh. *Fuck, I almost died.* My insides twist around. I open the window and let the cold air in on my face. I need to stay awake. My life isn't the only one to be concerned with. Something is out there.

~ * ~

A moan escapes from somewhere inside Heather. She can taste blood. Pain cracks out from a central point like how a windshield breaks from a rock strike. Her tongue touches the side of her mouth. She can feel sharp edges of where there had been teeth. The inside of her head spins round and round. Her eyes go wide. Stars are spinning in a wild spiral. Her eyes close tight again. She doesn't know where she is. For a second she doesn't know who she is. Then it all comes back. *Teddy. Blooming Point. Surprise.* The last thing she remembered was seeing movement out of the corner of her eye. He was moving. It was a fist.

He punched her.

What did she walk into? Panic rises inside her chest with a red heat. She starts to count in her head. *One, two.* She can't let the panic overtake her. If she lets it win and pulls her soul into that state of no wits or conscious thought she'll never see her daughters again. *Three, four.* The burn sticks in her chest. It reaches out and starts to circle her heart. She has to think. She can't stay here. She can't let this happen. *Five.*

Tap.

Heather does a quick inventory of what she knows. Smells. The only scent she can smell for certain is the brininess of her own blood fresh in her nostrils. Sight. She struggles to push her eyes open. They go wide. *Tap.* Pain emitting from behind them and through her skull. There isn't much light. She's laying on her front on a hardwood floor at the edge of a rug – the right side of her face is down. There is a table leg in front of her, a coffee table. Sounds. Her heart is pounding so loud someone has to hear it. A clock is ticking. There's a humming noise that sounds like a refrigerator running. There's a tapping noise. *Tap.* Something on the hardwood floor. *Tap.* What is that noise? She knows it from somewhere. Feel. Pain. She has a massive headache radiating out from the left side of her face. Her cheekbone feels like it must be broken. She can feel wetness. Her pants and top are wet, probably from where she hit the ground. She feels cold. *Tap.* She isn't wearing her jacket any more. She didn't take that off. *Tap.* Her feet are cold. She's not wearing her shoes or socks.

A shoe. The tapping sound is a shoe on the hardwood floor like someone keeping beat to a really slow song. Or they are waiting for something.

Heather moves her hand.

"Oh, you're up." The voice is very familiar. *Teddy.* There's the creek of springs in a chair being let free to return to a dormant state. The tapping has stopped. *Footsteps.*

Heather feels something solid slide under her armpit. The shoed foot lifts her up and turns her over to her back. The pain flares. Her eyes stare up at the nice photographer staring back down at her. His face is calm. His lips are not a smile, but they go up slightly at the ends. A red snake comes out and licks them.

He lets out a loud breath. "I apologize for hitting you. It was the only way I could think of to shut you up."

She bites her lip. She tries to look around him to see, where she is. Heather went through women's self-defense. She would need to know details if she got out. There are pictures on the walls, furniture, little things on ledges. There isn't enough light to get details and her eyes can't focus. He bends over then straightens again. A bright flash lights the room and temporarily blinds her. A camera flash. He took her picture. The word, "why," slips from her lips before she can stop it.

"Why?" Teddy puts something aside and stands over her. His fists are clenched. One holds something. "Because this is my world and I want to. Your kids ever say that? Because I want to? It's their world and that is a good enough reason for them." He moves his hand. Light from behind him shines off of something.

"You're number four. Reid stopped the other one at four. He won't do it this time. This is my world."

It's a knife.

Teddy kneels down over her body. Heather tightens. Her eyes stare at the large knife in his hand. It has a wooden handle and a blade made for hunting. Made for gutting. He points it down toward her stomach. The tip touches her skin. Her stomach tightens. She has good abs, but there is still a little left from the two babies. He flicks the knife. She feels the small cut at her navel then feels her tank-top tighten and then loosen completely. The ripping sound echo's through the room. The knife shines up as it continues its cut through her top. Her small breasts feel the cold air. His eyes change to slits as he stares at her white flesh. He runs the flat of the cold blade down over her left nipple. In one move he rolls her onto her front again and pulls the top off her shoulders. Heather closes her eyes. She feels a hand on the back of her neck and another on her buttocks. The one down there pushes the handle of the knife between her cheeks. The tip of the blade touches the small of her back.

Help me.

Something wet touches the spot where she has a rosary tattooed behind her shoulder. Teeth graze her skin. He brings his tongue down again and licks the spot. Her body shakes.

The knife slices below her tattoo cutting a red line three inches long. Heather screams. Her back arches. Why? He spins her onto her back. His hand pushes down on her shoulder so that the cut presses against the hardwood floor. Heather screams again. The pain shoots down through her arm and down her body. His other hand pulls down her pants. The knife slices into her leg with small accidental cuts. Sticky heat trickles around her leg. Her leg moves up. His fist punches down into her inner thigh. The muscle goes numb. Her pants tie up her legs. He pulls the thong she wore especially for him down. She feels the cold of steel against her crotch.

Oh God, he's going to stab me inside.

Heather closes her eyes. She pictures her daughters playing in the sandbox. She pictures them holding her fingers. She imagines their first birthday and how they got chocolate cake from head to toe. Somehow one of them got it on the ceiling.

He didn't stab her inside. She had no choice but to let him do what he wanted. He was in her. She tried to force her mind to go to its own place to take her away from what was happening. The pain wouldn't let her. As he thrust he pushed down on her shoulder and shot fire through her body. She felt her blood going out of her.

"I thought you'd be better," Teddy says after finishing.

He sits at Heather's feet. She keeps her eyes closed and tries to put herself somewhere else. She doesn't know how much time has passed. She doesn't know what day it is.

"All that experience you'd think you would put something into it." He lets out a little laugh. "You're pathetic." *Pathetic.*

The tip of the blade runs up the bottom of her foot slicing the pad from the heel to the ball. Her leg curls in. She screams. The inside of her throat is raw. She's going to die.

"Your husband should have talked to my Grandpa. He's lost control of you. My Grandpa once said that women are like horses. You have to ride them often or they'll think they can do whatever they want."

He takes her pants completely off. He takes a whiff of the crotch and then tosses it aside. His hands grab her ankles and pull her toward him. Heather feels slivers dig into her backside. "Once I'm done. We'll tie you up and have real fun." He pushes himself inside her again. This time she can't put her mind somewhere else. She is going to die.

Her babies. She thinks about her babies.

Heather opens her eyes. She can feel his hands. One holds her waist, one holds an arm down. She wants nothing more than to pull away from them. She doesn't want him to touch her. She can't feel the knife in his hand any more. She can get him. She can claw his eyes out. She has to get free. On a forward thrust. *One. Two.*

The fingers on her free hand form into a claw. She drives it up. The acrylic nails dig into his skin above and around the eyes. *Missed.*

He stops.

She drags her nails down. There's blood and soft tissue. A nail breaks off. He pushes back off of her. He lets out a scream of anger. Heather pulls both legs to her chest. She kicks out. One foot hits his stomach. The other hits his still hard groin. He stumbles back. Heather rolls onto her front and pushes herself up. She hears a crash and things falling, a call of pain, but doesn't look back.

She stumbles forward. Her knee connects with something hard. Her hands reach out. She doesn't care about clothes or her bleeding shoulder or the sticky wet on her leg or the pain with every step her foot makes. She has to get out. Her hands find something. A door handle.

She's outside. The cold air shocks her body. She's awake now. It is dark now. The stars are out. *What time is it?* There are noises behind her. Don't look back. Her feet touch the deck. There are stars. She leaves bloodied footsteps on gravel. She almost falls as a rock digs into the cut. She can hear the ocean thundering against the shore. The moon lights little. She knows the bay is to her right. The paved road is down a long gravel road to her left. Trees are all around. She lunges forward for the trees. Her knee touches down in a ditch.

"Heather," the yell comes from inside the house.

She scrambles up and into the woods. Her hands get cut by rock and thorns. A branch slaps her face and sends her back a step. She raises her arms to block her face. Her shoulder calls out in pain. Pine branches scrape at her bare body. Her legs, arms, stomach, breasts, everything gets slapped with bare branches. She steps on something solid with her cut foot and almost falls. She wants to scream out. Evening dew soaks her feet and lower legs. Her body starts to shiver.

There's a light behind her. It moves right and left. It cuts into the branches. The trees pull in around her as they take back their space. She lands on her hands and knees, scrambles a few feet, and gets up. He's coming. She has to keep moving. She has to find a way out. She can't die this way. *Her babies.* She has to stay alive for her babies.

"Heather."

Chapter 23

"Caesar? Manuel? Pierre? Have I asked about that one before?" Eckhart pushes his glasses up with the back of his hand.

Marilyn and I have continued with interviews all week and working on the Ted Mosby angle. We get missing person calls every day and have to look into all of them right away. All of them so far have turned up. This morning we were settling into the office when we got a call from Stratford RCMP about a woman's body found by her husband.

I shake my head at Eckhart. "You're never going to figure it out."

"You can't have a name that odd that nobody can guess it. Elvis? Willow?"

"I would love to be called Elvis." My head slowly moves from side to side to get different views of the object of our attention.

In the center of the garage a woman hangs from the rafters by her wrists. She doesn't move. There is no wind in here. This woman is older than the previous three. She is in her forties. Her age shows around her eyes and on her smile lines. Her short brown hair, professionally coiffed, has lines of grey. She has white tipped finger and toe nails. She has cuts up her legs, over her torso, and on her arms. I count about thirteen stab wounds and maybe a couple of lacerations. Her face is clear of cuts and clean except for a few specks of crimson. Her bare breasts hang a little. There are no cuts there. *Drip*. Blood drips from her bare feet into a puddle on the concrete floor.

The garage is organized. One side wall has tools on a peg board and a set of small boxes on a table holding nails, screws, and other tidbits. The other side wall has homemade shelves; each holding sporting equipment like skis, cricket mallets and wickets, baseball bats, and tennis rackets. The top one has a box showing an artificial Christmas tree on the side and a few other boxes with Xmas written in black marker. There is a white refrigerator beside the door leading into the house. There are four bikes hanging off the back wall. I have rarely seen a clean garage. My aunt's was so full of junk that everyone in the car beside the driver had to get out before pulling the car in. This one is a garage owned by orderly people.

"Hey, I guess I should apologize for when I blew up. We haven't had much interaction since then. I'm sorry."

"Don't worry about it, Hector. No? This guy's got everyone working extra hours. And he's threatening you so –"

"Actually he never threatened me. He just called. And he was in my house." I watch my booty covered feet step on the path already checked out by Eckhart and Ashley. I look up at the body. *Chloe.* Her name is Wendy Parker, married to Charlie Parker. He found her. I don't even want to think about what that must have been like.

Last night Hillary and I talked for two hours on the phone just about what Ontario is like in the spring and the adventures Leigh has been having.

This killer has talked about my family. Just thinking about what Mr. Parker is going through – I want to kill him.

"Reid, look at this."

I blink and look away from the body. Eckhart stares at me from behind the woman. She was good-looking. She had muscle tone, in some places she looks like she had excess skin, but still good. She wasn't over weight. She didn't seem to have any scars. I let my eyes ride around her as I step up to Eckhart. It's what is not there that is the thing he wants to show me.

Eckhart points his gloved finger. "These look like hesitation marks here and here. And look at this."

"She doesn't have a tattoo. This isn't right. This whole thing isn't right. As soon as the doc gets here I need you guys to estimate a time of death. I'll be outside."

As I walk out of the house into the mid-morning air, I pull off the hood of the bunny suit. It is our first hot day of spring with temperatures well above normal. Weather on PEI is a moody beast. Summers take their sweet time getting here, and when they do the heat can be intense with weeklong heat-waves. Labor Day weekend in September announces the end of summer, and the end of tourist season and weather. The Tuesday after the weekend is usually cold and autumn starts instantly. The winters are not as cold as in some other parts of Canada but the wind is always wet. It dampens through your *Thinsulate* jackets and layers of clothes making you feel colder than you really should. Spring arrives with a rollercoaster of cold and warm and rain. The last couple of days were cold. Today is hot enough for no jacket, so I left mine in the car. I can feel the sweat caking to my shirt under the thin bunny suit.

"What's it look like?" Marilyn stands outside the side door waiting in the sun. It shines off of her hair.

"Something's off." I stop beside her and shove my hands deep in my pockets. I look down the driveway where a man sits in the back seat of one of the cars at the end of the driveway. His feet are on the ground. His elbows sit on his knees, head in his hands.

The garage is attached to a nice house on a nice residential street in the town of Stratford across the Hillsborough River from Charlottetown. You take the *TransCanada Highway* over the Hillsborough River with *Tim Horton's* and *Wendy's* on the Charlottetown side and a store with a *McDonald's* on the other. The highway continues on until reaching Wood Islands and the Ferry across to Caribou, Nova Scotia. It is also the main strip in the town with all the basics: a grocery store, *Home Hardware*, liquor store, and a couple of quick restaurants. Stratford, - a town of beauty and opportunity – is Prince Edward Island's fastest growing community. It has a long history dating back to the settlement of the Acadians. Today it grows as an extension of the

251

capital city while still holding its own identity. New apartment buildings, condominiums, and housing units are always going up. The majority of the people living there are middle class, white collars living in the bigger fancier houses near the water.

The only reasons I have ever had to go to Stratford were to go to the *½ Price Steak* store, a golf course for a charity game last summer, and the *Soccer Complex* where Leigh plays indoor soccer during the winter.

"What do you mean something's off?" Marilyn unbuttons her jacked.

A blue Pontiac Grand Am sits in the driveway in front of the garage. Eckhart's truck is behind it. The street is lined with RCMP patrol cars. Officers go door to door asking if anyone heard anything, saw anything, knew anything. The neighbors collect behind the cars trying to see what is going on. Other officers are trying to keep the media at a distance. I can make out Catherine Arsenault and her camera guy in the crowd of reporters. For the past week the only big news they've had to report is that the RCMP still had no apparent leads and was seemingly no closer to arresting a suspect than they were the day before. They want more. The *jackals* are hungry. McIntyre is walking slowly toward them to feed the gulls a fish.

I lean in to Marilyn. She has diamond studs in her earlobes. Her hair is pulled back exposing her long neck. My eyes trace the line of her white skin until it disappears in her collar. "Something just is. A feeling. I don't think our boy," I stop myself. My words get stuck deep in my throat.

"You don't think this is the same killer? It's not contagious, Reid. You're saying that murder has become a fad."

"She didn't have a tattoo."

"Maybe he ran out of tattooed beauties. She's a lot older too. Don't forget he said he was going to cover the island in blood. Maybe he grabbed the first woman he could find."

"Look at where we are," even I am surprised by the excitement in my voice. "The first two were out in an abandoned summer house and the middle of the bush. The third was in a historical site which nobody lives around. This is a garage on a full street of houses and witnesses. This isn't his thing."

"Well, he didn't make his threat until we started the Atlantic Fitness interviews so maybe we're closing in on him. Maybe he had to break his usual routine. Let's go talk to the husband."

He wears jeans and a white t-shirt with blood smeared down the front. A brown suede jacket hangs off his shoulders as they slump forward. He has a bit of a pot belly threatening to fall over his belt. His hair is thin and grey. He looks tired like he has been up for days straight. He doesn't look up until we stop in front of him. His eyes are red, cheeks puffy. He looks at us like a puppy dog unsure of what is happening.

"Mr. Parker, I'm Sgt. Reid, this is Sgt. Moore." I pause but he doesn't make any move to speak or even acknowledge that he understands what I have said. "You were the one that found your wife?"

He squeezes his eyelids together then opens them again with a look of surprise. They droop down again. He pulls in a jagged breath. "Yes. I should have been here."

"Sir?"

"Yesterday I went to Moncton. My buddy, he is getting married in, um, a month, so we had his bachelor party last night. We went to a strip club. Oh Jesus." He runs a hand back through his hair. PEI does not have any strip clubs. It has a church on almost every corner so I guess there isn't any room for that type of depravity. Luckily just over the thirteen kilometer long Confederation Bridge straddling the Northumberland Strait to New Brunswick and two hour drive to Moncton you can join the ranks of the immoral, as some see it.

"When did you last see your wife?"

"Wendy. I saw her yesterday at three. I kissed her and said I would see her today. I left New Brunswick first thing this morning to surprise her." I ask him to tell us what happened when he got home. "I pulled in the driveway and pushed the remote to open the garage. She was hanging there. I jumped out of the car and ran to her. I tried to lift her. I tried to wake her. Then I called the police and an ambulance."

"Your hands are clean."

He opens up his hands palm up and stares down at them. He looks up at me. "What?"

"Your hands are clean," I repeat. "You said you went to her body and tried to lift her. Your shirt is covered in blood, but your hands are clean."

"I washed them. I couldn't look at her blood on my hands."

"Did you touch anything else?"

"No, why? This killer, this Red Island Killer guy killed my wife. Why are you asking me these questions? Shouldn't you ask me something about people watching us or people mad at us or something?"

My eyebrows go up. I keep staring down at him. I want him to feel uncomfortable. "Well, has somebody been watching you?"

"Yeah, I don't –" He gets to his feet and takes a step away. "I really don't like the way you're talking to me. I'm a management consultant. I know about tone of voice. I teach people about tone of voice and I don't like yours."

Marilyn puts her hand on my lower back signaling me she is taking over. She takes a step in front of me. "Do you think anyone you've worked with may have had a grudge against you?"

Charlie Parker keeps looking at me for a few long seconds. His gaze moves to my partner. "No, nobody has anything against me."

"What about your wife? Did anyone have a grudge against her?"

"I thought this was that serial killer. That's how he does it right? Hanging from something? All cut up? My God, did you see her?" He puts a hand over his face again. He falls back against the car as if he can't stand to be on his own two legs without some support.

I look away from this scene and down toward the reporters. They snap pictures of nothing hoping to have something they can use. Video cameras keep panning everywhere. McIntyre talks to the line briefly, probably something like we have no comment at this time and we will make a statement when we do, blah, blah, and turns towards us and starts walking. He is dressed in his uniform all freshly pressed. The past couple of days he has needed his official uniform a lot.

"We don't know who the killer is," Marilyn continues. "We have to go down every avenue to see what we can find. Does anyone have a grudge against you? Have you received any threats?"

"You asked that already. No."

I walk away from the two of them in McIntyre's direction. I can feel Parker's eyes on me. He wants to know where I'm going and why I'm not more interested in what he has to say. I don't really give a damn. Everything is wrong about this murder. No tattoo, no cuts to her face, in suburbia, she's hanging by her wrists and not her neck, her left breast is still completely attached. This woman was stabbed, yes, multiple times, but her body still doesn't show the brutality of the others. If our killer is going to give us another body so soon he is going to make it a brutal one. He feels he has to make a point.

"Give this one to Dispirito or LeBlanc," I say to McIntyre without any salutation. His brow furrows and mouth drops. I lower my voice and turn my back to the reporters just in case. "Our guy didn't do this. The signatures aren't there."

"Who?"

"I'd check into their married life. Maybe he was sick of his wife so he saw an opportunity to get rid of her and blame it on somebody else. I don't know. My guy didn't do this. I'm going back to the office."

"What? You can't just leave. Arsenault will follow you, you know."

I make a scrunched face in her direction. "Either she follows me back to Headquarters or I waste all day here on something most likely not connected." My phone calls out to be answered. I push the button, say my name, and listen.

"It's Kyle," Longfellow, "we just got a call about a woman at QEH who was assaulted last night."

I roll my eyes. "Look, I'm busy with three murders. Get someone else to go talk to her."

255

"Reid, it happened out at Blooming Point."

I turn my head and yell for Marilyn.

~ * ~

We each squirt a little hand sanitizer in our palms as we walk through the sliding door into the emergency room. I flash my badge at the first nurse we see. She ignores me. The second one stops so that I can announce who we are and that we are looking for a woman brought in from the Blooming Point area. Other police should be with her. She tells us to give her a few minutes and walks off. Half of the seats in the waiting room have someone sitting in them with different stages of injuries or sickness. There is a television attached to the wall in the corner over a drink and snack machine and water fountain. The television show *Saved by the Bell* plays on the screen.

"You ever watch that show?" I nod my head towards the corner.

Marilyn is absently checking her fingernails. She looks up at the television then puts her attention back to the nails. "Of course I have. Who hasn't?"

"Hillary never saw any of them until like two years ago. I was sick and some kids channel was having a marathon so I made her sit with me and watch them all."

"Aren't you a bit old for watching that show? When did it come out?"

"89," I look behind us. The ER security guard stands by his desk talking to a nurse. I turn back to Marilyn. She stares down at me with a quizzical expression. "What? We were curious what the actors were doing all these years after. *Saved by the Bell* was an important part in television history. What?"

"Nothing." She looks away from me and puts her light green eyes back on the television.

I check my watch. What the hell is taking so long? "So were you a Zack lover or Slater?"

"Slater. I love my jocks," she replies.

"Oh come on, Zack was the man. Here comes Longfellow." I give him an upward head nod. "What's going on? Where is she?"

"This way." He turns on his heel and leads us back the way he came. One hand waggles his black notebook at his side while the other hangs on to his tie. "Sarah Burry came home after driving her kids to school at nine-thirty, they slept in and missed the bus, and found a woman curled up in the fetal position on her deck outside her front door, naked and bleeding. EMT's and RCMP were called. She had hypothermia as well as all the cuts. She looks like she had the crap beaten out of her. She hasn't said much though. We know her name is Heather. That's it." He enters a private room. "Heather," his voice becomes soft and soothing instantly, "these are the other officers I said would be coming to talk to you."

The woman lies on her side on a hospital bed with her head up on two pillows. She is completely covered by a blue blanket pulled up to her neck, but we can tell her knees are pulled up to her chest. Her arms are probably wrapped around them. Her hair hangs down over her shoulder and onto her face. The soft brown does little to hide what is underneath. She looks like the left side of it exploded in a monstrous purple zit. Purple isn't the right color. I count a dozen shades of purple from blue through black from the tip of her mouth to her temple. The left eye is swollen and dark. Dry blood has collected at the end of her nostril. She moves her head a little to get a look at us. The right eye is blue, the left is stained red and pink. Dark streaks of mascara mark her cheeks. I can see a dry leaf in the strands of her hair along with a few pine needles hiding in there. The metallic smell of blood is in the air. I fight back the urge to step forward, remove the leaf from her hair, and caress the fair-haired woman telling her it will all be okay.

The doctor stands at the side table typing into her tablet. She looks up. Her chestnut hair tied back bounces from her shoulder to her back. She wears pale green hospital scrubs with a long white coat overtop. Her stethoscope rides the back of her neck from shoulder to shoulder. She puts the computer pad against her chest and holds it with both arms. "She may not wish to talk. All she's told us so far was her first name. Do you want to talk to the police officers Heather?"

There is no movement or sign from the patient. She continues staring at us.

The doctor continues, "I've given her a mild sedative so she may get sleepy. Excuse me."

I look at Marilyn and give her a wink. I give Longfellow a twist of my head toward the door. We both walk out to the hallway giving Marilyn a chance to talk to the young woman and gain her trust without any men around. I quickly catch up to the doctor. "Can I ask you some questions, Doc?"

She turns quickly and I almost run into her. I'm close enough to tell her left eye is hazel and her right is brown. She has freckles on her nose.

"I have a lot of people to see so make it quick," she says.

"Right, did you get a last name for Heather?"

"Not yet. I'm hoping the sedative will help her relax and maybe she'll be freer to talk."

"Can you tell me what injuries she has?"

She stares at me for a second or two. Her eyes search my face for something. "She has facial fractures on her left side. There is a large laceration on the back of her shoulder below a tattoo." Oh yes. "Small lacerations to her back, inner thigh, and a long cut straight up the bottom of her foot. Multiple small cuts, contusions, and bruises. There are also signs of rape trauma. I don't know what happened to this young woman, but she went through hell. Is that enough for you, Constable?"

"It's Sergeant Reid, you are?"

"Doctor Brandi Mooney."

"Brandi with an I or Y?" I give her a smile.

"I, is it really important?"

I look back at Longfellow he cocks his head to the side and lifts his shoulders. I turn back to the doctor. "Did I do something to piss you off? Women are being harmed and we're just trying to help."

She adjusts the tablet putting it in one hand. The other hand goes to her hip and she cocks it out to the side. She probably weighs a buck thirty, *130 pounds in my father's language*. She has a serious look to her face. People around here probably either think of her as a wonderful person and doctor or that she's a bitch.

"As long as she's in my care I'm responsible for her well-being," she says. "She's been through a lot and needs to rest before being barraged with questions making her relive the whole trauma over again."

"There's a killer out there taking young women and torturing them then killing them." I stop talking as a man and woman walk past. The man does not look good. When they go into a room I get close to the doctor and whisper, "do you have a tattoo on the back of your shoulder?"

"No."

"Then at least you're safe."

I turn away and put my hand on Longfellow's arm to get him to do the same. Before going back to the room I tell him to head back to headquarters. I knock on the room door with two quick raps before popping my head in. Marilyn motions for me to come in. She now sits in a chair in front of Heather.

"Heather," her voice is soft to, "this is my partner. He doesn't let anyone know his first name."

Her lips move. The top lip is swollen. It takes her a few tries to get out the word, "why?" A tear falls from her swollen eye, travels down her nose a little and then falls to the pillow beneath her head.

I slowly step behind Marilyn and put my hands behind my back. "I'm not a fan of it," I say

"Reid, this is Heather Blais. She works at Giorg."

Mosby.

Heather pushes herself up on one arm. The good eye is wide. The other strains to open. Her lips quiver. "Reid? Reid. You stopped him at four. I'm number four. You stopped him at four." She raises her voice until it reaches a violent scream. Her body shakes. Marilyn reaches out for her. Heather's arms swing back

259

at her. She opens her mouth and yells out, "Reid stopped him at four."

I take a step back. Marilyn purses her lips and makes the same sounds Hillary used to make to quiet Leigh. A nurse and Doctor Mooney come through the door. The doctor pushes me back. "What the hell did you do?"

"I didn't do-"

"Reid, wait outside." Marilyn points to the door. "Go."

I stumble out into the hallway. I'm certain there is a look on my face that says, *What did I do?*

In ten minutes the nurse and doctor come out. I'm told to go wait in the waiting room down the hall until I am needed. I don't like waiting rooms, I get impatient, I get fidgety. Since the latest flu outbreak, all magazines were removed from the waiting room to try and stop the spread of germs. Nothing to read. The security guard has complete and total control so nobody has much say of what channel is on the television. It is still a family network. *Saved by the Bell* has been replaced by *The Fresh Prince of Bel Air*. I sit and watch Will and Carlton compete over the same girl to ask to their Halloween party. After that I step outside and call McIntyre to find out what is happening with Wendy Parker and to fill him in on what is going on here.

A little boy crawls underneath the rows of connected chairs. I get ready to jump up and save him when it looks like he's stuck, but he wiggles his hips around and slips through a small opening.

Dr. Ferron would have called this part of my minor super hero complex where I need to save the day. Da-da-da-da. I shot and killed the guy in BC because I needed to stop him from taking any more children. I chase the bad guy with the gun because I have to be the hero. I have to save the little boy under the chairs. I have to stop in the pouring rain to help someone with a flat tire. Da-da-da-da.

I so want this case to end. I should get Hillary and Leigh back home as soon as I can so at least their lives can go back to normal. I miss my wife. I know it may be hard to believe, all things considered, but I do miss her. In a way, we needed this time apart. I don't know what will happen once we are back together again living each day the same as the ones before all of this happened, but for now I miss her. You can't predict what will happen. I always hated job interviews when they got to the part where they ask where you see yourself in five years. Does it really matter? Where you see yourself now, may seem silly in five years.

I miss having my dog at home.

"Hey,"

I turn to see Marilyn walking through the sliding doors. We both watch an ambulance come in through the ER loop and do their thing by their own entrance.

"So I got her to talk a little." She pauses and I nod for her to continue. She tells me how Heather said she got picked up for a date by a man who wasn't her husband. He drove her to a summer cottage out by Blooming Point where he hit her, raped her, and cut her. Then she got away and ran into the woods. "She heard him calling her name and he yelled out that he was going to kill her and her children. She found a small group of evergreens and curled up inside them. She heard him walk past where she was. She was so exhausted that she fell asleep. When she woke it was morning and she couldn't hear him anymore. She walked out, went to the house, and banged on the door. When no one answered she fell down and just laid there."

I get back on the phone and make the necessary calls to get a K-9 unit out to where Heather Blais was found and to get police units to her house to watch her children. The dog will follow her blood back to the cabin where she was held. Maybe, just maybe, we'll be lucky enough to find out who the killer is through the summer cottage. Of course he tortured and killed Casey Marsh in an abandoned summer home.

"Did she give us a name?"

"She wants you to come in and talk to her." I stare at Marilyn for what seems like a long time before nodding and letting her lead the way.

Heather is still on her side, but this time her hands are outside of the blanket. One of her white tipped nails is missing. Her good eye looks drooping and relaxed as the drugs take hold of her. She doesn't want to give in and go to sleep. It's in those initial steps of sleep where your dreams, your nightmares, are most real. That's where *Freddy* can get you.

Marilyn sits down. I stand and smile at her.

Marilyn turns her head to look between us. "Heather, can you tell us your attacker's name?"

For a moment it looks as if Heather didn't hear her, then she blinks and settles her head further into her pillow. "T-T-T-T-T-Teddy."

I step forward. An excitement swells inside me. I have to try and suppress it down. I say, "Mosby? Ted Mosby from Giorg?"

Her head shakes slightly from side to side.

"Heather told me she met him in the Confederation Court Mall," Marilyn tells me.

Hillary's bank is in that mall.

Marilyn continues, "She doesn't go to Atlantic Fitness."

Heather's throat chokes. She says, "He has pictures of my babies," and her hands reach for her face. Large sobs shake her whole body. It takes ten minutes before she calms herself. "He, he said you stopped the other one at four."

I stare down at her. I flip through the files in my head trying to figure out what she is talking about. I find it in a box hidden away in a dark dusty corner where I always try to hide it, but someone always manages to drag it out in the open and dig through what's inside. Lately it's been Catherine Arsenault digging out the BC case and all the dirty goings on. This time it is this hurt and broken woman.

"Are you going to stop him?" she asks.

I can feel her staring inside me. She wants answers. I have nothing to give her except my promise that I will stop him. Only inside myself, hidden away where she can't find, is doubt.

Chapter 24

Catherine Arsenault stares out of the television. Her brown hair sits elegantly on her shoulders. Her eyes squint from the sun. Little lines creep out on each side.

"Today, terror has once again gripped the island as police investigate a suspected homicide here in Stratford."

Images of a two story house with an attached garage and a blue car in the driveway, roll across the screen. There is an ambulance and Royal Canadian Mounted Police cars with flashing lights. Reid and Moore are there.

Reid stares in the direction of the camera.

Arsenault goes on, "Police have not confirmed any identification as of yet, but this is the home of Charlie and Wendy Parker. Mrs. Parker is believed to be the fourth victim of the Red Island Killer."

"No." The yell surprises Ben. It takes a few moments before he realizes it came from deep inside him. A glass shatters against the far wall. Pellets of glass and splashes of orange juice spray over the wall and cascade onto the floor. He throws the table beside his chair. It skids across the floor and comes to a stop beside the television. The CD/DVD stand teeters back and forth. The cool damp cloth covering the scratches on the side of his face drops to the floor.

"Sgt. Wayne McIntyre of the RCMP Major Crimes Unit will be delivering a statement to the press within the hour with the official identification of this fourth victim."

Ben's nostrils flare. His teeth grind until his jaw hurts. His eyes burn through the television. This isn't happening. This isn't his. He didn't do this. Someone is trying to take all that he has done and make it their own. *This. Can't. Happen.*

Pathetic.

He pushes up from the chair. He takes one step. *How dare they?* He takes a second step. This is his world damn it. His knee curls up to his chest. His foot bursts forward. It connects hard with the picture tube of the television. The box takes to the air. It shoots backward and deflects off the wall with a loud crack. Ben pushes the small television stand down. His fingertips curl around the video stand and sends it into the air. He runs his hand along the wall knocking every photograph loose of their nails. They crash on the floor sending more glass skidding out all over the place. His feet land on them. The glass cracks. His hand grabs one of Shannon and Frisbees it across the room. Ben's fingers grip the large scenic pictures. He pulls them forward. The nails take gyprock with them. His women's photos scatter over the hardwood floor.

Sweat drips from his body. It seeps into the new scars on his face, but he can't feel it. This is wrong. This is all wrong. Last night was wrong. He spent hours searching the forest for that woman and then drove up and down the road hoping she would come out looking for help. Everything is falling apart. His hands form tight fists and all the muscles in his arms and chest flex and stress until the tendons hurt.

What if she lived the night? Can she tell Reid who I am? Where is she?

Ben rubs his head as the thoughts run wild inside his brain. How can this be happening? This is HIS world. His world should be moving the way he sees it. The way *he* wants it. *Chloe.* This is like when he was young and getting pushed around and thrown to the ground and stomped on. He didn't have any control over what was going on. They had control over him. They played with him. That wasn't his world. This is his world.

He can hear his breath pushing out his nostrils. The anger feels like an animal inside him wanting to get out. It wants to taste fear and blood and *death*. Number four got away. They think they have number four, but they have nothing. They have an imitation. They have a joke. They will learn. They will see.

Ben leaves the mess he has made. He knows Reid will soon be here, he can't fight that. He walks to the stairs, his hands in tight fists at his side, knuckles going white. He stops at the top where a full length mirror hangs on the wall. He looks at his face and stares into his own eyes. Three scratches run down the left side of his face, the middle one starting at the corner of his eye. The white of his left eye is now red. He can't see himself. He sees through himself. He knows what he has to do.

He has to kill.

~ * ~

"Say excuse me honey." A woman with long red hair, pushing a young girl with the same red hair, steps around Ben and starts down the stairs. He follows. He watches the back of her head. He watches the older woman's hand on the shoulder of what he assumes is her daughter. A perfume comes back and touches his nose. It is something floral with something sharp inside it. The woman wears chunky heels. The daughter has on a white frilly skirt. *I bet she'd scream*, Ben thought. If he grabbed the little girl the woman would follow without question. That would show Reid. That would show everyone.

Reid.

He'd go crazy. He wouldn't know what to do with himself. In her pictures he'd see his own daughter's face. He'd get lost in the cuts and stabs all over her young body. This time he'd cut the little girls breast off. He would see his own reflection in all the blood. And to top it off the mother would be there tied to a chair, still alive, to tell the police exactly what he did to her daughter.

Chloe.

He stares at their backs as they get in their car and drive away.

Ben gets in his SUV and drives away. He knows where to find his women. Reid can't stop him. Catherine Arsenault can't stop him. Everything is spinning. He feels like his limbs are attached by loose rubber bands.

He drives down Queen Street toward the downtown. It's hot out. People are walking. Women are wearing skirts and short sleeves. He stares at the police officers outside Atlantic Fitness on Kent. They don't know him. They don't know what he's about. They don't know the hunger inside him.

He turns onto University then onto Grafton heading back toward Queen. She'll be down at Victoria Park walking the boardwalk. He'll take her. *Pegasus*. She'll be number four. Then he'll deal with Reid. This is something they'll report. They'll do it right.

Chapter 25

Marilyn hates being in the passenger seat of the car. She feels it is the passenger's obligation to hold up and keep moving any form of conversation so that nobody gets bored. As I turn off of the Charlottetown By-pass onto St. Peters Road, or Highway Two, she says, "So have you talked to Hillary lately?"

We haven't talked much since going to see Dakota.

"Yeah, we talk every night. We've probably talked more since they've been gone than we have in the past six months."

She reads the sign outside a church. Every week, or so, they change what is written there. Today it's, *Put down Facebook and pick up Faith book*.

"So things are good with you two? Do you still want to cheat?"

The other side of the church sign says, *Jesus Satisfies*.

I look at her with one eyebrow raised.

"I'm not offering so get that look off your face."

We are in no hurry to get out to where Heather Blais was attacked. The K-9 unit is out there and constables have the sight secured. Ident is still working in Stratford and neither of them can come out to Blooming Point until they are done there and everything is put away.

I don't say anything for a while so Marilyn feels the need to add more. "Didn't you sow enough oats before getting married?"

"What? I don't know. I've only had three partners, so there wasn't much oat sowing."

"Are you serious?"

"What?"

"You've only had sex with three women? How old are you? Thirty-seven? How long have you been with Hillary?"

As I turn a corner, I shift my foot to the brake and slow the car down. A red tractor with huge rear tires lumbers along beside us. I think for a moment of shifting my foot back to the gas pedal, flipping on the flashing lights and leaving the tractor and everyone else behind us. Instead I settle in and wait for the next safe place to go around.

"Fifteen years. Married for ten. I've only had three women, is that bad? How many guys were you with?"

Marilyn smiles and turns her head to the side window. I swear her face goes red. She runs a hand back through her hair and waves it out over her shoulder. I catch the scent of her shampoo. It smells floral and delicate. She taps the hand rest of the passenger side door with her nails.

I look at the three cars out front of *Lilly's Convenience Store.* No SUV's.

"I've had a few."

"How many?" I look over at her. "Double digits? More than twenty?"

She turns to me. "No, not more than twenty, well, no. Is that bad?"

"I'm a prude, so who am I to say?"

We pass through a part of the island called Ten-mile House which is really nothing more than a spot on the map and a blue sign on the side of the road. The island is a patchwork quilt of township like areas. Every small place has its own name. In some cases they are small towns or villages but most are nothing but a spot. Ten-mile House is known for having some of the worst weather along St. Peter's Road. In the winter just a small two kilometer area can seem to have its own blizzard closing the cross island highway while the rest of the highway is clear. It has to do with open fields and wind coming off of the north shore and through Tracadie Bay. I turn the car left onto Highway 218, or Blooming Point Road, depending on what you want to call it. Islander's wouldn't know the number or realize the name. You'd have to tell them to turn left at the big red house. If you reach the

268

gas station with the *Robin's Donuts* in Scotchford you went too far.

"Chris came by last night," Marilyn says. I look away from her to the tall white church at Tracadie Cross corner. At night it has a spotlight shooting up the steeple into the sky that you can see for miles around. "We talked."

"Yeah was he there in the morning?" Right away I know I shouldn't have said it. I can feel her eyes on me.

"You don't have to be an ass, Reid."

"What do you want me to say? The guy hits you. Last week you wanted to sleep with me."

"Oh and you didn't me? My memory says you brought it up first."

Yeah, I get to be lucky number twenty. I don't say it. I'm not that stupid. "I'm going through things. Don't listen to half of what I say."

"You're unhappy. Everyone gets like that sometime."

"I'm not unhappy." I think about it for a few seconds as I swerve through the corners. "I'm frustrated."

I stop talking.

Marilyn doesn't say anything for a couple of minutes then says, "Do you know how thin we're stretched right now?" She shifts herself so that she's facing me more. "This guy has us running all over the island. Blooming Point. Stratford. Blooming Point again."

"He didn't do Stratford."

She opens her mouth to argue with me shakes her head. "Either way, we're screwed. Eckhart's going to bitch at you if you start throwing him a scene every five minutes."

"It's not me."

"You know what I mean."

I look at Marilyn. Her eyes glare. I look back at the road and swerve to stay straight. As we round a corner, the large white house where Heather Blais was found is on our left. Up ahead from it an RCMP car sits on the side of the road. A constable pushes himself up off the hood as I slow down and pull in front of him, two wheels on the grass. A sign reads *Windy Road*. Behind

269

his car is the white SUV used by the Charlottetown City Police K9 unit. L Division does not have its own dog unit so we often borrow the city police dog. Before getting out, I stare up the road to where 3231 Blooming Point Road is. People drove past it and never knew. People will drive past this road all summer and never know.

"How's it going?" I nod at the constable.

"Good." He straightens himself out and nods back. A bead of sweat runs down his temple.

"Where's Renier?" I ask.

He cocks his head toward the rough road heading into the woods.

I walk down the road with Marilyn following in my footsteps. We watch where we step staying out of tire tracks. The grass is growing. Ferns are starting to pop out of the underbrush in half extension. Fiddleheads, young ferns, are big in the grocery stores right now. My dad always tried to get me out in the woods when I was young to look for them. They're great with butter and bacon. The woods on either side are instantly thick a foot away from the worn path of the road. The pines and spruce stand together like soldiers guarding their bare brothers until they have the time to grow leaves and take their own forms. In the late afternoon the grass is still wet from the morning dew and frost. The sun can't reach down this far. By the time we get to the end where the road splits to go to different summer cottages my feet are soaked to the sock. The air is fresh. You can smell things starting to grow and you can actually smell the green of the island. From spring through summer I swear the island goes through thousands of shades of green.

I call over my shoulder, "There wasn't a moon last night was there?"

"No I don't think so."

"Imagine being in these woods in the middle of the night. You wouldn't see the trees until you walked into them. I can see how she didn't get caught, but she probably should be a lot more hurt than she is."

"I think the prick hurt her enough." I'm surprised at the harshness in her voice.

As soon as we walk out into the clearing a breeze from the bay softly lays a hand on our cheeks. The smell of salt water and musty seaweed fills the air.

"There's tire tracks here in the mud." I look back at Marilyn pointing down to a patch where ridges are clearly visible coming out of a mud puddle. "Eckhart will have fun with those."

Assuming that not too many vehicles come down here, Ident can take photographs and possibly take an imprint of the tread. They can then hopefully identify the type of tire and possibly what type of vehicle drove down here. Everything helps.

Up ahead Constable Albert Renier tosses a ball up in the air. His midnight black Labrador, named Hancuf jumps into the air. He tips it off his nose, lands on its feet, and quickly twists its body around and grabs the ball and brings it back. Renier sees us and gives a sharp command. The dog instantly sits beside his partner with its hip touching the officer's ankle. It stares at us, tongue sticking out of the side of its mouth. Hancuf looks up at the K9 officer waiting for him to throw the ball again or put him to work.

"Hey, guys. The blood trail took me through the woods to this small white cottage. Is your Vic still alive?"

"Yeah, why?"

"She bled like a stuck pig. There's blood everywhere in the woods. She made a lot of circles too. It was an easy trail to follow though."

"Killer probably couldn't see the blood in the dark," Marilyn adds.

"Anyway, it led us here. She came out of the house and right across the road to the woods on this side." He indicates the spot where he has tied yellow caution tape to a tree. "We circled the building, at a safe distance, and didn't see any movement. Hancuf hasn't even popped an ear up at any sounds. I've just been waiting for you guys so that I could go. You have the scene?"

I nod and he walks away.

The cottage is one of the one story prefab sorts of bungalows found all over the island. It has white siding and a black shingled roof. The trim around the windows and door is a nice charcoal color. A deck is out in front with a blue painted railing. A small pile of dried firewood, chopped and stacked in a triangle, is between the door and the railing. Blood has dried to the wood deck and down the stairs. Wooden flower boxes have been built on the top of the railing, two in front and one on each side. Dead plants still remain, their lifeless bodies hanging over the edges. A large bay window sits on the right side of the front door. It has beige curtains inside curving from the top center to the outside. A red brick chimney stands firm on the side of the house. No smoke comes out. There is a metal swing set off the side. The red and white paint is flaking off and no swings hang from it. The black and green garbage bins that every home on the island has sit beside the side of the deck. Someone has painted a large eye on each with blue eyeliner and lashes so that when they are put side-by-side, as they are, it looks like someone looking at you. I wonder if the garbage trucks come down here in the summer or if they have to drag their bins all the way up to the highway. The other cottages are about one hundred meters away. Close enough to have neighbors but far enough so that you have your space. It looks like a nice place. A nice place you would take your family on weekends during the summer. You can walk to the beach, have a bar-b-que on the deck, and just relax enjoying the ocean air.

We keep our distance. The gravel at the base of the stairs from the deck looks like it has been disturbed as if someone fell or was dragged through it. I walk around the house keeping my eyes on the windows. The grass all around the house has not been mowed since fall, to make a three meter square all the way around the building except on the side where the swing set is. The grass there has been mowed all around the A frames. Nothing has been disturbed. The windows all have curtains covering what is inside.

I finish my circle and stand next to Marilyn. She inspects a finger nail for a moment then bites some skin from the side. "It has a nice view." She looks out toward the water.

We are on the Northeast shore of Tracadie Bay looking out at the small opening to the Atlantic left by the peninsula made by Blooming Point Beach and the sand dunes. An old fence barely stands before the grass ends and a small beach starts. One of the posts, stained dark from time and weather leans a little to the side. The barbed wire fence goes down the tall grass and then is seen again where another post leans far to the side. Something inside my head clicks, but the thought won't form. It's like a *déjà vous* feeling. I've been here before. Or I've seen it before.

"Where the hell's Ident?"

~ * ~

Eckhart shows up about forty minutes later. Ashley follows thirty minutes after that and tells us she dropped Heather Blais' rape kit off at the Maypoint RCMP office. It takes a full hour before they are in the summer cottage and another twenty minutes before Eckhart lets us in.

Eckhart says, "There was no forced entry. Any idea who owns this place?"

"We're looking into it," I announce.

We have to step over bloody footprints as we walk in the door. The living room and kitchen are all one open area divided by a breakfast island. It looks like all the action took place in the living room. There is a small white couch with only two cushions and two chairs. All three have the same tall grass and leaf pattern in the beige fabric. An oval coffee table probably sat in front of the couch at some time but now it was pushed half-way across the room. The floor is gold colored hardwood with a lot of grain accents. A lamp is on the floor with a broken light bulb. Blood has been pushed and smeared into the floor in front of the couch. There's more on one cushion and then the footsteps toward the door. The rest of the room is not that impressive. It has the typical things a home would have all around.

273

"There's a glass here." Eckhart takes photographs of a glass sitting on the mantle above the open fireplace. There is a little water still in the glass.

"Look at these photographs."

Marilyn stands in front of a wall with a dozen photographs in wood frames of different colors all over the wall. They show different views of the island's coastline. I step up beside her and take a look. Something pokes away inside me.

She turns back to the center of the room. "So Heather was probably here in front of the couch. She didn't say much about the inside of this place. She said he didn't have the lights on." She walks back and points down. "This is probably from her shoulder." The blood is smeared all around. Red splashes up the couch. "He probably sliced her and followed through. Look at the spatter."

"Check this whole area for DNA. He raped her right here. There has to be something. This guy fucked up here. He didn't think Heather was going to fight back. Something here has to have the answers." I walk in the kitchen area. I am careful where I step. As I reach a gloved hand out for the kitchen cupboard, I can feel Eckhart's eyes on my back. I slide the knife drawer open. Everything looks in place. There is a large carving knife and steak knives and all the rest of the normal utensils. "I think he brought his knife with him. Did Heather say anything about the knife?"

"Yeah, that it was the biggest thing she had ever seen."

"That's what she said."

"That's not funny Greg."

"Give me a break, Marilyn. All I've had today is bodies and blood."

"Did you get anything from Stratford?"

Eckhart starts taking samples. "Killer used a knife that was in the garage already." He explains all that he found at that scene, but I only half listen.

I slowly step around the room taking in everything. The killer sat either on the end of the couch or one of the chairs tapping his foot waiting to pounce. Why didn't he take her to the bedroom?

There are two bedrooms in the cottage, but neither has been disturbed. He used the bathroom. There is blood in the sink and on the liquid soap dispenser. Did he wear gloves or does this mean he was bare handed? Why did so much go wrong with this one? He had Johanna Bowers for a week and nothing went wrong. The only reason we have anything on that case was because he gave it to us. Why didn't he tie up Heather Blais? Is he that confident in himself?

My phone rings. Longfellow tells me who owns the summer cottage and their address. Marilyn and I leave Eckhart and Ashley with the instructions to call if they find anything.

~ * ~

We don't really talk on the way back to the city. She insists on driving. We discuss movies that we are looking forward to seeing and whether the *Barenaked Ladies* should have kept the name or changed it when Stephen Page left the group. We don't really come to a conclusion on that one. At the top of the hour, when the news is coming on, I turn the radio off. We stay as far from the murders as we can.

Will and Kathy Hanson live in the Hillsborough Park area of Charlottetown on the far side of the Bypass between KFC and the Queen Elizabeth Hospital. They live in a nice house with a nice garage and a nice car out in the driveway. They have a nice summer cottage out in Blooming Point with a nice blood stain in the living room. We walk past their metallic green BMW. A dog barks inside when I ring the bell. It sounds like a little dog. Within a few seconds there is a woman's voice inside telling the dog to quiet down.

"Can I help you?" Kathy Hanson is an average sized woman, but the skin of her face lightly slides to her neck as if she doesn't have a jaw. There is no jaw definition. Her hair is a light brown with some grey sneaking in there. It is in a loose perm that goes flat as it crests over the top. She has large breasts under a pink blouse. Cradled between them she holds a tan Chihuahua with a red collar around its neck. The little rat wiggles until it can see us. Mrs. Hanson has yellow painted fingernails and wears at least one ring on every finger, and on one thumb. Around her neck are two gold chains.

"Sergeants Reid and Moore with the RCMP. We need to talk to you about your summer cottage in Blooming Point.

"Oh my God. Did someone break in? Did it burn down? Will hates the fact that we can't go there during the winter." You can tell she wants to put a hand to her face, but the dog squirms.

"No ma'am, nothing like that. Not really. Does anyone have access to the cottage?"

The dog wiggles enough so that it can stick a tongue out and lick her round neck. "Pompey," she snaps at the dog. "No, no one. I don't think Will gave anyone a key. He's at work. He sells real estate."

"Mrs. Hanson, last night someone got into your cottage. They took a woman there and attacked her." I watch her face change to genuine surprise. "Do you know anyone who would have access to the cottage at all?"

"Attacked a girl? The Red Island Killer. It was him, wasn't it? Oh my Lord." Her skin comes over pale. She squeezes the Chihuahua into her chest.

Marilyn says, "We don't know. Would you like to sit down?"

"We'll need a list of everyone who may have been in your cottage or may have access to it," I request.

"I have to call my husband."

Marilyn leads her in and sits her down in a chair. I close the door and follow. I know we probably won't get anything useful here but you can't really tell someone that a serial killer used their summer cottage and then walk away. She lets the dog free. It instantly goes for my soaked and cold feet and sniffs to its heart's content. After Kathy Hanson calls her husband we accept a cup of tea while we wait for him to come home. When he does we go through the same thing and find out that nobody else has keys to the cottage. They were last there in October.

~ * ~

276

"How long are you going to stare at that wall? Reid?"

Eyes the color of faded green are staring into mine. Behind her are pictures of bloodied women and lists of everything from their lives, nothing seeming to match. My eyelids flutter like a hummingbird's wings. My eyes strain to focus. Where am I? MCU. How long have I been standing here in front of the white board wall? I don't know. What time did we get back here? I don't know. What time is it now? I don't know.

"What?"

Marilyn snaps her fingers by my ear. "You've been staring at the board for a while. You okay? Have you figured anything out? Do you see something?"

I look at the board a little longer then let out some air. "No. Hand me that dry erase." I point at a blue and white marker sitting on the ledge near the end. I take it and move to the next blank white board. On the left side I write Casey Marsh near the top. Below that I write Johanna Bowers. Nicolle Theresa Pereira next. Heather Blais at the bottom. To Marilyn I say, "Let's start from the beginning. Something has to connect these women. Casey and Nicolle were members of Atlantic Fitness." I write AF beside both of their names. "Heather met her attacker at the Confed Mall." I write that beside her name. Beside Johanna I put a question mark. I draw a line down after that and put hair up at the top. Next I write eyes, body, nails, age, height, weight, tattoo, relationship, home address, and location found with a line between each column. "Let's go over them all. Casey's hair?"

Marilyn checks her specifics. "Sandy, shoulder length. Johanna had long blond hair, Nicolle long black with brown, and Heather's is fair and shoulder length." I write them all down in the same row as the names. "Eyes are blue, green, brown, blue." We continue writing down every detail that may be similar between the women. At the end the white board is full of my scribbled handwriting. Some things are similar between a couple of the women but nothing seems to connect all of them.

Casey Marsh was twenty five, single with no children. She had sandy shoulder length hair, green eyes, a thin frame with larger breasts, and had a tattoo of three hearts on a dagger on the back of her left shoulder. She disappeared three months ago. She was found on May first hanging from a ceiling fan inside 3231 Blooming Point Road. She had over forty lacerations to her body. Her left breast was almost completely cut off. Cause of death, massive blood loss.

Johanna Bowers, age twenty-two, single as of one hour before abduction, no kids. Long blond hair, blue eyes, thin frame with a nice figure. She had a black and grey rose tattoo on the back of her left shoulder. She disappeared April 10 walking on a street in downtown Charlottetown. Her body was found over a week later hanging from a tree a kilometer from Blooming Point Beach. She had between forty and fifty cuts and lacerations over her body, most superficial, and her left breast was almost completely cut off. Cause of death, massive blood loss.

Nicolle Theresa Pereira was twenty years old, dating, no children. She has long black hair with brown highlights, brown eyes, and a fit body that is a little rounder than the other two. On the back of her right shoulder is a Portuguese quote tattoo. She last spoke to her family at 6 pm on April 28 and was abducted forcibly from Victoria Park. Her body was found three days later at Port-la-Joye Fort Amherst Historical Park lying on the ground in the center of the old fort site. Multiple lacerations, left breast almost cut off, death by stabbing of the lungs.

Heather Blais is twenty-five, married, two children, fair-haired, with blue eyes and a good body. She has smaller breasts than the others. Her tattoo is of a cross and rosary beads. She went on a date on May 12th to a summer cottage in Blooming Point. Lacerations to her body. She escaped.

Marilyn crosses her arms over her chest and stands beside me looking at the board. She says, "So they all have tattoos on the backs of their shoulders, not always the same shoulder, and they're all in shape. Except for Heather he practically takes off their left breast. And she didn't get tied down. I don't see anything new."

"We have to look outside the obvious." I talk more to myself than to my partner. Behind us I can feel McIntyre and the other's eyes on us watching every move we make. He's waiting for something to click. Something has to light up and make sense. We're running out of time. After my call from the killer; I know in my soul that he is out there either killing or looking for another victim.

My eyes focus on something. "Look here," I move to the map of Charlottetown. I pick up a florescent pink highlighter. "Casey Marsh's house is here. Johanna Bowers here. Nicolle Pereira. And Heather Blais." With the fourth pink dot I draw a circle around all of the downtown at least a centimeter wider than the furthest out dot.

"This is his hunting grounds. Johanna was taken in that circle. Nicolle just on the edge," I say and take a step back to look at everything together. There is so much it makes my head spin. So many scenes had to be processed and most of it is here on the wall. All of their autopsy reports and photographs are either on the wall or in a file folder in Marilyn's hands.

Suddenly. "What about this?" I move to the map of all Prince Edward Island. I look for Blooming Point Beach along the north shore. "Casey Marsh was found here at 3231." Pink dot. "Johanna Bowers here near the beach and Heather Blais attacked here." Two more pink dots go on the map. I draw a line to each of the dots making a small pink triangle. "Okay, we know this is his hunting area, right?" I continue without getting an answer. "This triangle is his kill zone. Nicolle was found way over here, but she was done in a rush. He wanted to leave a message with her. This triangle. He has to have a connection to this area. Bodies are usually dumped within fifty feet of where they were killed. I'll bet he lives in this circle where he hunts the women and that he has something to do with this Blooming Point area."

"Non, we interviewed everyone in that area," LeBlanc says from his desk. "Are you saying Longfellow and I missed something?" He sounds defensive.

I looked at every interview they did along the Blooming Point Road after we found Johanna Bowers' body was discovered. They asked all the right questions. They documented everything. I explain that we have suspects now. "We know more than we did then. All we asked then was if they saw any strange vehicles or anything out of the ordinary. We have more to actually ask. Maybe something will stick out"

McIntyre stands outside his office door. His arms cross his chest. He stares absorbedly at me and the boards behind me. "Did we send a sketch artist to see Heather yet?"

"Dr. Mooney says she's still sedated. When she wakes up, she starts crying hysterically and screaming. We'll have to try tomorrow."

"Then head out to Blooming Point tomorrow. Tonight, get some rest. I think you all need some sleep."

~ * ~

I don't know what to do with myself. Marilyn leaves before I do. I stay behind to pretend to be working. I spend over an hour staring at the dry erase board with the pictures and lists of known facts and the rough spreadsheet I wrote with the dry erase. The bright pink triangle on the map almost comes out of me in 3D. Wendy Parker's name is off to one side with all of her information listed below in black dry erase marker. Dispirito agrees that my guy probably didn't kill her. He's leaning toward the husband, but needs to nail down a motive. Sometimes, "she was a bitch," isn't enough to for the crown to prosecute. I am the last one to leave. The dashboard clock says 8:15.

I pick up a *Captain Hook* burger with onion rings and a chocolate milkshake from *Peter Pan's* before going to the hotel. It used to be the snack bar at a drive-in restaurant. Now it is a restaurant at the corner of University Ave. and Capital Dr. The burger is juicy and fantastic. It hits the spot. I try watching television for a while, but nothing holds my interest. Hillary calls and we get into a fight about her wanting to sleep with me and missing the dog and Leigh missing her horse. It ends with her saying, "I'm tired of talking to dead air," and hanging up without a goodbye or an, *I love you.* So I guess I'm an ass. *Shame on me for not catching the bad guy. Shame on me.* At 11pm the evening news comes on and I really need to avoid it. Something in me decides to go for a drive.

In fifteen minutes I am parked at the curb outside of Marilyn's place. The lights are out. I look down the street at the trees and how the leaves cast shadows from the street lights. I do everything I can to not look at her windows or Chris's truck in the driveway. I just stare into the dark.

I jump when my phone rings. It's probably Hillary calling to talk again. "Hello."

"I know your name." It's a man's voice.

At first I'm a little confused and then I realize it's him.

"What?"

He makes a noise. "I knew my world was falling apart when I couldn't find out what your first name was. It took some searching, but I found it." There's a long pause. I don't know what I should be saying back. After a while he says, "I didn't kill that woman."

"What?"

"Have you been drinking, Sgt. Reid? Because you can't seem to come up with a viable sentence. Maybe that's why you can't catch me. If this is how you are when you're interviewing people no wonder you're not even close. I wanted to tell you I didn't kill that woman, the one in Stratford. I didn't kill her."

I shake my head to get rid of the cobwebs. I have to get this guy to talk to me. I have to find out something. "But you attacked Heather Blais."

"She was part of my falling apart world. She got away because I couldn't find your name. Now I have it."

"So what are going to do then?" Everything I learned through my six months at depot and any other classes on hostage negotiations or criminal interviews are completely gone from my head.

He laughs over the phone like I said something sarcastic and he has to force it. "I'm going to kill someone and get it right."

"You're pathetic." I'm pissed off. I don't want to play his games any more. I'm tired of it.

"Don't call me that." His voice is hard. He doesn't like it.

"What? Pathetic?"

I can almost hear him growling over the phone. He doesn't say anything for a while. I think about saying it again to rile him up. Before I can he says, "You're pathetic, Reid. Do you want to know why?"

"Sure, you tell me."

"You're pathetic because you're sitting outside your partners place when you'd rather be inside licking her ginger pussy like you did your wife." The phone goes dead.

My hand goes to my gun. I look in the rear view mirror. I look out the windshield and turn my body to look out the rear window. I still hold the cell phone to my ear. There are no sounds there. There are a couple of vehicles on the street, but none are running. I step out and look both ways. I can't hear any engines. I can't see any people. This is still his game. He has full control. All I can do is take it day by day and hope he screws up or takes his hand off the piece without checking every path.

I don't think I'll sleep tonight.

Chapter 26

"Hello? Talk to me."

The sobs come and shake her entire body. Snot runs from her nose. Tears soak her face from her eyes back to her ears. Ben watches her shake her head. She pulls at her arms. Her elbows thump against the floor beneath her.

"Why are you doing this?"

Her hands are in fists. She yanks them forward. They don't move. The ropes dig into her wrists. She can't bend her knees. They are tied apart.

"Why?" Her voice screams high until it breaks and she begins to cough.

"Why do you let them do this to you, Benny?" His mom sat on the toilet lid. She squeezed a sponge over his shoulder. Hot soapy water cascaded over his chest and back into the bathtub. Ben cried. His body trembled with the tears he tried to hold in. His chest hurt. He couldn't pull air in. He was naked in the tub – his dirty and torn Sunday clothes were on the bathroom floor. "I told you before, you have to stand up to these bullies."

He tried to say something. He couldn't pull in the oxygen needed to speak. A couple sounds come out. His mother just shook her head.

She made the "sh" sound over and over. "Shshshshsh." She pulled the sponge down his cheek. Brown drips of mud and bits of grass fell to the soapy water around his feet. The blood hadn't reached the water yet. His stung. The pain ran through his wrists into his lower arms. "Do you want to tell me who did this?"

He shook his head. Ben sucked back a snot bubble into his nostril.

"I can't help you then." His Mom ran the sponge over his body. She put it into one hand and squeezed the water out. She reached down to saturate the purple sponge and did it again in the other hand.

It felt good. Ben didn't want to talk to her. He didn't want to tell her who beat him up. What the hell was she going to do?

"You have to stand up to them Benny." She put a finger under his chin so that he was looking in her eyes. He pulled his face away. "If you don't stand up to them it becomes your fault. They see you as a target."

It was all your fault Ben.

She got him out of the tub and went over him with a rough towel. She was careful on the cuts and scrapes. She repeated her mantra of standing up to the bullies. All he had to do was show them he wasn't afraid.

The woman lets out a moan. Her head stretches back. Ben looks down at her and lets his eyes walk over her face and body, looking at the shadows made by the dim light. She has blood on her face. It sparkles like glitter make-up. It might have come from the cut to her back underneath the Pegasus tattoo or it could be from the other cuts and nicks on her skin. He hit this one in the back of the head instead of the face. Her face is defined. She has high cheekbones, deep eyes, and sculpted brows thin and perfect. She has round shoulders and toned arms. Small, perfectly shaped breasts sit on her chest; they fall a little to the sides. Her stomach is solid and flat with no pouch at all. Her legs are muscled and sleek. All of her skin has a light tan. He's been in her. He's tasted her. She may be his favorite yet.

Kathy Welsley opens her eyes and catches her breath. The dark brown open wide. Blood lines spider-web the whites. Ben stands above her. He is naked with smears of her blood on his hands and chest. His equipment glistens in the light. He smiles down at her. He knows her eyes are on the hunting knife his hand. The blade is now red.

"What are you doing? Please stop. Please let me go." She draws her head back and screeches out the word help. She looks back at him. She raises her head off the floor to look closer at him. She yells, "What are you doing?"

What are you doing?

Ben looked up and felt a charge through his body. His hard groin tingled. He thought he heard a car pull up. He listened for a few seconds that seemed to drag on. There was nothing. He looked down the length of his parents long open closet at the door to their bedroom. He didn't go in their bedroom without asking. They weren't home. They could be home at any moment. He didn't hear any car doors closing or any keys in the lock.

He put his head down. Behind the old brown suitcase with darker brown re-enforced corners that held his Mom's knickknacks, childhood memories and newspapers from when Prince Charles and Princes Diana got married and then from her death, under his Mom's fur coat is a cardboard box. At the top of the bigger box was a small yellow one a little askew to the back. It had Dad's slides in it from when he was in the navy in the early seventies. Under the yellow box was a red safety helmet from when his father worked construction. Under all of those things, he memorized their exact position and angle so that he could replace them the exact same way when he was finished, were six VHS tapes and a stack of sixteen magazines.

The first two video tapes were all black. The next two had a white sticker label on their front. They each had a number in the top right corner of the sticker. Number two was the best. It had three movies on it. The first was of a bus of football players and cheerleaders and coaches on a trip to a game. The quarterback and the head cheerleader start things off in the back seat of the bus. The first time he watched the porn he didn't get past that scene before his pants were wet. All of the video tapes are full of pornographic movies with bad story lines and grainy pictures. The magazines range from the tame, popular nudie mags to the more graphic ones with close-up pictures of vaginas and hard dicks. He stroked the hard spot in his sweatpants.

He heard a car door slam. He put the magazines back. He dropped a video tape, grabbed it back up, and put them back in the box. A second car door. Safety helmet. Yellow box askew to the back. Suitcase back on top. Fix the fur coat to cover the gap. Keys in the lock. He walked out of his parent's bedroom and into the bathroom.

"Ben, we're home. What are you doing?"

Ben touches the flat tip of his hunting knife on her forehead. The woman below the honed steel goes silent and still. He can smell the fear radiating out from her pores. He's in control. What is he going to do with the knife this time? He starts dragging it down her forehead, enough to touch her skin but not cut, over the bridge of her nose. Her wide eyes watch it, almost cross-eyed, travel down her nose and drop from the upturned tip. The pointed blade end pushes in her top lip. The moisture from the steel sticks to her dry bottom lip. It pulls it down and out stretching her lip until the dull pink rips free and falls back. Ben keeps his eyes on hers. He can taste her fear. It mixes with the smell of sweat and sex in the air to make something sickly sweet. He doesn't notice the thin red line the knife tip draws straight down her chin.

It drops.

The tip sinks into the soft spot just above her sternum. It comes back out like a raft in the sea cresting a high wave. A slow red crimson boils over the edges of the cut sending strings down both sides of her neck like a bright red necklace.

He turns the blade flat side down and trails it onto the right side of her chest. Her pale skin erupts in goose bumps. *Oh, she likes it.*

She keeps staring up at his face. The knife slides down over her right breast. Ben smiles at the little white bumps of her perfect breast. He sees the dark round first. Then the hard nipple snaps back and erect. His groin tenses.

Maybe he should put himself back in her again. He could satisfy her. He was that good.

Chloe.

It is his world after all. He rules everything he sees.

Reid.

Ben rammed the knife forward as hard as he could. He felt flesh give way to muscle to the wood behind. He felt hot blood spray out over his hand. The animal squealed a high pitch screech that hurt his teeth. White eyes stared out through a black mask. The raccoon kicked and clawed at the air around it.

Ben cocked his head to the side and watched the animal struggle to survive. Moving wall art. *He actually laughed out loud. What reaction would he get from an art gallery if he wanted to do a show of animals stuck to the walls with hunting knives?*

He pulled a second knife from his back pocket. He took it from its sheath. He rammed the knife blade into the animal. Ben's teeth glared. His eyebrows went to a point above his nose. His eyes glassed over and shone. He loved this. The raccoon squealed. Ben stabbed again. He stabbed. He stabbed. He stabbed. The raccoon stopped screaming out. It stopped moving.

"Ben, are you out here?" Grandpa called out.

Ben watched his grandfather's coffin start to lower into the ground. He was dead. He was gone. His eyes flicked up. There was a woman on the far side of the coffin watching the casket slowly drop. Who was she? He didn't know. He didn't really care. She wore a dark dress that went to a point over her chest. Her cleavage line was dark. Fuck her. How dare she dress like that? What the hell was she doing? He licked his dry lips. He wanted to be between her large breasts. What the hell was he doing? This was his world. His World. He hated her. He hated Grandpa for dying. He hated his dad for making him look at the body. He hated it. His world.

His world.

He plunges the knife into Kathy Welsley's side. She jerks her body and screams in pain. The sound echoes around the walls of his SUV. He stabs her thigh. The hot blood touches his fingers.

Pathetic.

He slices the skin holding her bicep in. A stream instantly flows out onto the floor of his automobile. Kathy's head turns left and right. Her hair flies over her face. A scream escapes from somewhere deep inside her.

Chloe.

They're laughing at you.

He draws the knife over her breasts.

Stand up to them. *Pathetic.*

Reid.

Pathetic.

He's got control of the world now. It's not Ben's anymore. He's lost control. He's never had control. It never was his world. *Pathetic.* It's all gone. Everything's different. No, no. No.

He stabs her. He stabs her.

Oh he loves this. This is his. He can do this.

His body jerks. He drops the knife to the floor as he drops to his hands and knees and ejaculates into her blood. This is the feeling. This is what makes his world complete. Kathy moans. She bites her lip. He hasn't done enough to kill her. In a few moments he'll put himself inside her again keep at her until his anger builds again. Who knows how long this could take.

His world is done. Done. Done. Reid can have it. He opens his mouth wide and screams Reid's name in Kathy Welsley's face. Spit flies from his mouth.

"Reid."

Done.

Chapter 27

I select a mug from the cupboard, a generic one nobody will miss for a day or two, since I forgot mine downstairs in MCU.

Today I need slow roast coffee from the second floor lunch room. The Folgers stuff we have downstairs just isn't doing the trick. No offence to Folgers, but sometimes you just need what you want.

The lunch room has a couch and a couple of chairs along the outside. There are two round tables with chairs around them. It has a full kitchen counter with a small stove and oven, fridge, and a sink. Two bowls and two coffee mugs sit on the plastic drying rack. Two spoon handles stick out of the cup for utensils. On the right side of the counter is a deluxe coffee machine. Beside that is a box of different coffee pouches that you put in the machine and let the hot water seep through it like a tea bag. This room is where we have a small Christmas party for the kids of the RCMP members. Back in the day this room was called the officer's mess. It was where officers could come and have a drink before going home. Then someone drove home drunk and got into an accident. Now it is only for lunch.

Nothing is going right. Between the RCMP and Charlottetown Police, Ted Mosby has been under surveillance for a week and all we know is that he works and goes home and sleeps. The only thing illegal he may do is take food from the restaurant which he does almost every night. Eckhart found fingerprints at the cottage; most belong to the Hanson's with a few unknowns. They could have had friends in there during the summer or the killer could have been there before. We are waiting to see if Heather Blais has calmed down enough to give a description to the sketch guy we brought in from Halifax. Who knows what she will be able to give us. It's all so frustrating. We're sitting on the edge and just need that one thing to get us over. We need that one flash to explode and send us on the right path.

I put the little coffee packet in the machine, put the mug in the cup rest, and push a button. The machine whirs to action. A red light comes on and hot water begins to filter through the slow roasted pouch. The smell of coffee beans fills the air and wakes my senses. I missed something. It's in my head somewhere. I have that tip of the tongue feeling. I know something; I just can't form it inside my head. There's just a bunch of clouds and colors. There's water. There are the colors of sunset.

"Hey, Reid, hey."

My skin jumps a little. Dispirito crosses from the door to the candy display. We have a collection of gums, chocolate bars, and little snacks. The drawer underneath has a money tray inside. If you can't trust cops, who can you trust? He looks through the bars and selects an *Oh Henry*. He writes his name on a small scrap of paper, puts IOU bar below it, and puts it in the money drawer.

"Where have you been today?"

I put my attention back to coffee maker. My cup is half full.

"Interviewing Mr. Parker again. Got a confession." His face lights up. His fucking pretty boy smile makes him look like a young Brad Pitt.

I don't think he's rubbing it in, but what the fuck? He gets a confession in less than twenty-four hours and I can't even get a suspect on three murders. I barely have a single viable clue. Where's Sherlock Holmes when you need him? *I say Watson, that smudge of dirt means the killer is that guy.*

He continues, "He didn't want to give it up, but I stayed on him. We have him dead to rights. Sorry for the pun." He smiles and lets out a little laugh.

Tall son of a bitch with his blond hair and scar and good looks.

"Mr. Parker said he got tired of his wife controlling his life, telling him what to do, what to wear, and making all the decisions. Neighbors said they witnessed a couple of her controlling blowouts when she let him have it. His co-workers said he flinched when she called the office. He saw these murders as his time to do something for himself. He gathered all the news reports he could and thought he had it all down. I guess he didn't think about our hold back details. Anyway, he confessed to killing her before leaving for Moncton the day before. Dr. Norton confirmed liver temperature that she was killed fourteen to sixteen hours before discovery."

I nod and watch my coffee mug fill up. The machine makes a final noise and the light goes out.

Dispirito gets tired of waiting for me to say something. "How's the Red Island Killer case going? Maybe my case will take the press off your back for a day or two."

I want to spit out, *don't call it that,* but bite my tongue instead. I don't know what to tell him. He wants us to put this case away to give Sierra West some peace. I need to give Heather Blais peace and to bring my family home. I sip my coffee. The hot liquid burns my upper lip. "Fuck. I don't know. It's like this guy's playing us. He knows what he's doing, I'm sure of it." In my head I've forgotten about Dispirito being there. "We'll only catch him if he wants us to."

"Are you serious?"

I stare at him for close to a minute before focusing in on his face. He has a stunned look over his features. I say, "I don't know. It's just something I feel."

"You think he let Heather Blais go free?"

My eyes connect with his. Since the moment we got the call from the hospital I have been thinking the same thing. I shake my head and shrug my shoulders. That's the only answer I can give him.

"What purpose would he have for letting her go?"

"Who the hell knows? Maybe this guy wants to get caught but for some screwed up reason can't just turn himself in. They say when Ted Bundy escaped he went and killed in Florida because they had the death penalty. Who knows what twisted crap goes on in these guy's heads."

Maybe when I catch the prick I'll have the time to ask him. Or maybe I'll beat him to within an inch of his life. Either way we have to find him first. I leave the lunch room and head down to grab Marilyn and head to Blooming Point.

~ * ~

We start with the big white house near the entry to Windy Road where Heather Blais was found the morning after her attack. As we get out of the car a dog inside the house lets out a yappy bark through an open window. You can see the spot on the deck where yesterday a young woman was found bleeding. I can still see some dried red on the wall of the house where it has dripped down between the deck and the wall. The smell of bleach touches the inside of my nose. A woman with short blond hair looks through a white curtain covering a square window on the door before opening it. We show her our identification so that she opens the door.

"Yes?" He asks in a timid tone. She pulls at her white blouse. The top three buttons are open. She has a dishtowel hanging over her shoulder.

"Sgt. Reid, Sgt. Moore, we need to talk –"

"I talked to the police yesterday. I told them everything."

"I know you did, Mrs. Burry, but we have some other small details to ask about."

She looks both of us in the face as if she is trying to see if our questions are there. With a huge sigh that lifts and drops her chest she turns back to the inside of the house and lets us in the door. This is a kid house. There are toys in the nooks and crannies. A red die sits hiding under the overhang of the third stair going up to the second floor. The number four looks at me in small white dots.

"I don't know what else I can tell you. The kids missed the bus so I drove them to school and when I came back there she was. I don't know anything else," she says

292

"I wanted to ask you more about the night before. Did you see or hear anything? Maybe your dog barked in the middle of the night?"

"Oh no, she only barks if something or someone comes in her yard." A white and black spaniel sniffs at our ankles. She has two spots on her back. I've been to Deborah English's to see Frix a few times so maybe she is smelling her.

This seemed like a great idea while we were back in headquarters, but now that we are here I don't know what questions to ask. For I moment I listen to the television noise coming from the near living room. The ladies from *The View* sit around their table talking about the latest news headline. The volume is up loud enough so that she can probably hear it from the kitchen.

"I wish I could help you out." She throws her arms out to her side. "I talked to my husband and neither of us heard anything. The kids slept through the night."

"Mrs. Burry, I believe the person who attacked Heather may have had some connection with the area out here. Do you know anyone who either lives out here or visits on a regular basis that is a little sketchy or gives you a bad feeling?" *Bad feeling.*

She shakes her head.

I have to continue probing to see if something is there. "It's probably someone you wouldn't suspect. Male, probably in his late twenties or early thirties, nice looking, quiet but still charismatic, anything like that?"

She shakes her head again. "Most people around here tend to stick to their own business. You can try Gwen Lachance down the road in the farm house with the old barn. She's lived out here for years and knows a little of everything that goes on. Oh, the baby's up. I'm sorry I can't help you."

~ * ~

"Yes, can I help you?" The older lady curls her white hair back behind her ears. She smiles with only the front six teeth still remaining in her mouth. Her eyes are friendly. A spider web of lines stretches out over her temples from her eyes and her cheeks from the corners of her smile. An overwhelming cloud of perfume comes out the open front door. It smells of soap and baby powder. She must be in her seventies maybe older.

This farm house is similar to the one Marilyn's parents own in Rustico. It makes a small L shape and has no deck but it does have a platform with stairs in front of the front door with a roof over top. The second story has tall rectangular windows. The roof cuts the walls at sharp angles. Downstairs has a lot of windows that probably bathes the inside in natural light. A wind chime of metal rods hangs from the roof over the stair platform. It makes an echoing tin noise every time the light breeze blows across the front. Off to the side of the house is a barn that was once painted red but has long faded and peeled away. The whole building sags to the right. It is one of those buildings that if my friends and I saw it we would have wanted to sneak into it to see what forgotten treasures were inside. A large opening up high on the end of the barn is blocked by a wood door. There is fencing around a large field behind the house. It looks like they had animals at one time. There are none here now. A small rectangular garden has been cut out of the lawn on the other side of the house. The dirt has been freshly tilled and now it waits to be tended to.

Marilyn introduces us. "We are working on a case and were wondering if we could talk about anything you may have seen. We were told you know what is going on in the neighborhood." Marilyn clasps her hands in front of her and shows her sweet side. I nod my head with tight lips. I straighten my tie and feel awkward in my own skin.

In the porch there is a pair of old, ladies shoes, sandals, generic white running shoes, and a pair of brown work boots three sizes bigger than the other shoes, all lined up perfectly. A small closet is lined with different men's and women's coats. Opposite the closet is a small pile of tools caked in dust.

The inside of the house is warm and inviting. There are framed photographs on every surface. Amongst them are glass figurines. People always bought them for my grandmother on holidays and her birthday. A large one of two dolphins jumping over waves sits on a small table as we walk from the porch into the kitchen.

A glass candy dish holds the keys to the Cavalier outside.

There are plants and flowers around the room. A green vine climbs from a hanging pot on one side of a large window over the curtain rod to the other side. The smell of coffee is faint in the kitchen. A small twelve inch television sits on the far corner of the dining table. Whoopi Goldberg is introducing a new guest to the show.

A large white and black cat is rolled up on the cushion covering a wooden chair. She pushes it off with the back of her hand. "What can I do for you?" She asks. The cat jumps quickly onto her lap and settles in over her legs. Its tail twitches up into the air and makes figure eights. "Oh, would you like coffee?" She pushes herself up from the table. The cat hits the floor hard on its feet and instantly looks up at us with contempt. "I always have coffee brewing. Gordon started me doing that."

"Gordon?"

"My husband, God bless him. He's been gone twelve years now. He always wanted coffee on the stove. When he was out with the animals or down plowing the fields he wanted to make sure there was always coffee on, so that it would be there when he came in. Would you like a cup?" She looks from Marilyn to me.

I shake my head.

"I could use a cup." Marilyn gives her a warm smile.

As soon as Mrs. Lachance makes the cup she places it in front of my partner and sits herself back down. The surface of the table is covered in thin loops of thread and crocheted doilies of all different designs and colors.

"Do you like these? I sell these at craft stores and at the church."

"They're very nice," I reply. "Have you heard of anything odd around the area or anyone new?"

"Besides the evil things that have been going on?" Her hand goes up and down and then crosses her shoulders. I notice the crosses on the wall and a small statue of the Virgin Mary on the mantle. "I don't think so. Cars go by that I don't know. Summer times coming now. It used to be only a few cars going up to the beach. Now on the hot days they don't stop. Gordon used to say, it was getting to the point he couldn't step out in the back yard to pee."

I let my eyes walk around the room. I take in everything on the walls and surfaces.

"So you haven't noticed or heard anything out of the ordinary?"

"Besides the cars going by at all hours with loud music playing? Nothing out of the ordinary. Everyone around here keeps to themselves."

"Where did you get this picture?" I get up and cross the room. A large photograph with an ornate wood frame is centered on the far wall. It is a scenic photo. The sky goes from yellow to orange to red before meeting with the horizon. Only a black cloud poking in from the right breaks the rainbow. Standing up from the ground is a fence post that leans over to the left. I've seen this.

"Do you like it? That's one of my favorites."

I keep my eyes on the photo trying to take in every part of it. I've seen this. The little clerk in my head starts walking through the stacks of files trying to figure out where I saw it. I picture him looking like Einstein in khaki coveralls. I think I'm going crazy. The cat walks in and out around my ankles. "Where did you get the picture?"

"My grandson took it. He's a photographer, you know. He comes out here all the time taking photos. He brought me these flowers yesterday." She points to a domed glass orb holding three chrysanthemums. He brought it yesterday.

"What's your grandson's name, Mrs. Lachance?" Marilyn asks.

"Call me Gwen."

"Yes, Gwen, what is your grandson's name?"

"Ben Cooper, my little Benny." She smiles bright. Even some of the lines seem to smooth out across her face.

The file clerk climbs up a ladder quickly. He grabs a cardboard box and scurries down. Ben Cooper was on the Atlantic Fitness list. My stomach tenses. I had a bad feeling about him when we met, but, to be honest, Ted Mosby got in my way. Shit, I got in my own way. Cooper didn't have any connection to any of the women except for the gym and no criminal record. Damn it. There's something else. The clerk is flipping through the pages. There has to be something there. It won't click in. How would he be connected to Johanna Bowers? I picture the photograph on her refrigerator. What is it? What is it? He came here yesterday. He drove right past the officers at the end of Windy Road. He could have driven past us.

"He sells photographs, you know. Do you like that picture?"

"I do," I say. "Does Ben come out to see you often?"

She twists in her chair to get a better look at me. The old wood creeks. "He tries as often as he can. He's very busy with taking pictures and all of his girlfriends." Her face brightens. She smiles with her mouth open, eyes wide. "He's a very popular boy, that one. Always telling me about new girls he's dating."

Photographer. Heather Blais said he was a photographer. Her guy said his name was Teddy. Why would he use his real name? Of course if the plan is to kill the woman why wouldn't he? I look at Marilyn and she gives me a nod. She's come to the same conclusion. This could be our man. My jaw clenches. I have to stay calm.

"Has he ever brought any of his girls out here?" I smile and look from her to the photograph.

"Only Shannon. Why are you asking about Benny?" Her voice goes hard and suspicious. The smile lines disappear instantly and the glow to her cheeks fades away. She stares at my face as if she is looking for her own answers there.

My tongue trips over itself a couple of times before I get out, "Just curious. Tell us a little about Shannon."

"Lovely girl that one. Her parents own a summer cottage near here. That's where they met. Benny was taking pictures and he took her's. They dated for, oh my, it must have been seven, eight years. Long time."

"Why did they break up?"

She puts her hands on her lap and stares past me out the window. In studies people have questioned if a killer's family subconsciously knows what he is doing. Her eyes sort of go blank and glassy. After a few moments she says, "Benny never told me and I didn't ask.

"We should get going, right Reid?" Marilyn pushes away from the table. The old woman looks at her for a moment. She stares at her blankly. She turns back to me.

"Reid, is that your name?" It's almost a whisper. Her soft eyes stare into mine. "I've heard that before."

"Come on, Reid. Thank you for your time, Mrs. Lachance." Marilyn pushes me out the door. I can feel the old woman's eyes on me the whole way.

Marilyn drives. Instead of heading to the next house down the road we turn back the way we came and make our way toward Charlottetown. I give Kathy Hanson a phone call and ask her flat out if she knows Ben Cooper. She does. He was dating her daughter for a few years until about three or four months ago. She doesn't know why their relationship ended. Very nice young man. A gentleman. She gives us Shannon's address and phone number.

"Do you believe this?" I think I'm talking to myself, but it is all coming out loud. "I had this guy. I knew he had something strange about him."

~ * ~

Shannon Hanson is a student at the University of Prince Edward Island. Before we even get back to the capital city she calls my cellular phone. I tell her we will meet out in the courtyard between the buildings of UPEI. We park the car in front of the W. A. Murphy Student Center and quickly find her waiting by the bus stop. We all sit at a bench amongst the tall trees that have been growing here forever. I keep my eye on the dark clouds moving in from the west threatening a wet evening.

"Hi, Shannon. Did your parents tell you what we needed to talk to you about?" I keep my hands in my pockets.

Marilyn sits with Shannon.

"The cottage." She rubs her palms along her thighs. She has a little spare tire hanging over her pants. Her thighs push against the fabric. A dark line of cleavage shows inside the V-neck opening of her white sweater. A pearl necklace hangs down over her chest where a tied knot hangs in the air. It sways forward and back.

"Do you know anyone who has access to the cottage other than your parents?"

"I don't know." Her eyes drop to the ground.

"We heard you had a boyfriend not long ago," Marilyn says.

We talked in the car how we wanted to do this. You never know about people after they break up. Sometimes they are vindictive and sometimes they still want to hide things.

Shannon looks at Marilyn's face. Her blond hair is cut in odd angles almost as if she did it herself. There is surprise across her face. "Ah, yes, Ben."

"Ben Cooper?" I state.

"How did you know?"

"Does he have access to the cottage?" I ask.

"What?" She looks away from me.

I feel my insides swirling around. This is it. This has to be it. We are getting there. LeBlanc and Longfellow are sitting outside of Ben Cooper's apartment building watching in case he makes a move. Things are clicking. "Does Ben have access to the cottage? Does he have a key or know where one is?"

She runs a hand back through her hair. "He might, I don't know. I haven't talked to him in a while. He used to like taking pictures out there. It's a good place to watch the sunset."

"Can you tell us a bit about him?" I feel excited like we are coming to the end.

"Why are you asking about Ben?" She looks to each of us. Her hands go to the bench ready to push herself up.

I nod to Marilyn.

"We are investigating a case where he is a person of interest. Can you please tell us about him?" Marilyn glares at her.

Shannon makes a move as if she is going to push herself off the bench and leave us so I take a step to block any escape. She looks up at me. I stare into her green eyes and try passing on the seriousness of what this is about.

"The murders. You're investigating the murders?" Shannon pulls her eyes off of me and turns them to my partner.

I turn away and look around the open area between buildings. Students walk across the grass going to classes or the student union. I look at the girls all seeming to be in their twenties, all pretty, all in shape. How many of those have a tattoo on the back of their shoulders. How many could become known as victims of the Red Island Killer? Is Ben Cooper the Red Island Killer? That little clerk in my head is jumping up and down waving his arms around. My groin is tingling.

Shannon takes a deep breath and lets it out slow. The pearl necklace swings out and then back until it touches her belly. "Ben's a nice guy." She rubs her hands together. "He opens doors and bought me things. He, um, he treated me good. It was –" She drops her eyes to the ground again.

"Why did you two break up, Shannon?"

She keeps her eyes on the ground. "He was my first." She looks up and back down. Her foot kicks at the grass under the bench. "He used to be very loving. In the past year things started changing. He wanted to play games in the bedroom. He wanted things to get a little rougher. He wanted to tie me up. I let him. And then he started getting rough, but only when we were making love. He never hit me or anything aside from that." Her fingers play with the knot in her necklace. I notice that her nails are rough from being chewed. She continues, "I didn't like it so I started wanting to do it less. One time he was," her voice drops to a whisper, "on top of me and he started choking me. I couldn't breathe. I was afraid for my life. I thought he was trying to kill me or something. After we were done I told him I didn't want to be with him anymore."

"How did he take that?" I ask.

"He stopped talking to me. I still love him. Did he, did he do these things to those women?"

"We don't know. Right now we just want to talk to him. When did you two break up?" Marilyn uses her softest voice to keep the woman calm.

"Almost four months ago."

Right before Casey Marsh was killed. That's what did it. That's what set him off.

~ * ~

I follow Marilyn into the main lobby of the hospital. In her pocket is a small picture of Ben Cooper that Shannon Hanson had in her purse. We ask at the information booth for Heather Blais' room and take the stairs up to the second floor. We walk down the hallway. I nod at the guard we have outside her door as we knock and enter. McIntyre had to argue with the CO to get a constable sitting outside her door. If the killer can get into my house, then he can find the one that got away.

"Reid," I turn to the sound of Longfellow walking fast down the hallway. He swerves around a nurse, letting his eyes linger. "I have those photos for you."

"And a board?"

"Yeah." He holds up a white board and a manila envelope. Inside the envelope are casual photographs of men in their late twenties or early forties. Dispirito's picture is in there at a baseball game last summer. We put the nine photos on the board along with the one of Ben Cooper. They all had to be casual pictures to match the one we took from Shannon.

"Thanks, Gordon."

"Good luck."

I nod to Marilyn and she opens the door. Inside the room an older woman sits beside the bed where Heather is propped up on pillows. She is introduced as her mother. I stay back and let Marilyn take the lead.

"How are you feeling Heather?" Marilyn asks using her caring, soft tones again.

Her cheeks are pink from crying and rubbing the tears away. She tells us about her nightmares that kept her moving all night and how the stitches on her back opened up.

"We have some pictures we want you to look at. We want you to tell us if you recognize anyone of these men and where you recognize them from."

She takes a breath that makes her entire body shake. Her eyes close tight. When they open again huge tears fall and run down her face. She looks like she has aged twenty years over night.

Marilyn nods to me.

I hold up the board with the ten photographs attached to it in two rows of five. I look over the top of the board and watch her eyes move from left to right over all of the pictures.

Her hand goes up fast and she turns away. Her lips tighten. Her head nods quickly. "That's him. That's Teddy."

Her finger shakes over the picture of Ben Cooper.

"Thank you, Heather." Marilyn turns away and walks out of the hospital room.

I am locked. My feet don't want to move. My arms lower the board down so it is out of her sight. I stare at this distraught woman as I had stared at the lifeless bodies of Nicole Tait, Sara McDonald, Tracy Field, and then Allison Crenshaw lying on the morgue slabs back in British Colombia and saw my own daughter lying there and here now. She is so vulnerable. She looks up at me and we stare into each other's eyes. Her's are a mixture of fear and anger and hatred. In the blue eyes I see every father's nightmare, a terrified child. In this world how can I stop my daughter from running into a man like this? How do I help her to see what I see now? What I didn't see when we interviewed him? Blue eyes shining with more tears look at me and I don't know what to do. I don't have the answer. They beg me to find this man. They want me to kill this man. I nod my head and walk out of the room.

"I'm on the phone with McIntyre trying to get the Crown to give us a warrant for Cooper's apartment. You okay?" Marilyn asks

I gaze into light green eyes this time and feel a new rush of emotion. I want to kiss her, I want to hold her, I want to be in her, and I want everything else to go away. I don't want to hate the world and feel this confusion of why it is the way it is. I just want to escape my reality.

I give Marilyn a nod. "Let's get down there."

Chapter 28

As if on cue, the rain starts the moment we pull out of the hospital parking lot onto the Bypass.

In one instant the world seems to go from bright white clouds and muted sunlight to dark gloom and wet. The sun goes dim in the late afternoon like someone threw a sheet over a lamp.

Headlights come on. We turn left onto St. Peter's heading into the city. The streets are instantly spotted with puddles. The wipers try their best to beat in time with the song on the radio, but soon fall behind. I turn the radio off.

Marilyn maneuvers the car through the Brackley corner. You can come into that intersection from five different directions, only three meet at the same place.

The wind picks up pushing the rain sideways. We go through the round-a-bout in front of the *Farmer's Market* and water splashes onto the hood. As we pass *Burger King,* I get a good whiff of flame broiled beef. It wakes me to the fact that I haven't eaten anything today except a microwave bowl of oatmeal this morning during the Triangle meeting.

Marilyn turns the car into the *Atlantic Superstore* parking lot and quickly makes her way down and across to the apartment building of Ben Cooper. I try to see his window but all of them look dark.

I can't help but wonder if he is really the one? Us getting his name and some facts came awfully quick. Did he do that or did we? Why didn't we ask the right questions the first time? How did he know Johanna Bowers? He is a photographer. Heather Blais went on a date with a photographer and was raped and cut by this man. She says the picture of Ben Cooper matches that man. He works out at Atlantic Fitness on Kent where Casey Marsh and Nicolle Teresa Pereira also went and he admitted to talking to Casey. He has to be the guy. We have no one else. Ted Mosby has an alibi for Heather Blais and she works with him so she would know if that was who she was out with. There is nobody else. We have been interviewing known sex offenders on the island to no avail. The Charlottetown police have gone around talking to the usual suspects. I know it has to be Ben Cooper, but I have some confidence issues. To this day, I don't know if I was right with what happened in BC. And there I killed the suspect.

Marilyn drives around to the front and parks on a side street behind the car with LeBlanc and Longfellow. One of them waves through their foggy rear window.

"Do you think if I wait long enough one of them will come out in the rain to talk?" I say.

Marilyn shakes her head at me.

"I'll be right back," I say and step out into the rain. My jacket and pants are soaked through almost instantly. My feet splash through every puddle on the sidewalk. Nobody else is walking around. I take a quick look at the building main entrance then slip in the back seat behind the other MCU officers. I wipe the rain water off my head.

"A little wet, eh?" Longfellow offers me a napkin.

"Yeah, any luck?" I want to get right to business. The sooner we get this done, the sooner my family comes back.

"No we haven't seen him. That's his SUV there on the third row of cars. It was there when we got here and nobody has gone near it at all. There's a unit around back watching his windows. They haven't seen him come out the fire exit or even walk in front of the window. What's the plan?" Both of them turn in their seats to look at me.

I stare at the front doors. My eyes move to the black *KIA* sport utility vehicle just sitting there sort of away from the building and away from the most popular parking spots. "We wait for a warrant I guess. I don't know. I don't want to go in there and have the lawyers come back and blast us." I open the door and step back into the rain.

This is him. Ben Cooper has to be the Red Island Killer because I have no one else. What happens if it's not him? We search his vehicle, search his apartment, and put him under twenty-four hour surveillance and it's not him. Then what? I don't have anyone else. I put my hand on the door handle. It has to be him. I saw it in Heather Blais's eyes. Could he have only attacked her and not the other ones? Is the fact that she has a tattoo on her back shoulder just a coincidence? No, he licked it. That has to mean something. I open the door and tell Marilyn I am going to take a look in his KIA and that I will be right back.

I pull my jacket in close around me. It isn't any good. My body shivers from the intense cold. I cross the street and walk into the open parking lot. In the middle, the driveway makes a loop in front of the door. The front door to the apartment building opens. My body tenses. A woman walks out and opens a red and white sectioned umbrella over her head. A little girl with long red hair clings close to her side. They walk with purpose to their car and quickly leave the parking lot without a look in my direction. I stop and watch them drive away. Water splashes up from their tires.

I feel really nervous. Something is working around in my stomach and pushing up into my chest. If someone were to come up behind me and yell, *Boo*, I'd probably piss myself. I can feel the eyes of the others watching me. Mine flip from the SUV to the front doors of the building. He's in there. He has to be in there. What if he took a walk somewhere before LeBlanc and Longfellow were out front? What if he comes around the corner and sees me before we see him? Walking over here just to look in his vehicle is a big mistake.

There is no movement near the door. I look at the corners of the building and see no movement. Rain hits my face on the side. I look through the back window of the SUV. They are tinted so I have to put my face close to the glass. Something is back there covered in a blanket. I move around the side, hidden from the front door, and keep trying to look through the glass. What was inside? What was under the blanket? I know Eckhart will bitch at me later, but I have no choice. I put my hands on the side of my face and press my nose against the window. The dark light and the dark window make it hard to see. I move a little to the side. Something is there sticking out from under the blanket. It's a hand.

It's a hand.

I try the door handle. It moves, but nothing happens. I look around the ground. *Nothing.* My fist hammers against the window. I take my pistol from inside my jacket, grasp the top, and hammer the base of the handle against the window. *Nothing.* I have to get in there. I hit again. *Nothing.* I hear a door close behind me. I have to get in this vehicle. I have to get in. I hit again. *Crack.* There are footsteps in water. My hand goes back. It goes forward again. The butt of the gun hits the glass. The glass fractures in. My hand follows through. I feel the sharp glass dig into my forearm. A strong metallic smell and stale sweat escapes from inside. I smash more of the glass until I can reach in and unlock the door.

"Reid, what are you doing? Marilyn comes to a stop behind me. Puddle water splashes up my legs.

My fingers fumble inside the side door. They find the lock. I open the door. My blood mixes with the water on the ground. I stop.

Marilyn stops asking me what is wrong. She can see what the hell is wrong. The back seats to the SUV are not there. A pale blue blanket lays there covering something. A dark red stain has formed in the middle of it. Just a foot away from the door is a hand, palm up with fingers curled. There is blood on the fingers. Dark bruises circle around the wrist. The fingernails are manicured. There is dried blood beneath them. The hand isn't moving. I reach out to touch the vein in the wrist going to the thumb.

Marilyn grabs my arm. Pain shoots up to my shoulder.

"You've got blood running down over your hand." Bright red streams run from inside my jacket and drip down to the ground from my fingertips. It is a far more vibrant color than the stain in the blanket. "What did you do? You can't touch anything. You'll contaminate the scene."

"What?" I stare at the blood dripping down and disappearing in a stream of water flowing under the SUV. Now that I see it I feel the pain. It is the back of my forearm. I pull my jacket sleeve up my left arm. The jagged cut has my skin open with blood running out like the water under the car. "Check her." I have no doubt the hand sticking out is attached to Ben Cooper's latest victim.

Marilyn takes a latex glove from her pocket and slips it on her hand quickly. She reaches a finger down and touches the wrist. She looks at me and shakes her head. A chill makes my whole body shudder with utter cold. My clothes are soaked through. My coat, my shirt, my pants, my underwear are all wet through and clinging to my body with ice crystals. But my body is freezing from inside out. She's dead.

"Are you going to be okay with this one?" Marilyn undoes my tie and uses it as a tourniquet to try and stem the blood flow from the cut in my arm. I can't tell yet if it's helping.

"Pull the blanket back. I want to see her." She stares at me for a moment, but one look at my face would tell her that I am in no mood to wait.

She reaches down and slowly pulls the blanket down of off the lump we assume to be the head. The face there under the blanket has high cheek bones, dark bruises around the eyes, cuts and blood splatters. She was young. She had a life and expected to have a much longer life and this son of a bitch took it away from her. When did he kill her? She's been sitting here this whole time.

"Is she cold?"

"What?" Marilyn looks at me with wide eyes. She leans into the vehicle and puts a finger on the woman's face. "She's cold."

"We've had cars on both sides of the building for over an hour now. She's been here the whole time. We've been sitting outside here the whole time," I say.

There are footsteps around us. I don't want to deal with LeBlanc and Longfellow right now. Their faces show flashes of confusion. The rain runs down their faces in waves. They stare into the SUV.

"You two were sitting in your car with this woman here the whole time. You didn't fucking think to come take a look? She could have been alive when you first got here."

"No, Reid. We were told to sit in the car and wait for you. Don't you yell at us." Longfellow gets in my face.

"Reid, we have to call an ambulance," Marilyn states.

It's too late.

She continues, "We have to get that warrant and then get in there."

"Exigent circumstances," I say and bolt toward the apartment building.

Section 487.11 of the Criminal Code of Canada states that peace officers can search without a warrant if the conditions for obtaining the warrant exist but by reasons of exigent circumstances it would be impractical to obtain a warrant. Basically this means I would be able to argue with the lawyers and judge that standing here in the rain waiting for the suits to get us a warrant, when they are probably already gone for the day, would be a waste of time. Our suspect could be up there destroying evidence while we are getting webbed feet. A dead body in the back of a SUV is a good definition of exigent circumstances.

I push apartment buzzers at the security door and wait for someone to answer. "This is the RCMP; I need access to the building." There's a buzz and the lock clicks open. I yank the door open and race for the stairs. I hear footsteps behind me, but I don't look to see who is with me. As soon as we are on the third floor, we flatten our backs against the wall. I keep my eyes on Ben Cooper's door.

LeBlanc taps my shoulder.

I take a quick look at him.

We nod. Then we move forward.

Inside my body my nerves are all on edge. I am starting to really feel the pain from the cut on my arm. The fingers on my left hand tingle with pins and needles. I put my right hand on the handle of my gun in its holster. What is this guy going to do? We don't know that if we knock on the door if he will start shooting or what. Maybe he wouldn't expect us to find the body.

"The door's open." There is a one inch gap between the door and the frame. Time stands still. I try not to hold my breath. I pull my Smith and Wesson 9mm and hold it in front pointing down. My left hand sits under the gun handle. The fingertips feel like someone is poking them with sharp needles. LeBlanc pulls his own gun out and holds it at the ready. He taps my shoulder telling me he is ready.

What if this guy is in there waiting for us?

You're not taking me alive, coppers.

Why would he have his door open? He could have guns and is waiting to ambush us. Should we go in there guns blazing like some cop show? Shoot first. Ask questions later. Not like it would be the first time.

I can't breathe. I have to keep calm. My heart is pounding so loud I can hear it echoing up and down the hallway. I reach my foot forward and give the door a little kick. It moves inward and stops shortly after. A dim light comes out of the room, I think from the windows. I look in. My left hand pushes the door open further, my pistol out in front.

"Clear," I signal to the others.

LeBlanc steps across the open door to the other side. He takes his position behind the door frame with his own gun out and ready, eyes searching the inside of the room.

"Go," he says.

I move quickly into the room a little hunched over with my hands holding the gun pointing down a little in front of me. Where I look, the gun looks. When I was a kid I hated going into a room with the sense of dread that a friend was hiding somewhere waiting to jump out and scare me. I hate being scared. LeBlanc moves in behind me as we check the bathroom and the bedroom. Clear. He is not here. We search under the bed and in the closets and he is not here. Without a warrant we really can only search the large spaces where a person of his size could possibly hide and he's not here. Where the hell is Ben Cooper?

The living room is a mess. The framed photographs that were on all of the walls when we first came are now scattered across the floor. A television in the corner has been smashed. There is glass on the floor from the television and frames. I recognize Shannon now in a picture on the floor near the front door. Was this a struggle? Maybe someone else got here first.

"Reid," LeBlanc stands in the middle of the room looking down at a large frame that had once been on the wall. "This is your daughter, no? And this is you and your wife."

There we are in full living color on our couch, in our home. In our *safe* home. Did he stand right outside our window watching us? And we are thumb-tacked next to photos of Johanna Bowers, Nicolle Theresa Pereira, Casey Marsh, Sierra West, Heather Blais, and other women. A picture near the bottom shows a lively picture of the face down in the SUV. It all starts with one in the top corner developed from real film. *Chloe.* There are so many of them that they overlap. Some I recognize from Dispirito's rape files, but a lot I don't. Did we really find his first or have there been others?

"Is this, ah, you and Marilyn?"

I can see Marilyn and me kissing. He was outside her house then. He has been everywhere. That probably was him in the field behind headquarters the night he called the hotline. He's been watching me. He could be watching us now. I want to reach down and pull the photos off the corkboard, tacks and all. They are my life. He had no right to take those pictures, to be watching us, to put them here. My first time staying home alone when my parents went on vacation someone called and hung-up three times in a row. They scared the death out of me. They had no right. Ben Cooper has no right. I don't want to live in fear. The women out there don't want to live in fear. Heather Blais shouldn't have to live that way. Ident is going to be here soon and they will have to take the photos and place them in their evidence bags. Everyone is going to know.

I can't take it. I can't give the lawyers a reason to doubt me.

My breathing calms. The feeling in my chest is beginning to subside. I look down at my hand. The blood is moving again, faster now. I watch a drop grow on the tip of my middle finger and fall to the floor. It splashes onto scattered photos. "We should get downstairs."

"You go down and get your arm looked at. I'll stay up here and watch the room. Send up another officer." LeBlanc's French accent is thick.

The parking lot of the apartment building quickly becomes a circus of police vehicles and gawking civilians.

The large Mobile Command Post is parked close to the suspect's vehicle. Yellow tape goes up in a wide square around the dark KIA Sorrento SUV. Shortly after that, a couple of people come and complain because their vehicles are being used to hold the ends of the tape.

I climb in the ambulance, sit down, get a blanket draped over my shoulders, and wait for them to bandage my arm. I need stitches. Eckhart arrives and goes straight to work on the SUV. His partner Ashley goes into the building. The Halifax Ident officers split up as well, one with each. The first thing they do is set up a tent over the vehicle so that they can work without rain diluting their scene. Charlottetown City Police arrive and are asked to set up a perimeter by Marilyn. When the first reporters arrive it is their job to keep them back. There is no way Ben Cooper will even try to come in now. McIntyre parks his car on the street behind our cars. Right away he takes over the direction of who is doing what.

"You okay?" he asks.

I don't want to look at him. "It's just pain," I say. *Pain and cold.* The blanket over me helps to keep my body heat in its cocoon, but with my clothes soaked completely through I still shiver uncontrollably. I squeeze my nose with my finger and thumb to clean out the snot threatening to run.

"So what happened? Where is he?" McIntyre puts his arm out at his sides and turns his head back and forth like a football coach looking for an answer to why the team lost the big game.

"I don't know. He should have been there. LeBlanc and Longfellow were out front and we had a car out back. He didn't come out the front door and he didn't go out his window or the back door. Somebody must have looked away. I don't know." I look at Longfellow. Hazel eyes stare back at me, his lips slightly parted.

"We didn't look away from anything." Longfellow crosses his arms in front of him. He straightens his back and makes himself look bigger. "Maybe your guy wasn't in there. You didn't take the time to do an in-depth background check on this guy. Maybe he has a second vehicle."

I get to my feet. I adjust the blanket on my shoulders. "Excuse me? There wasn't time. This guy would have bolted if we started digging around." I feel my face go tight. My teeth push against each other and my brow furrows. "I didn't have the time to sit on my hands watching this guy and going through the steps. His killing schedule is erratic at best. With Casey Marsh and Johanna Bowers he tortured them for days before finishing them off. Then Nicole Pereira is killed in a couple days. Two weeks later he goes after another woman just to make a point. He didn't think we could touch him. He thinks he's smarter than us. Why else would he call me *and* the tip line? Why else would he go in my *home*? Why else would he kill the day after Heather Blais got away? He's out of control. He's angry at us." *At me.*

"You don't go blaming us for this." Longfellow takes a step forward. His nostrils flare.

"Don't get in my face Gordon," I retort.

"Don't blame us because we didn't know something." He puts his face close to mine. I can feel his hot breath on my cheek. There's a mix of hamburger and ketchup.

"Alright that's enough. The press is watching so don't the both of you pull them out to see who's biggest." McIntyre moves his glare from one to the other. He keeps looking over our shoulders to where the press is gathering behind the tape. Catherine Arsenault is already here. "Gordon, go back to headquarters and get ready for all the information coming in. I want T's crossed and I's dotted."

Longfellow nods at McIntyre then turns and heads off to where the cars are parked. As the files manager for this case, it is his job to make sure all the paperwork is correctly placed onto computer and CD-ROM for the attorneys. With a new body and the suspect's apartment he will have a lot to do.

"We should send a car out to his grandparents place in Blooming Point. The girlfriend's too. He knows we're closing in on him so he'll have to find someone to help." I'm supposed to be in charge, but my head is spinning.

"I already had CrOps send cars to the Confederation Bridge, ferry, and airport with Ben Cooper's photograph. An APB has been put out across the island." McIntyre is in charge. He knows what to do.

The street lamps are all lit. When did that happen? Sometime while I was inside the apartment building the sun went down somewhere behind the clouds. Night is quickly creeping up on us. Large lights, the same ones used at the Johanna Bowers scene, are being brought out of the MCP and set up around the Sorrento.

"Reid," Eckhart yells out from under the tent. McIntyre and I walk over to join him without getting ourselves in the immediate crime scene. Marilyn stands beside the Ident tech dressed in her bunny suit. Eckhart pushes his glasses up his nose with the back of his hand. "You bled all over my crime scene."

"Things had to be done."

He stares at me for a moment. "Yeah, well, I'm going to need your blood sample later." I nod and wait. "Okay, she's the same as the other vics. She is naked and was beaten, tied up, cut, and stabbed. Her left breast is almost cut off. In fact I can't even tell how it is still attached. She has a tattoo on the back of her left shoulder of a Pegasus. It's only a rough count, but she's was stabbed at least twenty-seven times. This guy is brutal." He pushes his glasses up. "I also think the back of the SUV is the murder scene. Her ankles are still tied and the amount of blood back there is astounding. I think she lost all of it."

"Reid," Marilyn has her phone up. "We have something on Cooper. Benjamin Cooper, age twenty-eight. No police record.

He's an Islander. The Sorrento is the only vehicle in his name. His grandmother though had the Cavalier, which we saw out at her place, and a blue Ford pick-up. I don't remember that out there. Do you?"

I shake my head. "No, there was no pick-up." Damn it. Why didn't I take the time to check this guy out? Longfellow was right. *Shit.* I won't tell him that, of course.

The rain has died down to a constant drizzle that doesn't really seem to fall but more hangs in midair dampening everything. The blanket over my shoulders is heavy from the wet. With the sun down the temperature has dropped noticeably. Jackets are being zipped up. A few of the officers pull on toques and gloves. All I can think about is when I will get to change my clothes. It'll probably take thirty minutes in a hot shower before my body feels right. I guess *right* isn't the right phrase. With this guy out there, I won't feel right even after my entire body is warm and the shivering stops.

A city police officer walks under the yellow police tape and quickly strolls toward where we are standing. Marilyn is still telling us what little information we have on Cooper. Right now it seems like he is either brand new to killing and raping, which most killers of this type are not, or he is so good that he just never got caught. The experts say that he should have started with smaller crimes, misdemeanors like peeping through windows, steeling underwear off of clothes lines, making phone calls, and maybe taking hidden pictures or videos of women pissing in public toilets. He should have been caught doing those things and either cleaned up or evolved into what he is now. If we are right about our profile, he did do assaults and rapes before taking Casey Marsh to 3231 Blooming Point Road. I guess he really is smart.

"Sergeant Reid?" The Charlottetown cop looks at each of us in turn until I nod. "There's a kid over here, says he has an envelope for you. Says a guy in the building gave it to him then used his outside door. He lives on that side." He points to the bottom part of the L shaped building. It's the other wing from where Ben Cooper's apartment is. Right away I know what he's

316

talking about. We didn't have anyone watching that side. On that side is the side Atlantic Superstore parking lot where the delivery transports park their trailers. He could have had Grandma's truck sitting over there as a just in case measure. All he had to do was make sure there was an apartment he could go through without too many questions. The officer brings me over to the kid.

He's around thirteen. There are red acne bumps over his greasy forehead. "Are, are you Reid?" His voice quivers. An older woman stands behind him with one hand holding her coat closed and the other holding a black umbrella above their heads.

"I'm Sgt. Reid. What's your name?"

"W-Wylie. Mr. Cooper knocked on our door and said he had to use our back door. He said to wait until Mom got home then bring this to you." He hands me a letter sized envelope. I take the corner of it with my finger and thumb.

"Do you know Mr. Cooper?" I ask.

"Yeah, he's a nice guy. He lets me use one of cameras sometimes. And he gives me advice on girls."

Marilyn lets out a small noise.

"Thank you, Wylie. You may want to get some other advice though. Excuse us." We quickly cross to the mobile unit and run up the ramp.

In the farthest forward of the command post, in what was the main bedroom of the RV unit it was made from, is an office with a desk and chairs. I put the envelope down on the desk. It is a little heavier than something with just a piece of paper in it. Marilyn brings me latex gloves. On the front of the envelope in blue ink is one word, *REID*. The flap is sealed with a yellow smiley face sticker.

"Maybe we'll be lucky and it's a full confession with instructions on where to find him." McIntyre runs a hand through his black hair using the rain to slick it down and make it shine.

I look up and smile in time to see Marilyn shake her hair out. She looks like a drowned rat.

"I don't think it's anything like that." I carefully un-stick the sticker and lift the flap. The envelope puffs out a little as what is inside tries to unfold and make room. My hands start to shake. He left this for me after giving himself enough time to get away. He knew we were there. How long had he had this escape plan? I lift open the envelope and with latex covered fingers pull out what is inside. I unfold it. My eyes go wide. My mouth drops. What the hell is this doing here? This shouldn't be here. What does this mean?

"Jesus, no."

Chapter 29

I look from the phone to the road. The wipers whomp over the windshield clearing the water splashed from other cars passing. *Whomp, whomp.* I look to the phone and press the green send button. The front wheels catch in a puddle and pull the car to the right. I pull it back. Because of the rain, the highway is a slick black mass with hidden puddles that I can't see by the beam from my headlights. I can barely see the yellow and white lines. I hold the phone up to my ear with the other hand on the top of the steering wheel. The car's lights flash.

"She's not answering." I take the phone down, press the red button then the green twice to redial the last number. The car swerves. I straighten it out.

"Do you want me to drive? Or make the call?" Marilyn has one hand on the dashboard.

I hang up the phone. Both hands grasp the wheel, the right still holding the phone as well. The rain has all but stopped. The only water now comes up from vehicles. *Whomp.*

I look at the speed limit signs change from ninety kilometers per hour to seventy to fifty as we come into Hunter River. We start down the hill into the valley that is the main center of the area. On a pole halfway down is a two digit digital readout of the cars speed limit reminding people to slow down to the assigned fifty. A Yellow 99 is on the readout as we drive past. My speed is well over one hundred kilometers per hour. I swerve into the other lane to avoid someone living to the law. Most people pull over when they see our flashing lights in their rear view. We start up the other end of the valley and my foot pushes down the gas pedal to keep up the momentum. I swerve around another car.

"Are you sure we should be doing this, Reid? McIntyre has units at your house and he's getting the OPP to look in on your family. We don't know what that picture meant." I can feel Marilyn's eyes on me. The moment we pulled the photograph out of the envelope she looked at me and has barely taken her eyes off me since.

I slowly unfolded the photograph and looked at it. They all looked at it. There was a copy of the photo in my daughter's room of Leigh riding her horse on the beach. I stared at it for a few moments going over everything in my head. Ben Cooper had Heather Blais just two nights ago. She never said anything about seeing anything in the back of his SUV. Was this other woman already there? No, he must have killed her after. Did he kill the new girl out of anger for Heather? Where is he now? Why the picture? There's no way he could have gone all the way to Ontario to go after Leigh. I supposed it was possible if he drove non-stop, but this is where he lives. This is where he is most familiar. What would the picture mean then? I didn't listen to McIntyre talking about what he was going to do.

I turned and left the Mobile Command Post and headed for the car. I heard footsteps behind me and knew it was Marilyn trying to keep up. We got in the car and left.

I pull the car into the passing lane and quickly get around a transport. *Whomp, whomp.* The wipers clean off the windshield. The phone in my hand vibrates then rings. I take a quick look. McIntyre. I press the button to ignore the call.

Marilyn's phone starts ringing. She looks at the call display and won't raise her eyes to me. I know its McIntyre. She pushes a button and the phone goes silent.

"You better know what you're doing, Reid. Are we calling for back-up any time soon?"

"When we get there. When I know if he's there."

"Where?"

There were only two things in the picture. Maybe he only left the picture for me to lead me into a trap, but still I have to go. He knows that. Does he know Leigh will hate me if anything happens to her horse?

He's here. We pull into the driveway at Circle K Ranch and right away see a blue Ford pick-up. Our eyes start working on looking for any movement. Kenneth would have put the horses in their individual stalls in the barn shortly before sunset and fed them all a bucket of grain. There are no horses in the fenced fields. There are no lights on in the house or barn. The clouds have completely cleared leaving a cloudless sky sprinkled with stars. The moon is a couple of slivers from full and lights up the ground with long shadows. Marilyn gets on the radio and calls for back-up. I stop the car with the headlights on the opening to the barn.

We both get out of the car with our guns in our hands and hunker down beside the car. Marilyn crouches as she moves around the back of the car until she is behind me. Her hand touches my back. My skin jumps. He could be anywhere. He could be watching us right now and we wouldn't know.

"What's the plan?" Marilyn asks.

The light from the moon is enough to see a grey landscape in front of us. Every crook and corner has a black shadow inside it. I know where I would be. I know where he is waiting for me.

"Let's check the house and see if the Olivers are okay. Have a flashlight?"

Marilyn answers by clicking it on.

The door to the house is wide open. Staying low we move quickly to the owner's mini-van. We both try holding our breath. I swear I can hear my partner's heart beating through her chest. She holds the flashlight with her left hand and rests her right with her gun over top of it. Marilyn leads the way up the small set of steps to the front door. I stay close behind. One step creaks. The noise seems to echo through the buildings and over the fields. My eyes search the grey shadows for any movement at all. My own heart races. I can feel my skin tingling beneath my wet clothes. I know Kenneth does hunt so he probably has rifles in the house. Would Ben Cooper exchange his knife for a gun? He could be sitting there in the shadows with his finger ready to squeeze the trigger and shoot us in the back.

Something moved. Where was it? I saw something move at the edge of my vision. Where? There. In the barn. That's him.

"Reid?" Marilyn whispers.

"He's in the barn." I keep my eyes on the opening to the barn door. I can see him sure as I saw him in the field between headquarters and the Farmer's Market. Our eyes meet and we stare at each other for a moment. A moment is all it takes. He spins on his heel and heads into the black of the barn. "Search the house."

"Reid."

I head off before she can say anything else.

I get back behind the mini-van and look around the back end. My Smith & Wesson 9mm Model 5946 feels heavy in my hand. I try resting the right in the left, but that arm does not feel strong. The wrapping the paramedics put around it shows a stain of red like the blanket covering the body in Cooper's SUV. He could be out there. He could be waiting just inside the black darkness waiting to blast me with a rifle. I run across, hunched over, until I am against the open doorway to the barn.

I know what is inside here, but it is dark. The moon barely lights two feet into the door. First up are storage stables on both sides, feed on one side, manure on the right, and then there are a couple of stables with the Oliver's horses. I try to will my eyes to adjust to the lack of light. There are dark grey shadows to my right and left and then black. I can see a couple of things in the dark. A bucket. A wheelbarrow, I think. Ben Cooper could be standing right on the other side of the wall and I wouldn't know it until I take my next step. The fear builds up in my chest and threatens to take hold of my brain. There is only one monster out there. I move forward.

My left hand reaches out to the side and I take a few steps until I touch something. Ropes dance at the touch of my fingers. Metal clasps thump against the wood. There's a noise somewhere ahead. It sounds familiar. It is like metal rolling in metal. Then there is a thump of wood on wood. I stop. My eyes strain to see what is right in front of me. A horse moves in a stall up and on my right. Its hooves thump against the sawdust covering the floor. There's that sound again. I know I've heard it before. It's right there in my head, but I can't place it. A horse whinnies somewhere down the hall going left at the end of this one. The noise again. I move forward keeping one hand at my side running against the wall. It loses touch as I move past the open feed stall. I take a couple of steps. My hand connects again.

I stop breathing. I stumble to my right. My feet buckle underneath me. My right elbow touches the concrete floor and then my right hip. The gun stays in my hand. My heart is in my throat. Somewhere in the dark beside me a mare has her head out of a small opening in the stall bars.

There is that noise again. Metal rolling in metal and wood on wood. I know that sound. I push up onto my knees. My left arm almost gives way sending me back on my face into the concrete. That noise, I hear that noise all the time when we are here. It is when Leigh puts Dakota in her stall. The stall door.

Metal smashes on metal down the long hall. Someone starts yelling. The metal bangs against wood. The sounds echo down the halls. There is thumping somewhere up and down the left. It joins more thumping like the hooves of the stallion in its stall. The thunder rises up. There are loud breathing noises and snorts. Hooves hit the concrete floor hard and fast. I have to move. I have to get out of the way. I get to my feet. The thumping is getting closer. I move to my left. The first horse is there out of the darkness like a hell rider, a white strip down its dark nose. Its flank hits me. I stumble more and hit something hard. Horses run behind me with powerful hooves on the concrete. Another hits me. My temple hits the sharp point of a wood post. Pain shoots all around the inside of my head. In the black all I see are flashing colors of light inside my eyes. A foot hits my shin. I pull my legs in close and squeeze against the door. I don't know how many horses are there. Something hits my back. Lightning shoots up my spine to the base of my skull.

The thunder stops.

My eyes are open. I know it is dark in here, but all I see are flashes of red right inside of my eyes. I roll onto my back. Pain shoots up and down my spine. My toes are tingling. He could be coming at me. I have to get up. I can feel sticky heat on the left side of my face. Something is crawling into my eye, blood. My hands flatten against the rough concrete floor and push my body up onto my knees.

My gun is gone. It's not in my hand. I grope around on the floor like Velma from *Scooby-doo* looking for her glasses. The concrete is cold and hard against my palms. I strain to hear something, but all I hear is a ringing in my head. I can't tell if there are any more horses coming or if there are footsteps bearing down on me. I think I'm in the center of the hall between the two walls. If more horses come now there is no place to go. My tongue stretches out and tastes blood. My left arm hurts, my head spins in colors and pain, and my right leg hurts where the horse kicked on my shin. I don't want to put weight on it, but I know I have to get up. I put my left leg underneath myself and push up.

My mouth opens and lets out a massive scream. Pain shoots all up my right leg and through my body. The bones in my leg grind against each other inside my skin. I have to move. My hands grope for the side. This should be near the manure shoot out to the old truck. I touch wood. I touch air. My arm hits something round. My fingers circle around the shaft of something. I feel around until the image of a shovel enters my mind. It will have to do. I have to move forward. The killer is out there. Dakota is out there.

I step forward. With every step pain soars through my body and sparks fly in front of my eyes. I lean on the shovel as I walk forward. Something is seriously wrong in my leg. I shouldn't be moving, but I have to. He's out there. He killed women for sport. He wants me to finish this game.

My hand runs against the stall. I feel the corner and turn. This hall with stalls on the left side and a flat wall on the right is nothing but darkness. There is a little light up ahead, the moon coming in from the far open door down the third hallway. I know there are boxes along the right wall with peoples riding equipment. I keep my left hand on the left wall of stalls. All of the sliding stall doors are open. That was what the metal rolling in metal sound was and then the wood hitting was the door getting to the end and hitting back against the stall. The stalls are empty now because he made them stampede toward me. He's playing with me.

It's dark. I hate the dark. I hate the night. Things come out at you in the dark. Your imagination can put things there. It's hard to breath. The air doesn't want to stay inside my body. My lungs don't want to work.

The knife slices my left thigh from back to front. There's a scream. There's movement in front of me. My legs collapse completely and I sink to the floor. The scream was from me.

There's noise up ahead. Feet scraping on concrete. Someone running.

My left leg is wet. My head spins and the world seems to go in and out. I can't lose consciousness. If I do I'm dead. I hear a voice. I shake my head. It doesn't help any.

"Come on Reid." The voice echoes through my head from ear to ear. I push myself up for what seems like the twentieth time. "Come on, Reid, get up. This is my world. You're doing it my way."

I'm on my hands and knees. I can feel the hot wet running over my thigh. I don't know which leg to put my weight on first. I know it was a thin quick slice, but in my head I picture a large gaping crevasse with blood gushing out. My mind is my weakness. My mind is my strength.

"Where's your wife hiding, Reid?" The voice is coming from down near the corner. Dakota is down that hall. "Your wife's a nice piece of ass. Did you see my pictures Reid? I know you were in my place." There's an air of laughter in his voice. "Did your buddies see them? Your partner?"

My hand finds the shovel. I crawl up the handle until I am on my feet. My knees feel like they are floating in water. The right leg feels like bone shards are loose and jingling between my skin like change in a glass jar. With every twitch of movement they stab into my muscles. My left leg is hot and wet. I take a step and let out a groan.

"What's wrong, Reid? You in a little bit of pain? That's what happens when you try and fight horses." There's a clinking sound of something metal touching something metal then skipping to the next. A knife on the stall bars. "That moaning of yours is going to be nothing compared to the sounds I'm going to make your daughter make. She's going to be a nice piece too. You better watch that one."

A growl rises inside me. "Shut up."

"And where's your partner? I can't believe you turned that down."

I can see his outline standing at the corner. My mind is clearing. The threat of falling again is still there, but I can think. I have to think. My mind *is* my strength. "You're a joke, Ben. You're pathetic." I pause, but he doesn't say anything else. "So why did you do all this?" I take a step and let out a grunt. I have to fight to speak again, "Your Mommy slap you with the good book? Is that why you did all this?" I stumble forward and fight the urge to scream.

"You don't know anything about me. You don't know what I went through. You don't know who I am." His outline is gone from the corner and his voice sounds farther away.

"Did Grandpa take you up in the barn and make you a man?"

"You shut up. You shut up." I imagine spit flying from his mouth and clinging to his lips. "Fight back. Stand up to the bullies. You don't know what they did. You don't know what it was like."

"What? You got picked on as a kid? Who didn't?" There's no response. I take another step and clench my teeth to hold in a scream. I ask, "Did you start peeping first?" My voice goes up high as I put my foot down and pain shoots to my brain. I can feel the fog starting to take over. "I bet you did. I bet you were a little pervert. You gonna blame that on the bullies also?"

No time passes. "I was beaten. I was tortured. They were jealous of me, of my brains. This is my world. They didn't have the right to do that to me. You think you have a clue as to who I am? You don't know anything. I'm not pathetic," he screamed so loud the walls seemed to vibrate.

I get to the corner of the hall. In front of me is the black square used to wash horses down. I turn to my right. There is light at the end of the tunnel. Framed in the open doorway with moonlight behind him is the outline of Ben Cooper. My face is drenched with sweat and blood. My legs are a circus of pain and weakness. I really want to lie down. My head spins. The fog is closing in so much that all around my vision is mottled and fuzzy. I have to stay conscious. Back-up is coming.

I take a step and bite my lip to keep from yelling out. "I know how you found Casey and Nicolle and Heather. How did you find Johanna? You just like women who would never have anything to do with you? Is that it?" I step. "None of them would have anything to do with you, would they? That's why you had to force it. You're," I think I know the word that sets him off, "Pathetic."

The outline starts to move. It is slow at first then it quickens. I brace myself ready to move or get hit. My mind swims. My body sways. I think about moving, but I'm too slow. His fingers twist into my shirt. His muscles flex. Suddenly my feet lift. My body moves without any force of my own. All that time working out in the gym looking for victims has worked out. My body hits the closest stall. The bars in the upper half dig into my back and shoulder blades. The horse inside makes a noise of annoyance. Pain shoots through my body. My head swims. The fog closes over my eyes. My arms fall to my sides. I can feel his breath on my face. Have to stay awake.

There's a pain in the right side of my chest. A sharp pain. I look down and see the glint of steel. A knife. It pushes farther into my chest.

"I'm going to find your Marilyn." His words fight through grinding teeth. His breath comes fast and hard as his anger tries to hold itself back. Each breath is hot against my face. In the half-light I can see his eyes. The pupils are dark as the night and the whites seem full of red. Or it could all be my imagination. The knife pushes deeper into my chest. I let out a yell. He says,

"I'm going to find her and fuck her." Spit hits my face. The fog is taking me. "Then I'm going to bring her in here and fuck her right in front of you. I'll give you a little show of what you missed. I'll fuck her then I'll make her scream. You think she'll scream for you? You think she'll scream for-"

Something explodes. The thunder cracks in my ear. Ben flies back and to his right. I get pulled forward. My hands react too slowly. My face hits wood then concrete. Pain shoots from my face around to the back of my head.

"Reid." A voice. A woman's voice.

Hillary?

Chloe?

"Are you okay? Reid?" Marilyn, it's Marilyn.

I can feel the darkness coming. It's a darkness blacker than the hallways of the barn. Blacker than the center of his eyes. There's a light above me. I can see a handgun. I can't see her eyes. Her eyes are on something else. The fog slips in.

"Hold on, Reid. Don't move. Hold on, Reid."

I can't fight it any more. I let the fog slide over my eyes.

Chapter 30

It has been three months and I can still see his eyes.

My body has healed, for the most part. My left forearm will probably always have a scar from where the window cut me open. My left thigh is no longer wrapped. The mountain range where he sliced my leg is still there. I am sure I'll be wearing Bermuda shorts all summer. I got the cast off my right leg two days ago. The fractured bones have healed. Now I have to get my muscles back in shape. I will always have a scar on my chest. The blade didn't go in too far. Marilyn shot him before he could do any real damage. The scars inside are worse than the physical ones.

I slide my legs out of the car and push myself up to standing. An old man's moan forces out from the back of my throat. There's pain inside my leg. I rest a hand on the roof of the car and stable myself until I'm sure nothing is going to buckle underneath me. People walk or run by on the boardwalk. Now that the warmer weather is here, more and more people are getting out. Two women jog past with a small dog on a leash leading the way.

Frix perks up in the back seat of the car. Her nubby tail moves as fast as she can make it go. I reach in, clip on her leash, and let her jump out. She looks one way then goes the other and wraps the leash around my legs. Unsure of what to do the old pup looks up at me and waits. Her white and brown lines are surprisingly like Dakota the horse. Her ears are down flat. She's ready for anything.

"Which way do you want to go?" Hillary asks. She closes the driver's door and joins me on the boardwalk.

Across the water from where we are I can see the green point that is Port-la-Joye Fort Amherst Historical Park. At the top of the crest is where the old fort is located, where Nicolle Teresa Pereira's body was found. I only let my eyes linger there for a moment. "Let's take Frix to the park and walk around," I suggest and lead the way across the street to Victoria Park. Hillary takes my hand the moment we are on the grass.

I wasn't awake when Hillary and Leigh got back to the island. I was in a hospital bed slipping in and out of consciousness. I felt butterfly kisses on my cheek and a hand squeeze mine. I heard the voices of everyone I worked with come in and talk to my wife. I wanted to open my eyes but it wouldn't happen.

I heard Catherine Arsenault ask for a quote from the sergeant's wife. She was told to go fuck herself and given a few suggestions where she could put her microphone.

After I did wake, Kenneth Oliver came by with flowers from his wife. He had bruises on his face, but otherwise looked well. Ben Cooper told them they weren't part of his world.

The moment I was awake I asked about Cooper and then was glad for pain medication. Marilyn told me she shot him in the side. He lived. I moaned about that and complained about the pain.

Pain heals. Chicks dig scars. Thanks coach.

Frix sniffs at the ground looking for anything interesting or the perfect place to squat and poop. To our left is the public pool with change rooms that will soon be open and full every day with screaming kids splashing and having fun. Leaves are getting full in the trees on the far side of the open grass. There are two jungle gyms with slides and swings for the little kids. One is surrounded by beach sand, the other is on asphalt. Further down are more swings and see saws for bigger kids. Some kids are playing on the plastic jungle gym equipment. A girl goes down the blue slide.

"You okay?"

I look at Hill and smile. "I'm good." I haven't gone back to work yet. I should soon. Hillary and I have talked about Marilyn. I'm pretty sure she believes there is nothing there. I'm pretty sure I believe the same. "All of started with a dream, you know."

"What do you mean?"

"On some cases I have dreams just before we get them." I stare across the park without seeing anyone. "In BC I had dreams of little girls calling out from the dark. This time I dreamed of someone named Chloe, but it was Johanna." *Chloe.*

"You don't have dreams, Reid, you have nightmares. Did you ever find out who this Chloe was?"

I shake my head no. During the search of Ben Cooper's apartment they found boxes of notebooks that he had used as a journal. In many of the pages he went off in crazy rants about a girl named Chloe, but they aren't sure who she was and what she meant to him. There were a lot of journals to read.

"That woman is staring at you." Hillary nods toward the jungle gym. A woman in black jeans and a long red coat stands on the grass outside the sanded area around the large set. Heather Blais. We walk over and I make introductions. My wife says, "Reid told me what happened to you. You were so brave."

She brushes her hair back behind her ear. Her lips twitch. "I had to get back to them." The blond girl I saw go down the slide chases a second child around the whole apparatus. "They were all I thought about." Her face softens and blue eyes glow as she watches them. She looks calmer now, at ease, but still with something inside ready to burst.

I bet if she saw a man staring at her, her entire body would break out in a cold sweat. She turns to Hillary, "You call him Reid too?"

"He won't answer to anything else."

"What is his first name?"

"Have you, um, been watching the news?" I don't know if I should go there. She may not be ready to deal with what has been going on. I really want to ask her if she sees Ben Cooper's eyes every time she closes hers.

"A little." She goes back to her children.

He started out by crying about bullying and prejudice against the small and different. Then when Marilyn and LeBlanc probed further he changed tactics and took full blame for what he had done. I think he found it was a way to take back control of his world. If he pleaded insanity it would be up to the judge and jury. Taking blame and admitting guilt put the control in his hands. He admitted to the rapes and then murders. He told about seeing Johanna Bowers by chance at the beach and then how he stalked her for months. The only thing he wouldn't talk about was the torture of Casey Marsh and Johanna. Those secrets he kept for himself. He told how he met and took Kathy Welsley, his last victim. He is probably going to be paraded in front of the media like Colonel Williams in Ontario in 2010. The people want to know why and how. They need to know that monsters like this are one in a million and not common place neighbors next door. I don't know what they will think when they find out he is just an average guy who went down the left path instead of the right. He didn't have parents who beat him or molested him. He didn't appear mentally imbalanced. He is average. Nobody wants to read that. Nobody wants to realize that the kid mowing your lawn could snap, rape your daughter, and torture your wife.

She stutters to say, "How long will he be in prison?"

"Twenty-five years to life. We're making up a few CD-ROM's with all the evidence and photographs taken at every scene so that when he comes up for parole in the future we will have something to show the board and keep him behind bars. We'll keep him there." I nod and try to smile. We all watch the children for a while. Frix sits at my feet and tilts her head to the side and watches too. "How are things at home?"

She lets out a long shaky breath. "Strained."

It amazes me how many lives have been affected by this one man being unhappy with his life and needing to rape and kill to get a high. A couple on the boardwalk points their digital camera at the opening of the harbor and snaps pictures of a sailboat coming in. Tourist season has started. It will most likely take a hit because of this, but I'm sure the island will heal and tourists will come again for fresh seafood, beaches, fishing, and Anne of Green Gables.

Hillary tells Heather how things take time. When trusts are stretched or damaged it takes time to build things back up. They talk about kids and schools.

I look around at the people and the trees. I wonder if someone could be standing in there watching us. For three months I've felt so dissatisfied. It's like I didn't do something. I didn't kill the killer this time. But that is a good thing.

"Reid."

I blink fast. Both women are staring at me. I'm not sure where I was. "What?"

"Heather has a question for you."

"What's your first name?"

I look around the area. I say, "I don't use that name."

"I just want to know."

"Come on Reid, you can tell her."

I stare into my wife's eyes for a moment or two. I turn to Heather, smile, and open my mouth to speak.

═══════════════════════════════════════

A Note from the Author

Look at that, you made it to the end of the book. Or you're like me and flipped to the end to see who the heck this Lorne Oliver is. Either way, you have the book so that's awesome. Thanks.

I hope you enjoyed Red Island. Tell your friends, tell your enemies, give your long lost relatives a call and tell them about this great book.

I would love to hear your thoughts or answer any questions you may have on this book or any of my other writing. Email me here: redislandnovel@gmail.com

If you want to keep up to date with my writing you can check me out at: lorneoliver.blogspot.ca or at facebook.com/oliverauthor and follow me on twitter @lorneoliver

Keep on the lookout for the next couple of books with Sgt. Reid – Red Serge (due out late August 2013) and Red Rover (due out in 2014) In between there also look forward to my novel, The Cistern, with a set of new characters due out winter 2013/2014. You can read the journey I have taked writing it on my blog.

23905573R90181